PATRIOT HEARTS

A Novel of
the Founding Mothers

⤳⤶

BARBARA HAMBLY

<small>DOUBLEDAY LARGE PRINT HOME LIBRARY EDITION</small>

This Large Print Edition, prepared especially for
Doubleday Large Print Home Library, contains
the complete, unabridged text of the original
Publisher's Edition.

PATRIOT HEARTS
A Bantam Book / February 2007

Published by Bantam Dell
A Division of Random House, Inc.
New York, New York

ISBN: 978-0-7394-7874-5

Printed in the United States of America
Published simultaneously in Canada

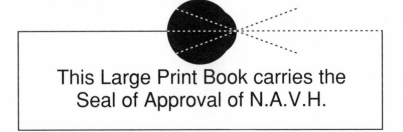

This Large Print Book carries the
Seal of Approval of N.A.V.H.

For my parents

ACKNOWLEDGMENTS

Far too many people contributed to the final version of this book for all of them to be listed here, but I would like to express my appreciation of the staffs at Mount Vernon, Monticello, Montpelier, Philadelphia's Congress Hall, and Colonial Williamsburg for the way in which they have brought the past to life. Special thanks go to Buzz Harris and the staff of the Arisia Science Fiction Convention in Boston, for getting me into the Adams houses in the middle of winter and for taking me out to Old Sturbridge Village. Thanks also to Nancy Smith with the National Park Service at the two Adams houses in Quincy, Massachusetts.

Thank you to my dear friends Laurie, Hazel, Ev, and Nina for putting up with me on the Colonial Death-March through Virginia doing research: I could not have done it without you.

And as always, thanks to my agent Fran Collin; to my editor Kate Miciak; to Kathleen Baldonado for her untiring devotion to detail in preparing the manuscript; and to Nita Taublib, for the original idea of this novel.

AUTHOR'S NOTE

Patriot Hearts is a work of fiction. It is not—and cannot be—a history of the United States in the Revolutionary and Federalist periods; it cannot even be a comprehensive fictionalized biography of any of the four women about whom it is written. There are acres of territory I would have loved to cover, had my intent been simply to write the accounts of four women's lives (and to end up with about half a million words at the lowest reasonable estimate).

I would have loved to go on at greater length about the scandal that rocked the Washington Administration in the aftermath of the Whiskey Rebellion, about the circus-like atmosphere of Congress in the 1790s, about the skullduggery surrounding the treaty that ended the Revolution. I would have loved to include Abigail Adams's reaction to Ben Franklin's Parisian girlfriend, the details concerning Martha Washington's illegitimate half-caste East Indian stepgrandchildren, and the more Gothic ramifications of the eccentric family into which Jefferson's daughter Patsy married.

But all of these things, I found, wandered from the focus of the story.

Patriot Hearts is a book about the relationships of four women—Martha Washington, Abigail Adams, Sally Hemings, and Dolley Madison—with their families, with their men, with the societies they lived in, with the choices their men made . . . and with one another. They were four women who lived in astonishing times, and they were called upon, as women usually are, to perform the age-old juggling-act of caring for their children while following their hearts, insofar as they were permitted to do so by the world in which they lived.

"My children give me more pain
than all my enemies."
—JOHN ADAMS

PATRIOT
HEARTS

1814

DOLLEY

⚭

Crowds started to gather outside the President's House not long after breakfast.

" 'Tis a good sign," remarked Dolley Madison, setting down her coffeecup with a hand she hoped wasn't visibly shaking.

When they were girls together in Hanover County, Virginia, Dolley had always striven to live up to her friend Sophia Sparling's elegance, and Sophie, she observed now, almost forty years later, awaited news of the invasion with perfect calm.

Because she hath less to lose?

Or for some other reason entirely?

It was true that Sophie was only a dressmaker these days, and Dolley the wife of the

President—the man whom the British commander had sworn to bring back to London in chains.

Jemmy Madison had ridden out in the black predawn cool, to join the militia camped by the Navy Yard. Since first light, Dolley had been at the window with her spyglass, watching the road from the Chesapeake shore.

Sophie half-turned from the parlor window, raised an eyebrow. Even in the thick summer heat she wore her usual widow's black. "They're waiting to see if you'll flee. Taking bets, I shouldn't wonder."

"Excellent." Dolley touched the coffeepot's gay green-and-cream cheek with expert fingers, poured another half-cup for her friend while the brew was still warm. In spite of the grinding millstone of anxiety behind her breastbone, she made her voice light. "If enough people remain in the town to loiter about watching what *I* shall do, the British can't be all *that* near. When *they* flee—" She nodded toward the windows, through which, beyond the ragged lawn and groves of half-grown poplar trees, could be seen the southern wall of the grounds topped with a frieze of boys and young men, "—I shall know to worry."

A gunshot cracked the morning air and Dolley's hand jerked, giving the lie to her calm. The coffee-pot's foot caught the handle of her cup and sent the smaller vessel and its saucer somersaulting to the floor. In her cage beside the open window, Polly spread her gaudy wings and screamed appreciatively, *"Merde alors!"*

The hall door flew open and Paul came in, fifteen, slender, and very grave in his new duties as valet. "It's all right, ma'am," he said quickly, hurrying to the table as if it were a point of honor to clean up the mess before his mistress could stir from her chair. "Some of those white gentlemen outside the house got guns, and more than one been drinkin' by the sound of it. That's all it is."

He whipped the folded towel from its place on his shoulder and wiped the spilled coffee from the woven straw mat that was the parlor's summer flooring. "If it was the British, you'd be hearin' more than one shot, that's for sure. I get you a clean cup, ma'am."

"Don't trouble thyself, dear," said Dolley.

"Mrs. Hallam and I are quite finished here, are we not, Sophie?"

As she gathered the newspapers she'd been perusing when Freeman the butler had announced Sophie, her eye touched again the printed columns: *We feel assured that the number and bravery of our men will afford complete protection to the city . . . It is highly improbable that the enemy . . . would advance nearer to the capital . . .*

"*Will* you flee?" Sophie asked abruptly.

Dolley turned to face her. Grilling sunlight already made the yellow parlor uncomfortably hot, and her light muslin gown—fashionably "Greek" and mercifully appropriate for Washington City's swampy summer climate—stuck to her thighs. The parlor windows, open to catch the slightest whisper of breeze, admitted no sound but the occasional uneasy mutter of voices beyond the trees and the wall.

Further than that, silence lay on the Federal City's marshy acres of woods and cow-pastures like fevered sleep.

"No," she answered quietly. "No, I am staying."

"To meet Admiral Cockburn? I'm sure he'll be flattered." Fifteen months ago, Cockburn's marines had sacked and burned the Maryland port of Havre de Grace. In addition to parading James Madison through the streets of London as a trophy, the Admiral had announced his intention to bring Dolley Madison—the Presidentress, they called her, and foremost hostess of the upstart Republic—to walk in fetters at her husband's side.

When Jemmy had come back late last night from a day in the saddle at the militia camp, he'd been so exhausted he could barely speak: A forced journey even under the mildest of conditions would surely kill him.

And she knew, from her own experience and that of a dozen of her acquaintance, how swiftly situations could deteriorate to violence, among armed men savage with victory.

"Not the Admiral," she replied. "To meet Jemmy." She moved into the cavernous gloom of the Presidential Mansion's long central hall. "And the Generals of the militia, and the members of the Cabinet, will be coming here to dine—"

"Don't tell me you believe that newspaper pap about how the British will turn north to

Baltimore." Sophie strode to catch up. She did so easily—she and Dolley had been the two tallest girls in Hanover County and had suffered together through nicknames like "maypole" and "giraffe." In her impatience she caught her friend's wrist halfway to the little stair that wound its way up to the bed-rooms on the second floor; beside them, one of Mr. Jefferson's iron heating-stoves, coyly concealed behind a concrete vase, gave forth the ghostly whisper of last win-ter's ashes. Through the doorway of the great oval parlor, the full-length portrait of George Washington, like a grave king in black velvet, watched them with wise and weary eyes.

"The British are angry, Dolley, and quite rightly so. After those Massachusetts imbe-ciles burned the Canadian Parliament build-ings in York last year, they'll not settle for sacking a lesser town."

"Dost thou know this?" Dolley's eyes searched her friend's.

If Sophie read anything into the tone of her voice she didn't show it by so much as the flicker of an eyelid. "I should be a fool if I didn't guess."

Dolley turned from her, and ascended the

stair. *And why should I think that Sophie should know? Because her father was a Loyalist? Because her family was ruined and driven out of this country, for adhering to the King?*

Before he had left this morning, Jemmy himself had told her that the troops were far fewer than needed to resist invasion: twenty-five hundred from Baltimore when six thousand had been frantically requested; seven hundred from Virginia in place of the two thousand promised.

Sophie is my friend, and hath been so for forty years.

She would not betray me.

When they reached the upper hallway, Sophie's mobile eyebrows quirked again, for here, out of the sight of whoever might come to call, hastily filled trunks lined the corridor.

"As the Arabs say, *Trust in Allah, but tie up thy camel,*" Dolley told her. "I spent yesterday packing all the Cabinet papers into the carriage. Sukey is like to shake me, for there isn't a cranny now in which to thrust so much as a rolled-up petticoat, and our gardener hath been out since dawn. He hath yet to find another cart or wagon for the rest of the State papers, and a valise of clothing. But whatever he doth find, I will not leave this house until Jemmy comes back."

"Do you really believe you can save him?"

"I believe I can be there to care for him, if he is . . ." Dolley's voice faltered at possibilities her mind wouldn't face.

No President of the country had ever taken the battlefield as President. Sickly and subject to seizures, migraines, and debilitating rheumatism, Jemmy had not been well enough to carry a gun against the British thirty-nine years before. Now, at sixty-three . . .

"I can be there for him if he is taken ill," she finished. "He is not strong."

"Neither apparently are the men who swore they'd guard this house." There was an edge of contempt in Sophie's retort. "Unless they've concealed themselves in the trees and I simply missed seeing them. You'll—"

She bit off her words with instinctive caution as they entered the bedroom and Dolley's maid Sukey turned from the northeastern window, spyglass in hand. "No sign yet, ma'am." Still handsome, though now in her sixties, Sukey had been Dolley's first concrete intimation of the ongoing dilemma of marriage to a plantation-owner. Jemmy had presented her with the woman upon their marriage. As a Quaker born and bred, Dolley abhorred the idea of owning another woman. As a Virginia politician's wife, it was not a sentiment she could ever make publicly known.

"I thank thee, Sukey. Not even smoke?"

The maid shook her head. "Miz Jones's butler Lou says they got that bridge over Goose Creek heaped up with gunpowder an' brushwood, ready to burn if'n they's drove back."

"Provided they can find some brave soul to go back under musket-fire and light the fuse," Sophie commented. "They'd have done better to burn it first."

"I told Jemmy that as well," Dolley said. "General Armstrong hath it that to do so would impede our pursuit of them."

"I shall be sorry indeed to miss the spectacle of veterans who held their ground at Waterloo fleeing in panic before the Virginia militia," said Sophie drily. "Dolley, you should at least make room in the carriage for one trunk of clothing—"

"I *told* her that, ma'am! We may not *get* a

chance for clean clothes, 'twixt here an' Leesburg—"

"We shall see," temporized Dolley, and inwardly flinched that the ultimate destination of Congress had been mentioned so casually. "I thank thee, Sukey." She handed the maid the newspapers, took the spyglass in her hand. "Dost think thou couldst get Freeman's son Danny to watch from the attic? 'Tis hot, I know, but 'tis a higher view—"

"Roof'd be higher," said the maid, evidently unconcerned that Danny would fry like an egg on the roof. The butler's twelve-year-old son was no kin of hers.

After Sukey left Dolley said, "I would sooner make room for the things that the others left here, things that belong to the country." She turned to the window, as she had again and again since dawn. Focused the spyglass on the familiar gap in the hills where the Bladensburg road wound through toward the bridge over Goose Creek—a meager stream which Congress had renamed, with no apparent sense of irony, the Tiber.

As Sukey had said, the sky to the east was clear and empty, like pale blue china. *It would ring if I tapped it with my nail.*

"Did they leave things?" Behind her, Sophie's voice was cool. "General Washington never spent a night beneath this roof, insofar as I know, and I was under the impression that everything Mr. Adams left, Mr. Jefferson had taken out with the trash."

"I don't mean them." Dolley lowered the glass, but stood still gazing through the window, to the hot clear stillness of the east. "I mean Lady Washington, and Mrs. Adams. I mean things a man would not think important, perhaps. Things that are part of what they were, of what *we* were. Insignificant things, meaningless as the dolls and ribbons and the cups we drank from as children. We need those, as much as papers and speeches, to remember where we came from, and who we were, if our hearts are to survive."

"I wouldn't know about that." The jeer in her friend's voice brought Dolley around with a stab of remorse at having spoken her thought. In her friend's chill eyes she saw the flames of a burning plantation-house, swarming with the shadows of looting patriot militia.

"Forgive me—"

Sophie dismissed the images with a

shrug, scornful even of her own pain. And yet, thought Dolley despite herself, the coldness in Sophie's face was to Dolley proof beyond words of the need for such dolls and ribbons and baby cups. *Would she be different—would her eyes be less hard—had she had time to snatch up even one fragment of the vanishing world she had loved?*

Or would her pain be only of a different kind?

Already Sophie was looking around her at the crimson silk bedroom with an appraising eye. *"Did* they leave things here? I don't imagine Lady Washington did . . ."

Dolley forced herself away from the window: *Watching the road all the day shalt make him no safer . . .* "The coffee-set was Lady Washington's."

"So it was." The triangular, thin-lipped mouth relaxed into a smile of genuine kindness. "I remember now. When I came back to this country eighteen years ago she served me coffee from it on my first visit to her. As mementos go, it's rather bulky. Did she keep the mirror, I wonder? The one the Queen of France sent her?"

"The Queen of France?" Movement on the

road caught Dolley's eye and she swung the spyglass back, her heart in her throat. It couldn't be soldiers, couldn't be the British already, those deadly lines of marching men whose coats had flashed like blood among the brown Virginia woods . . .

It wasn't. Through the thin young trees and across the whitewashed railings on the unpaved track grandiosely named Pennsylvania Avenue, Dolley could see two carriages. Their roofs were heaped with roped parcels and their teams were laboring as if the vehicles were jammed with people and goods. Behind them, three men pushed laden wheelbarrows through the dust.

Her hands trembled as she turned back to meet Sophie's enigmatic gaze. She drew a deep breath, asked, "Marie Antoinette, Queen of France?"

"I don't imagine it was Marie de Medici. It was a hand-mirror, the kind they make for travelers' toiletry-sets—it was originally part of one, you know. You've seen the sort of thing: brushes and combs, pins in a fancy box, night-light, candles, mirrors, sometimes nightcaps and a nightgown. This one was in gold, with blue enamel and dia-

monds, and the Queen's portrait in miniature on the back, and the words—"

"Liberté—Amitié," Dolley finished, a little
breathless. "I know. Mrs. Washington gave
it to me, almost the last time I saw her." Her
throat tightened, remembering plump small
competent hands in their lace mitts, the
bright squirrel-brown eyes. How white her
old friend's skin had seemed against the
black of mourning.

"Did she indeed?" Sophie raised her
brows. "I'm surprised she let it go again, after all the hands it passed through, to come
to her. It was lost, you know, on its way to
her. The War was still going on, and the ship
the Queen sent it on was captured by
British privateers."

"Martha said it had a story to it, that she'd
tell me one day. But after that she was ill.
And she never was the same, after the General died. I suppose she'd rather the mirror
were saved, than the coffee-set. People
were always sending General Washington
gifts after the War—I think the coffee-set
came from one of the French generals—but
the mirror was special, she insisted." Dolley
led the way toward the stairs again, trying to
picture in her mind where she had seen that

exquisite little looking-glass last. The curio cabinet in the yellow parlor? In among Mr. Jefferson's seashells and fossils on the glass-fronted shelves in the dining-room that had once been his office?

"The coffee-set was the one she used to serve all the members of that first Congress, after the General's inauguration as President," Dolley went on as they descended, into the heavy stillness of the great house. Would Martha have fled? she wondered.

She didn't think so.

"She told me she could scarcely stand to look at it. Had it not been a gift, she said, she would have taken it out into the yard and broken every piece of it to bits with a poker, and thrown them all down the privy."

"Good Lord, why?"

"Because of what befell her and her family, when her General became President." The windows of the great dining-room—formerly Jefferson's office—faced north onto Pennsylvania Avenue; even with the casements closed, she could hear the voices of the men before the house, the rattle of the carriage-traces and the creak of more wheelbarrows and handcarts being pushed along. A reminder of her peril. Like the Devil constantly whispering, *Thou'lt never see Jemmy again.*

Would Martha have whispered, *And serve him right?*

As she opened the cabinet between the windows, swiftly scanned its contents, she went on softly, " 'Twas Jemmy who brought him—*them*—out of retirement, after the General swore to Martha and to all the nation no more to meddle in public affairs. It was the end, Martha told me once, of her happiness, and her family's . . . and of the General's as well."

Out on the Avenue a man detached himself from one of the knots of idlers watching the face of the house, stopped one of the barrow-men. There was a brief dumb-show, arms gesturing, hands pointing back to the gap in the hills, the Bladensburg road.

Dolley's heart froze. Then the man turned and ran off up the Avenue. The barrow-pusher spat on his hands, picked up the handles of his load again. Two more men from the watching idlers raced away, toward their own houses, their own families, perhaps.

To gather their possessions and flee.

❧ 1787 ❧

MARTHA

⚭

Mount Vernon Plantation
Fairfax County, Virginia
Thursday, January 25, 1787

The Negroes always said a barking dog was the sign of ill luck on its way.

Martha Washington's father, London born and educated there til the age of fifteen, might scoff at this superstition, but her childhood fifty years ago in the isolated little plantation of Chestnut Grove had taught her its wisdom. A barking dog meant a stranger coming onto the place.

And a stranger could mean anything.

A visitor with ill news.

A letter with a request that could not be denied.

Dread flared behind her breastbone like the spark struck from steel and flint, but the fire that blossomed there was the flame of pure rage.

Not again.

I will not let him do this to me twice.

The bedroom windows looked more or less south, toward the river and the wharf past the lane of outbuildings: smokehouse, washhouse, coachhouse, and stables. That way, too, lay the river road that wound south along the Potomac, half-hidden by the slope of the ground and the gray lacework of winter trees. But the windows of the two small dressing-rooms adjoining the bedroom commanded the drive where it circled up to the gate.

A girl's trick, she thought, annoyed with herself as she rose from her chair and crossed the room. Like a child impatient to grab at a future that was, good or ill, inevitably on its way.

What would be, would be.

But at least I can ready my heart.

The dressing-room was icily cold. As the familiar scents of well-worn wool, herb sachets, and hair-powder drifted around her, the wish flitted through her mind that she might have a nice Kentucky long-rifle, of the sort the men at the camps at Cambridge and

Valley Forge had borne, a foot longer than her own diminutive height and deadly at a distance of two hundred yards. From this window she could pick off the rider the instant he appeared between the gate-posts.

She guessed who it would be.

She dismissed the wish briskly—*Don't be silly, Patsie, what an appalling example to set for the children!*—but wasn't shocked at it. She had long believed God never blamed you for your first thought, only your second.

Please, God, don't let it be James Madison. She changed her wish to a prayer.

It might, of course, be someone else. Since the end of the War it seemed that everyone in the thirteen States felt entitled to come to Mount Vernon to see the man who had led the Continental Army to victory. In addition to assorted Dandridges and Bassetts—her own family—and the General's brother Jack and sister Betty and their adult offspring, men arrived whom Martha had known from her winters in the Army camps with the General. Not only the officers like stout Harry Knox and dour-faced disapproving Timothy Pickering, but common soldiers, men from all walks of life whom she'd nursed in camp hospitals or knitted stockings for. Martha had grown accustomed to the constant stream of visitors, and to never really knowing how many to tell Uncle Hercules would be sitting down to dinner, to say nothing of the expense.

But since October, the bark of dogs and the crunch of hooves on the drive had filled her with foreboding that sometimes turned her cold with fear, and sometimes hot with rage.

A child's voice sliced the air. Half a dozen small figures milled excitedly into sight from the curved walkway that led to the kitchen, trampling last week's muddy snow. The little ones who helped with chores in the shops and, in summer, in the wide vegetable gardens near the wharf were always on hand to take messages to the house, and could dash up the steep hill from the river long before horses could take the drive. Shivering in the raw cold by the dressing-room window, Martha heard her niece Fanny's gentle exclamations from the walkway. At nineteen, as the wife of the General's nephew Augustine, Fanny had stepped into the role of auxiliary hostess at Mount Vernon.

Martha caught the words, ". . . Mr. Madison," and her small firm jaw clenched until it ached. The General's niece Harriot—one of several family members now dwelling under the Mount Vernon roof—cried, "Let's go tell Aunt!" and Fanny murmured something in reply and, Martha hoped, an admonition about how ladies didn't shout.

What am I ever going to do with that girl?

The thought of Harriot—of Fanny with her first baby on the way, of the two children of her dead son Jacky whom Martha had taken in as her own, and of the older sisters of those two, who'd journeyed down from Alexandria to have some relief from their mother's constant illnesses and pregnancies—the thought of Harriot's older brothers who'd have to be provided for and looked after—suddenly weighed on Martha's thoughts, and she closed the window without even waiting to see who was arriving at Mount Vernon that morning.

But her knees shook as she returned to her chair by the fire. Her breath was coming fast.

He promised.

Promised not only me, but the Congress and every one of his officers, every one of his soldiers.

I will not become a dictator, he had promised her. *A Cincinnatus, not a Caesar. We have not spent eight years ridding ourselves of one despot, to exchange for another. My own vine and fig tree, shared in peace with you, are more precious to me than any palace, any crown.*

Martha closed her eyes. She felt thankful beyond measure for her own long-standing rule that the hour after breakfast, when the General rode out to supervise the work on Mount Vernon's outlying farms, was inviolate. Even Fanny whom she loved like a daughter, even her treasured granddaughter Nelly, knew enough not to knock at her bedroom door during that hour of solitude. When the French clock on the mantelpiece spoke its small sweet note at ten, that would be time enough to take up her weapons and learn what battle it was that she would have to fight.

But her instincts told her that in this inclement season, with Congress reconvening soon, the visitor had to be James Madison. And for a bleak silent moment Martha Dandridge Custis Washington wished the little man dead.

Eight years.

In the fairy-tales of which her daughter—her beautiful Patcy—had been so fond, days of trial and testing for hero and heroine concluded with "happily ever after" and were presumably followed by a lifetime of peace (although, reflected Martha, Heaven only knew what one would talk about with a man who'd spent his youth hopping from lily-pad to lily-pad in the guise of a frog). She'd never read one in which the deserving couple had their years of peace first, their trials and tribulations afterwards, and no end to them in sight.

Her first marriage, at nineteen, to Daniel Custis could certainly not be counted a tribulation, once his frightful father was dead. Plump, middle-aged Daniel had adored her and had showered her with gifts. The only trials she'd passed through had been the deaths of two of their four beautiful children before they reached the age of four . . . and the appalling legal mess of his Parke grandmother's legacy, which had fallen upon her, ensnarled in the vast Custis fortune, when Daniel had suddenly died.

As for the General . . .

George had his trials and his tribulations,

reflected Martha. But he was a soldier. Of course there had been times when he'd lain in the hand of Death. Ambushed by the French and Indians in the days before the French had been driven out of Canada, he had brought a division of confused and panicky English soldiers out of the wilderness to safety. When first she'd seen him, stepping out into the sunlight of the Palace Green in Williamsburg in his blue-and-scarlet militia uniform, that was what Daniel had said of him: *That's Colonel Washington, the man who saved Braddock's troops.*

Two years after that they'd been formally introduced, at a ball to celebrate her sister Anna Maria's wedding to Burwell Bassett of Eltham Plantation: Fanny's mother. He'd asked her to dance—quite properly soliciting her husband's permission—and led her out to the floor, a very tall man who seemed taller yet because of the straightness of his carriage, and because of the Indian-like litheness with which he moved. Only a month before that she had lost her daughter, sweet four-year-old Frances. She had almost declined to attend the wedding or the dance.

But when George bowed over her hand,

and looked down at her with those remarkable eyes, pale chilly blue like spring sky when the clouds first break, she would no more have refused a request to dance—or a request that he carry her out of the ballroom and away from Williamsburg over the crupper of his horse, for that matter—than she'd have turned away from the warmth of a fire on a freezing night.

She later learned that George had that effect on most women.

As it was, the impact of his presence confused her, because she still did quite sincerely love Daniel. . . .

But this was different. When she thought about it later, she realized this must be what people meant when they spoke of *charisma,* the potent magic that some people had that made you want to be near them, that made you want to do as they asked.

When he thanked her for the dance—and he danced with the leashed power of a well-schooled hunting-horse going over jumps— his voice was like brown velvet, but she saw that his teeth were very bad. The reason, she understood at once, for his tight-lipped expression, and his snorting, close-mouthed laugh.

He was self-conscious.

And though she continued to love Daniel til he died, the memory of that dance was like a little piece of warmed amber, tucked away in a pocket, that she could touch, in the months that followed, when her hands or her heart felt cold.

Some eight months after Daniel's death, George came to call on her at the home of mutual friends. During those months she'd been wrestling with the maddening difficulties of keeping the overseers of four plantations from either stealing her blind or half-killing the slaves in order to get work out of them, and with the legal complications of finding a guardian for four-year-old Jacky and two-year-old Patcy, since Daniel had died intestate. In George, she had recognized at once both great strength and great patience, and an intelligence similar to her own. Neither of them was bookish, nor could either be called a philosophical genius. But George, like herself, had a keen understanding of how things worked, and a sharp vision of what was most important in any situation.

And, they laughed at the same things.

The fact that he was twenty-five years old

and the most breath-taking man she'd ever seen didn't hurt matters either.

Happily ever after.

⚓

The woods below the house wore their winter-dress of gray, brown, and white; in the mornings the water in the bedroom ewer would be skinned with ice. With the dressing-room windows shut Martha couldn't hear whether it was a single horse's hooves that crunched the gravel by the mansion house's western door, or the creak of harness and the grind of carriage-wheels. But through the shut door of her room the sounds of the house came to her, comforting and familiar as a heartbeat.

Sal's measured footfalls in Nelly's bedroom on the other side of the wall, and the scratch of her broom on the bare pine floors. The faint clinking as Caro gathered up chamber-pots to bear down the backstairs and out to the scullery. The creak of bedropes and the dawdling tread of the young girls—Sinah and Annie—as they passed and repassed, making up the beds. Taking their time: From childhood Martha had understood that it was useless to expect any slave, from the lowest field-hand up to house-servants like George's valet Billy and her own dear Nan, to hurry. It drove the General frantic. He'd take his watch out to the fields and time the men at their tasks, trying to arrive at new methods to make the work go more efficiently. The men in the fields, the women in the weaving-rooms, would merely look at him when he'd explain how they could actually accomplish twice as much in the same amount of time, increasing the productivity of the plantation . . .

And would then go back to doing as they'd always done.

Their voices came to Martha in snatches, since they spoke quietly, respecting her hour of peace. She heard Mr. Madison's name, and the phrase, ". . . the blue bedroom." Had their visitor been only a messenger, the man would have been accommodated in the attic room next to that of the children's tutor, young Mr. Lear. Harriot's footsteps galloped wildly up the main stair, vibrating the house, with Nelly's a swift-pattering echo.

"Is Uncle going to Philadelphia?" demanded Harriot. "Do you think he'll take us?

We never get to go anywhere, and I'm so bored with Mr. Lear's lessons I could *scream!*"

"Well, don't scream in the house," responded Nelly, two years younger and sounding like the elder by several years. "Sal, I'm sorry, did you see Harriot's copybook up here? It's not down in the parlor."

"I ain't seen it, child—"

"I told you, Wash took it! Wash is always taking and hiding things!"

Seven-year-old George Washington Parke Custis was Nelly's brother, known throughout the family as Mr. Tub. The footsteps retreated, out of the bedroom and down the stairs; Martha reflected that more probably Harriot herself was the culprit. Her own son—Daniel's son—Jacky would do the same thing, many years ago in those peaceful days when he and Patcy were schoolchildren, "losing" his copybook or hiding it and blaming poor Patcy for its theft, with no other purpose than to delay or disrupt unwanted lessons. Of course, Wash was more than ready to pilfer copybooks on his own, or do whatever was necessary to disrupt lessons, being no more of a scholar than his father Jacky had been.

Martha smiled to herself even as she sighed with exasperation at her child, her grandchildren, George's obstreperous niece.

THIS is my world. Family and home, children growing up and bearing children of their own. Fanny's first was due in March, and Eleanor, Jacky's widow, was expecting yet again by her second husband Dr. Stuart. . . . Something would have to be done about introducing Jacky's oldest daughter Eliza into society when the time came, if Eleanor continued to be so preoccupied with her second family. Though there was plenty of time to think of that.

This was the world Martha would have chosen, if offered every fairy-tale realm from Camelot to the Moon and the splendors of Egypt and Rome. Mount Vernon in the quiet of winter, with the fields bare and the woods and lawn patched with snow. George riding out wrapped in his Army coat to survey the fields for next spring's plowing, his dapple gelding puffing smoke through its nostrils like a dragon.

A world of mending and knitting, of black icy mornings rank with the smell of wood smoke from the kitchen. Of the soft chatter of the women in the weaving-room by candle-glow and firelight, of counting out bulbs and seeds and planning next year's garden.

A world where in earlier years her sister Anna Maria or her brother Bart or George's brothers or sister or the Fairfaxes or the Masons from across the river would ride over for dinner and a few days' stay or a few weeks'. A world where she'd be waked in the dark of predawn by George's soft-footed rising and the soft clank of the poker as he stirred up the fire, so that the bedroom would be warm for her.

That world had been theirs for seventeen years, all the "happily ever after" she'd ever wanted. There had been the recurring worry about her daughter Patcy's seizures, which the shy, beautiful girl had suffered from childhood. But somewhere, Martha had always felt—perhaps in England—there must exist a cure. At the time it had seemed to her that these days of happiness would go on forever, until she and George were old.

But they had lasted only seventeen years.

⚜

The mantel-clock struck ten. It was time to get up, and go downstairs, and ask Fanny in the most natural-sounding voice she could contrive, "Who was that, whose horse I heard in the drive?"

So it seemed to her, Martha thought, that in 1774 a clock had struck somewhere and it was time to get up from their quiet life of family and home and watching the river flow past the foot of the hill, and step out the door and into the War.

The War had ended four years ago. But as she shook out the folds of her dark skirts, and glanced at her looking-glass to make sure her cap was straight, it seemed to Martha that the War was once again waiting downstairs, as alive as it ever had been. Ready to sink its claws into George and drag him away from her.

Drag them both away, never to return.

Never, she vowed in her heart. *I saw what it did to them—to Fanny, to Jacky, to those children whom I most love.*

He promised, and I will hold him to that promise. Nothing—nothing—will take us again from this place, and from these people who need us.

⚜

As she came down the stairs into the paneled shadows of the hall, Martha heard

James Madison's voice in the West Parlor. Barely a murmur from that small slight man, like a mouse nibbling in a wainscot. A wet, rasping cough told her Madison was talking with George's nephew Augustine—Fanny's husband, about whose health Martha was increasingly worried.

"In the States that have paper money, it's worth half what specie is, if that," she heard as she came nearer. "But the States make laws that this paper must be accepted, and those who've lent in good faith are being driven to bankruptcy. In the States that don't have it, you can't lay hands on a shilling and creditors are calling in their debts by taking a man's land. They're saying in New York that if it weren't for the western counties rising in rebellion, Massachusetts would have gone to war with Connecticut over trade between them."

"Madness," said Augustine, and coughed again. Augustine had been part of the General's staff during the closing years of the War, a slender young man whose succession of feverish chest-colds had kept him a wanderer in search of that elusive "change of air" that all doctors prescribed. He'd come to Mount Vernon last year to take up again his position as the General's secretary, and in so doing, had met once more his childhood sweetheart, Fanny.

His usual task at this hour was to be in the General's study copying letters. But since, unlike Fanny, Augustine wasn't six and a half months gone with child, the task of entertaining the visitor until Martha came downstairs fell to him.

"It is more than madness; it is the death-knell of all we have fought for," said Madison. "In Richmond they talk of a moratorium on taxes, because no one will or can pay them. How we're to deal with the British—"

He broke off, set down his glass of Madeira, and got to his feet as Martha appeared in the doorway. "Lady Washington."

"Mr. Madison, I'm so pleased to see you!" It was a complete lie, of course. But in Virginia, where everyone was related to everyone else and everyone's welfare depended on that cat's cradle of friendships, alliances, and marriage, there was no point in expressing personal animosities about which one could do nothing. "And how is the Colonel?"

"My father is well, ma'am, thank you for asking." Madison bowed. Though only three years older than Martha's son Jacky would have been, had he lived, James Madison—small, thin, prematurely wrinkled, and with gray already thick in his brown hair—had the look of a little old man. And in fact, Martha quite liked him, or would have done so, she told herself, had he kept to his own business of the Virginia Assembly and the Continental Congress, and not tried to drag George back into it, to fix the mess they'd made.

Back in October, Madison and his friend James Monroe had stopped at Mount Vernon on their way back from the Congress, and after dinner the two men had sat in the dining-room, talking to George far into the night. Martha knew Monroe, as she knew Madison, from the War: While Madison's health had been too frail to sustain the rigors of camp-life, Monroe had been part of the force that George had taken across the ice-filled Delaware River on Christmas night, 1776, to counterattack the Hessian mercenaries. The Hessians had been so incapacitated by holiday cheer that they'd managed only to get off a handful of shots before surrendering: One of those shots had hit Jim Monroe.

That was the kind of person Jim Monroe was.

After that dinner in October, George had been very quiet.

In her heart, Martha had always known Madison would try again.

Still, her own fears and her own rage—rage at men who shouted and waved their arms and complained of taxation without representation, and then when they *got* representation didn't want to be taxed anyway—were no excuse for incivility. "My dear sir, you must be frozen! Augustine, I trust Frank is having a good fire made up in the blue bedroom for our guest? The General has ridden over to Dogue Run Farm this morning, to see what condition the fields are in, but he shall be back for dinner. Please do make yourself at home here, Mr. Madison—Surely you aren't riding on to New York tomorrow? All the Negroes are saying there is another storm on its way."

"I fear I must, ma'am, thank you. There are matters pending in Congress that cannot wait. I have not even been home, on my way from Richmond—a night is all I can stop."

More time than enough, thought Martha grimly, *to convince George to go to Philadelphia with you once the spring crops are in the ground. More time than enough to de-*

stroy what we have here, the peace that we have earned.

She had learned, to her cost, how quickly—in three minutes or less—the whole of the world could change.

⚜

"All shall be well, Aunt Patsie."

Fanny slipped an arm around Martha's waist as she emerged from the parlor and gathered up her heaviest shawl to walk to the kitchen. In the shadows of the hall, for a moment it was as if Martha's sister Anna Maria, and not Anna Maria's daughter, stood beside her: Anna Maria come to life again, with her brown curls slightly tumbled, her hazel eyes kind. Despite the exhaustion of her pregnancy, Fanny had been in the kitchen, making sure dinner would include in its inevitable bounty items suitable for Mr. Madison's delicate digestion. Her clothing held the scents of wood smoke, cinnamon, and baking meats.

"Even though Uncle's retired, you know he's still interested in politics. You know how he's been following all this talk about another convention to straighten things out between the States. Even if he doesn't go to

Philadelphia, he *was* elected as part of the delegation. Of course he'll want to tell Mr. Madison what to say."

Fanny gathered up her own shawl from its peg on the wall as she followed Martha into the little hallway at the south end of the house that ran next to the General's study; even with a fire burning in the study, the hall was brutally cold. In the little parlor behind them, the voices of the children could be heard, reciting their lessons with the stocky young New Englander George had taken on as tutor: Jacky's children, and restless, noisy Harriot.

Martha's responsibility, and George's. With no one to look after them, if they did not.

"Uncle knows how much he's needed here." Fanny took her hands, the way Anna Maria used to, when she wanted to coax Martha into letting her do something. "Augustine has told me how deeply in debt we are, because of Uncle being away all those years. And though of course if Augustine had been manager during the War instead of poor Cousin Lund the place would have made money hand over fist—"

"Of course," responded Martha, stifling a

grin in spite of herself. At the start of the War, Augustine had been twelve years old.

"—even he will tell you that any plantation will suffer, if its master isn't on hand to oversee things in person. Uncle knows this."

Fanny was so earnest, and so anxious that her favorite aunt be reassured, that Martha gave her a smile which she hoped displayed relief, and laid a small, lace-mitted hand to Fanny's cheek. "Of course you're right, dearest. And now don't you *dare* come out to the kitchen again with me: You'll catch your death. You should be upstairs resting."

Fanny's—and Augustine's—argument could be made, she reflected, for the entity that had been born in Philadelphia, that wretched sweltering summer only eleven years ago. That the so-called United States of America would suffer, if its master wasn't on hand to oversee things in person.

And Jemmy Madison had determined that the only master all would obey was George.

⚜

There was a great deal about the year before the War that Martha simply didn't remember.

Looking back on it, as she went about her morning routine of doling out kitchen supplies of sugar, tea, coffee, and spices from their locked chests—of checking that the women in the weaving-and-spinning rooms were doing their work quickly and neatly—it seemed to Martha that one day she and George had been happy in the sunny world of family and work, and that the next, George was a self-declared traitor, riding away to war against the King.

It hadn't been that quick, of course.

In the plantation account-books for 1774 and the later half of 1773, she would still find entries in her own handwriting concerning dinners she had no recollection of giving, dresses she had made with her own hands whose cut and color and construction she remembered nothing of.

What she did remember, as if it were only hours ago, was the muggy June afternoon in '73 that had followed what turned out to be their last morning of that peaceful happily ever after. George's younger brother John Augustine ("The only one with a lick of sense," said George) and his family had journeyed from Bushfield Plantation to stay for a few days, to meet pretty Eleanor Calvert, her son Jacky's intended bride.

That in itself had been a source of tension. On the eve of being sent away to college the previous winter, Jacky—then nineteen years old and determined to profit as little as possible from a succession of tutors and boarding establishments—had announced to his appalled parents that he was engaged to the fifteen-year-old daughter of a Maryland planter. George had managed to talk his stepson out of immediate matrimony, on the grounds that he needed *some* modicum of education to fit him for the responsibilities due his young bride. And, when Eleanor and her sister Elizabeth had come to visit, the girl turned out to be the sweetest of young ladies, if overly sensitive and rather featherbrained.

Over dinner in the little dining-room—that was long before the big one was built—Martha had mentioned the new sheet-music that had arrived from England for Patcy's harpsichord. "Oh, do play them for us!" Eleanor cried. "I do so love music and I'm such a fool at it myself. My poor teacher says it's as if my hands were all thumbs!"

And Patcy had blushed, laughed: "Only if

you'll play with me. I'll show you how! You'll have to learn if we're going to be sisters." Still smiling she got to her feet—"May I just get my music, Mama?"—took three steps toward the doorway and stopped, her hand going to her throat. . . .

For years Martha dreamed that scene, over and over, as if that fragment of sunny dining-room, of languid June heat and the scents of new-cut hay and baked ham, had somehow become trapped in some secret chamber in her mind into which she wandered, unable to get out. The way her elfin dark-haired daughter stopped in mid-step, thin hand flying up to her throat, and the look of terror and despair that flashed across her face as she understood that another one of her seizures was coming on.

Sometimes in her dreams Martha was able to wake herself up before Patcy fell. Before she began to jerk and spasm like a landed fish dying in air, eyes huge with fright and shame and hands slapping and flinging aimlessly. Before George was on his feet and to her side, his reactions quicker than anyone's at the table, gathering into his arms the seventeen-year-old stepdaughter who'd always called him "Papa . . ."

In her dreams Martha screamed. She didn't remember whether she'd actually done so that afternoon or not.

But in her dreams, when she saw Patcy sag down suddenly limp in George's arms, her disheveled dark hair tumbling down over his elbow—when she saw George's face alter from concern to realization and grief—then she would scream, screaming and screaming in the hopes that George would wake her, would hold her against him, would rock her gently while she cried.

⚜

Jacky married his Eleanor the following Christmas, of 1773. Martha did not attend the wedding. For many months after Patcy's death she found even the company of much-loved friends and members of her family more than she could bear. And though Jacky came often to visit her, he had moved to Maryland, to be near his bride's family. Martha had vague memories of hearing about the ninety thousand dollars' worth of British-taxed tea that the Massachusetts Sons of Liberty dumped into Boston Harbor, but like many things during that year, it seemed to her no more real than scenes in a play in which a woman named Martha Washington was one of the players.

During the "public times" in Williamsburg that year, when the House of Burgesses was in session, there was great furor over the King's decision to retaliate upon the port of Boston for the destruction of the tea: Courts were placed under direct British control, local officials would now be appointed by the Crown, and town meetings were outlawed throughout all thirteen colonies.

"What on earth had *we* to do with it?" Martha protested to George's fellow Burgess, lanky red-haired Tom Jefferson, one evening. "Why punish Virginians for something those people up in Massachusetts did?"

In July of '74 there was a general Congress of the thirteen colonies in Philadelphia, and as a war hero of unquestioned honesty and probity—not to mention being the man who'd married the wealthiest widow in the colony—George was elected one of Virginia's seven delegates. Martha remembered being worried, because in the climate of royal vengefulness there was no telling who might get punished for what, but even then she had no real sense that their lives had changed.

Like a boat in a squall, even after Patcy's death she had expected things to right themselves eventually. Even though she knew that George was helping to drill the State militia, and that weapons, ammunition, cartridge-paper, spades, and food were being stockpiled, she thought of the matter as a passing "flap," as her father used to call such alarms. Certainly less critical than the ever-present whispered threat of slave insurrection, a fear that had run like a dark undercurrent through the whole of her childhood.

Then in April of '75, as George was preparing to leave for a second Congress in Philadelphia, Royal Governor Dunmore ordered the marines from a warship in the James River off of Williamsburg to seize the powder that was traditionally kept in the Williamsburg Magazine against the threat of an uprising among the slaves. The local patriots protested, triggering a near-riot on the Palace green.

And at almost the same time, General Gage, in charge of occupied Boston, sent eight hundred of his men to destroy a patriot cache of arms in the town of Concord.

And instead of a concerned magistrate riding to a conference on the subject of finding some means to redress colonial grievances, when George rode away down Mount Vernon's shallow hill in his new blue-and-buff uniform, he was a man who placed himself in the camp of those who had taken up arms against their King.

A traitor, who would face sentence of death.

⚜

George returned a little before three. Martha was in the kitchen, putting the finishing dashes of cinnamon into a custard that she knew was her granddaughter's favorite—not that Uncle Hercules couldn't make equally marvelous desserts, but it gave her great pleasure to make the treats for her grandchildren herself. There was always a commotion when the General rode into the stable-yard, audible from the kitchen. Martha raised her head sharply, and with a smile the big, handsome cook took the spice-caddy from her hand.

"If her Ladyship'll trust a poor ignorant

savage to finish pepperin' up that custard, I promise you I won't poison them poor children."

In spite of her apprehension, Martha smiled up at Uncle Hercules. From the walkway that led to the house, Harriot's voice shrilled, "I'm going to *kill* you, Tub!" Footsteps pounded.

Uncle Hercules widened his eyes at Martha and added conspiratorially, "Not unless you want me to, that is, ma'am."

"Get along with you." Martha's heart beat quickly as she dried her hands on her apron, picked up her shawl, and stepped through the door into the brittle cold of the open walkway.

Saw him striding up the row of outbuildings through the slush, coat flapping about his calves and dogs caracoling ecstatically around his boots. Saw him turn his head to greet Doll and Sal where steam billowed out the door of the laundry, and old Bristol as the gardener crossed the path with an armload of fresh-cut stakes.

She'd been married to him for almost thirty years, and he still took her breath away. She'd seen him laid low by intestinal flux and reading in bed without his teeth in,

and it didn't matter. He was still the handsomest man she'd ever seen.

Her husband.

Her George.

He took her hands, bent down to kiss her.
Even wearing the tallest of her collection of
bouffant lace caps, the top of her head
didn't reach his broad shoulder, and her
small hands were lost in a grip powerful
enough to crack walnuts. "Bounce, *down,*"
she ordered, in the voice that invariably silenced the loudest quarrels in the kitchen.
"Fang, York, *sit.*"

The hounds abased themselves instantly
in the half-frozen mud. George's eyes
danced above his tight-closed smile.

"I always said you were wasted, knitting
stockings for the men." He kissed her again.
"Baron von Steuben could have used you
on the drill-grounds at Valley Forge."

"His Lordship would have been less impressed with my talents if he'd ever tried to
out-shout my brothers and sisters." Martha
reached up to take his arm. "Mr. Madison is
here."

She watched his face as she spoke, her
voice carefully neutral. Saw how the muscles in his jaw hardened, and how for a mo-

ment his eyes took on the faraway look of a man who scans the invisible horizon of the future, for what he hopes he will not see.

Knowing how he hated to be pressed on matters about which he hadn't made up his mind, she immediately went on, "I've put him in the blue bedroom and his man in the attic, but he says he must ride on at once in the morning, though I did tell him that Doll's back has been warning her since yesterday of more snow on the way. Why is it that men will believe a barometer, when they mostly have *no* idea how it works—*I* certainly haven't—and will not believe a perfectly trustworthy human being whose back *always* begins to hurt twenty-four hours before the onset of a storm? Fanny came up with Augustine this morning, and considering how bad the weather has been, would it perhaps not be better if they moved back into the house with us, at least until the baby comes? I'm sure that cottage of theirs isn't nearly warm enough for an infant."

George nodded as they entered the house. Billy had hot water, clean clothes, the powdering-cloth and powder-cone ready in the dressing-room. While George changed, Martha kept up the soft light chatter of the small inconsequences of the day: A letter had come from their lawyer in Port Tobacco. Austin the coachman's wife was laid up with rheumatism again. Harriot had ruined yet another petticoat and gotten stains of ink and mud on her yellow dress: "Honestly, the way that child destroys everything she touches it's no wonder your poor brother died insolvent! I've put her to mending her own petticoats when she tears them but I'm not sure what to do about the dress. . . . Oh, and we've had a letter from the head-master in Georgetown. Steptoe is doing a little better but Lawrence is definitely Harriot's brother, only for him it's books he demolishes, not dresses! And both boys sneaked away last week to go sailing. . . ."

And as she spoke she continued to observe his face. He was usually silent while she chattered—he'd once likened her and Anna Maria's family gossip to the voices of birds in the spring woods—but she could see today his thoughts were only partly on what she said. January was the time for planning next year's crops, for estimating seed and guessing what the markets in Europe, in New York, in England would bear: an anxious time. Tobacco prices had never been the same since the War, and like many other places in the Tidewater, Mount Vernon's ability to produce quality tobacco had declined. In addition to the financial disarray left by eight years of absence during the War—not to mention having come within a hair's breadth of having the house burned to the ground by British warships—they owed considerable money to British tobacco-factors from before the War. All planters did. That was part of the ongoing squabble in Congress.

Money for farm equipment and carriages. Money for dishes and corsets and paint, for window-glass and paper, medicine and tea. Every book in the library had come from England, and most of George's guns. Prior to the War, it had been the only way to live. The planter wrote the factor to buy a plow, the factor bought one and billed the planter, and took out the cost of the plow when the next year's tobacco-crop came in. They'd fought the War, in part, because England's laws forbade the colonists from seeking cheaper Dutch and French goods: It was the function of colonies to support their Mother Country. And though they'd theoretically won the War, everyone still owed money to their factors and everyone still mostly bought British goods because that's what they'd always done.

Only now everything cost more and the British factors refused to take anything but "hard" coin, gold or silver, of which almost no one had any. George had always been a conscientious farmer, keeping up with every advance in agriculture and inventing some of his own, like a new type of threshing-floor (which the Negroes refused to use, preferring to do things their own way); Martha knew he wouldn't truly relax until the harvest was safely in.

She knew, too, that the chaos and dissension between the States made trade all the harder, a situation that drove him wild. Maryland was currently claiming that it owned not only the north bank of the Potomac, but the south bank as well. According to the Maryland legislature, the Virginia legislature would have to petition them for navigation rights—which struck Martha as exactly the sort of imbecilic quarrel that had used to be solved by the King.

Above all else, George hated waste and inefficiency. Watching him clean his guns after shooting, or supervise the repair of the

grinding-wheels at the grist-mill, or con-
struct a pinwheel for little Wash, Martha was
well aware of that aspect of his character:
that he liked to build things, to fix things. To
make things run better, for the benefit of all.

James Madison was a clever man. He,
too, knew this.

They said the Devil called you in the
voices of your loved ones. What he offered
you in trade for your soul was whatever you
wanted most.

Nan came in, the pretty mulatto girl who'd
been Martha's servant from her girlhood—
who was, Martha knew (everybody knew,
though no one talked about such things, of
course), her own father's daughter by one of
the Chestnut Grove housemaids. She took
Martha into the other dressing-room and
perched her on the stool there, removed her
fichu and lace cap, draped her with the
powdering-cloth and gave her the powder-
cone to cover her face. Hair-powder was
another thing that came from England,
though one *could* use flour; except that by
the time one had sifted it repeatedly through
a dozen bolting-cloths to get out fragments
of hulls and speckles of grit, it was easier
just to buy it—not to mention the issue of

bugs. Martha came from a generation that wouldn't dream of sitting down to dinner unpowdered, even if one's only company was a man one didn't want to see.

⚓

James Madison had powdered for dinner, too.

Though at thirty-six Madison was a confirmed bachelor, it was clear to Martha that he was the uncle of a vast number of nieces and nephews, up there in Orange County. He listened gravely to eleven-year-old Eliza's declamation, in accents of throbbing horror, of how Wash had put a baby mouse in her shoe ("Wherever did you get one at this season, Master Wash?"); gently drew out the timid Pattie on the subject of hair-ribbons; and coaxed Harriot from her care-for-nothing brashness with a query about the latest litter of puppies in the stables.

One did not, of course, discuss politics at table.

Martha could feel herself waiting for the meal to end, as the men were waiting, too.

Dinner at Mount Vernon.

Martha scanned the length of the table as Frank and Austin, resplendent now in their white liveries trimmed in scarlet, brought in the platters: smoked ham, mashed potatoes, the pigeon pie that was the staple of winter fare, spoon bread, yams. It was always difficult to put on a decent meal at this season of the year, without lettuces or spinach or any fresh greens, but Uncle Hercules had worked his usual miracles with dried peas, dried apples, and Martha's justly famous fruit conserves.

But it was the faces around the board, she decided, that were the true treasure of Mount Vernon, the real fruit of the Biblical "vine and fig tree" that George spoke of with such longing and love. Pale, too-thin Augustine leaned across to describe to Nelly the hurricanes that swept the island of Bermuda, where he had gone in quest of elusive health, while at the foot of the table, the tutor Tobias Lear was explaining some aspect of fortress-building to Wash. Fanny, pale and lovely in the voluminous flowered shawl that concealed her pregnancy, put in the observation that battlements were all very well, but what were the defenders going to do if the attackers managed to enlist a dragon or an evil wizard on their side?

Her family. Hers and George's. All that was

left to them of the children they had so dearly loved.

He had abandoned them once, to go and do his duty as men must do in troubled times.

The guilt that pierced her heart was that she had abandoned them, too; her only regret was the price they'd paid. The price she'd let these children pay, for her love of George.

⚜

George's letter had reached her just before her departure in October of 1775 for Eltham Plantation, to visit Anna Maria. Eltham was where the War really started, for her. All the way down from Mount Vernon to Eltham, six days' jolting by coach, Martha's heart had turned and twisted like a fish fighting a hook, trying to determine in which direction her duty lay.

. . . I ask whether it will be convenient to you, to join me at the camp in Cambridge this winter. . . .

The words had had the exact effect upon her as a glass of brandy: shock, elation, warmth that rose from her toes to the ends of her hair.

To the surprise of no one except those who'd thought themselves more qualified for the position—a largish group which included the Washingtons' neighbor Colonel Horatio Gates and the head of the Massachusetts Sons of Liberty, John Hancock—George had been made Commander in Chief of the new Continental Army. General Charles Lee—*no* relation to the Virginia Lees—had sneered that this had had much to do with the fact that George had attended every Congressional session wearing his militia uniform, the only man there to do so.

Having met General Lee, a former mercenary whose mouth was as filthy as his shirt, Martha could only suppose that this was what the man would have done himself, had anyone elected him to Congress or to anything else.

And knowing George, Martha guessed that in a way Lee was right. George had worn his uniform for the same reasons that he would have worn his best clothing and hair-powder to an assembly of men empowered to elect him to the House of Burgesses: because he knew that what a man is given depends largely on what he looks like he can handle. He had worn his uniform precisely to underscore in every delegate's mind that he had field experience in commanding men in battle, something John Hancock and a significant number of other contenders lacked.

The New Englanders couldn't really object, because he'd been nominated by a tubby little Massachusetts lawyer named John Adams.

Since the debacle at Lexington and Concord, the British army had been bottled up in Boston by the ever-growing bands of militiamen camped on the Boston Neck. An island town, Boston was connected with the mainland by a single narrow track of dry land that stretched between acres of salt-marshes. Some fifteen thousand patriots were camped in a ragged semicircle centered in the little towns of Cambridge and Roxbury, where the Neck debouched onto the mainland. Just before George went up to take command in June, the British made an attempt to break out by sea, crossing the harbor to a place called Charles Town below Breed's Hill. After savage fighting, they drove the militiamen from their makeshift emplacements on the hill, but were left too shattered to pursue their advantage. Which was just as well, Martha later gathered, because the militiamen had almost no ammunition. A further assault would have crushed them.

At about this same time, Royal Governor Dunmore retreated with his wife and children to the British man-of-war that was still sitting in the river off Williamsburg, and issued a call to Virginia Loyalists to form an army of his own. Along with this summons came the Governor's promise that any slave who escaped a patriot master would be enlisted, armed, and given his freedom.

All their lives, everyone Martha knew had lived in dread of slave insurrections. Hand in hand with fear of organized rebellion—and in some ways more deadly—went the threat of troublemaking by individual slaves, subtle and silent protests against bondage in general, or an unloved master in particular, that could involve anything from breaking tools and hamstringing plow-oxen to burning houses and poisoning their masters . . . or their masters' children. Fury and outrage swept not only the patriot planters, but men—not all of them slaveholders themselves—who felt no particular conviction about freedom from England one way or the other.

Dunmore was denounced in parlors and pulpits as a fomenter of slave insurrection. Hundreds of slaves decamped, from patriot and loyalist alike, to flock to the British standard.

At Dunmore's proclamation, George's brother John Augustine wrote Martha in a panic with schemes to carry her at once to safety, should Dunmore attack Mount Vernon. Martha wrote back that she considered herself perfectly safe where she was. Before leaving for Eltham in October, Martha packed up all George's papers and the account books, not only of Mount Vernon but of the much larger Custis estate that had been left in trust for Jacky's children, so that Cousin Lund, who'd been left in charge, could easily get them out of there.

"I cannot imagine Governor Dunmore besieging Mount Vernon with a troop of marines in order to capture one middle-aged lady knitting in her own drawing-room," remarked Martha, when she produced George's note for Anna Maria's perusal their first morning at Eltham. Jacky and his pretty Eleanor were still sleeping—Eleanor had borne, and lost, her first child in September, and was still in delicate health—and Jacky because it was never possible to get Jacky out of bed before nine in the morning. Anna Maria's two sons were at their lessons with their tutor, but eight-year-old Fanny had remained at the breakfast table while one of the housemaids brought in a basin of hot water and a towel, for Anna Maria to wash up the cups.

"And what would he do with me if he took me?" pursued Martha. "Chop off my fingers one by one, like a Turk, and send one to the General every day until he surrenders with all his army? Of course he wouldn't." She gave Fanny, round-eyed with horror, a reassuring smile. "One doesn't do such things to people who've had you and your family to dinner."

"The Governor might put you in a dungeon," suggested the child.

"He might," agreed Anna Maria, setting the cups to dry on the towel. Eltham was a larger house than the six-room wooden structure in which the Dandridge girls—and their five brothers and sisters—had grown up at Chestnut Grove. But though the china and silver lacked the elegance of those at Mount Vernon, still there were things that the lady of the house would not entrust to any slave. "He'd put your aunt Martha to mending sheets, and then your uncle George would have to send his army down to get her out."

And Martha smiled, at the thought of being rescued by George on a white horse at the head of a gaggle of the hairy-eared backwoods tosspots she'd heard described in letters from Boston.

"I don't suppose you'd be much safer in Cambridge," her sister added, picking up the note again. It was without superscription or address, delivered by one of George's Lewis in-laws. Already communications were being lost or, worse, intercepted by the British and published, with scurrilous additions, in London newspapers.

"From what I've been told, those so-called patriot soldiers haven't the sense to stay awake—or sober—on sentry-duty, and wander in and out of the camps as they choose. Relieve themselves where they choose, too: God forbid a Pennsylvanian would permit a New York officer to tell him where to piss. I understand smallpox is everywhere in Boston." Anna Maria's bright brown eyes, when Martha glanced up to meet them, regarded her older sister with a close and worried concern.

As if she heard in Martha's voice, or felt like an aura radiating from her flesh, the urgency of her desire to go to Cambridge, to fly like a girl in a ballad to be with her soldier.

As if she, not Martha, were the elder, puzzled at this wildness in one who had all their lives been the sober sister, the businesslike one who kept the household running and made sure everyone had a hot meal and clean socks.

She had never seen this side of Martha before.

Neither had Martha.

"It's a long way to Cambridge," Martha said slowly. "And it's late in the year. It will certainly be snowing by the time we arrive. Jacky says he'll escort me, and Eleanor, too, has offered to bear me company. I shouldn't, of course. Not just because Eleanor has been so ill, but I know how difficult it will be for Lund to run the plantation with both of us away. It would probably be better if I—"

"Mama," piped up Fanny, "why would Governor Dunmore and the Tories lock up

Aunt Patsie anyway? Aunt Patsie's a Tory herself."

"I most certainly am *not!*" Martha bristled with indignant shock.

Anna Maria put in hastily, "Now, you know that isn't true, dearest."

"It's what Scilly Randolph said. And Francine Chamberlayne. And Neddy Giviens."

Anna Maria's cheeks reddened with vexation at the mention of her daughter's closest playmates. "Well, it isn't true. It's just those roughnecks in the local militia, who don't understand that just because your aunt Patsie is looking after things for her friends the Fairfaxes while they're in England, that doesn't make her a Tory, too."

"But it *is* being said?" Martha asked.

The younger woman hesitated. Then she nodded.

Martha leaned across the table and plucked the note out of her hand, just as Eleanor and a rumpled and sleepy-looking Jacky appeared in the doorway. "That does it," Martha announced firmly. "Jacky, please let Austin know we're returning to Mount Vernon tomorrow, and then going on to Cambridge."

☙

"When I am married, and have a house of my own," Eliza announced to her end of the dining-table, "I shall have a ballroom large enough to dance fifty couples, *and* a private theater, so that all my friends may put on plays at Christmastime. Proper ones, with music and elegant costumes. *And* I shall go to the theater every night."

Pulled back to reality, Martha turned with a smile to meet Fanny's eyes, as bright as they'd been when she'd asked if Governor Dunmore would really lock up her aunt Patsie and make her sew sheets.

Mr. Madison responded gravely, "I take it you intend to live in Philadelphia or New York, then, Miss Custis? Or Charleston—I believe there's a theater in Charleston."

"Philadelphia," Eliza drawled grandly. "The heat in South Carolina does not agree with my constitution." She put a weary hand to her forehead, not that, at age eleven, she'd ever been to South Carolina in her life. "I shall have the grandest house in Philadelphia: forty rooms, and every one with a black marble fireplace and looking-glasses on the walls."

"You'll bankrupt your husband trying to heat it," remarked Nelly, and set aside her custard-spoon with the last morsel of the dessert uneaten, as good manners dictated.

Pattie, Eleanor's daughter, put down her spoon and slipped her hand into Martha's. "When I'm grown-up I'd like to have a house just like Aunt Patsie's." Her voice was wistful.

Martha put an arm around her and thought, *So would I, dearest. So would I.*

She looked along the board to make sure everyone was finished—little Wash had left a polite final morsel about half the size of a pixie's fingernail—then rose smiling. In her breast her heart was a nugget of slag. "If you'll excuse us, gentlemen?"

The men stood, moved back chairs for them. Had there been more company the children would have been relegated to a table of their own in the little dining-room, but Mr. Madison only bowed, and gave the four young girls a wink as they filed into the parlor where Sal had already built up the fire, and set out the sewing-boxes.

As she left the dining-room, Martha heard

George ask, "What's the news from Massa-chusetts?"

"Not good," answered Madison quietly. "The whole of the western counties are ris-ing in rebellion, and claiming their right to separate and form a state of their own. The legislature in Boston speaks of sending in troops, and hanging the leaders for trea-son."

"Treason?" George's deep voice was trou-bled. "That's a hard word, coming from men who were but lately called traitors them-selves."

Frank shut the door. It was not done, for a woman to listen in on the talk of the men once dinner was over, and Martha would never have dreamed of setting so scan-dalous an example for her granddaughters and Harriot—who had, God knew, poor enough examples of behavior in their own homes. But if they hadn't been there she wasn't sure that she wouldn't have snatched up a water-glass from the pantry sideboard and pressed it to the door to amplify to her ear the voices on the other side.

Tom Jefferson had taught her that trick.

For eight years she had waited to hear that her husband had, indeed, been taken prisoner and sent to England to be tried for treason.

For eight years she'd waited to hear that he'd been killed, without the slightest idea of what she would do, or how she would live, if he were gone.

⚜

It took her, Jacky, and Eleanor over three weeks to get to Cambridge in the winter of '75. They'd stopped for nearly a week in Philadelphia because both the horses and her daughter-in-law badly needed the rest. Snow lay thick on the ground when they finally joggled through the Army camp at dusk, hard powdery northern snow that squeaked underfoot, not like the wet soft snow of Virginia. Campfires glowed amber against the last lilac ghost of twilight, the dark shapes of huts and men standing out bare and black. The shelters seemed to be constructed, like Robinson Crusoe's, out of flotsam and salvage: boards of unequal shape and length, sailcloth, raw logs chinked with mud, discarded shutters, branches, brush. The men resembled their dwellings: grandpas who should have been dozing at their family hearths, boys who looked

scarcely older than Anna Maria's eleven-
year-old Burwell junior. Farmers in homespun, clerks huddled in thin town jackets,
hairy gimlet-eyed men from over the western
mountains, swilling rum from round-bellied
bottles. Women with petticoats tucked up to
their knees and their hair straggling loose.
Battalions of dogs. There were Indians
among them, too, and black men who
Martha earnestly hoped were freedmen and
not runaways.

The sight of blacks with rifles in their
hands was a new one to her, and profoundly
unnerving.

The men got up from around their fires
and followed the coach to a handsome
brick house not far from the Cambridge
common, with white pilasters to its porch
and a double staircase down to what had
been a lawn and was now a wasteland of
trampled snow. The carriage stopped, and
one of George's Lewis nephews—handsome in the blue uniform of a Headquarters
aide—helped her down.

Then she looked up, and the house door
opened, yellow lamplight spilling out onto
the snow around the tall black silhouetted
shape.

For eight years after that, it seemed to
Martha that she led two lives. They alter-
nated like dream and waking, summer and
winter: her actual self and a sort of simu-
lacrum who was waiting only to return to
"real life."

But it was the summers at Mount Vernon
that felt like the dream. She carried on her
duties as mistress of the plantation, tried to
adjudicate between the overseers' harsh-
ness and the exasperating passive contrari-
ness of the slaves, managed the finances of
the Custis estate as if George were simply
away at Williamsburg. She had looms set up
and put the female slaves to weaving for
the Army, and organized the women of
the neighborhood into a Society to knit
stockings and sew clothing for the soldiers,
since Congress couldn't seem to figure out
who was supposed to pay for equipping the
Army and the separate States all howled
about their individual poverty. She did what
she could to rally support at home, using
hospitality to settle political differences the
way all the landowners did, visiting and entertaining everyone whose support might

conceivably be of use to George and George's cause.

Yet it was only during the winters—in unfamiliar borrowed houses, surrounded by soldiers and secretaries and military aides, waiting for news of disaster and trying to achieve some kind of normalcy under the most bizarre conditions—that she felt truly like herself, at George's side.

Every autumn, she would load up a wagon with the produce of the plantation—smoked hams, preserved fruits, sacks of potatoes, yams, corn—and with whatever medicines she could obtain, before journeying off to wherever the Army was camped that year. There was never enough food at Headquarters and it was seldom good. That first winter in Cambridge, Martha heard from her friends in camp—the outspoken Lucy Knox, wife of George's trusted artillery general Henry, and General Greene's lovely, featherheaded wife Kitty—about the backbiting that had already begun to envenom the upper levels of command. In winter camp, men who thought they should have been put in charge of the Army had little to do but pick holes in George's methods of discipline, and find fault with all he did.

And many of the Generals' wives were as ambitious, or more so, than their men.

For this reason, almost the first thing Martha did was to establish a rota of entertaining officers and their wives to dinner, and set about making the house of the Commander in Chief the social as well as the command center of the camp.

As a Virginia planter's daughter—as a Virginia planter's wife—Martha had spent far too much time listening to the power politics of the House of Burgesses not to be aware that a man's power over others depended almost as much on his appearance of competent strength as on strength, or competence, itself, particularly in an emergency. This was an understanding she shared with George, on a level more profound than words could begin to fathom—something she wasn't sure that anyone else in the camp, or in the Congress for that matter, completely comprehended.

She felt, sometimes, presiding over those dinners with dour Massachusetts colonels and frivolous South Carolinians—and later French and German and Spanish officers who came to observe and aid anyone who was willing to make trouble for the British—

the curious sensation of her marrow-deep unity with George. It was as if they were dancing a dance long practiced together, or, like twins, could read one another's thoughts.

In making him Commander in Chief of the Continental Army, Congress had authorized George to flog and hang. Knowing what would become of the Army if the country-side turned against them, George disciplined without mercy. A veteran of battle himself, he knew that under combat conditions, only discipline can stand against panic. The men were accustomed to the idea that they could disobey any command they didn't like, so the potential for discontented officers stirring up trouble could not be ignored.

At the very least, Martha thought, even if her dinners didn't completely defuse the poisonous atmosphere, they would give everyone something to look forward to. In addition, the dinners let people see George in some other context than when he was giving orders or swearing at the troops.

Politics and social maneuvering aside, it was Martha's nature to want people to be comfortable. And she knew that comfort, especially in times of stress, depended to a large degree on things being organized and meals being served hot and on time.

Thus her Headquarters life felt like a curious extension of what she'd always done without thinking. The routine of a plantation mistress fit weirdly well into the context of war. And as a plantation mistress, Martha was as accustomed to looking out for the common soldiers as she was to smoothing things over between George and his officers. Her days at Cambridge—and on the New Jersey heights above New York the following winter, and at Valley Forge the winter after that—were spent in organizing the women of the district into committees to make clothing and knit stockings, as she did during the summers at home, and in visiting the men in their shelters or in the camp hospital with such small and necessary gifts. Even the men who growled about George's readiness with the lash came around, at first simply because they needed the stockings, and then when they began to observe for themselves that their General was absolutely consistent in his rules and his punishments. He played no favorites, he listened to both sides of every case, he never held back their pay or sold their rations for his own profit. He had no hidden end beyond keeping the Army together and in the field. He raged and swore as much as they did against the Congress and the States who expected them to fight well-fed professional troops with no food in their bellies and no powder in their guns.

And eight years passed.

⚜

As Martha stitched the microscopic hems of a shirt-ruffle for Wash, by the glow of the work-candles Frank brought into the West Parlor, she saw in the faces of her granddaughters and niece the reflection of those eight years.

Wintering in New Jersey and Pennsylvania and New York, not returning to Mount Vernon until summer firmed up the roads. In 1776 that had not been until almost harvest, so she'd still been in Philadelphia in July, to hear the church bells tolling and men shouting in the streets that Congress had proclaimed the colonies' independence from Britain.

That was the summer Eliza had been born. The girl's face, already bearing the promise of a fleshy beauty, was restless and discontented as she bent over her sewing: a neglected child from the outset, trying with tantrums to make herself heard. Eleanor had been ill and depressed after the birth, and Martha, who would naturally have stepped in to care for both her and the child, was still in Philadelphia. *How different would Eliza be now, had she not spent her first three months in the care of a succession of slave nurse-girls not much older than eight?*

On New Year's Eve of '77, when Pattie had been born, Martha had been packed already to leave for winter camp. Only a week before Pattie's birth, in the midst of caring for the bedridden Eleanor at Mount Vernon, word had reached Martha of the death of her sister Anna Maria, her most dear and treasured friend.

On her deathbed, Anna Maria had asked her family to send word to Martha, that Martha was to take in her daughter Fanny, barely turned eleven. "Raise her as your own," she had whispered.

Martha had refused. Three weeks later, she'd gotten into the carriage, to go to the camp in Pennsylvania. Because George needed her, and she needed George.

Fanny had been sent instead by her grief-stricken, elderly father to the care of whichever relatives could fit an extra girl into their households. Eleanor, withdrawn into her world of shadows and pain, had been left with Jacky, who was completely useless around the sick. Tiny Pattie and sixteen-month-old Eliza were again relegated to the care of such girls as were too young to be employed in the fields.

Throughout the bitter winter in that awful little stone house at Valley Forge, Martha remembered now, she had dreamed about them. Or, worse, had dreamed about Patcy. Dreamed that she'd left a baby girl somewhere—set her down in the woods or the stable or the house and wandered away—and was searching for her, frantically trying to get her back before night fell.

From that dream Martha would wake to freezing blackness, to the drums of reveille in the camp and the clack of flint and steel as George knelt by the hearth: it never took George more than one or two strikes to get a fire going. Aaron Burr, General Putnam's dapper young aide, used to say that all

George had to do was look at the kindling, for flame to spring to life. It wouldn't dare do otherwise.

⚜

Across the parlor now she considered them, in the comforting glow of candles and fire-light and happily ever after. Fanny so ex-actly like Anna Maria, smiling at Nelly's grave plans to find a sweetheart for her tu-tor. Eliza stitching away on an extravagantly embroidered crimson petticoat and detail-ing to her sister her plans for a career on the stage, while Pattie more prosaically knitted stockings. Harriot, stitching on the other side of the fire as far from Eliza as she could get, looked scornful but knew better than to get in a quarrel with her cousin when Martha was in the room.

How I wronged them. They needed me, and I wasn't there.

She'd been gone from home when Nelly was born, too.

She remembered her maid Sal, telling her what she'd heard from the maids in Jacky's household: that when Jacky's friends in Alexandria—and any convivial strangers who happened through the town—came for dinner, her son would lift the three-year-old Eliza up onto the dinner-table, and encourage her to sing bawdy songs at the top of her voice for the edification of the men as they drank. Eleanor, so frequently confined to her room, either didn't know or didn't have the energy to care.

Jacky was a good boy, Martha told herself sadly. *Sweet-natured, though his judgment wasn't good.*

But she knew that, too, was a lie.

She remembered how she had returned from the winter camp at Morristown in 1780 to find her beloved sewing-maid Nan with child. A white man, Nan had stammered, a white man came upon her in the woods beyond the grist-mill. The maid disclaimed all knowledge of who the man was, but had looked away from Martha with fear in her eyes. She would say only, "He said he'd make sure I never saw my family again, if I told."

When the child was born—Willy, seven now and learning to be a houseboy—he had looked like Jacky. He looked even more like him now.

I should have been here.

But it wasn't that easy.

In the months before Martha went to Valley Forge, leaving Fanny and Pattie, her own
ailing mother, Eliza and Nan and Eleanor all
to their fates, word had reached her that the
Continental Army had been defeated in battles along the Delaware River. Congress had
been driven out of Philadelphia only a day
before the British took the city, and the
British came within a hair's-breadth of capturing the Army—and George—after the
disastrous counterattack in the fog at Germantown. The year before, they had barely
escaped through the streets of New York
City as the British were landing on the Bat-
tery.

The last she had seen of him, as he'd
handed her into the carriage at Morristown
and had stood watching her out of sight,
might have been indeed the last time she
would see him, ever. The good-bye kiss he
gave her could have been the final adieu.
Even more than the knowledge that he
needed her support, what she could not
bear was the awareness that she might
never see him again.

Each winter that she took from Eliza, and
Pattie, and Fanny, was a treasure that she
was laying up within her own heart. The

treasure of being with him, for what might be the final time.

I could not be two places at once!

Each winter she had chosen. And those winters glimmered back to her now through Eliza's operatic angers, in Pattie's wistful clinginess and the note in Fanny's voice when she would speak of "having a home of our own." To say nothing, reflected Martha's more practical side, of the badly kept tangle of plantation records that George was still trying to sort out four years after war's end, and the terrifying tally of debts.

As the evening grew later, and the men remained talking in the dining-room, the anger congealed to a point of heat behind her heart.

I followed him for eight years. I left behind those who had reason to expect my help.

Does he really need me to remind him, that he laid down the sword of power with the understanding that he would not take it up again?

A Cincinnatus, not a Caesar, he had promised. *A farmer and not a ruler of men.*

By the end of the War, he could have become a Caesar. The charisma that drew her—and every woman who encountered George—combined with his good sense and calm integrity, to unite, at last, New York men who'd grown up despising Pennsylvanians, Massachusers to whom every Rhode Islander was a thief, South Carolinians who held their noses at the mention of Vermont boys. He had made of them one fighting force. Year by year, she saw how he became the embodiment of the cause that held them together, the cause for which more and more of them risked their lives simply because he was willing to risk his.

In September of 1781, word reached her at Mount Vernon that George was coming. On the way to join with the French fleet in a maneuver to trap the British army at Yorktown, he would have the chance to visit the home he had not seen in six years. The previous winter, one of George's most trusted generals, Benedict Arnold, had turned his coat and gone over to the British side, and had led their armies in raids on Virginia. Arnold had occupied the new capital, Richmond, and barely missed capturing Tom Jefferson, whose fragile baby daughter died as a result of the hardships of the family's escape. Martha had been with George at the winter camp in New Windsor at that time, frantic with worry about her own little granddaughters; about her mother, ill at Chestnut Grove; about Fanny.

That spring, moreover, Martha herself was ill, first at Headquarters and later in Philadelphia. She was still not feeling herself by the time she returned to Mount Vernon in June—having missed the birth of little George Washington Parke Custis—and had barely recovered her strength when George wrote in September that he would indeed be able to cross his own threshold for the first time since May of 1775.

He arrived on the ninth of September after everyone was in bed. Martha, for a week too excited to sleep, heard the dogs barking, and then hooves in the driveway. *It's one of his aides coming to announce his arrival tomorrow. . . .*

But from downstairs she heard a familiar deep voice say, "If she's asleep, for God's sake let her sleep! That's an order, Breechy. Just to see the roof-line and smell the gardens is worth the ride. . . ."

"General Washington—" Martha appeared

at the top of the stairs, her braid hanging forgotten over the embroidered homespun of her dressing-gown and hairpins still in her hand. "If you dared let me go six hours til dawn not knowing you were in the house, I should—I should write a letter to the *Times* in London saying that such conduct proved you to be *no* gentleman."

He grinned wide—something he almost never did because of his teeth—and reached the bottom of the stairs in two strides, in time to catch Martha in his arms.

He had ridden sixty miles from Baltimore that day, to sleep beneath his own roof at her side.

The French did arrive the following day, General Rochambeau handsome and courtly and a little too suave in his gorgeous uniform—George had written to her that he was too hard on his men, which was something, coming from George. The day after that—the eleventh of September—the rest of the French officers appeared, and on their heels, Jacky, Eleanor, and the grandchildren whom George had never seen. The French Comtes and Chevaliers in their gold-embroidered uniforms all smiled to see the tall, stern General scoop up five-year-old

Eliza and hold her like a kitten above his head.

Throughout dinner, Jacky hovered around the Generals like a smitten schoolgirl. He asked breathless questions about battles, gazed in rapture at the swords they wore and the gold of their epaulets.

Martha still remembered the men coming into the parlor—this same parlor where they now sat—after dinner that day, Jacky with his features radiant: "Papa's going to take me with him to Yorktown! I've been commissioned as one of his aides!"

Eleanor's gentle eyes flared with alarm, and her face paled. Jacky might towse the servant-girls, and waste his late father's fortune on imbecilic land-deals for currency that wasn't worth the paper it was printed on, but he was her husband. Without him to run Abingdon Plantation, neither Eleanor nor her four tiny children could survive.

Martha's first reaction to this announcement—that he was going to war, but only in the safest possible position, behind the combined French and Continental armies—was to roll her eyes. She longed to reassure her daughter-in-law that Jacky might go to war—and she was willing to bet his first act in the service of his country would be to purchase a dozen uniforms that put General Rochambeau's to shame—but she couldn't imagine her son actually doing anything to put himself into harm's way.

But he did. Martha had become so used to the sicknesses that ravaged the Army camps—at Morristown, at Valley Forge, at Trenton—that she seldom thought of them anymore. Her own illness had been more inconvenient than dangerous. The Knox and Greene babies whom her friends Lucy and Kitty now brought regularly to winter quarters seemed to thrive. George's favorite aide Alec Hamilton, goldenly handsome and a few years younger than Jacky, had never had so much as a cold (or the French pox, which was even more surprising).

By the seventeenth of October, however, when General Cornwallis sent an aide out of his fortress to surrender his sword to Washington, Jacky was so sick with camp-fever that he could only watch the capture of the British army from a carriage in the road. The same letter that brought Martha news of the British surrender urged her, and Eleanor, to come at once.

Through six years of war, she had often

lain awake in terror at the thought of losing George. She had never dreamed that she would lose Jacky. But at Eltham Plantation, where six years previously Martha had made her choice to follow George to war, less than three weeks after the defeat of Britain by her American colonists, Jacky Custis died.

⚓

Pattie dozed over her knitting; Nelly had fallen asleep. Outside the wind had begun to moan, puffing threads of smoke back down the chimney. On the side closer to the windows, Martha felt the air of the room growing cold. The rumble of the men's voices continued behind the dining-room door. Fanny gathered her shawl about her: "I'll get these little sleepyheads off to bed," and Eliza piped up immediately that she wasn't the least bit sleepy—

"My nerves are too delicate to let me sleep, Aunt Patsie."

And Harriot: "Why do men take so long over their wine?"

"It isn't polite to make observations about how long anyone lingers after dinner," replied

Fanny gently, and herded the girls from the room.

Why indeed?

Martha's breath felt stifled in her chest. They would come out soon.

The last time George had lingered so long over dinner had been the night last October, with Madison and Monroe.

Warily, Martha had watched them then, as she had watched Madison tonight. Too fragile to go to war, he had spent the years from 1775 to 1783 in the Virginia legislature; he knew the ins and outs of local politics with the brilliance of an Alexander viewing a battlefield. Last October, she had heard him speak of the relationship of Congress to the various States, and the States to each other, like a physician observing a dissection, pointing with a needle: *a cancer here, a lesion there, a muscular weakness there, and here gangrene is setting in . . . The patient will die.*

"No," George had said quietly that night, and had raised his eyes from the Madeira into whose golden depths he had been gazing as Madison talked. "We did not fight, and men did not die, that we should become the laughingstock of the world for our inability to hold what we won."

His eyes met Madison's, and Madison had made no reply. Martha had watched her husband's jaw harden, and the muscle in his temple twitch, as it did when he was holding hard to his temper. She had felt in his silence, that October night, the eight years of seeing his men starve because Congress had no power to raise money to feed them; eight years of maneuvering the logistics of fighting battles with only a few rounds of ammunition per man; eight years of keeping his temper as he explained to Congress yet one more time why he didn't storm into battle more often or why men who put their lives on the line for their country really ought to be recompensed for their pain.

Now, like a debtor's child, the new confederation calling itself the United States of America came into being owing a hundred and seventy million dollars to France, Russia, Spain, and the Netherlands—twenty-seven million of that payable only in gold. Without the threat of the British guns in the background, the Congress's financial pigeons all came home to roost. As a "firm league of friendship," not an actual government, Congress still had no power to tax, and no means of paying off those loans any more than they'd been able to pay the Continental troops.

The Convention of States' representatives in Annapolis had signally failed to resolve the trade differences separating them.

Another Convention, Madison had said in October, was being planned. It would meet in Philadelphia come May, to further discuss the issues that threatened to lay the divided States open to piecemeal conquest as soon as Britain or France or Spain or Russia thought it safe to do so.

"We cannot let it go for nothing," George had said, and Madison had folded his thin hands, wrinkled face alert in the candle-glow.

"Nor will we, sir," he said. "But we cannot go on as we have. And to bring the States together, we must have someone whose authority all will trust."

⚜

"Lady Washington . . ."

So profoundly had she been in her reverie that the opening of the dining-room door took her by surprise. Mr. Madison bowed deeply. "I abase myself, ma'am, for keeping your husband talking so long."

"What, has my wife given up and gone home?" Augustine coughed, and in the candlelight his face had the pallor that Martha didn't like, as if he were sickening for another of the colds that sometimes laid him up for months.

"I fear poor Fanny has the right of it." The corner of George's mouth tugged in a smile, but his eyes were gentle behind the shadow of infinite weariness. "Poor Patsie. I fear we've trespassed on your good nature, and will do so no more this evening." His big hands were warm, completely enfolding hers. "Frank—" He turned to the butler, who'd materialized to take the green Sèvres coffee-pot back to the kitchen to be refreshed. "Please show Mr. Madison to his room. Are you sure you will not remain, sir, at least until the weather promises better?"

Spits of sleet had begun to spatter the windows, and the shutters rattled sullenly on their hinges. Madison shook his head. "I cannot linger."

"Then I shall instruct Austin to have your horse ready after breakfast, that you may reach Georgetown easily by dinner-time."

Fanny returned from the nursery and she and Augustine kissed; it was agreed they would stay tonight, rather than walk back down to their own newly built little house in the bitter cold. All as if everything were normal, as if the little man in black bidding Fanny a courteous good-night now had not brought word that the nation George had risked his life on the battlefield to free was already falling apart.

Martha watched her niece and George's nephew, and then their guest, leave the parlor on the heels of candle-bearing servants. She shivered and was conscious of her hand trembling on her husband's arm.

Looking up at his profile in the candlelight, she found herself regarding him, as well as their diminutive guest, as an enemy. *I will not let you take me away from my family.*

I will not let you take me away from my home.

They went into the dark and freezing cold hall to bid everyone good-night, but when the flickering dabs of light disappeared around the turn of the stairs, George guided Martha back into the parlor, to wait for him by the fire's sinking warmth while he made his final patrol of the lower floor of the house, checking shutters, locking doors. Making surè all was safe, as was his invariable habit.

Just as, she recalled, he had walked around the camp every night, wrapped in as many cloaks as he could obtain and scarfed up to the eyes, to make certain the sentries were sober and the black woods beyond the picket-lines silent in the starlight.

How many nights, wondered Martha, had she waited up for him, knitting by the fires in those icy little bedrooms? How many nights had she studied the walls of some other woman's chamber in the dying light? She still recalled the silhouettes of a boy and girl that had decorated the house in Morristown: She had asked, but had never found out whose they were. In another place—Valley Forge?—a child's laborious cross-stitch had spelled out "The Lord is my shepherd, I shall not want."

Yea, though I walk through the valley of the shadow of death, I will fear no evil, for Thou art with me.

From the dining-room beyond the parlor came the creak of quiet footsteps, Frank, Sal, and Caro clearing up. A moment later Caro's shadow passed through the dark hall with a tray of glasses and a basket of broken nut-shells and cheese-rinds. In the kitchen the fire would be sinking low in the great chimney, Uncle Hercules waiting to bank it before going to bed himself. Abovestairs the girls and young Wash were sleeping under featherbeds, trusting there was someone in the world who would look after them and love them. Someone who wouldn't leave them with the servants yet one more time.

She heard George's step in the hall, light as an Indian's on a forest track.

He closed the parlor door, a reflex any white Virginian developed from earliest childhood: His valet Billy would be waiting for them outside their bedroom door, with her new little maid, Oney. The house, like any in Virginia, was always filled with listening ears. For a moment he stood with his back to the door, only looking at her in the deep shadows of the parlor, while the wind wept around the eaves.

All those years of working together with the Army had opened a passageway between their hearts. It was as if they had been talking of Mr. Madison's news all day. When Martha said, "You have done enough," there was no need for him to ask her what she meant. And no possibility to pretend that he did not know.

"I agree."

"What more does he want of you? That you should go back on your word? On the promise that you spoke before all your officers when you bade them good-bye, that you would retire from public life?" Her voice shook, but she knew exactly what troubled him most. The prospect of turning into a Caesar would not have weighed on his mind, had he not seen sword and crown hovering invisible before him, like Macbeth's dagger: promise and doom at once. "That wretched little kingmaker has said it himself. He wants you there because they all trust your authority." She added bitterly, "I thought it was *Congress* that had the authority, not you."

"Congress is losing that authority." George's voice was quiet. The powder in his hair glimmered in the gloom. It was as if face and hair were becoming only a marble memory of the man she loved. "The States despise it. In their turn, the counties of the West despise the States. If Congress hangs the Western rebels it may only bring on greater revolts."

"Massachusetts—"

"You know it isn't only Massachusetts we're talking about." He didn't raise his voice, but there was inexorability in his tone. "At the second Congress in Philadelphia, just before I left to take command, Dr. Franklin jested that 'we must all hang together, for if we do not we shall verily all hang separately.' That is as true today as it was eleven years ago, Patsie. Only this time it is we who are putting the noose around our own necks."

"And just what, exactly, do you think is going to happen if you go to this Convention to wield the . . . the *authority* Mr. Madison is asking you to wield?" she retorted. "You've talked about it before as if they're just going to make a few little changes in these famous Articles of theirs, to make things run better. If Mr. Madison needs your authority, it sounds like he has something up his sleeve other than *a few little changes.*"

"I think he does," said George. "Mr. Madison—and others, including Alec Hamilton, who as you know is no fool—want to entirely scrap the old Articles under which the States are united, and forge a central government. As a confederation, each state holds the sovereign power to go its own way. We must become a single nation, a united nation that will not be the laughingstock—or the blind victim—of every nation of Europe."

"And what then?" The edge of sarcasm in her own voice cut her heart like glass but she couldn't stop the words. "If you go to Philadelphia and lend your *authority* to the Congress—which I assume means telling those fools to shut up when they start squabbling—you know they'll elect you to preside. They might have declared us free, but you're the one who actually did the job of throwing the British out, while the rest of them sat on their chairs and called each other names. And then what? Who does Mr. Madison propose will *rule* that central government of his? Whose *authority* does he propose to keep it all together? Who will be King, do you think, with him and Hammy Hamilton standing behind the throne?"

He was silent. *I've hurt him,* she realized, and her first sensation was a bitter pleasure. *Now maybe he'll listen.*

For years, most of their visitors to Mount Vernon had been strangers, both American and European, who had come simply to marvel at the man who would not be King. Knowing that he could have made himself King in the wake of the War, he was deeply sensitive to the public declaration that he had repeatedly made, "never more to meddle in public matters." The declaration had been made not only to Congress, but to numerous gazettes and newspapers in the thirteen States.

"You know me better than that, Patsie." He sounded sad, rather than hurt. As if he understood that it was her fear that spoke. "I did not fight the King's troops for eight years in order to take his place on a throne. And if I did, there would be only one person standing behind it, and it wouldn't be Mr. Madison." He took her hand, and raised it to his lips. "It would be you."

"I don't want to stand behind your throne," she whispered. "I want to sit in a rocking-chair at your side, on our own piazza, watching the sun on the river in peace. Thrones kill the men who sit on them, George. All crowns are crowns of thorns. I don't think I could sit still and watch that happen to you."

He at least did not say, *It wouldn't.* Still holding her hand, still looking into her eyes, she could tell from his face that he knew that it would.

In the lengthening silence the fire sighed, with a kind of silky crumbling, and flares of its dying light flickered in his eyes.

At last he told her: "I must go, Patsie."

I could say: You can go without me, then. I'll remain here and care for my family and our property while you go do what you choose to do.

I could say: Don't make me choose to leave my home, to abandon the girls to their mother, and Fanny and her baby to a sickly husband with Death already at his elbow. Don't make me betray them again.

Jacky's death, and Patcy's, had taught her how swiftly things could disappear, once you turned your back on them even for a little time.

I could say: You have hurt me as nothing has hurt me in my life, save the death of my darling children. Do not hurt me again.

But looking into his face she saw that he knew all those things. For eight years, woven like a secret code into every letter he had sent her during those summers of war, had been his deep love for the quiet of Mount Vernon. When he'd write about the new dining-room, or which fields should be planted in wheat and corn, he wrote as a man who had every square foot of his land, every brick and floor-board of his house, engraved on his heart. Sleeping at night, he could walk about his home in his dreams.

This love—those dreams—were in his voice when he spoke again. "Mr. Madison informs me that last year the Congress wasn't even able to pay the interest on the loans we took out to buy weapons and feed our soldiers through the War." The distant tone reminded her of the way the men in the camp hospitals would talk to keep their minds from the pain of having a limb set. "Each state took out loans as well, you know, and are no more able than Congress either to pay in gold or to convince France and Spain to take the paper they're printing. Congress—and the States—paid many of the soldiers in land. How long do you think it will be before the nations of Europe start thinking it their right to claim *their* payments in our Western lands?"

It still doesn't mean YOU have to go.

Let Mr. Madison be his own authority, if he can.

She closed her eyes, rested her forehead against the big hand that still clasped her own.

If you go, this time I must stay behind. It was a very real threat, for a man already genuinely concerned that men would say *He seeks to make himself a Caesar after all.* As pointed as if she had packed her bags and abandoned his house, a truer supporter of the Republic than he. Maybe more so. People often remembered an action more clearly than any number of words. He couldn't let himself be seen as less of a Republican than his wife.

If I say it, will he stay?

And if he stays, what will it do to him?

And to us?

She supposed, if she were as true a supporter of the Republic as all that, she would have added—or thought first—*What will it do to our country?*

But she didn't.

Abigail Adams would have, she reflected. And had her heart been less sore, Martha would have smiled at the recollection of that small, sword-slim, beautiful woman who'd come to tea at the Cambridge camp one afternoon, all bundled up in a green wool cloak against the cold. A true New England patriot, that one: a passionate, intellectual Roman matron willing to lay her children, her home—maybe even her beloved little red-faced John—on the altar of her country.

It needs a heart like hers, thought Martha sadly, *to follow George where he now must go.*

Heaven only knew what God was thinking of, to have put her hand, not Abigail's, where now it lay.

Because she knew that even in the face of the one threat that would truly draw his blood, her husband would not turn aside from the need of his country.

So she asked only, "When do you leave?"

"Not until May."

"What can I do to help?"

"What you have always done, Patsie. Be there to guard my back."

And felt his kiss press her forehead, his arms gather her close.

Now make us a king to judge us like all the nations, the Israelites had cried, when even after soundly trouncing the Philistines and the Hittites and the who-all-else they were still disunited and living in tents.

And the prophet Samuel had gone and picked on poor Saul, who only wanted to get on with his farming but who was the most impressive-looking man in the countryside, and made him be King. *(Had Samuel been a*

withered little gentleman in black, with pre-maturely whitening hair?)
And look what had happened to Saul.

*Washington City
August 24, 1814*

"It was just after Jacky died, that the Queen of France sent her 'elegant gift,' as it was called, to Martha." Sophie shook her head over the wampum-belt, the fossilized mastodon-tooth, and the tiny bronze mechanism for calculating the appearances of comets that were all that the lowest drawer of the dining-room cabinet contained; Dolley closed the drawer again. "It ended up auctioned off on the docks at New York—which was still in British hands until the treaty was signed two years later—but I doubt poor Martha would have been much aware of it if it *had* made it safely to the American forces. Jacky was the last of her children."

"Then just before the General rode away to Philadelphia for the Convention in '87, Fanny's baby was born and died." Still empty-handed, Dolley passed between the tables, the dressmaker like a shadow at her heels. "I know it seemed to her even then that the world she treasured was already coming to pieces."

Sophie looked as if she would have made some remark about Martha Washington not being the only one to have lost her peace and her home, but held her tongue. As they crossed the hall, the butler came down the stairs, carrying the smallest of the trunks. He stood aside to let the ladies precede him into the yellow parlor. Throughout the house Dolley could feel, rather than hear, the tension stirring among the servants. Would any of them take the opportunity to flee?

"It was only weeks after Fanny's baby was born that Abigail's first grandchild arrived as well," Sophie said, as Dolley opened the curio cabinet by the parlor's sunny window. "Her daughter Nabby's baby—We should probably take this," she added, and crossed to the fireplace. Beside it hung a slightly faded drawing, carefully framed in gilt. Dolley had always liked it, though despite its elaborate frame it was plainly an amateur's work: a rather overgrown garden in autumn, with leaves scattering its paths and bright Chinese tubs filled with marigolds.

"Dost know who drew it?" she asked, surprised. "I've always wondered."

"Nabby Adams did," Sophie replied. "It was their garden, the year the family lived in Paris."

"Didst know them there?"

For an instant her friend's gray eyes filled with the memory of years she'd never spoken of to Dolley, the years between her own flight with her mother in Cornwallis's retreating ships, and her somewhat inexplicable return. Then she replied, "Oh, yes. Mr. Jefferson introduced us, because I had helped nurse his wife in her illness. Nabby and I used to sit on the bench by the old fountain, where that picture was drawn. I recognize the view. After they left Paris for London, Mrs. Adams and I corresponded. And of course I sewed for her when she returned to Philadelphia. I did not see this in her parlor in those days." Sophie's long fingers traced the little drawing. "I think Abigail must have given it to Mr. Jefferson, in the days when they were friends."

There was no sign of the little golden hand-mirror in the cabinet drawer. Dolley felt a stab of frustration, and a sort of panicky anger: It *had* to be here somewhere. It suddenly seemed critical to her to find the mirror, one of the few mementos she had, she realized, of the woman who had been her friend. To lose it would be like losing Martha all over again: not only Martha, but Martha's memories, of the War, and of the world as it had been.

"I've always wondered which was worse," she said softly. "To be perpetually living half normally, half in exile as Martha did all those years, or to live as Abigail did, for years at home without her John and then for years away from the rest of her family and every- one she knew and loved."

Sophie tucked the drawing carefully be- tween two large books and wedged it into a corner of the trunk. "I suppose that de- pends on how one feels about New England in the dead of winter. But if you think Abigail suffered for her family when she left them to follow John across the sea, you don't know her well."

"In fact, I never met her." But Dolley smiled in her heart at the recollection of tubby, short-tempered little Mr. Adams, holding forth at the dinner-table of that house in Philadelphia that she and Jemmy had rented from Jim Monroe. "She was ill and remained in Massachusetts when the government was in Philadelphia. Then Jemmy and I left Philadelphia two months before she arrived after Mr. Adams's election. I have always regretted that. Everyone said Mrs. Adams was so formidable. But from what Mr. Adams said of her, I think we would have gotten on well."

Sophie considered her friend for a moment, then smiled. "I suspect you're right. When one grew to know Abigail, behind the politics she was a great deal kinder than she seemed."

"Politics or not, I cannot imagine any woman not feeling pain when separated from her children, especially when they're young."

"I think she felt pain," Sophie replied. "But pain was never a thing that affected Abigail's judgment, when her principles were at stake. Her sins against her children were different sins. She—and they—paid a different price, Dolley."

ABIGAIL

⌒◌ざ

Grosvenor Square, London
Monday, April 2, 1787

"Mrs. Adams, ma'am!" A scurry of feet in the upstairs hall, as a mob-capped head poked around the door of the little second-floor parlor that Abigail had taken over as her office at 8 Grosvenor Square. "Becky's just come from Miss Nabby's—Mrs. Smith's," the maid Esther hastily corrected herself, and the tall, wide-shouldered form of Jack Briesler appeared in the doorway behind her. In spite of everything the Adamses' very proper English butler Mr. Spiller could do, he couldn't get Briesler to understand that he must don his powdered footman's wig every time he came upstairs.

To Briesler's credit, reflected Abigail, folding

her hands over the pages of her sister's letter and regarding her footman with an expression of mild enquiry that she was far from feeling. Briesler had served under Washington at Trenton and Brooklyn Heights; he wasn't about to wear any sissified wig if he didn't absolutely have to.

"Her time is on her, Miss Becky says," Briesler provided, and Esther's head bobbed in confirmation. Like Briesler, Esther had come to England with Abigail from Massachusetts four years ago, and the excitement in her face was as great as if it was her own sister, and not her employer's daughter, who was about to bear a child.

"Is she all right?" Abigail stowed the letter and her reply in their drawer, locked it, wiped her pen, and capped the ink-well with gestures as swift and automatic as smoothing her hair before she stood, shaking off the pinching cramp of rheumatism in her legs and back. *Really, I'm getting as stiff as an old lady.*

And why not? This day, God willing, I shall be a grandmother.

And as Esther nodded again, Abigail remembered her own pain, her own panic, the day her own first child was born.

But her mother, and her sixteen-year-old sister Betsey, had stayed with her all the previous week, she remembered, as she crossed the hall to her husband's study door, the two American servants right on her heels. Her sister-in-law had been just across the little dooryard of that small brown house on the Plymouth road: in and out of each other's kitchens all day the way everyone was in the tiny Massachusetts town of Braintree. There had also been Granny Susie, John's sweet-natured, bouncy, busy mother. *I wasn't alone in a foreign country, much less a country like England. . . .*

John wasn't in the corner room, whose wide window displayed the wet gray spectacle of Grosvenor Square's bare trees. The fire was embers in the grate, scruffy little Caesar curled in a tight gray ball before it with his nose hidden in his disreputable tail. The door to the gloomy cubbyhole generally occupied by John's secretary stood open, and that room was empty as well. "Mr. Briesler, please go downstairs and see if Mr. Adams is in his office. Let him know I'm going over to Mrs. Smith's right away. I shall probably be there all day, so he'll be on his own for dinner. And please tell Mrs. Stubbs and Mr. Spiller so." Even after four years, it felt strange to have to inform one's cook and one's butler *(of all things!)* if one was going to be away at dinner-time.

It crossed her mind to wonder if Nabby still had a cook. Nabby's husband Colonel Smith had been threatening for weeks to sack that wretched woman, and wasn't the man to think about the inconvenience of finding another, to a woman in the concluding stages of pregnancy.

In many ways, Abigail reflected as she ascended the stair to the front bedroom, things were a great deal simpler in that four-room farmhouse on the Boston-Plymouth road, war or no war.

War or no war. Another woman would have paused at the recollection of the phrase she'd used uncountable hundreds of times during those eight appalling years: *War or no war, this family has to eat; war or no war, you have to do your lessons, Johnny; war or no war, you have no excuse for punching your brother. . . .*

It wasn't in Abigail's nature to pause. Yet the phrase rang in her mind, as she collected a stouter pair of shoes from the wardrobe, plucked warmer stockings and a heavy India-goods shawl from the high-boy—it was always freezing in Nabby's house—and sent Esther flying down three flights to the kitchen for the bag she'd packed last week. *War or no war. . .*

The inner contradiction of those words came home to her now, and she realized she could not even imagine her life, her world, her children's lives, had there been *no war.*

The War had shaped her life and theirs. Everything had been a part of it, related to it. She was here in London because of the War. Her first grandchild was going to be born on enemy soil, because of the War.

Because of the War, she had not seen her two youngest children in almost three years.

Nor had those children seen her.

For eight years, there had been nothing but the War, and all that the War had brought. But it troubled her a little now to reflect that she literally could not imagine, *No war.*

That in her heart of hearts, the War was all there was.

⚜

That hot July morning in 1765 when she'd felt the birth-pangs of her own first child, she'd sat down for a moment after the milking, to read over the draft of one of John's articles for the *Boston Gazette.* For weeks John had been writing protests against the British Parliament's decision to levy a tax on all court documents, college diplomas, books, real estate certificates, newspapers—anything comprised of printed paper, even dice and playing cards. At the same time it had announced the tax, Parliament had informed the colonists, from Massachusetts down to Georgia, that they were now responsible for housing and feeding the ten thousand British soldiers who were to be sent to guard the colonial frontiers, either in their own homes or in barracks built at their expense.

Abigail well recalled the flame of anger that scorched her at the arbitrary imposition of these duties—*What did Parliament know about conditions in the colonies?*—and, hard on its heels, the stab of pain in her vitals, the warm wetness of her water breaking. She hadn't even had time to call out when her mother came in from the dairy with the milk-pans, saw her gasping, and rushed to her side.

The child who'd been born later that day,

twenty-two years ago come July, had been Nabby.

Nabby who would today—*Please, God, let it BE sometime today and not tomorrow or Wednesday!*—birth a child of her own.

⚜

Footsteps creaked in the hall of that tall gray stone town house that was so wildly different from the kitchen of her memory, the kitchen whose open back door had let in the scents of summer fields and orchards just beyond. John appeared in the bedroom doorway, stout, round-faced, blue eyes as bright and as sharp at fifty-seven as they'd been when first they'd met. In times of agitation his plump cheeks tended to turn red and they were like cherries now: "Is she all right?" were the first words out of his mouth.

"Esther seems to think so." Abigail was lacing up her boots.

"Esther has no more brain in her head than your finches do."

As if to confirm his opinion of them, Beatrice and Benedick went into a chirping flurry of self-induced hysteria in their gilt cage beside the window. Abigail made a shushing gesture to her husband, fearful that Esther might come up the stairs and hear this re-mark. John was probably the least diplo-matic diplomat since the Goths had sent their emissaries to ancient Rome, and didn't confine himself to referring to one of his fel-low delegates as "a demon of discord" whose life was "one continued insult to good manners and to decency." He'd gotten better over the years, but when enraged or annoyed he would still say pretty much any-thing to and about anyone, and had more than once had the servant-girl—who really did sometimes seem to have a brain the size of a grain of bird-shot—in tears.

But the servant who appeared behind John wasn't Esther, but prim Mr. Spiller the butler. "Shall I have Ned harness the car-riage, ma'am?"

"Don't be silly," retorted Abigail. "It's five minutes' walk to Wimpole Street." It took most people ten.

"It's also coming over cloudy again," John told her. "You've been ill most of the winter—"

"Nonsense," said Abigail, though it was perfectly true that since October she'd been racked by the worst bouts of rheumatism since the voyage from Boston. "I shall have

Esther bring along an umbrella. You may need the carriage."

John shook his head. "Surely the *mere* concerns of hearth and home haven't driven it from your mind that we're dining with Lord Carmarthen today? To give me one last chance at getting some satisfaction about those articles of the treaty that the Crown hasn't honored and shows not the slightest intention of honoring. . . ."

"Drat it!" Abigail had forgotten, though she'd been writing to her sister Mary about dining with the Foreign Secretary moments before Esther and Briesler had come in with the news. "You might as well stop at home, for all the good talking to Carmarthen is going to do. What good is negotiating a treaty, and having even the King sign it, if they refuse to comply with it? They're still keeping troops along our frontiers, they're still seizing our shipping and claiming it's smuggled, and still forcing American sailors into their navy." She finished lacing her other boot, straightened up to face her husband. "And if they've honored a single one of the claims of Americans here in London that you've petitioned for—"

She broke off, seeing Esther come up the stairs again, cloaked and hooded for a walk in the harsh spring chill and carrying the oiled-silk umbrella that Abigail had purchased in Paris rather than condemn herself to forever doling out shillings and sous for sedan-chairs when it came on to rain.

Nabby needed her. In Nabby's position, she herself would have been content to bear a child alone in an enemy land, if doing so would allow her mother to attend a gathering so potentially vital to the cause of the young Republic, always supposing her gentle mother would have done any such thing in her life. But Nabby, Abigail suspected, did not have her strength. She firmly pushed aside her disappointment at not being able to be in two places at once, and said, "Please tender my regrets, and Nabby's, to Lady Carmarthen. I shall send a note from Nabby's this afternoon." She wrapped the thicker India shawl around her shoulders, over the one she'd been wearing that morning already. Though she'd put on weight since coming to England, Abigail still felt the damp cold profoundly. There were weeks on end when it seemed to her that she never got warm.

"Would it help if I came?" John—and his maniacally inquisitive friend Tom Jefferson—were the only men Abigail had ever met who would actually volunteer to be present at a childbirth.

"It will help most, dear sir," said Abigail, laying a hand to his cheek, "if you do precisely as a minister should: Dine with Lord Carmarthen, and impress upon him the dishonor that he does to his country, and his country to itself, by disregarding the treaty. And let me deal with the *mere* concerns of hearth and home. I shall send word to you at once if there is . . ." She hesitated, unwilling even to say it. Instead, she finished with, "if there is anything you need to know."

For all her fine-boned thinness Abigail had birthed five children without trouble, but for a fleeting instant she saw the shadow in John's eyes. She knew exactly what was in his mind: the haunted look in Tom Jefferson's eyes, when anyone spoke of the beloved wife whose childbearing had taken her life. They descended the stairs in silence, to the hall where Briesler waited with heavy cloaks, broad-brimmed hats, tall iron shoe-pattens, stout gloves, and the basket of linen rags, lint, soap, spirits of wine, thread, and fine-honed scissors. Abigail had made sure the best midwife in London had been engaged but never left anything to chance.

On the way downstairs she added her Bible, a copy of Richardson's *Pamela* (which she knew to be one of Nabby's favorites), and Buchan's *Domestic Medicine.* John opened the door for the little party onto the chilly sparkle of the cloudy April day, and she turned back and put her hand to John's cheek again. "All will be well, dear sir," she promised.

Like her, she thought as she descended the front steps, John, too, wished to be in two places at once, both doing his duty to his country and sitting at his daughter's side.

⚜

London.

Abigail moved along Duke Street at a brisk pace. The pattens on her shoes scraped and clanked on flagstones slimy with the morning's rain and several days' accumulation of horse-droppings. London was a far cleaner city than Paris, where passersby had no hesitation about using the doorways and carriage-gates of strangers' houses as urinals, but even here on its northern edge the air was gritty with the smoke of too many chimneys, redolent of privies, horses, and garbage rotting in back-lanes. Her dressmaker spoke of London being "thin of company," as Parliament had not yet opened, but you couldn't tell it from the number of carts and carriages jostling for space along Duke Street, the shaggy louts carrying sedan-chairs, the vendors of everything from coal to hot pies bawling their wares at the top of their lungs.

Gulls cried overhead. Even so far from the river, the air smelled of the sea.

A wild scent that brought back to her the view of Boston, when she'd climb to the rock slabs on top of Penn's Hill and see it spread before her: the small brown wooden city under its haze of smoke, seeming to rise out of the shining stretches of water that surrounded it; the narrow dry strip of the Boston Neck that linked it with the mainland; the islands all floating in the brightness and the forest on the green hills beyond. The birds like clouds wheeling above the salt-marshes on either side of the Neck, and the white snips of sails clustering along the wharves.

Nabby had climbed Penn's Hill with her hundreds of times, during those days when John was riding the circuit of the courts, a sturdy little blond girl who'd laugh when the clouds broke and sunlight would sweep across the water as though driven by the wind.

Was it the War, Abigail wondered, *that made our daughter so silent?*

When the redcoats first swarmed on the Long Wharf to garrison Boston in October of 1768, she and John were living in the town. The rented house on Brattle Street lay close enough to the Commons so that she was waked each morning by the regimental drums. Nabby was three then, toddling about the sand-floored kitchen in stiff muslin pinafores or playing with her Boston cousins, for Abigail's family—the Smiths—was a large one, and had outposts from Salem all down the coast.

In the evenings John and his wily cousin Sam would argue before the parlor fire, and Abigail would put Nabby, and baby Johnny, to bed and come down to take part in the talk. Joseph Warren had come often, one of the masterminds behind the struggle for colonial liberties, and James Otis, like a half-mad Titan whose mind flashed primordial fire. She remembered elegant little John Hancock presenting her with his best smug-

gled tea, and quiet, steady Paul Revere going to the shed for another log. How many
nights had Nabby lain awake in her cot, listening open-eyed to the voices of the men?

When did she begin to understand?

Susanna was born at the end of that year,
named for John's mother, and died not long
after the end of the next. Even her recollection of that awful grief, and of the numb feeling of hollowness that followed, was mingled in Abigail's mind with the Revolution. A
month and a day after little Susanna's
death, a British captain was taunted by a
mob in King Street and shouted for rein-
forcements. To this day, nobody really knew
who fired the first shot.

She remembered Nabby's frantic silence
as the five-year-old clung to her in the
kitchen, listening to the crackling fusillade
of gunfire, the sea-roar of men shouting.
She'd tried to leave Nabby and three-year-
old Johnny with Pattie, the hired girl, but her
daughter had screamed and screamed until
Abigail took her along. Heavy already with
another pregnancy, she'd refused to accept
the woman's part of sitting at home with her
frightened children, waiting for someone to
tell her what had happened.

When she saw the bodies in the bloodied snow of King Street she'd bent to cover her daughter's eyes. Drifts of powder smoke still hung over the street when Abigail reached it, the gritty, sulfurous smell mingling with the metallic tang of blood. Abigail had been barely conscious of Nabby's arms tightening around her neck, of the little girl pressing her face to her shoulder, small hands gripping her hair.

John was asked to defend the soldiers at their trial. Cousin Sam had been outraged, but John had retorted, "Counsel is the very *last* thing *any* accused person should lack in a free country." Even Sam couldn't argue with that. Abigail was too far along with child to go to the courthouse—Charley was born in May—the very summation of why there were times when she wished with all her heart that she'd been born a man.

"Nonsense," sister Mary wrote back to her complaint. "If you'd been born a man, Abby, you'd never get to kiss John without the whole town talking."

Two years later they bought a house in Queen Street. They were still living there—Nabby nine by then, solemn Johnny seven, Charley a gay and sunny five, and Tommy a toddler of three—when the ships of the British East India Company sailed into the harbor with an immense cargo of tea that they had to sell to someone or go bankrupt. The Crown had decided to crack down on colonial smuggling in America and force the colonies to buy only Company tea, with a nominal Crown tax.

Abigail was ill that December, as she often was, with an inflamed chest and a fever. Beneath the quilts of their gloomy little salt-box of a bedroom, she tossed, unable to sleep through the long nights after the tea-ships docked. She'd listened to the church bells tolling endlessly, as if for a plague. The streets were eerily silent. Everyone knew something was coming.

Through her open door she heard the voices murmuring in the kitchen, at all hours of day or night during those two endless weeks. "What if they *do* fight?" she heard John ask. "What if they call out soldiers to protect the tea?"

"What a pamphlet *that* will make!" She could almost see Cousin Sam rub his hands, gloating over the prospect. He was a burly ruddy-faced man who'd failed in half a dozen businesses because he was far too interested in politics to pay attention to merely making a living, a man without fear for his own life nor with regard for the lives of those around him. From the small bedroom where the four children slept, all crowded together in one bed, she heard Nabby cry out softly in one of her nightmares—the child had not had nightmares, thought Abigail, when she was tiny.

"They won't do it though, my lad." Cousin Sam sounded regretful. Looking back on it, Abigail often remembered the scene not as something overheard, but as if she'd been down in the dark kitchen herself, seeing the two men's faces by the glow of the banked embers beneath the chimney's loops of pots and chains. Sam's square, mobile features with his short-cropped hair bristling up where his hat had disarrayed it, and the shoulders of his threadbare coat dark with rain; John's face half hidden in the shadow, expressionless, but his eyes very bright. "Good God, Johnny my boy, have you seen how many men have come in from the countryside? Five thousand! Some of them have walked clear down from Salem to be here—to make sure we stand too many together to be dispersed with a few volleys."

Sometimes when she'd dream about the scene, Abigail saw that Sam carried a bundle beneath his arm, three feet long and heavy, wrapped in a striped trade-blanket such as peddlers sold to the Indians of the western forests. Where it slipped aside she saw metal glint.

"There's another meeting at the Old South Church this afternoon," added a light tenor voice that Abigail knew as John Hancock's. "That's where the lobsterbacks will be looking. We're meeting in the back room of Edes and Gill's print-shop. As soon as it's dark we'll move out. When we pass the Old South we'll have as many men following us as we need. Believe me, there'll be no trouble."

"Oh, there'll be trouble." As Abigail drifted deeper into sleep she heard the lightness creep into John's voice, like a soldier who frets on the eve of battle but sings as the charge begins. "Just not right away."

⚜

Through the drizzling day that had followed those whispered conversations, Abigail remembered now as she turned along Oxford Street, Nabby had not spoken one word about what was going on in the city. The girl had gone about her chores and read her lessons in the indifferent silence that was becoming characteristic of her, in contrast to Johnny and Charley, who were in and out of their mother's room a hundred times. The boys were going to a nearby dame-school to learn their letters, but since men had been pouring into the town after the docking of the tea ships, and red-coated soldiers patrolled the streets, Abigail had kept them both at home. She'd insisted they keep up with their lessons nevertheless.

"You must be strong," she'd said to them, when with fall of darkness the voices of the men assembled outside Old South grew louder. She gathered them close to her on the bed, Charley and Nabby and Johnny, and Tommy a babe in the crib. "I expect all of you to be strong, to be worthy and to serve your country as your father is doing."

God help them, she had thought, *they will need strength, if anything goes wrong. If something happens to John.*

When Johnny and Charley had been put to bed, Nabby remained in Abigail's room, reading to her. Her young voice had barely paused, when torchlight had streamed past the window; she had not even looked up. Abigail had wanted to ask her then if she still had nightmares, but could not.

Later, when John had come in and Nabby had run to him to silently clasp him round the waist, he had laid a hand on her head but looked over her at Abigail. He had said only, "The die is cast."

⚜

A scruffy little boy dressed in men's cast-offs darted up to Abigail at the corner of Marylebone Road and offered, for a half-penny, to sweep the crossing: "Fine lady like you don't want to get 'er clogs all shitty," he explained with a winning smile. He didn't look any older than Johnny had been when the fighting started with England, and was probably as illiterate as Abigail's finches.

"Indeed I don't," she agreed, and handed him a farthing. "And the rest when we're safely across the road." Far from being offended, the boy gave her a dazzling grin and leaped into the traffic with his birch-broom, carving a path through the trampled swamp of dung while he dodged drays, riders, and the fast-moving phaetons of the rich. According to Abigail's closest London friend Sarah Atkinson, hundreds of parentless children slept under the bushes in the Park, or beneath the arches of the public buildings. They died of pneumonia every winter like the sparrows that fell from the frozen branches.

"You should be in school," she informed the boy, handing him the second installment of the fee when Briesler, in his stout boots, had steadied her across the slippery cobblestones to the far corner. "Surely you don't plan to still sweep a crossing when you're grown?"

The child took the coin with unimpaired cheer. "Lor' no, ma'am. When I'm growed I'll take the King's shillin' an' be a soldier."

Before she could reply he gave her a brisk salute, and dashed away to proposition his next customer, a stout gentleman emerging from a wine-shop. *And where will your King send YOU,* Abigail wondered, *the next time he needs to avenge ninety thousand dollars' worth of ruined tea?*

As she'd feared, her son-in-law had sacked the cook, and the young maidservant who answered the door at 10 Wimpole Street had the flustered look of one overwhelmed with too many jobs. "Ma'am, I'm that glad to see you, and so will Mrs. Smith be, too," exclaimed the girl as she opened the door, forgetting the cardinal rule that good servants were both invisible and mute. English servants, anyway—Abigail had never encountered an American servant who didn't think himself or herself the equal of their employer. "We sent Katie—that's the kitchenmaid, ma'am—out for the midwife, and she should be here any time now."

"Mama!" Colonel William Smith came striding down the stairs, holding out his hands to grasp Abigail's. "Thank God you've come!" Big, dark, and flamboyantly handsome, Colonel Smith looked concerned but not scared. When he kissed Abigail, his breath smelled of brandy.

"When did her pains begin?" asked Abigail, and her son-in-law looked completely nonplussed. "You're a soldier and you didn't note the time of the battle's opening guns? Shame, sir."

"Eight o'clock or thereabouts," provided the maid. "And nobbut a few moments long. I've got water on the boil, and made her some tea." And snatching up the apron she had clearly stripped off and dropped onto the hall table moments before opening the door, she vanished down the kitchen stairs again.

The house, Abigail observed as Colonel Smith escorted her volubly up the stairs, though a third the size of 8 Grosvenor Square, was ill-kept and a trifle dirty, and, as she'd feared, freezing cold. No one had cleaned the lamp-chimneys in days, and every candle-holder bore a burned-down stump of melted wax. Wax, she noted, and not the less expensive tallow that Abigail bought for every room in her own house where the smell of them wouldn't be detected by guests.

She understood, of course, the need to keep up appearances, but she knew also what Colonel Smith was paid as John's secretary. Though a hero of the War, the handsome New Yorker had no family money, a fact which had not entered into the discussion when Smith had asked for Nabby's hand. And indeed, in a new nation, with the Colonel's obvious ambition and drive, family money was less important. John's father had been a farmer, like the Colonel's, and a ropemaker in his spare time.

At all events, a cheerful fire burned in the bedroom where Nabby sat, propped among pillows, on a sheet-draped chair before the blaze. In spite of herself Abigail glanced at the sides of the hearth. She was relieved to find that it, at least, had been swept the previous day.

"Mama . . ." Nabby caught her mother's hands, and Abigail dropped to her knees to hold her.

It was as if the stiff, withdrawn silences, the indifferences of the war years had never been.

⚜

Abigail didn't know how she could have endured the War, if it had not been for Nabby at her side. Nabby had turned nine four months before the tea was dumped in Boston Harbor; the first shots were fired at Lexington bridge three months before her tenth birthday. *When a man weds, he gives hostages to fortune,* John Dryden had said a century and a half before. Unspoken in Abigail's partnership with John was the promise that it was she who would keep those hostages safe.

With the closing of the port of Boston after Cousin Sam's so-called Tea Party, John and Abigail had moved back to Braintree, to the house on the Plymouth road. Abigail was infinitely thankful for the move in April, when the Minutemen drove the British back into Boston and barricaded them there by encampments on the Boston Neck. Only weeks after that, while John was away at the Continental Congress in Philadelphia, four British warships dropped anchor not four miles from the house. Their goal was to seize hay stored on the nearby Grape Island as fodder for their horses in the town, but they could just as easily have come ashore in force and burned the farms.

All that summer, the countryside seethed. Refugees fled Boston and militiamen marched toward it, and all of them had to be provided with food, drink, and in many cases lodging for a night or a week. With her farm help disappearing into the Army and the tenant in the farm-cottage refusing to either pay rent or vacate, Abigail had been worked to a shadow milking, weeding, mending, cleaning. In June the British had tried to break the seige, and from the top of Penn's Hill, Abigail and eight-year-old Johnny had watched through her spyglass as crimson-coated British regulars had twice charged the patriot defense works on Breed's Hill, before the ragged militiamen had finally been driven away. Too mauled to follow up their victory, the British had returned to Boston. The settlement of Charles Town, beneath Breed's Hill, lay in ashes.

Keep your spirits composed and calm, John wrote her that summer, *and don't suffer yourself to be disturbed by idle reports and frivolous alarms.* Every refugee and soldier carried rumors. They spread them like an infestation of lice: of British attack, of smallpox in Boston, of Indians in British pay poised to murder. Moreover, every village and farmstead bubbled sullenly with suspicion, as patriots burned the barns and mutilated the stock of those who remained loyal to the Crown, and Loyalists fled to Boston carrying with them intelligence about the countryside and the disposal of patriot troops.

In case of real danger, John wrote, *fly to the woods with our children.* Abigail was aware that John's place was unquestionably with the Congress, fighting to unite the disparate colonies into an entity capable of fielding an army—

But if he'd been in the same room with her then, she'd have brained him with a stick of firewood.

Through all that, Nabby was at her side. Washing clothes and making soap, churning butter and dragging ashes to the ash-heap, trying to save pins and medicine, salt and tinware, coffee and fabric and all the other things that British trade had provided and British laws had forbidden the colonies to manufacture. Trying to make the tiny cache of "hard" currency hidden in the attic floor-boards last as long as it could.

Six-year-old Charley thought that another raid by the British would be a tremendous lark ("I'll kill 'em, Ma, you'll see!") and Johnny drew up intricate contingency plans on the sanded kitchen floor. But what Nabby thought of any of it, Abigail never knew.

At night she told them stories from Virgil and Horace and Livy, of Roman strength and Trojan determination: Horatio guarding the bridge, and Appius who stabbed his own daughter to death rather than have her live a slave. Or tales from the Bible: David and Gideon and Deborah, who led God's chosen people to victory.

My heart is toward the governors of Israel, that offered themselves willingly, the ancient prophetess had sung. *They fought from heaven; the stars in their courses fought against Sisera—the river Kishon swept them away.*

"We must be strong," she told her children, "and keep ourselves fit to be of use to our country." Johnny's eyes brooded in the firelight and Charley's shone, and even Tommy forgot his ever-present fear. Nabby quietly stitched at their shirts, or braided candlewicking, and said nothing. Abigail tried not to think of what would become of them during a British raid, or if she were killed.

Winter came. In its shadow, the pale horseman of sickness rode over the barren fields. John's brother Elihu died in the camp at Cambridge. Abigail's sharp-tongued sister Mary fell ill in Salem, and at the Weymouth parsonage, so did her younger sister Betsey, twenty-six that winter and still unwed. When John's mother fell ill, and Abigail's servant-girl Pattie and little Tommy, Abigail sent the older boys away to her sister in Salem. Eventually eight of their neighbors died. Some nights Abigail was so exhausted she could only cling to her daughter's shoulders and weep with weariness, feeling the girl's thin body stiff as a doll with fear. The day Pattie died, it was Nabby who brought Abigail word that Abigail's mother was sick as well.

John's mother recovered, tough as a little walnut.

Abigail's mother died.

⚜

"I'm sorry about the cook." Nabby winced, groped for her mother's hand. In her voice Abigail could hear the tremor of pain and fright. "Dinner on Sunday was absolutely frightful, and William went down to the kitchen and found her by the hearth, drunk—and on his brandy, too! It was the third time since Christmas—"

"Don't fret yourself about the cook." In Abigail's opinion William Smith should have been looking for a new cook since Christmas. She said instead, "It's all right."

Nabby shook her head, blond hair tangling against the pillows. Tears sprang into her eyes. "It isn't! I've tried—I've tried so hard . . ."

"Child, what are you talking about?" Abigail demanded, gripping her daughter's swollen hands. "You have done all that can be asked of any woman: to love and obey your parents, to be a good sister to your brothers, to marry a good man and bear strong sons and daughters for the new Republic. She'll be a new little American, you know," she added, with an encouraging smile. "One of the first of the new generation."

"Like those stories you used to tell us." Nabby managed a smile in reply. "Remember? I always liked Cloetia, escaping from the enemy and swimming across the Tiber under a hail of spears." Her breath caught and her fingers tightened on Abigail's. "But I always felt like I'd have been one of her friends, who got left behind as a hostage because Cloetia chose to free the young men, knowing Rome would need the soldiers. I always felt—"

"I daresay the Romans carried their patriotism a bit too far," responded Abigail firmly, looking down at her daughter's taut face. "Any woman who bears a child, of either sex, is doing far more for our country than the bravest soldier ever did, and enduring more pain as well. But you'll come through it, dearest. You're a Smith—*my* family Smith, as well as William's. And we Smith girls are tough as ponies."

Nabby's eyes pressed shut, her breath coming in gasps and her hands crushing Abigail's now as the wave of pain swept over her—*Where on earth is that miserable midwife?* The pains, though sharp, were still some minutes apart, but who knew how long that would last?

"It won't be long before she'll go home— we'll all go home—and see our country again," Abigail continued, remembering how desperately she'd needed to hear a friendly voice while she herself had been in labor. "Even your father knows what a waste of his time it is, trying to deal with Parliament. They have no more intention of living up to the terms of the treaty than they do of going back to wearing loincloths and painting themselves blue, though I daresay with the fashions I've seen here this season it may come to that. They haven't made a single reparation for American property seized at sea during the War. Your father has sent to Congress asking for his recall. If they do as they've said, and reorganize the government, they'll need him there. And if he goes, almost certainly Colonel Smith will be called home as well."

Nabby's body was racked with an aftermath of sobs. She whispered something, Abigail thought she said, "New York." Meaning, she guessed, that William Smith's mother, sister, and younger brothers lived outside New York City, a week's hard travel from Braintree. But when she leaned close and asked softly,

"What did you say, dear?" Nabby asked brokenly, "Did I do the right thing, Ma?"

Tears streamed down her face. As Abigail dried them with the clean spare handkerchief she invariably carried, she felt her own heart contract with guilt. She knew exactly what her daughter meant.

⚜

In the spring of 1782, Royall Tyler came to board with Abigail's sister Mary, who had by that time returned to Braintree to live. Nabby was sixteen.

John had been gone two and a half years by that time. The Congress had sent him to France early in 1778, when the French King had allied himself with the American cause. He'd taken Johnny, not quite eleven years old, ostensibly as an assistant but in truth so that there would be one soul at his side whom he could completely trust. He'd come home for four brief months late in the summer of '79, and had then departed. This time he took with him both Johnny and Charley.

Nine-year-old Charley had wept to leave Braintree, his cousins, his family, and his friends—Johnny at least had borne his own earlier departure with the stoicism of one who knows his duty to family, country, and his own future worth. No amount of parental encouragement about seeing a foreign land, learning a language that would serve him well in the future, and meeting friends who could put his feet on the road of profession and honor seemed to make a difference to Charley. In the end, all Abigail could do was tell her sobbing middle son that he must strive to excel, and hope.

Since the British had abandoned Boston in 1776, there had been no more fighting in Massachusetts. But the War had gone on. With many of the able-bodied men either in the State militia or the Continental Army, it was hard to find anyone to do the farm's heavy work, especially given the sharp increase in wages and the scarcity of any kind of real money. Both Congress and the State of Massachusetts had printing-presses instead of treasuries, and most people demanded either specie—of which almost no one had any—or payment in kind: crops, eggs, a lamb. It cost a hundred and fifty dollars just to get a new fence. John took to sending Abigail, from France, small packages of the kind of goods that were scarce

in Massachusetts: pins, silk gloves, handkerchiefs of fine muslin, ribbons, the occasional length of fine white lawn. All of these
she could sell, or trade.

Somehow, they survived.

Her loneliness, as the months stretched
into a year, then two years, was agony.
There were days when her longing for his
company yawned like a bottomless pit in
her soul; nights when sheer carnal hunger
for his body filled her with a fever no medicine could slake. Snow heaped around the
house in the winters and darkness closed
down by four in the afternoon. John's letters
were too often brief, for John had a horror of
the British intercepting his correspondence
on the high seas.

In the summer of 1781, only months before Cornwallis surrendered, John wrote
that he was sending Charley home: He had
"too exquisite a sensibility for Europe,"
meaning, Abigail guessed, that neither John
nor anyone else knew what to make of the
boy's sensitive nature and odd combination
of introversion and happy-go-lucky charm.
Fear of having the letter—and Charley—intercepted precluded John from saying how,
where, or when, which turned out to be just

as well for Abigail's peace of mind. Charley, and one of the two Americans John had entrusted him to, ended up stranded in Spain, caught in high-seas battle with privateers, and becalmed in mid-ocean for weeks before fetching up, five months after setting forth from France, in the shipping town of Beverly, a long day's journey north of Boston.

Abigail didn't know whether to fall to her knees praising God for the return of her son or to write her merchant cousin Will in Amsterdam and ask about hiring someone to break a broom over John's head for sending their boy off alone.

And a few months after that, Royall Tyler had come into her—and Nabby's—life.

Nabby had at first wanted to have little to do with the handsome young lawyer. Royall was twenty-five, and according to sister Mary—who admittedly had two marriageable daughters of her own to dispose of— had thoroughly disgraced himself at Harvard with drunkenness, profanity, fathering a bastard on the charwoman, and informing the faculty that he cared nothing for a "little paltry degree" which might be bought for twenty shillings anytime he really wanted one.

"My sins were a wild boy's sins," he admitted to Abigail, when he ran to catch up with her one summer afternoon on her way home from Mary's house. "Of them I can only ask, with the Psalmist, that you *remember not the sins of my youth, nor my transgressions . . . Pardon my iniquity, for it is great."* He bowed his head meekly before her, but his dark eyes laughed through his long lashes. "I adore your daughter, Mrs. Adams. Without your aid I am nothing. I cannot open my breast and lay my reformed heart before you on a tray for your inspection, though I would if I could. I ask only that you regard me as *tabula rasa,* and look upon my present actions with an open mind."

Abigail was perfectly well aware that she was being flirted with, but she also knew the effects of gossip in Braintree. Though Royall was said to have dissipated a substantial part of the fortune his father had left him ("Of course I did! I was fifteen!"), he was still in possession of a ship, a store, a chaise-and-pair, and a house in Boston, and was negotiating for purchase of the handsomest house in Braintree. It would be no bad thing, she thought, should Nabby wed a man who would be able to keep her well.

And, it was always hard for Abigail to turn a cold shoulder to an educated man. There were few enough people in Braintree with whom she could talk about Voltaire, Cicero, and Plutarch, as she did with John. Royall would drop in at the house on the Plymouth road, as if by accident on his way to and from Boston, to chat in the kitchen or the dairy with mother and daughter. Even when Nabby went to spend weeks in Boston with her Smith relatives, Royall would visit Abigail, to help with the legal business of collecting the long-overdue debts owed John, and to advise her on the details of running the farm and whether investing in land in Vermont would be wise. Afterwards Abigail would write to Nabby, saying that her suitor sent her his love.

She had, she admitted, high hopes for the match, if for no other reason than that Nabby's aloof silences had begun to worry her. She feared that something in Nabby had been changed or broken in the years of war and fear. If she could not love a man as devoted to her as Royall was, and as educated, clever, and witty, to whom would she ever gift her heart?

⚜

Was a part of her fear, she wondered now, looking down at her daughter's face, a fear for herself? Petals scattered on the wind of time can never be regathered. And her own mirror, that icy winter of 1783, showed her gray in her dark hair, and the spoor of age beginning in the corners of her eyes and lips. When she turned thirty-nine in November she wrote to John, *Who shall give me back my time? Who shall compensate me for the years I cannot recall?*

In France the treaty-wrangling with England dragged on. John sent letters filled with maddened frustration. Two of the other delegates at the Court of Versailles were completely untrustworthy and bickered like cat and dog; another member of the delegation, he suspected, was selling information to the British by means of a letter-drop in a hollow tree by the Tuileries garden. To make matters worse, he shared quarters in Paris with Benjamin Franklin, and the spectacle of the philosopher—who at seventy-seven was arguably too old for that sort of carrying-on—merrily leaping into and out of half the beds in Paris was almost more than he could stand.

In '81 John had been taken ill on a journey to Holland—"As near to death as any man ever approached without being grasped in his arms"—and since that time, Abigail had lived with fear.

No more letters signed *Portia* or *Lysander,* their old courting nicknames.

No more pillow-fights, followed by burning kisses that consumed the whole of her flesh; no more long evenings of talk and argument and jokes about Plutarch in bed until the candles burned out.

No more hope that she would one day look up from weeding the vegetable-garden and see him striding up the path.

⚓

Was that why I pushed you to marry Royall Tyler? Because I wanted you to have what I feared I would lose? Another woman would have gently stroked her daughter's sweat-damp hair—Abigail prosaically wrung out a washrag in the basin, and mopped Nabby's face. Rewarded by Nabby's faint shut-eyed smile, and the plump hand stealing up to briefly close around hers.

I only wanted what was best for you, my dearest child.

And at about the time Nabby at last began to unbend, and yield herself to Royall's enraptured kisses, the letter came from John.

Will you come to me this fall, and go home with me this spring?

⚜

"Lord, ma'am, I am that sorry."

Abigail looked up swiftly as the midwife came in, plump and wheezing and shadowed by a girl who carried a wicker basket bigger than Abigail's own.

"It's as if God sent out a circular letter to all the ladies in London at once, saying He wanted every baby birthed sharp this morning and no shilly-shallying about it. I've just got back from Clarges Street, with a fine young lady come into the world." The midwife beamed, and Abigail, who'd ascertained at a glance that the woman had taken the time to change not only her apron but her dress between deliveries, returned her smile.

"And I devoutly hope we shall see another

such before the day's much older," she replied, and held out her hand. "Mrs. Throckle, as I recall?"

"It is. And you're Mrs. Adams, if I remember aright, Mrs. Smith's good mother. I knew when I came home and found that girl of Mrs. Smith's there, and she told me you'd been sent for as well, I said to myself, 'Well, there's one I don't have to worry will come to harm before I arrive,' which I'm sorry to say in my business you can't always count on and that's the truth." After a brisk, firm clasp of Abigail's hand—a welcome change from the upper-class English habit of extending two limp fingers—she turned away at once and began her examination.

"Her waters broke not long after eight, her maid tells me," Abigail provided, kneeling at Nabby's other side. "So it's been—" She glanced at the elaborate little clock that decorated the bedroom's marble mantel, "—nearly three hours. The pains are about three minutes apart by my watch."

"Early days yet." Mrs. Throckle removed the clean towel that covered her basket, and began removing little flasks of olive oil, chamomile, belladonna.

Nabby gave a gasp and a stifled cry, and

her hand closed hard on Abigail's again, her back arching as if it would break. She sobbed, "Ma!" through gritted teeth, and then, desperately, *"Papa!"* She had been only seven when her youngest brother was born, too young to remain in the house during her mother's travails, but the knowledge of childbirth's pain was something it seemed to Abigail that every woman was born understanding. When the contraction was over she clung to Abigail, and shivered, sobbing.

From the street outside the bedroom window Abigail heard the jingle of harness, and rising, angled her head to look down. It was, as she'd half suspected, Nabby's husband Colonel Smith, just getting into a smart green-and-gold chaise behind a sleek bay gelding. Abigail thought, *Damn him,* and then, remembering the brandy on his breath as he'd hugged her, *Just as well.*

"Ma?" Nabby opened her eyes again, struggled to sit a little straighter, to keep her face composed. "Were you afraid? When you had us, I mean, me and Johnny and Charley and Tommy?"

"Of course." Abigail sat down again beside her. "I think every woman's afraid, no matter how many times she goes through it safely—as who wouldn't be?" She rubbed Nabby's hand, taking comfort, like her daughter, from Mrs. Throckle's competent bustling presence in the background. "I can assure you, though," she added, "I was never as afraid having a child as I was crossing the ocean to join your father."

And Nabby, as Abigail had hoped, blew out her breath in a shaky laugh. Perhaps at the idea of anyone being bothered that much by a sea-voyage—Nabby had been back on her feet and eating heartily within days of boarding the little ship. Perhaps at the idea of her incisive mother being afraid of anything at all.

⚓

By the time John's letter reached her in the fall of '83, it was too late to embark on the sea. All through the spring of '84 Abigail made preparations to leave, arranging for the farm to be looked after, and the small rent on the cottage to be collected by John's brother Peter. Jack Briesler, a veteran who for several years had cut kindling, fixed roofs, and mowed hay at the farm, would go with her, as would Esther Field, the daughter of one of her neighbors, horse-faced, mousy-haired, good-natured, and fifteen. One could not present oneself as the wife of the American Minister to France without servants of some sort, and Abigail wanted to have at least someone around her who could speak English. It was decided that Charley—fourteen now—and twelve-year-old Tommy would remain at the parsonage at Haverhill, fifty miles away near the Vermont border, where her sister Betsey—not an old maid after all—and Betsey's husband ran a school.

But though Royall Tyler pleaded ardently for an early marriage with Nabby, and pointed to the large and handsome house he'd bought with its eighty acres of farmland, Abigail was beginning to have her doubts. Part of this was due to her own sister. Though Nabby might now hotly defend her suitor, and retort that her aunt Mary had her eye on Royall for a son-in-law herself, as Royall's landlady Mary had a closer view of him than did anyone else in town. Sister Mary had spoken darkly, both to Abigail and to Nabby, of the young man still having some wild oats to sow. Abigail wondered, too, if Nabby's sudden "understanding" with Royall had something to do with wanting to remain behind in Braintree.

In the end, when Abigail journeyed to Boston with Briesler and Esther—and a stock of provisions for the voyage including mustard, wine, a barrel of apples, several dozen eggs, tea, coffee, pepper, brown sugar, a sack of Indian meal, and a cow for milk, plus all their bedding, ewers, and chamber-pots—Nabby went with her. For a day or two before the *Active* sailed, they stayed with Abigail's uncle Isaac Smith, and it was there, the day before their departure, that Abigail first met Thomas Jefferson.

"I have myself only just been appointed Minister Plenipotentiary in partnership with your husband," he told her, that summer evening in Uncle Isaac's wood-paneled company parlor. All the Smiths in Boston had come to bid her and Nabby farewell, and a wide assortment of Quincys, Storers, and Boylstons: that vast spun-steel kinship network that bound New England merchant families together. "Hearing you were in Boston, I came to offer you my escort to Paris."

"See, Nabby?" Abigail remarked as she extended her hand. "Strange men still accost me out of the blue with offers of elopement to Paris at first acquaintance—not bad for forty."

Nabby looked shocked, but appreciative laughter danced in Mr. Jefferson's hazel eyes. He bowed deeply over her hand.

Slender for his gawky height and scholarly-looking, he was one of those fair-skinned sandy redheads who freckle or burn rather than tan, but there was an energy to him, a sort of shy friendliness that Abigail found enormously attractive.

"I've made arrangements to cross on the *Ceres,* out of New York, on the fifth of July, I and my daughter," he went on, his soft, husky voice marked by slurry Virginia vowels and carelessness with the letter "r." "If Mrs. Adams would care to accompany me back—"

"That's very kind of you, Mr. Jefferson," said Abigail. "But my daughter and I sail tomorrow."

Jefferson looked disconcerted. *By the fact that a woman wouldn't wait for a gentleman's escort before crossing the sea? Or because anyone would go ahead and make plans without consulting him?* "I hadn't heard of another ship bound for France that was prepared to take on passengers," he drawled.

"The *Active* sails for London." And, seeing the way those sandy brows shot down over the bridge of his nose, "We're no longer at war with them, after all."

"Does that matter, when one counts the dead?"

"If it did, no treaty would have validity and we should never be able to sleep in peace," retorted Abigail, a little surprised at this prejudice from a man John had described as reasonable and educated. Then she took a second look at the lines of sleeplessness around his eyes, and recalled all she had heard of the viciousness of partisan fighting in the South. And she knew somehow it was his own dead of whom Jefferson spoke.

⚜

The *Active* put to sea on Sunday, June 20, 1784, and immediately began living up to her name. Her cargo was whale-oil and potash, and Abigail's cow was not the only animal on board. These underlying stenches combined with the ground-in reek of unwashed clothing, sweating bodies, and every meal served and beer spilled in the course of every previous voyage.

From the cabin two small doors let into two eight-by-eight cells, each jammed to the ceiling, it seemed, with trunks. Abigail learned very quickly that chamber-pots had to be emptied out the single porthole immediately, for the next lurch of the ship would inevitably capsize them. The male passengers, Captain Lyde had explained to her, would, like the crew, relieve themselves clinging among the netting draped at the bow.

In all things give thanks unto the Lord.

Abigail shared one cubicle with Esther, and Nabby the other with a woman known universally on board as The Other Mrs. Adams (or, privately, Mrs. Adams of Syracuse, with a nod to *Comedy of Errors*)—the only Mrs. Adams Abigail had ever met who wasn't somehow related to John. The Other Mrs. Adams's brother Lawrence had very gallantly given up his bunk there to Nabby, otherwise the crowding in Abigail and Esther's cabin would have been impossible. Abigail had intended to go over the bare wooden bunks with arsenic, soap, and camphor before putting a stitch of bedding on them, but even before they were out of the harbor she could only hang on to the door frame for dear life, and within a very few minutes was so sick she could barely stand.

There followed the worst two weeks of her life. In damp weather Abigail had always been prey to rheumatism and headaches, and since the ship was, by its nature, perpetually damp, there were days when, in addition to nausea and the dizziness from dehydration and starvation, her body ached so badly she couldn't have stood if she'd wanted to. She'd cling to the sides of her bunk, into which she frequently had to be tied because of the high seas and buffeting of the winds, and wonder blindly if she was going to die before she saw John again.

At least she had plenty of company. All night long she could hear the men in the main cabin, and smell them, heaving up such dinners as they'd managed to down in the afternoon. The two cabins allotted to the women were so tiny, so airless, and reeked so badly of the cargo in the holds beneath, that the doors had to be kept open unless their inhabitants were actually in the act of changing clothes or using the bedroom vessels. Whatever modesty had survived the bearing of five children and the housing of large numbers of fleeing refugees in every room of a four-room farmhouse vanished rapidly, Abigail found, when men she'd never seen before came in to assist her while she vomited. When she was able she would return the favor.

This must be, she thought, *how men develop the camaraderie they speak of at having passed through battle together.*

My strength is made perfect in weakness, Saint Paul had written. *Thrice I suffered shipwreck, a night and a day I have been in the deep . . . in perils of waters, in perils of robbers, in perils by mine own countrymen . . . in perils in the wilderness, in perils in the sea. . . .*

Abigail felt that the saint had never quite got the credit he deserved, if he went through this very often on his travels.

Then one morning she woke to feel the ship no longer "lively," as the sailors said, but moving with a steady surge, like a horse at a smooth gallop. Though she still ached in every joint, the absence of nausea was like the glow of health. She went up on deck, and found herself reborn, into a world of sparkling blue and silver, white clouds and shards of white foam and white sails, and a delicious open wildness of salty air. Everything seemed to be moving, dancing—balancing as she was learning to balance. Above the tangle of ropes and masts it seemed to her the whole of the universe exulted.

I'm actually on a ship, she thought, her mind freed for the first time in twelve days from the shackles of reeling sickness, the repeated blank shock of the fear of going to the bottom in a storm. *I'm crossing the ocean.*

And at the end of this voyage, I'm going to see John.

Journeys end in lovers' meetings—

I'm going to be in London, and in Paris. Cities dreamed of, read of, heard of as a child . . .

And I'm going to see John.

Enchanted, Abigail walked to the rail and clung to the bar of damp wood, watching the gray porpoises as they raced along in the wake, so near, it seemed, that she felt she could lean down and touch them. One turned a little as it dove, and for an instant regarded her with a black, wise, mischievous eye. Then it was gone.

"Mrs. Adams!" Captain Lyde sprang down the short steps from the quarterdeck, held out his hands to her. "Good to see you on your feet!"

"Good to *be* on my feet," she responded. "And good—you don't know *how* good—to be able to come out and breathe air!"

The captain laughed. He was a sturdy-built man, fair-haired and red-faced. Abigail couldn't imagine how he shaved on board without cutting his own throat, but obviously he did. "And your daughter? She's a bonny one, she is, and as good a sailor as you could ask for. You'll let me know if there's anything I can do for you?"

"I'm glad you mentioned that," responded Abigail briskly. "I hope you understand that I don't speak from personal animosity, Captain Lyde, but this ship is a disgrace. There's an inch of filth in the passageway outside the main cabin, the stench below-decks is enough to turn a Christian's stomach, and there are rats the size of pit-ponies scurrying back and forth across the rafters above my bunk every night."

"Er . . . Mrs. Adams, you won't find a ship afloat that doesn't have rats."

"No, but you don't have to make their lives easier for them. And you could at least have some of your men swab out the passage-way. I don't wonder I've been sick for nearly two weeks. If the ship was in dry dock I'd no doubt still have been sick, from the smell alone."

Within the hour, three deck-hands were at work below-decks with scrapers, mops, brushes, holystones, and buckets of soapy water and vinegar. If there was nothing that could be done to eliminate the ground-in stinks of tar, half-spoiled salt-pork, whale-oil, and potash, at least the boards of the passageway deck were visible again and Abigail no longer had to clean her shoes coming and going from the cabin. The men muttered, but since Abigail herself led the work team until Captain Lyde tugged her gently back into the cabin, there wasn't much they could say.

Her next project was the galley. The cook had been accustomed to bringing in what-ever foods were cooked in whatever order they got hot—a leg of pork, followed by sometimes a pudding, sometimes a pair of roast fowls, and then a quarter of an hour later, when everyone was finished, he'd reappear with a platter of potatoes. "If not for the sake of your own self-respect," declared Abigail, confronting the big scar-faced African in the mephitic dark of the galley, "I should think you'd want to learn how to serve a meal for the sake of your own future. What if Captain Lyde were to die of consumption? Then you'd have to go back to being a deck-hand."

She picked her way around the corner of the high-built sand-box where the fire burned, to the copper of water, which was only lukewarm. "Good heavens, a fire this stingy will never get water cleansing-hot! Anyone would think you were planning to sell the leftover charcoal at the end of the voyage."

The piggy eyes slitted resentfully; Abigail pretended not to notice.

"Let's get these dishes clean for a start. Then I'll show you how gentlemen—and ships' captains—like to be served their meals. And wash your hands. If Captain Lyde or anyone else ever saw you in daylight they'd never touch food you'd prepared again."

⚜

Ten days after that the sea roughened again. The passengers had to remain below. One of the sailors brought word that land had been sighted, but Captain Lyde didn't recommend anyone going on deck to see for themselves. The *Active* rocked like a barrel in a millrace, and twice that evening Abigail was flung from her chair at table, until she roped herself into it, as she did when she sat on deck. That night, Nabby clung to her in the swaying gloom and whispered, "Ma, I don't want to die! I don't want to die without seeing Royall again."

If after waiting four and a half years to see John's face, Abigail reflected, she and her daughter ended up drowned in the ocean a mere hundred miles from where he sat, her first act upon arrival in Heaven would be to ask God for an explanation, and it had better be a good one.

"It will be all right," she said, stroking the girl's fair curls. "It will be fine."

On the third day the shaken, exhausted passengers crept forth onto the deck. Far off to port, Abigail saw a line of green-rimmed white cliffs, that shallowed to gray beaches and a gray-walled town, and white surf like the ruffle of a petticoat. Between surged an enormous expanse of monstrous gray waves that fell away into still more monstrous troughs, like chasms opening down Neptune's root-cellar. The sails flapped and cracked like cannons. Spits of rain lashed her face as she stood. Overhead, the sky loured blacker still.

"We could stay beating here in the Channel for days, trying to get around into the Estuary," explained Captain Lyde, looking more cheerful than he had any right to be considering that nobody on board had had more than an hour's sleep in three days. "Since these gales sometimes blow for weeks, I'm having the pilot-boat lowered, to take you into Deal." And he pointed to the wet-black huddle of roofs, the castle that poked up so improbably pale against the drenched green slopes of the hills. "You can get a post-chaise to Canterbury and then on to London, and can be there in a day."

London, thought Abigail, dazed at the thought.

I'm going to be in LONDON . . .

In someplace that won't sink under me,

and drown me and Nabby before ever I see John again.

She looked down over the rail at the churning sea and her heart turned to water.

Only the thought of going down with the *Active* in the Channel, within touching distance of John's hand, got Abigail down the jerking, swaying, wooden wall of the hull and into the pilot-boat. This lurched and knocked and veered from the ship's side, leaving a gap of icy sea. Only her own courage, Abigail suspected, got Nabby, Esther, and The Other Mrs. Adams to follow her. The sailors at the oars seemed to treat the matter as all in a day's work, but with what Abigail knew of Mr. Blunt's cooking, she suspected life and death were as one to this crew.

Gray rain streamed down into the gray sea. The Other Mrs. Adams wailed that she was going to die, a prophecy she had made hourly for the past thirty days. As a wave the size of a church rose up under the boat like a wall, then dropped away to nothingness, Abigail was inclined to agree with her, though nothing would have induced her to say so. Soft-spoken fellow passenger Mr. Foster grabbed her in his arms and clung fast to the rail, Abigail embracing him as she'd only ever embraced John while spray and rain soaked them both to the skin.

Just let me see him again, she found herself praying. *Just let me see him—*

There was a noise like thunder and a wave swept the boat up broadside, black oars flailing in air. Mr. Foster's arms tightened around her and Abigail shut her eyes, and the next instant the keel ground on pebbles.

She opened her eyes to see gray stone beach and emerald hill above her, sailors jumping from the boat to drag it farther up the beach, water the color of steel rushing around their bare shins.

It was Tuesday, the twentieth of July, 1784, and they were in England at last.

⚜

Rain began to fall at about noon. Nabby's pains grew harder, yet the baby showed no signs of coming. Mrs. Throckle's businesslike cheerfulness settled into a watchful quiet. Exhausted, Nabby clung to Abigail's hands. Between pains she would ask about her aunt Mary or her cousins Bettie and Luce, or whether Mr. Jefferson had written from Paris—"Do you know if his little daughter is on her way to France, as he said she'd be?"

"She is, and she'll be landing in England first, to stay with us til he comes for her." Little Polly Jefferson was seven, too young, in Abigail's opinion, to suffer the rigors of a sea-voyage. But when news had reached the Virginian in Paris, over two years ago now, that Polly's tiny sister Lucie had died, Jefferson had been inconsolable. He had been counting the days until Polly was marginally old enough to send for; Abigail could not deny him that, even in her heart. "It will be nice," added Abigail, watching her daughter's face worriedly, "to have a child in the house again."

"Mrs. Jefferson died," whispered Nabby, "from having a child. That's what Patsy told me—" Patsy was Jefferson's oldest daughter, a tall and awkward twelve when Abigail had met her briefly in Boston before their departure. "She had her child early, after they fled from the British attack. She never got over it, Patsy said." Then as her face convulsed with pain, she cried out, "Johnny!"

Not her husband's name, reflected Abigail uneasily. Her brother's.

The house John had rented for them on the outskirts of Paris was huge, set amid a wilderness of tangled garden across the road from the Bois de Boulogne. "We're constantly discovering new rooms," Abigail said to Jefferson, when he came calling with a basket of apples, four bottles of wine, and a strange old book about clockwork homunculi that he'd found in a shop on the rue Cluny. "We'll freeze, come winter. Or starve, wandering about in search of the dining-room. Last night I stumbled upon a *theater* in the north wing!"

"That doesn't surprise me," said Jefferson in his soft voice. "The place was built by the Desmoiselles Verrières, a pair of thoroughly reprehensible sisters."

"Hmph. I shudder to think the use they'd put to that room on the second floor that's entirely paneled in mirrors. John says we'll need the space to entertain, but on twenty-five hundred pounds a year, after one has bought candles and coal and soap and fodder for the horses, I am at a loss as to what we'll serve our guests—herring and oatmeal, I suppose."

Jefferson's hazel eyes widened in alarm as if, just for a moment, he feared she'd actually do it. In the green dapple of the garden's light and shade, he looked better and more rested than he had in Uncle Isaac's parlor in Boston two months ago—he'd had a pleasant voyage on a sea as calm as a millpond, he said, drat him. John had told her of the death of Jefferson's wife, as a result of flight from the British too soon after childbearing; she understood now his cold anger at the British, the war in his heart that no treaty could ever amend.

"It would help if the servants would actually do some work. The cook won't hear of so much as washing a dish—it's all I can do to get him to wash the vegetables. Pauline the *coiffeuse*—and the Americans we met in London all insist that *no* woman with pretensions to good society simply hires an itinerant hairdresser or, God forbid, dresses her hair herself—Pauline refuses to sew or sweep or make a bed, not even her own. And our maître d'hôtel doesn't do anything but make sure that nobody on the staff robs the family but himself."

"How many do you have?" Jefferson looked back through the vine-covered trees toward the limestone walls, the glittering windows. "I can't imagine keeping up a house that large with fewer than fifty servants. The Spanish Ambassador has a hundred of them, fifty in livery—one feels as if one is about to be taken prisoner."

"We have eight," said Abigail incisively, "Esther and Briesler being worth five apiece. Briesler on the subject of 'Popish French layabouts that don't speak a Christian language' is a treat. Our footman Mr. Petit is at least some use, and young Arnaud is energetic—Arnaud is our *frotteur.* He spends the entire day swabbing the floors, and emptying and cleaning the chamber-pots. This garden is large enough to make a paying wheat-crop in, yet it doesn't seem to have occurred to anyone to install a necessary-house anywhere on the property."

"Perhaps you simply haven't discovered it yet," suggested Jefferson mischievously. "Who knows what *terra incognita* lies beyond that pergola there and away into the orchard? A scientific expedition must be mounted—"

"Go along with you!" Abigail poked him with her fan.

"Ma!" a voice called out, and two hurrying

figures appeared from around the ruined summerhouse, hand in hand like children. A gray-and-white mongrel—who seemed to have come with the house—romped happily around their feet. "Ma, there's a *fountain* back here!"

"You see?" asked Jefferson. "The American spirit will always seek new horizons to explore."

One of the greatest and most delightful surprises, on their arrival in Europe, had been Nabby's reunion with her brother Johnny—John Quincy, Abigail supposed she must learn to call him. That somber young gentleman who'd met them in London was a schoolboy no longer. The last time Nabby had seen her brother she'd been fourteen, and Johnny twelve. It had distressed Abigail during John's brief return in '79 to see the boy as withdrawn and aloof as his sister, as if he understood the need for sacrifice and excellence that had taken him from his family.

Now they were together again, an affianced young lady of nineteen and a well-traveled diplomatic assistant of seventeen, poking and teasing one another and laughing together as if their postponed childhood had been given back to them. Not even with Royall had Abigail seen her daughter so joyful.

Was it because neither of her older children formed close friendships easily, Abigail wondered, that they became so quickly inseparable? Coming from large and close-knit families themselves, she and John were both used to looking no further than the family for intimacy. In France that meant the small circle of themselves, Nabby, Johnny, and Thomas Jefferson and his daughter. John and Jefferson had worked together in the Philadelphia Congress, John's hard-headed practicality meshing perfectly with Jefferson's lyric idealism. But even in '76, Abigail had detected in their letters something deeper. Jefferson was like a brother neither she nor John had previously realized they'd had; Nabby and Johnny adopted gawky, twelve-year-old Patsy as a sister.

Jefferson, a naturalist to his bones, had a wide circle of friends in Paris. He spent many of his evenings with cronies from the Philosophical Society, and every day but Sunday Patsy lived at the convent school of the Abbaye Royale de Panthemont. There were, of course, no Protestant boarding-schools in France, and to Abigail's indignant protest, Jefferson replied that he would not have his daughter left alone for most of the day with only the servants.

For the most part, the four Adamses were the whole of each other's world. In the mornings, Abigail would wake her son and daughter with a brisk tap on their bedroom doors, at opposite ends of the long range of rooms that made up the main block of the house; together they would breakfast in the little red-and-white chamber adjacent to Johnny's room.

While John and John Quincy—and shaggy little Caesar—were taking a long walk in the Bois de Boulogne, Abigail would outline the day's chores to the maître d'hôtel, and go over the household accounts. Often she would have their superannuated coachman drive her and Nabby into the city, at an hour when the streets still swarmed with black-clothed lawyers and clerks on their way to the opening of the law-courts, and with barbers and barbers' assistants en route to customers in lodgings. After being invited to dine with the Swedish, Prussian, and Spanish ministers—with their battalions of liveried servants—Abigail knew that new linens, new china, and new silverware were in order, if the United States was going to appear as anything but a parcel of beggars.

Even with most of its better-off citizens in the country for the summer, Paris was an astonishing place. Its streets seemed perpetually crowded with carriages, carts, sedan-chairs, and vendors shouting their wares at the top of their lungs. The narrow lanes were a constant hazard to life and limb with the rattling speed of light English carriages frantically driven; every wall and fence was placarded with advertisements for plays, books, lost dogs, or lost diamonds, all of which had to be licensed by the chief of police and all of which were pulled down every night, to be reposted the next morning.

On these shopping expeditions she and Nabby were often accompanied by a young Virginia lady named Sophie Sparling, to whom Jefferson introduced them: Sophie's father had been a Loyalist, Jefferson explained, but his friend (and distant cousin) nevertheless. Miss Sparling, now a paid companion to an Englishwoman living in the Faubourg St.-Antoine, served not only as translator but as their guide to the shops of Paris.

Jefferson shopped, according to John, like an extremely tasteful army sacking a town. Linen for which the Virginian paid three hundred francs in the ultra-fashionable boutiques of the Palais Royale, Sophie showed them for a hundred in the Mont de Piété, the government-run pawnshop where used furniture, dishes, and linens in all states of wear or nonwear might be obtained.

"And whatever you do, don't buy pepper already ground," Sophie would advise in her aloof smoky voice. "The shopkeepers adulterate it with powdered dried dog-feces." Of equal value, to Abigail, were the young woman's briefings on French social usages: In France, one made calls upon one's arrival in town, rather than waiting to receive cards from one's social equals. Before she could undertake the daunting exercise of appearing in a total stranger's drawing-room in order to bow in French-less silence, Abigail was called upon in the more reassuring American fashion by several American ladies as they returned to Paris with the coming of fall, and the business of making calls and receiving them quickly settled into place in the early afternoons.

This enterprise of calling and being called

on, while John was at work in his study, was, to Abigail, the heart of the day and of her life: the business of being a diplomatic hostess, of being at the center of the young Republic's affairs. Dinner was at two, or a little later if they were invited to dine with other members of the diplomatic corps— Spanish, Swedish, Prussian, Russian. If they dined at home, guests could include Americans engaged in politics or trade in Paris, like the wealthy William Bingham and his beautiful wife Ann, or French favorable to the Americans, like the Duc de la Rochefoucauld.

The talk was of the young Republic, of the hopes men had for France. Abigail heard very quickly of the notorious Tax-Farmers, the financiers who actually ran the kingdom's economy and France's mounting and terrifying debts, many of them connected to the American War. Listening to the strange maze of pamphlet-driven demagoguery, special privileges to the King's friends, *salonnières* who used fashion to steer politics, and the rotating carousel of Finance Ministers, Abigail felt a deep uneasiness at being allied with these people, at being beholden to them, as a woman might feel upon discovering that the man she's married is a drunkard and a gambler.

And John, she could tell, felt the same.

After dinner John and Johnny would go to meet Jefferson at Benjamin Franklin's house to work on the European treaties. On these afternoons Abigail would write—to her sisters, to her nieces, to Uncle Isaac or Uncle Cotton or the friends she'd left behind in Massachusetts. Sometimes she would hear Nabby practicing on the pianoforte in the music-room, or through the windows of her little private parlor see her daughter sketching in the garden, before her mind returned to her correspondence. The gossip of Braintree and the family brought to her not only the tone and timbre of her sisters' voices; the affairs of the State of Massachusetts, the growing disunion among the States and the increasing snarl of paper-money finances and constant squabbling seemed to be slowly swallowing up the young nation that had so recently come through the fire.

In return, she wrote to Mary and Betsey of the things they'd never seen: the opera and the theater. She and her sisters had read plays, but had never seen them performed, and for Abigail, opera was like being transported to another world. A very different world from Massachusetts, she reflected, the first time the not-quite-clothed *corps de ballet* tripped out onto the stage. Her mother would have told her to hide her eyes but she was far too fascinated to do so.

But it was the evenings she loved best. Evenings spent at home with John and Johnny, with Nabby and sometimes Jefferson as well, in the candle-lit parlor, Caesar dozing at John's feet. It was the time for talk, of Paris's fads and fashions, or of politics with John while Johnny—Hercules, she had nicknamed him, for his sturdy frame— studied his Latin and Greek. In November her son had announced his intention to return to Massachusetts to attend college at Harvard, and no arguments she and John could conjure concerning the greater usefulness of diplomatic experience would sway him.

Those were the evenings, she thought, that for the first time in a decade she felt as if she were having a normal life again. As if the War that had shaped and bent all their lives were finally over, and she could be together with those she loved.

It wasn't true, she understood. Because of the War, because of the call of the new nation for her husband's aid, they were in France, far from her sisters and John's mother and brother—far from poor Charley and young Tommy, growing up as semi-orphans in their uncle's boarding-school in Haverhill.

Far from Royall Tyler, and the life Nabby would have had, as a young bride with a home of her own.

Between August, when they reached Paris, and their departure in May for John to take up his post as first United States Minister to England, Royall Tyler wrote exactly once to John—as Nabby's father—and once to Nabby herself. Abigail wrote to Royall a number of times, reminding him how much Nabby looked forward to hearing from him, but with no result. Moreover, her sister continued to provide a disquieting account of Royall's behavior. He would lose or mislay letters and legal papers sent to him, delay delivery of documents to other members of the family for months.

Abigail was aware that her sister Mary had never liked Royall. Was aware, too, from nearly ten years' experience with her own mail-pouch romance, how frequently letters went astray at sea. Yet her own disgust with Royall's light-mindedness was growing, as spring brought preparations for the move to London, and for Johnny's departure.

⚜

It was Johnny's departure—

The thought half formed itself in her mind, as the baby's protesting wail rose above the quiet bustle of the stuffy, rain-dark bedroom.

As her daughter's head fell back onto her breast, Abigail looked swiftly from the crumpled loosening of Nabby's features to the child in Mrs. Throckle's hands and back again. "It's a boy," she said, with happy wonder, and tiny William Steuben Smith sucked in a deep breath and let out his debut bellow as he dangled naked by his feet in the first lamplight of evening.

The midwife's girl and Nabby's maid began their clean-up of the inevitable mess of a new human being's entry into the mortal world. Esther, who'd kept herself busy in the kitchen through the whole of the endless day, peeped around the bedroom door with her long, horsy face wreathed in smiles.

Nabby leaned her head back against Abigail's shoulder, tears tracking down her cheeks.

My mother cried, Shakespeare's Beatrice said of her birth; *but then there was a star danced, and under that I was born. . . .*

Were you born, little grandson, under a dancing star?

"Hush, dear, it's all right," she whispered, and stroked Nabby's hair. "It's a boy, and it's all done and over."

But as Nabby held out her arms for Baby Will, Abigail thought again, *It was Johnny's departure, not Royall's inconstancy, that sent her into William Smith's strong arms.*

She frowned at the idea, wondering if it were true. Certainly Nabby had been desolated when her oldest brother sailed for Boston, just before the family left Paris for London. And in London, Colonel Smith had been waiting, big and handsome and self-confident; a hero of the War, and not a man to let letters and papers go undelivered and unanswered for months at a time. The Colonel had lived with them for a while when first they'd taken up residence in Grosvenor Square; he'd been attracted to Nabby instantly.

And just as quickly, Abigail admitted to herself, she herself had been drawn to Colonel Smith. She had favored the match, and encouraged it, glad, this time, that Nabby was being courted by a man who would care for her.

For Nabby needs someone, she thought, when a few minutes later deep voices boomed below in the hall. Seeing her re-united with Johnny—seeing her return to smiling wakefulness like the princess in a fairy-tale in Paris—had showed her that. And while Abigail might rail to John about the social laws that robbed a woman of an education, or the judicial ones that forbade her ownership of her own property, she was conscious enough of the world's ways to know that a woman alone would be subtly ostracized.

She was aware, too—and a little disap-pointed—that Nabby had not her own strength, nor the sharpness of mind that made her welcome John's temper-tantrums and the stimulation of politics and literature.

Nabby wanted a companion, the way our Johnny wanted one, all those years of travel to Russia and France. Johnny's latest letter from Harvard returned to Abigail's mind.

The unhappiness in it was unmistakable as he drove himself in his studies like a man possessed. *Nabby was as wretched without a companion as Johnny is now.*

Would Colonel Smith's suit have succeeded, had her brother been here for her to laugh with instead?

The thought was an unsettling one. Abigail tried to put it aside as she helped Esther clothe Nabby in a fresh nightdress and bore her to the bed while Mrs. Throckle wrapped little Will in the dress of tucked lawn that Nabby and Abigail had embroidered that winter. *Like the dresses I made for Nabby,* Abigail thought, remembering those evenings at the kitchen table, stitching while John wrote articles about the Stamp Act beside her.

So far we have come.

Then the men were in the room, Colonel Smith catching first his new son, then his wife, then Esther and Abigail and Mrs. Throckle and the little assistant each in his giant embrace, laughing all the while with one incompletely powdered lock of raven-black hair hanging in his eyes.

And John was quietly holding Nabby's hand, his gruff-tempered Yankee face glowing with the softness of absolute love as he looked down at his first grandchild. "We have a new little American," he said gently, and bent to kiss Nabby's cheek.

"A new citizen of a new Republic," agreed Abigail, and joined him by the bed, his arm slipping around her waist. "Colonel Smith works for the legation, which should qualify this house as American soil, I think."

From somewhere, Colonel Smith produced a decanter and a glass, which he filled and held high: "To America's newest citizen! May he bring confusion to that scoundrel Carmarthen and may he ram their wretched treaty down their throats!"

Nabby smiled at her parents' enthusiastic declarations of "Hear, hear!" and drew little Will's head to her breast. But the old withdrawn look was returning to her eyes, that aloof sadness that Abigail had never quite fathomed. As if, with her child in her arms, she still sought for something she had lost, could never retrieve from the river of the past.

⚜

Young William Steuben Smith had just begun to raise his head from the pillow, when the first letters reached John from his old

Continental Congress friend, birdlike little Elbridge Gerry, concerning the initial sessions of the Constitutional Convention in Philadelphia. The news from Massachusetts had been unsettling: rebellion in the western counties, rumors of separate governments, even, forming in the Ohio Valley, demands for more paper currency, for equal distribution of property, for summary annihilation of all debts. That at least would put paid to any hope of the British living up to their side of the Treaty of Paris. The Tories in London, who had begun their mockery of John Adams the moment he'd become Minister, jeered that the nation of rabble was clearly showing its true colors and speculated as to how long it would be before they either were conquered by England or returned to the fold of their own chastened accord.

"I should be there," said John. There was bitterness in his voice.

"In a way, you are." Abigail set down her pen: a note to Sophie Sparling in Paris, another to her niece Bettie, a third to Cousin Sam's wife Bess. All the friends whose love sustained her, when one too many Englishwomen exclaimed, "But surely you *must* prefer it here!" and when the newspapers

commented snidely on how "fat and flour-
ishing" the "so-called Ambassador" looked,
considering the paltry poverty of his official
entertainments.

"Hoping that some member of the Convention will have read my book," said John
drily, "is hardly the same as 'being there.' "
In January, John's *Defense of the Constitu-
tions of Government in the United States*
had been published in London, and copies
sent home—a distillation of all John's experience in the Continental Congress and as a
diplomat, of his voracious reading in the
field of government and history. Abigail,
who had read it over his shoulder, thought it
disorganized and prolix. She feared, too,
that those who read it would see in his im-
passioned demand for "a strong executive"
a thinly veiled euphemism for an American
monarchy to sort out the mess.

When she'd said so to John, however,
he'd snapped back at her that the book said
nothing of the kind. He defied her to show a
connection between a necessarily strong
central administrator and the well-meaning
blockhead that currently disgraced the
throne of France. Abigail had said no more.
Privately, she suspected that someone like

Tom Jefferson, who believed men were nobler at heart than she had ever actually seen them behave, would make the connection, too.

"I am sure the Convention will see things put right."

John sniffed. "Oh, you're sure, are you?" he mocked. "If you'd ever sat through a session of Congress, my girl, you wouldn't be 'sure.' If you'd listened to that pipsqueak Rutledge back in '76, whining that we should wait until the populace was 'ready' . . . How much readier could we have been, with British bayonets at our very throats? If you'd met some of the men who sit in Congress now, you'd be upstairs under the bed tearing your hair out."

"Then it's just as well that I haven't," responded Abigail mildly, and shook sand over her note. "And I can only hope that while they're about it, the gentlemen meeting in Philadelphia will have the sense to make it *possible* for people of my gender to sit through a session of Congress—"

"God save the mark, what a mess we'd be in then!" But it was an old argument between them, and even as he said the words he gave her the quickest glint of a smile. "Bad enough we have some of the *men* in

Congress that we do. And God knows what will happen if they decide to combine all the functions of the government into one Assembly, like that fool Frenchman Turgot is preaching. That way lies nothing but chaos and corruption, the way—"

"Mr. Adams?" The drawing-room door opened. Edward the footman stood framed in it.

"What is it?" barked John, interrupted mid-tirade.

"Sir, there's a Captain Ramsay downstairs, with a Miss Jefferson to see you. From America, sir."

Abigail heard their voices as she and John descended the stair.

"I *won't* stay here! You go to Hell, God blast your eyes!"

"Miss Jefferson, there'll be no more of that kind of talk!"

"You don't care! I *hate* you!"

And as Abigail, with a startled look at John, opened the door of John's receiving-room, she was cannoned into by a very disheveled little girl in a much-stained dress of white-and-green chintz, who drew back the next instant and started slapping furiously at Abigail's skirts, crying, "I hate you! I hate you *all*!"

"Now, Polly, that's enough!" The tall girl who'd been standing by the windows, gazing out into Grosvenor Square in amazed delight, reached the child in two long strides just as Abigail caught Polly's hands in her own. "You swear at me all you please, sugarbaby, but you don't swear at Mrs. Adams. I am so sorry, ma'am, please don't blame—"

"I HATE Mrs. Adams!" Polly jerked away from Abigail's grip and flung herself on the tall girl, hiding her face in her neat blue skirts and bursting into tears.

The girl cupped the back of Polly's head with one long-fingered hand, and met Abigail's gaze. Her eyes, Abigail saw, were a clear blue-green, like jewels.

At the same moment Captain Ramsay reached the group, caught the little girl by the arm, and jerked her gently but firmly around to face Abigail again. "Miss Jefferson, this is no way for a young lady to behave. Mrs. Adams is going to take care of you, you know, and we don't hate those who care for us. Mrs. Adams," he said, "may I present to you Miss Mary Jefferson? Miss Mary Jefferson, Mrs. Adams; Mr. Adams."

"Now, Miss Mary, whatever you feel in your heart is of course not my business," said Abigail, and held out her hand. "But we do have a rule that no one swears in this house. Even Mr. Adams has to obey it."

Polly raised velvet-brown eyes, profound suspicion dimmed by swimming tears. "Captain Ramsay, too?"

"Captain Ramsay, too."

Far prettier than her sister Patsy would ever be, Polly Jefferson bore the marks of considerable rough play on her porcelain-fine skin: scratches on her nose and temple, a bruise where she'd bumped her chin. Being Thomas Jefferson's daughter she had his fair redhead's skin, now covered with freckles from the sun, and her nails were bitten to the quick. Abigail glanced again at the tall girl she'd flown to for comfort, wondering where Polly's actual nurse was and how she'd been looking after the girl during the voyage, to let her get into this state. This girl, probably the nurserymaid, was—

Ramsay said, a touch of dryness in his voice, "This is Sally, Polly's—Miss Jefferson's—nurse."

Abigail's first shock was that this girl, who looked no more than sixteen, should have been put in charge of a child under any circumstances, much less in the dangers and discomforts of an ocean voyage. Only in the next moment did she realize belatedly that the girl was a Negro.

She'd heard Jefferson—and her own father, for that matter—refer to "light" or "bright" Negroes, though her father's two servants, more indentures than actual slaves, had been chocolate-dark of skin. Most of the black sailors she'd seen on the streets of Boston had been the same, with African features marking their ancestry. The single servant Jefferson had brought from Virginia, Jimmy, though very light of skin, had been unmistakable as to his race.

Sally, watching Abigail with a calm wariness under the long, curling lashes of her eyes, was only a little darker than some of the Italian beauties she'd seen in Paris. Her hair, which hung down her back in a style fashionable in both Paris and London, was a river of dark brown, silky curls.

Abigail said the first thing that came into her mind. "Good God, don't tell me they sent a chit your age across the ocean as Polly's only companion?" How dared "Aunt

Eppes" be so blithe about the safety of this tiny, too-thin girl?

"Yes, ma'am." Sally's speech, like Jefferson's, reflected the soft inflection of Virginia; otherwise there was in it only a whisper of the sloppy, almost slurring usage Abigail had heard among Boston's few slaves. "My aunty Isabel was going to come with her, but her time was near, so Mrs. Eppes asked, would I come instead?" She rested her hands on Polly's thin shoulders. "It was because Polly knew me best, ma'am, and so wouldn't be afraid."

"It sounds to me as if several persons should have been a great deal more afraid on Polly's behalf," Abigail snapped. "Edward, please tell Esther to have Miss Nabby's old room made up for Miss Mary, and ask Mr. Briesler to bring up her trunk there at once. Tell him to prepare a truckle-bed there for . . . for her nurse. While he's doing that, would you be so good as to take up some hot water for her? Sally, I'm sure Miss Jefferson will feel much better when her face has been washed and her hair combed, and she's in a clean frock."

"Yes, ma'am." Sally took Polly's hand. Polly wrenched away instantly and seized

Captain Ramsay's red, calloused fingers in a frantic grip. Defiance blazed in her eyes.

"I'll stay right here, child," promised the captain.

Polly's grip tightened. She began to tremble, and tears leaked down her face.

"Go," Ramsay ordered gently, and with inexorable strength turned his hand out of the little girl's grip. "I'll be waiting right here for you, when you come down."

Abigail saw his glance cross Sally's. The tall girl flinched the tiniest bit, and her green eyes turned aside. Polly Jefferson gazed back over her shoulder as Sally led her out of the room.

"The girl'll have her work cut out for her, just washing the bairn's face, never mind her dress," prophesied Ramsay, picking up his battered leather hat from the sideboard. "She wore that same dress when Mrs. Eppes and her family brought her aboard. Since her father's been writin' for her to come to France, she's said she wouldn't leave the Eppeses, so they told her they were just going for a picnic on board. They left as soon as she fell asleep, and damn—dashed if we could get her to change her frock for nigh onto a week. Sally's fond of the child, but the girl's never to be found when you want her: always off lookin' over the rail, or gettin' the mate to tell her how to shoot the sun or what the names of the sails and ropes are, or askin' the hands about places they've been. You'll need to keep a sharp eye on her, and keep her at her job. It's my opinion she should be sent back."

He shrugged, and held out his hand. "It's been good making your acquaintance, Mr. Adams, Mrs. Adams. Don't be too hard on the bairn," he added, as he strode into the hall, John and Abigail in his wake. "She and Sally have been pets of the whole ship, passengers and crew, and I'm afraid the men weren't as careful as they ought to have been about their language—not that they'd know how to speak proper if you clapped a gun to their heads. She'll lose her tongue-roughness as quick as she picked it up."

"Thank you," said Abigail, struggling with shocked outrage. "But won't you remain and bid your good-byes to the child, as you said? It's clear she is most fond of you."

"Aye, and if I stayed for a good-bye you'd be all the morning getting her to let go of me. It'd be more grief for her in the long run. Believe me, this way's best, ma'am. Your servant, sir." He clasped John's hand again and slipped out through the front door. Through the windows Abigail saw him striding away across Grosvenor Square.

"Of all the blackguards!" Abigail rounded on John, breathless at this casual betrayal. "I daresay that's how he takes leave of every woman in his life: 'If I stayed to say good-bye she'd only cry and make a fuss, so I'll just disappear and let someone else pick up the pieces.' Isn't *that* just like a man!"

John drew back in alarm. "Dearest, in all the years we've been together—"

"In all the years you've been deserting me for months—or years—at a time," retorted Abigail, "no, you've never skimped on honorable good-byes. . . ." She heard genuine anger flare in her voice, and made herself stop, and breathe. "And God knows you had plenty of practice at them, sir." She put her hands on his shoulders and kissed him, as running footsteps sounded on the stair, and Polly Jefferson's voice sang out.

"Captain Ramsay, come look! I'm to have the prettiest room, with flower curtains on the windows, and—"

The little girl stopped at the foot of the stair, looking in startlement at John and Abigail. Then, like a baby animal, she wheeled and plunged through the door back into John's receiving-room. Abigail heard her scream, "Captain Ramsay!" In a belated rush of skirts Sally came down the stair and made for the receiving-room door, as Polly came bursting out—face washed, hair combed, but still in the torn and dirty green dress—and flung herself at the front door. "Captain Ramsay!" Sally and Abigail caught her at the same time, as she seized the door handle to pull it open. Polly clung to the curving brass, howling—in grief, in betrayal, in despair at being only eight years old and the dupe of adults who'd trade her happiness for their convenience. When Abigail gently prized the child's fingers loose Polly struck at her, wordlessly sobbing, then turned and flung herself into Sally's arms.

DOLLEY

⚭

**Washington City
August 24, 1814**

"Now I think on't," said Dolley, with what she hoped was an expression of bright thoughtfulness, "I think I saw the mirror last week in one of the drawers of the sewing-table in the parlor upstairs. Wouldst go seek it, whilst I clear up here?"

Sophie is my friend, she chided herself as the other woman disappeared through the parlor door. *She is no spy!* But even as she thought this, Dolley strode to the writing-desk and pulled out Jemmy's most recent letters. Her hands shook with haste as she folded them into a tight packet, bound them with the first piece of string she could find. *And even were she so, what think I she'll do? Take Jemmy's letters from me at pistol-point?* She realized she was mentally timing Sophie's probable progress across the hall, up the stairs, into the big oval parlor. She was still wondering where she could thrust the letters that would be out of sight, when Sukey's voice nearly startled her out of her skin.

"Ma'am—"

She whirled, breathless, to see the maid-servant standing in the doorway.

"Ma'am, the men along the walls? They's gone."

Dolley reached the window in a swirl of muslin, and saw that the maid spoke true. The top of the wall was empty. She thrust Jemmy's papers back into the writing-desk and turned the key, kept it in her hand as she hastened across the cavernous hall to the vast "East Room." From its long windows she could see Pennsylvania Avenue.

The knots of watchers had gone. A cloud of dust now hung over the Avenue, through which carriages, wagons, and hurrying forms could dimly be made out. Fleeing toward Georgetown.

The sky above the eastern hills was still clear.

Trembling, Dolley crossed back through the hallway. From the entry-hall by the Mansion's great front doors she could hear her majordomo, M'sieu Sioussat—French John, the servants called him—talking to the butler, his voice measured and calm. French John had trained for the priesthood, sailed the seven seas, and had been held up by his father over the heads of the crowd to see the French King's execution, twenty years ago: Not much troubled him.

He will stand by me, thought Dolley. *And he'll know what to do, should worse come to worst.*

Surely I am not the first beneath this roof, who hath known trouble and fear.

To her left, through the door of the oval drawing-room, General Washington's portrait was visible. Someone had pulled from it the gauze that protected all the house's paintings and mirrors in summer, and from its rich, muted background of reds and grays, the General gazed out at the world. The throne he had refused stood in shadow behind him, the sword he had wielded transferred to his left hand while his right—the hand of power and intent—stretched out over the pens and papers of due process and law.

He seemed to wait calmly for the army that he had once defeated to make its appearance on the threshold of the house he had built.

And he looked remarkably, thought Dolley, as he had the first time she'd seen him.

Philadelphia, Pennsylvania
Sunday, May 13, 1787

The church bells began to ring while the family was still in Meeting. Hearing them through the walls of the Pine Street Meeting-House, nineteen-year-old Dolley Payne reflected that if she were a better-disciplined soul, the arrival of General George Washington in Philadelphia would be a matter of sublime indifference to her. Yet at the sound, her glance shot sidelong and caught that of her best friend Lizzie Collins, and saw in her eyes the reflection of the excitement effervescing in her own.

General Washington was coming to Philadelphia!

A buzz riffled the stuffy gloom of the meeting-house as every child in the gallery whispered, poked, and was silenced by the adults whose turn it was to keep order up there. On the way to Meeting that morning one of her ten-year-old sister Lucy's friends had dashed past them, calling out, "General Washington's coming today! The cavalry went out to meet him!"

"And why doth Andrew think that the assembly of soldiers to go greet another soldier—and a slave-owner to boot—would interest thee, Lucy?" their father had asked, when Lucy's blond head snapped around to follow her friend down Third Street.

Lucy had quickly faced front again, her younger siblings following suit like toys on a string: Anna, Mary, and Little Johnnie. Even the older boys, eighteen-year-old Isaac and William, who was twenty-one, kept their mouths shut.

Dolley, the eldest daughter, had turned to say something about the General to her mother, but saw her mother's glance cut to her father's face. A year ago, or two, her father would have put his question mildly, even playfully. It was the harsh note of danger that silenced the four youngsters and put the fear in her mother's eyes.

Now as the bells of Philadelphia rollicked

above the city's low red roofs, Dolley's eyes went to her father's face. In the muted light of the meeting-house it seemed to have grown dark and lumpy with anger. So frightening, so alien, was the glare of his eyes that she returned her gaze swiftly to the whitewashed front wall, her heart beating hard. For a moment she wondered if he would stand up, break the meditative silence of the Meeting with the furious words he'd muttered all morning: *Vanity of vanities, all is vanity! What does it profit a man to gain the whole world, if he lose his soul?*

But he didn't. And on the far side of his blunt, tense profile, she could almost feel how rigidly her mother sat, as if she, too, feared what she didn't understand.

The moment passed, but the bells continued. Voices in the street outside, a clamor very unlike Sunday morning in Philadelphia, and with the day's clouds even the usual mark of slanted sunlight on the meeting-house wall was gone. It was impossible, thought Dolley, keeping her hands demurely folded, her glance carefully schooled away from Lizzie's, to gauge how much longer the Meeting had to run or whether she'd have time, after she walked back to the house with her family, to coax them into letting her go see the cavalcade ride in.

Vanity of vanities, all is vanity, and yes, General Washington is a soldier and a slaveholder who buyeth and selleth his fellow men, but he is still the hero who captured the British army, who won the war that set this country free.

Dolley remembered clearly the red-coated files of riders, glimpsed through the brown autumn woods of Hanover County. Remembered lying in a thicket behind the house, face pressed to the prickly leaf-mold with two-year-old Lucy clutched against her body, praying baby Anna in her arms wouldn't cry. At eleven, and tall for her age, she had been dimly aware that her mother feared more for her than rough mishandling at the hands of Banastre Tarleton's dragoons.

Worse by far than the British raiding had been the bitter, constant warfare between the local Tories and those who supported the Congress. Small battles and vicious betrayals, ambush and revenge: the constant anxiety of not knowing whom one could trust. When the patriot militia burned out the plantation of her friend Sophie Sparling's grandparents, it was to Dolley's parents that

Sophie and her mother had fled. Dolley still had dreams of waking in the dead of night with the flare of torchlight visible through the cracks of the shutter, hearing the trample of hooves outside, and men cursing in the yard. Patrick Henry, firebrand of the patriots and first Governor of the new State, was her mother's cousin, and they'd lived at his backwoods plantation when first her family had returned to Virginia from North Carolina. Even the knowledge that as Quakers the Paynes took no part in the War might not have been enough to save them.

General Washington's victory had ended all that.

And all gratitude aside, Dolley simply loved the sight of sleekly groomed horses, the brilliance of gold-braided uniforms, the stir and lilt of the music that a band was sure to play as the General rode up to be greeted at the State House door. An avid reader of newspapers, she was curious about the delegates who had been arriving for two weeks now for the Convention of the States, longing to put faces to the names she'd heard discussed among her friends.

The two Morrises she knew by sight, sleek peg-legged young Gouverneur and his not-related business partner, stocky and extremely wealthy Robert, one of the city's most prominent merchants. On warm spring evenings, when she'd walk with Lizzie and their dear friend Sarah Parker, they'd often see Robert Morris's carriage rattle past on the cobblestones of Market Street, bright with gilding and varnish. And everyone in the city knew old Benjamin Franklin, at least by sight. He'd smiled at Dolley and spoken to her any number of times in the market, on those days when he was well enough to be about: Even at eighty-one, thought Dolley with a smile, he clearly retained a lively interest in a well-turned ankle.

But the others, of whom she had only read and heard—Elbridge Gerry of Massachusetts and George Wythe the Virginia lawyer; Roger Sherman and Oliver Ellsworth of Connecticut; Alexander Hamilton, who'd fought at Washington's side and was supposed to be dazzlingly handsome—these were the men who would change the way life was lived in Philadelphia and all throughout the country. The men of the Meeting like Lizzie's father, and young Anthony Morris (no relation to either of the more famous ones), and his friend the sobersided John Todd, might be content with debating the writings of these men, but Dolley wanted to see their faces. To see what they looked like, how they stood, how they dressed. Who they actually *were.*

"It should matter nothing, what they look like," John Todd had argued earlier that week, when she'd walked down to the Indian Queen Tavern on Fourth Street because she'd heard that George Wythe was there. (And he had been, lean and white-haired with a nose like an ax-blade, talking gravely with the proprietor about cheese.) "It is what they have done, and will do—what they have written and thought—that will count." He'd encountered Dolley on her way home from the tavern, when it had started to drizzle, and had offered her his escort back to her house with his umbrella.

John was the sort of young man who always had an umbrella.

"What be the difference, if a man be short or tall, young or venerable, if his eyes be brown or blue or if his skin be white or black for that matter, so that he love God, and do good in the world?" he'd asked.

Dolley had sighed, and said at once,

"Thou art right, John," because she knew he was.

Nevertheless, she wanted to know.

⚜

She was still smiling over this encounter—and John's complete incomprehension of the female mind—when the Friends filed quietly from the meeting-house into the clamor of Pine Street. Church bells kept their delighted riot from every steeple in town, men and women hastened by them in their Sunday-bests toward the end of Market Street, where the Baltimore road ran in from Chester. Lizzie, walking sedately among her own family, cast her a glance filled with query, and Dolley nodded: *Of course I'll go!* Lucy, Anna, Mary, and Little John knew better than to cluster around their parents on the way out of Meeting, but whispers whipped among them: *General Washington—General Washington!*

Two years ago her father would merely have sighed, and shaken his head. Now he whirled like a baited bull, and snapped at their mother, "Canst thou not keep their minds on God, even on God's own day?" And as the four little ones halted in their tracks, appalled at his fury, he suddenly shouted at them, *"Even a child is known by his doings, whether his work be pure. A high look, a proud heart, and the plowing of the wicked*—ay, and riding forth under arms to war!—*these are sin. The man that wandereth out of the way of understanding shall remain in the congregation of the dead!"*

"John . . ." Molly Payne put a quieting hand on her husband's arm. Those of their closer friends in Meeting who'd begun to move toward them to admonish saw her frown, and stepped back. "John, they are only children. And every day is God's own day. *When I was a child, I spake as a child and I reasoned as a child . . .* and nowhere doth Paul in his Epistle say that it is ill to do so."

Dolley's father drew in a deep breath, then shook his head as if to clear it. "I—Yes. Thou art correct, Molly, and I—I spoke harsh." For a moment, as he faced the younger children, huddled around Mother Amy, the only one of her father's slaves who had remained in the family when he'd freed them, his face bore the puzzled expression of a man newly waked. Then he reached out a big hand, with its bleached, cracked calluses, to Lucy, who stood nearest him, an offer of reconciliation. Lucy clasped it, and smiled her sunny smile.

And at that moment, John Todd, who'd lingered inside the meeting-house to chat with the scholarly Henry Drinker, came hurrying down the steps to catch up with Dolley. "Might I join my steps to thy family's, Neighbor Payne?" he asked her father, and his open glance included her mother in the request. When dealing with his clients, the fledgling lawyer wore a more modern coat than the one he kept for Meetings, and a three-cornered hat instead of the broadbrim that the men of the congregation considered less worldly, as if setting aside even Quaker plainness in order to make his clothing less noticeable.

But the longer-skirted fashion of an earlier year suited him well, Dolley reflected. And if he had to ask a few times too often if she was making a joke, or quoted Biblical Kings rather frequently on the subject of forward women, the kindness of his heart made up for a great deal.

And, because he hadn't a deceitful bone in his body, when her father beamingly nodded his assent—Dolley knew he was hoping to make a match between herself and

John—John turned to her and said, "And if thou wilt, afterwards, I offer my arm to thee, Friend Dolley, to walk out to the end of Market Street, that thou may see General Washington ride in."

Dolley could have screamed.

"Thou shalt do nothing of the kind!" Her father whirled, his face suffused with fury. "Bad enough that the children tug and whine to see this slaveholder, this warmonger, with the whole town yelping about him like a pack of brats! *When I was a child I spake as a child,* thy mother saith! But thou art no child, Dolley, and thou shalt spend God's Sabbath as a woman ought, among her family!"

Dolley stepped back, her eyes flooding with tears, not of disappointment—though she could have shaken John for his tactlessness—but of shock. When John opened his mouth to protest she caught his arm and squeezed it hard, and when he looked at her, baffled, shook her head. Her father had already turned and stormed away, still dragging the frightened Lucy by the hand; her mother strode forward to catch the little girl's other hand. Mother Amy gathered the younger children like a hen collecting chicks beneath her ample wing. Dolley was aware that her hand was trembling where it still lay on John's arm.

John, for his part, looked like he hadn't the slightest idea what was going on, but walked, obediently silent, at her side down Pine Street, and then along Third. As they crossed Market Street a carriage passed them by, varnished green and drawn by a spanking team of bays: Dolley recognized the livery of the black coachman as belonging to the Willings, glimpsed in the back two of the daughters of the house whose dresses, at any other time, she'd have felt a pang of regret at missing. Her father checked his stride as if he would have spoken, then moved on.

"What—?" John began, but Dolley shook her head again.

They continued in silence to the small brick row-house that for two years now had been her home. "I thank thee for thy company, Friend John," she said, on the doorstep of the little shop that occupied the two downstairs rooms. "I hope we shall meet again soon."

When she went inside, her father had already gone upstairs. Her mother was herding the little ones into the narrow staircase after him, but stopped when Dolley came through from the front shop into the workroom behind it. "Mother Amy, see the children into the parlor, an't please thee," she said, and took Dolley's arm. "And see they keep quiet," she called up after the retreating group. "Friend Payne hath a headache."

But when she turned back to her oldest daughter, Dolley saw in her eyes that her mother lied. Molly Payne's face had a weariness in it that Dolley hadn't seen even during the worst of the War.

For a time the two women stood in the little workroom, gloomy despite the wide windows that looked onto the small yard. With the day's gray overcast, yard and workroom had become a monochrome still-life, sacks of rice piled in one corner and the grinding-quern standing near the door, the sieves of graduated fineness, from brass wire down to the finest silk, making a pattern of circles on the whitewashed wall. Because of the rain, on and off all last week, the long, shallow settling-trays had been moved into the workroom from the yard, and in their shallow riffles the first rime of starch grayed the wood like a thin frost.

Six days a week this room, the yard, and

the kitchen at the back of the yard were the heart of the house. Now they were still, like a heart that rests in meditation.

Dolley saw tears in her mother's eyes.

"Thy father meant no . . ."

Tears tightened Dolley's throat at the recollection of his rebuke that had been like a slap in the face. She kept her voice to a whisper. "What's *wrong* with him, Mama?"

Her mother shook her head, but in her shut eyes, and the slump of her shoulders, Dolley saw the sheer relief in the knowledge that someone else, at least, understood that there *was* something wrong with John Payne. That it wasn't just a bout of indigestion, or headache, or, worst of all, only their own womanish imaginations.

"He didn't used to be like this," Dolley went on softly. "*Is* he ill?"

"I asked him if he would see Dr. Rush, and he said there was naught amiss. He needeth only to think, he said."

"Is that what he doth, when he doth shut himself into the bedroom?" Dolley slowly removed her bonnet, the wide-brimmed plain white muslin sunbonnet that was the only headgear a good Quaker girl could wear without drawing whispers from the rest of the Meeting. There were some, like Lizzie's cousin Hannah, who managed to coax their fathers into buying them brighter colored chintzes and muslins, and even silk, and who wore fashionable hats during the week and dressed their hair in curls. But these "wet" Quakers were treading a dangerous line. Back in Virginia, Dolley had seen members "read out of the Congregation"—cut off from their fellow Quakers, their families, the friends who made up the fabric of their lives—for "following the corrupt ways of the world" and partaking of "vain fashions and customs of the world," as well as for the more usual offenses such as fighting, defaulting on one's creditors, committing adultery, using ill words, or marrying one who was not a Quaker.

"I know not what he doth." Her mother removed her own bonnet, pressed her fingertips to her forehead, as if to crush away some ache there, then looked up into her tall daughter's eyes. "Reads the Bible, I think. But when he goeth up early, and I'm down here until after dark, I'll go up and there will be no candle lit and no smell of smoke in the room, as if he hath sat there in the darkness all that time. Sometimes he sitteth in his chair by the window, when I go to bed, and cometh not in with me until nearly dawn."

Dolley looked into her mother's face and saw in the bruised circles beneath her eyes, the hollows under her cheekbones, that she, too, did not sleep until nearly dawn. But while more and more often her father remained in the bedroom in the dark of the mornings, her mother was always the one to come down and open the little shop that sold starch and gum arabic, and the fine small irons that ladies'-maids used to press the stiffened ruffles of collars and caps.

"It could just be worry," she said, seeking the illusion of a comfort in which neither of them really believed. "Thou knowst since the end of the War things have been hard everywhere. I've heard Father say the tariffs on rice from the Carolinas are ruining him, and many of the rice-growers won't accept Pennsylvania currency."

Her mother's eyes asked bitterly, *Dost thou truly believe 'tis that simple?* But Molly Payne patted her daughter's cheek. " 'Tis possible," she agreed. She turned her head as movement flickered in the yard: Lizzie slipping through the narrow gate beside the kitchen, her gray dress like a paler shadow in the gray of the afternoon. She saw Dolley's mother and halted, guilt all over her face.

Molly Payne smiled. "Go along, then," she said softly.

"Thou'lt need help getting dinner—"

"I put dinners on the table before thou wert born, girl, and shall do so after thou'rt wedded and gone away. Now hurry, or all thy sisters and brothers will be yapping to go as well."

Dolley caught up her bonnet, ducked into the yard. She would have liked to unearth the tiny cache of worldly baubles she wore for festive occasions—a gold necklace given her by her non-Quaker granny Anna, a ruffled lace collar she'd stitched herself— but didn't dare delay. The sound of church bells followed the two gray-clothed girls as they raced down the little alleyway and out into Third Street, where Sarah Parker and Beth Brooke waited for them, then blended into the larger crowd on its way to Market Street.

⚜

Cannon had begun to boom, fired by the ships along the wharves, and in the square before the State House, Dolley could hear the sound of cheering ahead. Around them, men and women in fine broadcloths or gay sprig-muslins pressed and craned for a glimpse up Market Street, and crowded past the line of posts that marked the pedestrian flagway to choke the street itself. Every doorstep was three deep, every window along the route occupied. Carriages further blocked the way, but the pressing crowds made the horses pull at their reins, and it would be a miracle, thought Dolley, if the morning passed without someone being bitten or kicked. She and her friends had to dodge and slip between market-women, citizens, wealthy gentlemen in fine coats and powdered wigs, along the walls where the press was thinner.

They'd almost reached Fifth Street, still clinging to one another's hands in a line like children playing crack-the-whip, when someone shouted, "Here they come!"

Dolley pressed forward, to where half a dozen people jammed the step of old Mrs. House's big red-brick residence. A gentleman on the lowest step, turning to protest, took a second look at her, changed his glare to an ingratiating smile, and raised his hat.

She gave him a dazzling smile in return, and he edged back off the step, gallantly surrendering his place to the girls.

Like a country stream in winter, half choked by ice and snow, Market Street had been reduced to a single narrow channel of brick. Dolley could see the flags, and the mounts of the Pennsylvania Light Horse, even in the wan gloom seeming to gleam like burnished copper and bronze; see the men looking out straight before them with their swords drawn and held upright, and the gold of buttons and braid sparkling bright.

Even had General Washington not ridden in the place of honor in their midst, Dolley was certain she would have known it was he. He wore, not the blue-and-buff uniform of the Continental Army, but the plain black suit of a private citizen—an act of modesty which would not, Dolley suspected, earn him the slightest indulgence from John Todd. *The man proclaimed before all the world that he would retire to private life, never more to meddle in the affairs of the nation,* the young lawyer had pointed out, when the subject of the National Convention had arisen. *To go back so upon his*

word would be to admit himself a Caesar
before all the nation, ambitious for a crown!

But there was nothing, thought Dolley, of
the Caesar in this man who came riding
down Market Street through the thunder of
cannon-fire and church bells. Though he sat
straight on his dapple-gray stallion, there
was no triumph in his face. He looked, if
anything, tired and a little grim, as anyone
would, she supposed, after a week's journey up from Virginia.

But would not a Caesar have stretched
out his arms to the welcoming crowd,
whose cheers reverberated against the flat
pink brick of the house-fronts? A Caesar at
least would have looked pleased.

The General looked like a knight calculating what he's going to need to take with him
to fight a very dangerous dragon; a knight
who, alone among the clamoring crowd,
doubts his own strength to prevail.

Even surrounded by loyal troops and
howling admirers, Dolley was startled at
how alone he seemed.

Beside her on the step the crowd stirred
and pushed as the door opened behind
them. Old Mrs. House, who had rented
rooms to members of the Congress since

the days of the War, emerged, beaming and attired in the half-mourning she'd worn for as long as Dolley had known her. She was escorted by a thin, shy-looking little gentleman in black, whose graying hair was braided in a neat queue. Everyone on the step was jostled back, as those who'd thought themselves secure in possession of higher ground jockeyed for position. Dolley teetered, her heel slipping off the granite step, and as she staggered the little black-clothed gentleman turned with surprising swiftness to catch her elbow in a steadying hand.

"Easy," he said.

She smiled her thanks as he helped her down and their eyes briefly met: a young man's eyes, bright blue-gray in the settled lines of old illnesses and lack of sleep.

Then from the street an officer cried a sharp "Company halt!" and Dolley looked around, startled, to see General Washington sitting his horse at the foot of Mrs. House's front steps, close enough that had she put out her hand she might have touched his knee.

The little gentleman in black turned from her, and with Mrs. House descended the step. Dolley pressed quickly back into the crowd as the General dismounted and said, "Mr. Madison." He had a voice like Jove, deep and very quiet.

"General." The little gentleman bowed, tiny fingers like bird-bones disappearing into the General's large, firm grip. "Please allow me to introduce you to Mrs. House. I've arranged lodgings here for you."

"But I hope you will take your dinner with Mrs. Morris and myself this afternoon." Robert Morris, plump and smiling in his cherry-colored velvet and powdered wig, stepped out of the crowd almost at Dolley's elbow. This, Dolley thought, was completely unfair: Mrs. House was a notable cook, but Mr. Morris's chef was renowned throughout the State.

The General inclined his head. Dismounted, he was the tallest man Dolley had ever seen, and looked just like the engravings: the slight curve of the nose, the tight-lipped mouth, strong chin, wide-set cheekbones under those piercing pale eyes. But as the cavalcade formed up again to proceed to the State House for the official welcome, Morris stepped close to the General and Dolley stood near enough to hear him murmur, "I do hope you'll reconsider my offer and stay with myself and Mrs. Morris, General. We're quite counting on you."

And on Mrs. House's front steps, little Mr. Madison—whom Dolley recalled was one of the organizing delegates from Virginia—for one unguarded instant wore the protesting look of a schoolboy who is too well-mannered to speak when a larger boy takes from under his nose that last cookie on the plate.

⚜

"I'd best go back," she said, as the crowds began to surge off after the retreating Light Horse in the direction of the State House. "Mama needs my help to put dinner on the table." The church bells still caroled, and with the sky so gray it was difficult to guess the time, but Dolley had the uncomfortable suspicion she'd been gone too long already.

"All the delegates will be at the State House," pointed out Lizzie, who'd been following accounts of the upcoming convention in the *Philadelphia Packet.*

"Oh, there goes Mr. Morris!" cried Sarah, pointing as the red-lacquered carriage edged its way out of Fifth Street and fell in behind the Light Horse, as if Mr. Morris were proclaiming his position within the Convention. "Didst see the dress Mrs. Morris wore the other day, walking along Chestnut Street? All white gauze, with a little green satin coat like a jockey's, and the most monstrous beautiful hat!" Her hands sketched the shape of a tall crown, a flowerbed of plumes.

Mrs. Morris, hat and all, would probably be at the State House, and the temptation was severe. Dolley shook her head. "I must go," she said. "Tomorrow, dear friends . . ." She kissed her hands to them. "Go," she added, waving them off as Lizzie made a move to walk home with her. It wasn't quite the thing to walk about by oneself, but it wasn't far and Dolley had a vague stab of discomfort—almost fear—of what her father would say should he come down and realize she had disobeyed him, whatever her mother had said.

That thought, too, disquieted her: that she should feel fear of her father.

Or did she fear the man she sensed her father was becoming?

She hastened her steps, turning her wide shoulders to slip sidelong through the crowd that pressed the other way. Most of them she knew, and those who might at another time have winked or whistled or tried to accost a young lady walking alone—mechanics and apprentices and sailors from the wharves—were far too intent on following General Washington to take the slightest notice of her.

And in any case, Dolley was not much impressed by would-be accosters. She'd heard too much barnyard language from her rural neighbors in Hanover County to be shocked, and too many of Mother Amy's forthright opinions about men to be overcome with maidenly modesty. She dressed neatly enough now to pass for a Philadelphia girl, but she'd grown up working hard on her parents' farm at Coles Hill. She'd been eight when her father had freed all his slaves, in the wake of the Declaration of Independence. She had learned to cook and cut kindling and do everything that, in Philadelphia, servants did.

In those days her father had been different. When she thought of him, that was the man she remembered. Big and rather heavily built, he'd bequeathed her his height, and the Irish brightness of his blue eyes.

He'd always been a man of strong passions—one of her most vivid memories was of him shouting down a gaggle of the local patriots when they jeered at him for not joining the militia. Strong as an ox, he'd worked "from can't-see to can't-see," as the fieldhands said, to plow and plant corn and wheat, after he'd given the slaves their freedom. God had guided him, he'd told Dolley and her brothers, to take on his own shoulders the yoke of his own upkeep. Of the former slaves who stayed on to farm portions of Coles Hill, he'd charged a crop-rent as low as he could manage, knowing they all had families of their own to support.

Did he regret his decision? Dolley wondered as she turned onto the quiet of Third Street. "Besides turning those poor Negroes off into the world to look after theirselves, which they ain't fit to do," had argued her cousin Catherine in horror, "what's he going to leave you and the boys if he should die? Land's no good without Negroes to work it!"

"We work it ourselves," Dolley had replied, annoyed, mostly because it was clear to her that Jonas, Cuffe, Quashie, and their families were doing a perfectly decent job of farming on the land they'd once tilled as slaves.

But Catherine had only gazed at her with aching pity and whispered, "Oh, you poor dear! How *could* your papa have done that to you?"

At the time—she'd been ten, in 1778— Dolley had thought Catherine a fool and a bit of a sissy. Sophie Sparling, three years older and the only girl in the neighborhood to treat her as an equal, had remarked, "Cathy only thinks it's horrible because she couldn't make a kitchen fire to save her own life." Sophie's doctor father had also freed his few slaves, though her grandparents had kept theirs—for all the good that had done them.

As the War dragged on, and Dolley had seen her parents' shoulders acquire the slump of tiredness that never finds rest—as she'd seen how Isaac had to wear patched rags inherited from Walter and William, and how she herself had no garments that had not been worn shapeless by either her mother or one of the other women in the Meeting—Dolley had wondered what her father thought of his decision. "It's all very well for a man to follow where the Spirit leads him, darling," one of her well-dressed Payne aunts said to her mother. "It's him dragging you, and his poor children, along after him that I cannot stomach."

The Paynes were wealthy, and owned many slaves. The fact that her family had coffee or occasional dress-lengths of new calico during the War, or pins and needles to sew with, had been due to that aunt. Her father refused to drink the coffee, Dolley recalled.

In any case, when Dolley was fifteen her father had sold the little farm. He'd announced that they were going to live in Philadelphia, now that the War was done and there was no further danger of the British burning the town.

At that point the truth of her cousin's assertion had been borne on Dolley: a farm of close to two hundred acres, without slaves, brought barely enough to acquire the small house on Third Street and the equipment to make starch. Her mother ran the shop in front, Dolley and Lucy keeping house while Mother Amy looked after the little ones. Dolley still wore dresses handed down to her from her mother, sewing ruffles at the hems, for none of them were ever long enough for

her unmaidenly height. William and Isaac
helped their father grind and pulverize the
Carolina rice, then patiently sieve and settle,
sieve and settle, until the fine powder of
starch collected on the riffles of the shallow
pans. Nobody in the family could ever get
new clothes at the same time. Coffee was
still adulterated with parched corn.

But in Philadelphia there were friends,
both in the Meeting and outside of it, to
whom it didn't matter that Dolley helped
Mother Amy with the cooking and the mar-
keting and the bed-making. In Philadelphia
she could buy newspapers the day they
were printed, instead of having to wait
weeks for secondhand information. She
could see all manner of people in the
streets, admire and make mental notes of
the newest fashions; talk and listen to people who had been other places, seen and
done other things.

As a tiny child, Dolley had dreamed of flying. In her dreams she would stretch forth
her arms and run, and feel her feet thrust
away the earth; feel the wind stroke her hair.
She would look down from above at the
trees and fields, then look ahead, to a beautiful city filled with light. Philadelphia might

not be Paris or London, but here she felt alive as she never had in the countryside.

John Todd, God bless his sober heart, might temperately agree that the polish of conversation was to be desired in that it made a woman tolerant and gave her a certain experience with others. This would in turn make her a better wife and mother— the only criteria, as far as Dolley could see, upon which Friend John judged any accomplishment, either in a woman or a man. Love of talk for its own sake, the desire to hear what Rome looked like, and what ladies wore in the south of France, puzzled him as much as her desire to learn whether Roger Sherman of Connecticut was clean or grubby in his person, or her satisfaction in knowing that James Madison, spearhead of the movement to not simply repair the government but to reconstitute it entirely, had kindly eyes.

Her father wanted her to marry John Todd. He'd made that clear, from the moment John—then reading law and preparing to open an office of his own—had first asked his permission to walk the sixteen-year-old Dolley home after Meeting one warm summer day three years ago. "He shall give thee a good home, Daughter, and make a fine father for thy children."

Like John Todd, John Payne saw others in terms of what they could be to their families. But when Dolley had replied—that had been in the fall of 1784, some three months after John had begun seeking out the spot beside hers when they encountered one another at picnics—"A man can give a woman a good home and healthy children, and still not make her happy, Papa," he had nodded, as if he understood.

"Yet I cannot see John Todd would make thee unhappy, were all the world given to him in return for it."

"Not *un*happy," Dolley had said, not entirely sure how to put into words what it was that her heart sought. "Just . . ."

How to explain that though she was deeply fond of John, she wasn't sure she would be happy as his wife? How to explain the sensation she sometimes had—of living in a cage and looking out through the bars at an astonishing world whose paths she longed to walk? That year she was sixteen, she'd already seen one of the first friends she'd made at the Pine Street Meeting, a girl named Anne Selby only a year older than she, marry a well-meaning young tailor: Anne was already with child. It wasn't that she didn't want children: Dolley loved children.

Was it frivolous not to want them just yet?

Selfish, and foolish, to dream of a life other than the one she had? A life no more possible to her than her dreams of flight?

Her eyes returned helplessly to her father, and he'd taken her hand and leaned close, so that not even the wind in the chestnut tree could hear. "Just that the Spirit murmurs in thy heart, 'Wait,' without telling thee what for?"

Dolley had closed her eyes, and nodded, her heart at rest.

"John Todd is a good man," her father had told her. "And he loveth thee very much. But the Spirit models Time the way an artist models clay, and there is indeed a time for every purpose under Heaven. How can we not believe this, when the same sky is sometimes blue and sometimes golden and betimes grows black, the better to show us the glory of God's stars?" Drawing her closer, he'd kissed her cheek. "The Spirit will never lead thee wrong, Dolley. Just remember that John is led, too."

That was the father she remembered.

⚜

She heard him shouting, as she neared the house. The note of insane rage in his voice pierced her, more than the echoes and snippets of his words: ". . . obeyed in my own house . . . uniforms . . . wild unbeliever with a worldly heart . . ." She'd been holding her skirts up as much as modesty would permit, to speed her steps; now she snatched them almost up to her knees and ran.

"Will you take this away from me, too?" Her father towered over her mother with both fists raised. "Tell the boys what to do, make the damned starch as well as sell it and spend the money as you think best? Send me off to some corner until you need something else from me?"

"And what am I to do to put bread on the table?" her mother slashed back, in the voice of one goaded beyond all endurance. "It wasn't I who sent thee off to a corner, ever! That corner where thou hidest half the day and all the night!"

"*It is better to dwell in a corner of the house-top, than with a brawling woman in a wide house!* There is no place in this house where I can go to get away from the sound of strife! And you, who want to be the man here—"

"I don't want to be the man! I want *thee* to be the man!"

"Is that why you let my daughter run after soldiers like a common trull?" He whirled, his face distorted, his finger pointing at Dolley as she stood in the doorway. The blue eyes she remembered with such love stared wildly at her, as if at a stranger. *"She is loud and stubborn; her feet abide not in her house: now is she without, now in the streets, and lieth in wait at every corner!"* The grip of his hand on her arm nearly pulled Dolley off her feet. Like a rag he shook her in her mother's face.

"Is that what you will have your daughters come to, woman? To go chasing after the vainglory of the world? Is that why you will be the man of this house? So that you can let them run about the streets like harlots?"

"I beg a thousand pardons, Neighbor Payne."

John Todd's stout, sensible shoes creaked on the wooden floor of the shop; his voice was pleasant and soft, as if in a chance encounter outside the meeting-house. "I apologize for bringing thy daughter home later than I told her mother I would; doubly so, for importuning her to go walking with me to begin with. I beg thee to make allowances, for myself and for them both. Both were most kind in indulging my pleas."

He must have been behind me in the street, thought Dolley. She had had the impression, just before she heard her father's voice, of quick footfalls hurrying to catch her up. Her eyes thanked him as he concluded, "And now I must go. I should not have come in at all, save that I feared to leave behind me a misunderstanding that would cause strife."

"No," said her father uncertainly. "No, you—thou didst right, Neighbor Todd. I knew not . . . I . . . I am sorry, Daughter. Molly." He blinked and held out his hand to his wife, and looking at his face Dolley realized he had not the slightest idea of what he had just said. His cheeks were ashen. "Neighbor Todd, thou wilt stay to dine? We spoke of it, did we not, at Meeting?"

"We did, friend," John responded. "But the matter was left uncertain, and I would not make extra work for thy good wife."

Molly Payne was still shaking with anger. In the stairwell door, Dolley was aware of eighteen-year-old Isaac, of Lucy, of the younger children all pressed on one another to listen, frightened and bewildered. It was Mother Amy who said, "I think it will be no great matter to set an extra plate, will it, Mrs. Payne?"

"No," said Molly Payne, in a voice that sounded to Dolley oddly like her father's: hesitant, as if she were waking and wasn't entirely certain where she was. Then, smiling, she went on more strongly, "Thou art entirely welcome, Friend John, and thou knowst it. To dinner, or at any other time."

⚜

Her father was an invisible presence, like a shadow on dinner, and none of the children dared raise their voice or ask what General Washington had looked like.

John, to Dolley's utter relief, maintained a measured conversation with her mother on the subject of the Meeting's school committee, boring as dust and, like dust, blanketing all jagged edges in a smoothing mask. Dolley had never been so grateful to anyone in her life. Afterwards he stayed to play Fox and Geese with Lucy and the children while the women cleared the table and carried the dishes back down to the kitchen to wash, so things felt normal and relatively cheerful by the time he took his departure at four.

Her parents' bedroom at the front of the house was still filled with the gray light of the late-spring afternoon, when Dolley knocked gently at the door. " 'Tis Dolley, Papa."

There was silence within. The children had gone out to the yard; Isaac was as usual trouncing William at dominoes; on her way upstairs Dolley had passed her mother in the kitchen, talking with Mother Amy by the open door.

At last a voice replied, "Come, Daughter."

He sat in the chair by the window. The window was shut and the room airless. Footsteps patted in the street; a woman's voice chimed plaintively, "But if he'd only agree to sit next to her the whole problem could be avoided!" Her father winced. He moved his head as if the sound were a bodkin, pricking at his ear.

Doth he miss the stillness of our country evenings at Coles Hill?

When you stepped outside in Philadelphia, it was like stepping into a giant open-air drawing-room full of chattering people.

That was one of the things Dolley loved about Philadelphia.

Her father looked weary, and she could see where white had touched his dark hair.

"I'm so sorry I disobeyed thee, Father. Sorry that my feet were so quick to run away when Mama said that I might. She meant nothing by it, truly she did not. The fault was mine. Please forgive me."

"John Todd is a good man," he said softly. "And a brave one. Why dost thou turn thy face aside from his love?" He spoke like a man speaking from the dark of a cell he knows he'll never leave.

Dolley wanted to protest, *I don't,* but knew that would be a falsehood. Every look John Todd gave her asked for something that she avoided.

"What more dost thou want in this life?"

"Father, I know not."

"I want to see thee safe," he said, after a silence so lengthy she wondered if he wished her to go. "Thy mother is right, Daughter. I hide in this corner. The voices of men are an abomination to me. The Spirit will guide me, the Spirit will show me the path I must take, but listen as I may there is only silence. I am tired, Daughter, more tired than I was when I plowed all day behind a team of oxen, and I think if I were to come into the presence of anyone, man or woman, I would—" He hesitated.

Weep? wondered Dolley.

Scream?

Curse God and die?

"I know it sounds like madness, but I am not mad, Daughter. I know I am of little use to thy mother and the children, yet this is all that I am or can be now. Thy mother says to work on in spite of my melancholy and the good people of the Meeting advise this and that, and yet it is all to me like men describing color to a man who hath lost his eyes. *How shall one season salt that hath lost its savor?* Please do not give me advice, Daughter." His eyes were bleak.

Dolley shook her head, then pulled up the little stool that stood beside the tall bed, so that she could sit beside him, and take his hand.

"Child, I want only thy happiness. Thou art made for better things than to lose thy days in poverty, and I fear that this is what is to come. This is why I say to thee, *Marry John Todd.* Marry him now. His heart is faithful, yet disappointment breaks even the strongest back in the end. Then what shalt become of thee?"

"Papa, what woman would have any use for a man who deserted her in the face of adversity?" Dolley spoke playfully, and his mouth tugged a little at the corner in response. Since she was fourteen, he'd been joking her about the number of young gentlemen who came calling on her, and the number of requests he'd gotten, from men who wanted permission to seek her hand.

Personally, Dolley never could see why. She was too tall, and inclined to bossiness. She knew she had pretty coloring, white and black and blue, but knew also that she lacked the fineness of feature that made true beauty. She enjoyed the attention, and enjoyed flirting, but it was hard to take any man seriously who threw himself on his knees before her and went into raptures about how lovely she was.

For all his sober stuffiness, and his inability to see a jest, she never had the feeling that John Todd gazed at her thinking, *I am looking at the most beautiful woman in the world.*

Just, *I am looking at my friend Dolley Payne.*

But her father's responsive smile faded before it reached his eyes. "Times are cruel, Dolley. More cruel than we knew when all we had to fear was the redcoats and the Tories. I fear thou shalt find that few men— maybe none—will seek to wed a woman who must work for her bread and who can bring nothing to the marriage, no matter how pretty she be. I do not know what the future holds for this family, but when I look ahead I see only blackness. I say again, Dolley, John Todd is a good man. What more dost thou want in this life? For what dost thou wait?"

For a wider world?

For a girl of even middling means, the world was never wide. As a youngster in Hanover County she'd been enchanted by the books in Sophie Sparling's grandfather's library, but not, as Sophie was, out of a steely hunger for learning. It was the stories that delighted her, the dizziness of looking through an infinity of windows into other experiences, other places and times. Living in Philadelphia, especially at such a time and with such events going on, was surely to be living in the widest world she would ever see.

For a man I can laugh with?

But it was silly, to wish for a man who shared her mirth above a man who would treat her and her children well. And while the Friends were far from humorless, she had never met a young man in the Meeting yet who had her zesty curiosity, her love of laughter.

And to look outside the Meeting was unthinkable.

So all she could say was, "I know not what I wait for, Father. Maybe for just the guidance of the Spirit?"

Once he would have agreed with her. Now he frowned. "Dost not think that *this* is the guidance of the Spirit? As a mother will push a child out of the path of danger, or into a safe and sunny garden, if from timidity or foolishness that child will not be coaxed?"

She heard her mother's voice in the parlor next door, and William answering something. Footsteps creaked, and Dolley was standing by the time a light tap sounded on the bedroom door. Her father closed his eyes briefly, as if the sound were the scrape of nails on slate. He whispered, "Go, Daughter. Think of what I have said. It is for thine own good that I speak."

But as she climbed to the stuffy heat of the attic bedroom she shared with her sisters, and opened the window there onto the wilderness of roofs and birds, Dolley felt only a great sense of confusion, and longing for something for which she had no name. *Timid and foolish,* her father had said. *And,* she mentally added, remembering her mother's tired face, *selfish as well.*

For what dost thou wait?

She knew John Todd would make her a good husband.

Did she really think some dashingly handsome Friend was going to come striding into the Meeting one morn, take her hand, and lead her into a world where she could read and talk, surround herself with music and bright colors, and not meekly grind away her days in work that had no end and little relief?

She had prayed often for guidance concerning John Todd, as she had prayed for guidance about her father. Now she rested her forehead on her window sash and whispered to the shining light that she saw within her heart, *Send me where I'll do the most good, by the route that doth seem best to You.*

Over the rooftops of Philadelphia, the church bells were silent. The cannons by the State House were stilled. The sky was beginning to darken at the end of the long afternoon. Dolley pictured the candlelight and mirrors of Robert Morris's elegant dining-room, and General Washington, resplendent in black velvet and powder. Delighted, she was sure, to be at his destination and able to partake of a decent meal—Would he write to his wife tonight and tell her he'd arrived safe?

Thunder rumbled grumpily over the hills west of town. Big, thick drops of rain began to fall.

Robert Morris had the finest mansion in Philadelphia, whose red-tiled roof and gleaming third-floor windows Dolley could see, a few streets over on Fourth Street. The British General Howe had occupied it as his own, the winter the British held Philadelphia in their grip. Now the merchant would be rubbing his chubby hands at the prospect of having the General's prestigious presence and the General's undivided attention on his own arguments and plans.

Dolley had been around meeting-house committees long enough to know that most of what got decided got decided over dinner or punch in some congenial parlor, not over debates in a sweltering meeting room.

Poor little Mr. Madison. He so clearly intended for precisely that reason to keep the whole of the powerful Virginia delegation together under his eye. Now he'd been left to wait at Mrs. House's boardinghouse, outjockeyed by the Philadelphia merchant.

It was going to be a long, hot summer for everyone in Philadelphia.

Washington City
August 24, 1814

Light footfalls under the cold high hanging lamps of the hall: Dolley turned her head. "Didst find it?" she asked, a little surprised, seeing Sophie holding something small, cupped in the palm of one hand. In the other she held a slender bundle of letters.

"These weren't in the sewing-table," Sophie replied as she approached. "They were shoved in behind the cabinet—when was that cabinet last moved?—They're unsigned."

She held them out, after the briefest pause. Dolley saw the top one was in English, though it started out, *Ma mie—My little one—* written in a clear strong hand. The superscription was "Rotterdam." "Dost know the hand?" she asked, and Sophie replied without hesitation.

"Of course not. This was with them," she added, and held out three broken fragments of ivory, and a few bits of ornamental gold. Put together, Dolley could see that it had once been a miniature: a beautiful girl in the simple white costume so popular in France in the 1780s. A girl with clear eyes of bright turquoise-green, and long dark curly hair hanging down her back.

She looked up, and met Sophie's eyes for a long moment; then turned the pieces over again in her hand. On the back of the miniature was written only, *Paris 1788.* The delicate paint was scratched and smudged, as if the girl's painted image had been shattered by being stomped again and again beneath a furious heel.

SALLY

❦

"Do you remember my mama, Sally?"

Polly Jefferson had been quiet for so long that Sally Hemings had thought the little girl asleep. The woods through which the post-chaise drove did little to mitigate the heat of the day; the vehicle's swaying was like the rocking of a cradle. At the beginning of the journey from Le Havre, Polly had been as wildly excited as Sally by every new glimpse of farmhouses, trees, and distant châteaus; after four days, she had grown accustomed enough to doze.

Sally could have looked forever, marveling at each half-seen roof or unfamiliar shrub. But she heard the wistfulness in her charge's voice, and tore her eyes from the green shadows of what M'sieu Petit had told them was the forest of St.-Germain—or at least that's what Sally thought he'd said. After the tricked parting from Captain Ramsay, Polly had become quieter than she'd been on the *Arundel.* Mrs. Adams at least hadn't tricked or lied to the girl, to get her to leave the house at Grosvenor Square with the dapper little Frenchman Mr. Jefferson had sent. Still, Sally was aware of long silences where there had been nonstop, childish chatter before.

It was the first time Sally had heard her ask about her mother.

"That I do, sugarbaby." She put her arm around Polly's thin shoulders. "I think your mother was about the most beautiful lady I've ever seen in my life." Because of the longing in the little girl's face, Sally probably would have said so even had it not been true, but in fact Mrs. Jefferson—Miss Patty, she'd been called in the quarters—had been truly lovely.

"Did she look like Aunt Eppes?" Polly sat up a little straighter, tugged at the brim of her sunbonnet, as if still worried about her father's admonition not to let herself get freckled. "Jack says Aunt Eppes was Mama's sister."

Jack was Aunt Eppes's fourteen-year-old son, and the idol of Polly's young life. On the voyage from Virginia, snuggled together in the curtained bunk she and Sally shared, Polly had asked to hear almost as many stories about Cousin Jack as about her father and her sister Patsy. In addition to listening to Sally's recollections, Polly would make up tales herself, some of them quite fantastic, involving the slaughter of dragons or the defeat of the armies of the King of Spain. Back at Eppington Plantation, Aunt Eppes used to frown at Polly's tales and scold primly, *Now you know that isn't so. . . .*

Sally knew she ought to do the same. But it was more fun to pitch in and add magical birds and the Platt-Eye Devil to the mix.

Besides, Polly knew perfectly well that their stories were only stories.

"You look more like her than your Aunt Eppes does," said Sally. She did not add that she herself looked more like the long-dead Patty Jefferson than either Miss Patty's white half-sister or younger daughter did.

It was one reason, Sally suspected, Aunt Eppes had been just as happy to get her out of the house. There were many white Virginia ladies who simply accepted the fact that their fathers took slave-women into their beds—sometimes for a night or two, sometimes, in the case of Sally's mother Betty and old Jack Wayles, for years. Patty Wayles Jefferson had treated Betty's "bright" children—Sally's brothers and sisters—if not as members of the immediate family, at least as a privileged sub-branch, and after her father's death Sally's mother had been Miss Patty's maid and confidante.

For Elizabeth Wayles Eppes, this had not been the case, perhaps because Sally *did* so much resemble their mutual half-sister. Once when Polly was five she'd asked Sally, "Ranney says you're kin to me—" Ranney being one of the kitchenmaids. Even at age ten, Sally had known enough to reply, "You go way back in the Bible, back to Noah and the Ark, and you'll see we're all kin to each other." Whether the little girl had pursued enquiries with her aunt, Sally didn't know.

Now she went on, "Your mama had curly hair like yours, dark red like yours, not bright like your papa and sister. And her eyes were sort of green that looked gold in some lights, like your papa, or M'sieu Petit." And she nodded through the windows toward the trim Frenchman who rode beside the chaise, just far enough behind so that the hooves of his mount would not kick extra dust to drift in through the open windows.

M'sieu Petit was Mr. Jefferson's valet, and Sally had to smile to herself at the very evident fact that white French valets seemed to stand just as high in their own self-importance as the high-yellow "fancies" generally picked for the job in Virginia. That reflection made her wonder how her brother Jimmy was getting along, among all those French servants.

Her heart twitched with joy at the thought of seeing him again.

"Your mama and papa used to play together, her on the harpsichord, him on his fiddle." She stroked Polly's hair, tucked the stray locks back under the linen cap she wore beneath her bonnet. "When they'd sing together in Italian, all the mockingbirds in the trees would stop singing and line up on the windowsill to listen, it was so beautiful. And if the sun had gone down, all the flowers in the garden would open up again just a little wee bit—" She demonstrated with her fingers, to make Polly laugh, "—just to hear one more verse before they had to go to sleep."

"Silly." Polly tried to look prim. "Flowers don't do that."

"For your mama they did."

Polly giggled, and settled her head comfortably on Sally's shoulder, blinking out at the green-and-gold dapple of the sunlight, the soft haze of the dust.

Were it not for Polly Jefferson—nobody ever called the child Mary—Sally thought she would have broken her heart with loneliness, these past two months. Of course, if it weren't for Polly she'd still be back in Virginia, and not in a coach on the way to Paris, that storybook capital of a storybook, magical land. She wouldn't be on the verge of seeing her brother again, for the first time in four years.

Every time Polly wrote a letter to her aunt Carr at Monticello, on shipboard and in London at Mrs. Adams's marvelous house, Sally had enclosed a short note to be read to her friends and family at the mountaintop plantation. She wished she might do the same for the friends she'd made at Eppington, but though Mr. Eppes was on the whole a kindly master, he didn't hold with slaves knowing how to read and write. She had merely asked Polly to write at the end of her letters, *Sally asks to be remembered with love to you all.* That way they would know at least that she was alive and well.

It was Mr. Jefferson who'd first taught Sally her letters. He loved to teach, and had instructed dozens of the slave-children on Monticello, though most of them—especially the ones who ended up out in the tobacco fields—let the skill go rusty. Destined from childhood to be a house-servant, Sally had kept it up. Because Sally had been reared as much by Miss Patty as by her own mother, she'd spent most of her time in the family house, whether it was at Monticello or one of the other Jefferson plantations, Shadwell or Poplar Grove, or for one astonishing season in the big governor's palace in Williamsburg. Mr. Jefferson's older daughter Patsy—only a year older than Sally—had delighted in passing along her own lessons to the younger girl. When Patsy grew old enough to be trusted in her father's library, she'd often bring

Sally along with her: a paradise of histo-
ries, stories, poems.

And at the center of it, like a wizard in an
enchanted garden, was Mr. Jefferson himself.

⚜

A ripple of something—not quite heat and
not quite the shivers, neither truly anger nor
sadness—went through her at the thought
of Mr. Jefferson.

Sally couldn't remember back before
she'd loved him, though the day she'd quit
doing so was vivid as yesterday in her mind.
It still filled her with sadness, and a sense of
confusion for which she had no name.
She'd seen them so often together, Mr. Jefferson and Miss Patty. Had been aware of
how deeply they loved one another, like the
red rose and the briar in the old ballad, inex-
tricably twined.

She had seen, too, the grief, loneliness,
and—once the War began—the constant
quiet terror in which her mistress lived, each
time Mr. Jefferson went away.

Miss Patty was all things beautiful, lovely
as the dogwood blossoms, sweet-scented,
filled with music. Mr. Jefferson, with his

tales of ancient Kings and Indian lore and the secret lives of every bird and grass-blade, was wise and quirkily marvelous. Kind, too. He was firm and reasonable with his slaves, both field-hands and house-servants: he would threaten whippings, but in fact the worst that would happen was that he'd sell an offender away. This was bad enough, and not simply because it meant losing every friend and relative you had. Everyone in the quarters along Mulberry Row knew that pretty much anywhere in the State would be worse than Monticello. At the time, it had seemed to Sally that she'd loved Mr. Jefferson merely for the fact that he didn't assume she was simple-minded, just because she was a little girl and a slave. Though she was always being scolded by her mother and Miss Patty for wandering off into the garden to look at plants when she should have been practicing her stitching, Mr. Jefferson always took her side. "It's rare enough to find any child, black or white, who will read Nature's text-books so avidly," he'd tell them. He'd joked with her, and laughed when she gave him back clever answers. Like a good father he'd always been happy to answer her endless questions, to explain the clouds and the winds—and the War.

In the snowy January of 1781, when Sally was eight, the family had been in Richmond, where Mr. Jefferson was Governor of the state. He had come back from the Congress, Sally's mother had said, because Miss Patty had begged him to, because she could not live with him gone all the time. Sally guessed her mistress feared that if the British took the Congress prisoner, Mr. Jefferson would be hanged. So he'd come back to Virginia, first to Williamsburg and then to Richmond, and the British invaded the state anyway. They'd seized Richmond, and the family barely got away; Sally remembered clinging to her mother's skirt as the servants huddled around the wagons, and hearing baby Lucie Elizabeth, who'd only been born the previous November, wailing thinly in the cold.

Three days later the British riddled the house with bullets at point-blank range, then rounded up the servants who'd remained there, and sold them off for cash. Both Miss Patty and baby Lucie Elizabeth came down sick as a result of the flight through the freezing countryside. In April, Lucie Elizabeth died.

Eighteen months later, just after Mr. Jefferson's term as Governor was ended and he returned to Monticello, a militia captain came tearing up the mountain one June morning at dawn, shouting that the British were but three hours behind him and had already taken Charlottesville. Mr. Jefferson woke his wife and daughters and got them into the carriage, carrying Polly down the stairs wrapped in a blanket. Aunt Carr, Mr. Jefferson's sister who had lived with him since the death of her husband, wailed prophecies of doom as her older boys Peter and Sam struggled to keep the younger ones calm, and Miss Patty's parrot Shadwell shrieked and swore.

Sally and her older sister Critta, and their sixteen-year-old brother Jimmy, helped load the farm wagon with food, blankets, clothing. Mr. Jefferson lifted her and Critta into the wagon, but their mother went in the carriage with Miss Patty, to quiet their mistress's terror as the vehicles went jolting down the breakneck, rutted road. Sally later heard from her oldest brother—Martin, the butler—that Mr. Jefferson had tried to pack up some of his papers and had gotten away from the house only minutes before the first red-coated dragoons emerged from the woods.

After the first flight from Richmond, Miss Patty had never been well. By the time they'd escaped from Monticello, the bones of her cheeks stood out through the sunken skin and her hands were like dead leaves.

Yet when Mr. Jefferson was there, Miss Patty would laugh and twine ribbons in her beautiful dark red hair, and insist she was much better; that there was really nothing wrong. Even as a child, Sally had sensed how desperately they both needed to believe this was true. By the fall of 1782 Miss Patty was with child again, her seventh, according to Sally's mother, counting the little boy she had borne to her first husband. She'd put on weight for the baby's birth— the second little Lucie Elizabeth—but even Sally could see it was unhealthy bloat, not the smoothness of returning health.

Those last four months, between Lucie's birth in May and September, when Miss Patty died, had a nightmare quality in Sally's memory. What they must have been for Mr. Jefferson she could not imagine. There was no more playing school with Patsy, or reading in the library, or learning fine stitching or the art of dressing hair. Sally had been put in charge of Polly—then four—sleeping on a pallet on the floor of the girls' room and helping Aunty Isabel in the nursery with baby Lucie.

Even little Polly sensed something was amiss, though Patsy whispered through gritted teeth that no one was to tell her sister how desperately ill their mother was. At night, when Polly couldn't sleep, Patsy would tell her stories, enlisting Sally's aid when her own limited invention flagged. Afterwards, when the younger girl drifted off to sleep and Sally returned to her pallet, Sally could hear the heartbreaking liquid sweetness of Mr. Jefferson's violin from downstairs, as he played for his wife in the darkness.

⚜

"Did Mama have freckles?" Polly sat up suddenly, her small, oval face puckered with sudden fright at the recurring concern. "Papa said he wouldn't love me, if I let myself get freckled."

"Your papa only said that because he'd

heard that pirates on the high seas look especially for freckled ladies, to haul away into captivity," Sally informed her gravely. "He just didn't want to scare you by saying so." And when Polly gave her a suspicious look, she laughed and said, "Sugarbaby, when your papa sees you, he'll be so glad he won't care if you're covered all over with spots like a bird's egg."

⚜

For three weeks after Miss Patty's death, Mr. Jefferson kept to his room. Passing the door, Sally had heard him weeping, or pacing incessantly, like an injured animal trying to outwalk pain. It was whispered in the slave-quarters that he would follow his beloved into her grave, from the sheer shock of his grief. Often Patsy would be with her father in his room nearly all night, as she was most of the day. Then it would fall to Sally to tell Polly stories, and hold her in bed until the little girl slept.

One afternoon he went through the whole of the house, gathering every letter, every list, every scrap of his wife's handwriting, and burned them all in the kitchen fire; cut to pieces the single small likeness of her that had been painted the year before. Sally remembered waking one fog-wrapped dawn, hearing a door close softly somewhere in the house, and Patsy's voice downstairs call hesitantly, "Papa?" Long familiar strides, first in the hall, then grinding on the gravel outside, heading toward the stables at the far end of Mulberry Row. Sally slipped out of her blanket and ran to the window in time to see Mr. Jefferson plunge down the drive on his fast bay stallion Caratacus. Tall and thin and stiff in her rumpled dress, Patsy stood by the back door with her rufous hair hanging down her shoulders. The pink of her shawl in the gray fog had been like the last flower of a summer gone.

⚜

Not long after that Mr. Jefferson had taken the family to his friend Mr. Cary's home near Richmond, for the girls and the Carr children to be inoculated against the smallpox. Baby Lucie had been left with Aunt Eppes. Sally, Critta, Jimmy, and Thenia, their youngest sister, were inoculated as well. Mr. Jefferson and Polly's nurse Aunty Isabel acted as sick-nurses to the whole group,

the first time Sally had seen her master begin to emerge from the desperate isolation
of his grief.

It was there that Mr. Jefferson got the letter from the Congress that his friend, the
fragile Mr. Madison who Sally always
thought looked like a wizened old man, had
put her master's name forward to be one of
the ministers to France. With Miss Patty
dead, there was no reason why he shouldn't
accept.

He'd gone to Philadelphia with Patsy. Sally
had hoped to be taken along as Patsy's
maid, or at least as a sewing-girl to the
household. Instead, when he came back,
she heard in the kitchen that she was going
to be sent with Polly and Lucie, not back to
Monticello, where she had friends and family, but to Eppington.

"Is it true?" she demanded of her mother,
when she'd raced in a flurry out to the sunny
room across the yard from the kitchen,
where the Cary slaves and those of their
guests gathered to do the mending and
ironing and stitching of clothing for the
household. The Cary slaves had regarded
her in mingled pity and surprise, that at age
nine she still seemed to think it would cross

any white person's mind to even ask if she wanted to leave her family or not.

"It's true," her mother had answered. And then, when Sally turned to run from the room, "Where you goin', girl?" She'd caught Sally by the arm, led her outside into the yard behind the big Cary house at Ampthill, the air cold after the frowsty sewing-room's warmth. "You thinkin' of runnin' in to Mr. Jefferson, to ask him not to send you to Eppington? Are you?"

When Sally didn't reply, Betty Hemings shook her, not roughly but urgently, pulling her eyes back to her own. "Don't you even think about it, girl. Don't you even *think* that because he teaches you your letters, and talks kindly to you, and answers all your fool questions, that he really cares even *that* much—" She measured the width of a lemon-pip between forefinger and thumb, "—where you want to go, or what you'd rather do than what he tells you to. Not him, not any white, man, woman, or child. They got a word for niggers that think they can ask not to do things they don't want to do and that word is *spoiled.* And once they start thinkin' you're a *spoiled nigger,* then they start lookin' around for ways to un-spoil you. To teach you real hard not to talk to 'em as if you wasn't black. You understand?"

Sally, trembling with defiance, looked up at her mother's face and saw there fear as well as anger: a terrible, piercing fear. She thought, *What does she think he'll do? Sell me?*

And the thought succeeded it as instantly as the following heartbeat, *He could.*

It was indeed what her mother feared.

"It's like that Decoration of Independence Martin was tellin' us about," her mother went on, her voice low and tense. "Mr. Jefferson wrote, *All men is created equal,* but what he meant was, *All white Americans is created equal to all white Englishmen.* Can you give me the name of any one of his slaves that he's turned loose since he wrote that?"

Sally whispered, "No, ma'am."

"You're damn lucky you're just goin' with Polly, and not bein' sold to Mrs. Eppes." Betty's voice was low, and she glanced at the back door of the Cary house, where young Peter Carr, just shooting up from boy to young man, could be seen flirting with one of the light-complected housemaids. "If

Mr. Jefferson was to die tomorrow, every one of us would be sold off to pay his debts. You better get used to it, girl, and thank God it's no worse yet."

Sally had returned quietly with her mother to the sewing-room, and had taken up work on a shirt for Sam Carr, as a way to quiet her mind and her hands. But later that evening, when the men had finished their port and were going in to join Mrs. Cary and the older girls in the parlor, seeing Mr. Jefferson walking behind the others Sally slipped from the shadows and tugged his sleeve, whispered, "Mr. Jefferson, sir—*must* I go to Eppington?"

He paused in his steps and looked down at her. His tall loose-jointed form seemed to loom against the candle-glow and gloom of the early-falling winter darkness. She was at the age when the slave-children began to be given real jobs, and had graduated from short calico shifts to a real dress of printed muslin, her hair—which was like a white woman's, silky and long—braided tidily up under a linen cap. In the half-dark she was aware that, being taller than the other girls her age (except for Patsy, who at ten was as tall as little Mr. Madison), she seemed already one of the adult servants, and not a child who can ask for things because she doesn't know any better.

Mr. Jefferson's voice was gentle and kind. "Now, Sally, Polly asked specially that you go with her to her aunt Eppes. She knows you, and loves you. I'm sending you with her so that she won't be lonely there."

He didn't sound in the least as if he even comprehended that she, too, might be lonely there. Shock, anger, disappointment pierced her heart like a thorn, but looking up into his eyes she saw there was no arguing. She'd seen that side of him as he'd dealt with other people, but never before had he turned that kindly implacability on her.

He simply didn't want to hear there was a problem. His hands rested briefly, warmly, on her shoulders. "You're a good girl, Sally, and I'm trusting you to take care of my daughter. And it won't be for very long."

It was to be four years.

And for those four years, Sally had hated Thomas Jefferson.

☙

The carriage emerged from the woods. Sunlight dyed the dust egg-yolk gold. They passed through a village: white stucco houses, brown tile roofs patched with green moss, a thick smell of pissy gutters, smoke, and pigs. A few of the people wore town-folks' clothes, like the people Sally had seen in Williamsburg and in the fascinating bed-lam of London, but they looked patched and threadbare. Most wore smocks and breeches, ragged and baggy and without stockings, like the field-hands.

But if they were field-hands, Sally reflected uneasily, somebody was short-feeding 'em and selling off the rations. One man spat af-ter the carriage as it clattered by.

Looking back, Sally had to admit that painful as it had been, her sojourn at Ep-pington had been for the best. If she hadn't been there when Mr. Jefferson's letters had come, insisting that Polly be sent to join him in France—if Aunty Isabel hadn't been with child and unable to make the voyage—she wouldn't be sitting here now. She wouldn't be about to see Jimmy again, her favorite brother. Lazy, handsome, prankish, trouble-making Jimmy: She almost laughed out loud at the thought of him. Her mother had sent her word that Mr. Jefferson was having him taught French cooking, which was supposed to be the best in the world, though Sally couldn't imagine better cooking than what her Aunty Lita could produce in a single pot over the fire.

She wondered if he'd learned to speak French like the lofty M'sieu Petit. *(Enough to cheat at cards and find every alehouse for five miles around, anyway!)*

She wondered if he'd changed.

A stone bridge, and the deep glitter of water; a speckled flotilla of ducks. Then woods again, like the wooded mountaintop of Monticello, crisscrossed with paths and dotted with lawn and flowers. A park, like the great parks in London, Hyde Park and Grosvenor Square where Mr. and Mrs. Adams would go walking with Polly, during the ten days they'd stayed in that wonder-filled metropolis.

Mrs. Eppes, and Aunty Isabel, had given Sally strict instructions about staying at Polly's side and staying in the house when Polly was out with the white folks—by the time it was known Sally would accompany her charge to France, Mrs. Eppes was as familiar as Aunty Isabel was with Sally's boundless curiosity, her omnivorous craving to find out about anything she didn't know. Neither the white aunt nor the black nurse

had ever been to a city bigger than Williamsburg, but they'd guessed what temptations
would flaunt themselves across Sally's path.

"The girl's never to be found when you
want her," the delicate, formidable Mrs.
Adams had complained, on their second
day beneath her roof. "A fine nursemaid for
a child Polly's age!"

But London—!

Even the birds were different in London:
cocky little brown sparrows, instead of the
silvery doves Sally knew in Virginia. The summer night-noise, too, was different, watch-
men and carts and vendors all yelling, instead of the incessant clamor of night-crying
insects. Her heart hurt for the songs of the
mockingbirds, but in Grosvenor Square,
walking in the twilight (when she should have
been back at Mrs. Adams's house!) she'd
heard the indescribable sweet voice of the
nightingale, that all the fairy-tales talked
about.

All those crowded houses had their stables along separate alleyways that begged
to be investigated. The Square and every
street around it was alive with vendors who
brought not only milk and eggs and vegetables from the markets but also hot pies,

scarves, slippers, quills for making pens. The markets were jaw-dropping carnivals of activity, produce, servants, housewives, whores—Sally had never seen a whore, and had to quietly confirm with Mrs. Adams's maid Esther that yes, those women with bright clothes and hair that startling color made their living by coupling with men.

Sally loved Virginia with the whole of her heart—loved its stillness, the sweetness of the woods, and the soft peaceful twilights. But the world was a marvel-filled place. Even Mrs. Adams had unbent, when Sally had asked, a little fearfully, if she might be permitted to read some of the books in Mr. Adams's library: Coming back to books after four years without them was like sitting down at table starving. Like Mr. Jefferson, fat, grumpy Mr. Adams loved books, and like Mr. Jefferson both he and his beautiful wife were born schoolteachers.

There would be books in Mr. Jefferson's house.

Had Mr. Jefferson changed?

⚜

Though her resentment at him had burned bitter in her for four years, she had never been able to eradicate from her heart the memory of his violin echoing in the darkness for his dying wife. The tireless months Mr. Jefferson had spent in Miss Patty's room watching her fade from life returned to Sally's mind, confusing the simplicity of her anger at all he had done. And not only to her: Even as a child of eight, Sally knew it took two to make a baby. It was impossible that Mr. Jefferson, a grown man who had read books and talked to doctors, wouldn't know it, too.

"She was afraid, if she put him out of her bed, that he'd start lyin' with Iris or Jenny," Sally's mother had said, naming the light-skinned housemaid, and the young wife of the plantation cobbler. Both had shown Mr. Jefferson—and a number of his guests at one time or another—their willingness. Being the master's woman was a good way to get extra food and gifts, and to pass along to any offspring the inestimable gift of preference in an unfair world.

"Why you think she always smiled, and made herself pretty the way she did?" her mother asked. "It's not just so he wouldn't fret. It was to draw him back to her, to bind him. To keep him from going away. She'd rather risk death than lose him."

Sally still thought Mr. Jefferson should have known better. And maybe, she reflected, recalling not only despair but horror in his eyes as fevers, weakness, infections ravaged the beautiful woman he had loved—maybe he had guessed at last what he had so frantically told himself wasn't true.

On that last morning, on the threshold of autumn of 1782, nine-year-old Sally had been in the room when Miss Patty reached for Mr. Jefferson's hand and whispered, "Swear to me that you will never give my girls a stepmother." Miss Patty had had two stepmothers in succession. From what her mother had told her of them, Sally wasn't surprised that the young woman had been grateful to Betty Hemings for her kindness and for the fact that she'd kept old Jack Wayles from needing to marry a third.

Mr. Jefferson had fainted from grief, and had been carried into the library next to Miss Patty's room. Everyone went back into the sickroom—Mrs. Eppes and Aunt Carr and Miss Sparling, the young nurse that the doctor from Yorktown had left to care for

Miss Patty—but Sally had lingered. She'd looked down at the ravaged unshaven face, the straight red eyelashes like gold against the discolored bruises of sleeplessness. *He knows it's true. He knows that it's he who killed her by possessing her.*

Later she'd overheard some of his friends remark on the excessiveness of his pain, that in those first few weeks he could not even look at his own children without collapsing, and she knew why he couldn't look at them.

Those things she'd remembered in her days at Eppington, even when her hunger for her family had been at its worst. She'd hated him, when she felt herself going half crazy with longing to be able to read again and when Mrs. Eppes came up with extra tasks and duties in the kitchen and the scullery to "un-spoil" a slave she considered inattentive and uppity. Yet she never could hate him with the whole of her heart.

In time her anger had altered, changed to a kind of slow-burning frustrated grief. For she knew that all things were the way all things were.

She had come to love Polly, and sunny-hearted baby Lucie, as if they were her own sisters. Mrs. Eppes had a baby daughter named Lucie as well: Polly would braid ribbons of identical color into both toddlers' hair, and say the Lucies were her own twin babies.

Then in early October of 1784, shortly after Mr. Jefferson left for France with Patsy, whooping cough swept over Eppington Plantation.

Both little Lucies died.

⚜

"Mesdemoiselles, les voilà!" M'sieu Petit nudged his horse up close to the chaise window, bent from the saddle, and pointed through the trees with his quirt. *"Les murailles de Paris.* How you say . . .?" He mislaid the English word, and shook his head with a wry smile, but pride and happiness sparkled in his eyes. Then he simply explained, "Paris."

For the past mile, Sally had seen through the trees the tall walls of houses—palaces— set back from the road at the end of aisles of trees. Now ahead of them she saw the gray stone wall Mrs. Adams had told them about, which the French King had let his friends build so they could charge every farmer and merchant a fee to bring goods into Paris. Sure enough, a knot of carts and donkeys and wagons was clumped in front of the small gatehouse, while uniformed officials pawed through their contents.

And beyond the wall, distant over yet more trees, could be glimpsed rooftops, chimneys, church steeples. It looked like a fairy-tale, but it was a city, no mistake. The stench was too real for it to be a dream.

Polly's face contorted with disgust. "Pew!"

And M'sieu Petit's eyes twinkled. *"Ah, la puanteur de Paris! Ça te fait forte!"* He thumped his chest. "It make strong!"

Stench, movement, shouting as if everyone at the Tower of Babel were being slaughtered at once all rolled in with the braying of asses, the bleating of sheep, the barking of a thousand dogs . . .

Paris.

An official strolled over to let them through the gate, M'sieu Petit slipping him a coin to let them through without being searched. The farmers to whom the man had been speaking—or who'd been shouting at him— followed, still shouting, filthy barefoot men, unshaven and carrying sticks. The official in his blue uniform ignored them, like a white overseer brushing off the impotent anger of field-hands. Sally couldn't tell what the problem was, but as the chaise went through the gate she saw their eyes: like the eyes of slaves who're burning to torch the kitchen some night.

But on the plantations around Charlottesville, a slave with such anger in him generally worked alone. She'd never seen that many men—that many sets of smoldering eyes—together.

She was house-servant enough to be frightened.

Whatever was going on, somebody was going to catch it bad.

On the other side of the gate lay a great circular open space, surrounded by rows of trees, with streets radiating in all directions. Among the milling farm-carts and gaggles of sheep, elegant carriages maneuvered. The long avenue beyond was almost like a country road, lined with trees and kitchen-gardens. Here, too, were both market-carts and fancy carriages, strollers in bright silks and farmers in faded rags. Less than a mile along, the coachman drew rein at the first courtyard wall. M'sieu Petit sprang from his horse as the porter ran from the lodge to open the gates.

With a breathless start, Sally realized, *We're here.*

Polly understood at the same moment, sat up very straight, her eyes huge with panic, her hands pressing guiltily to her freckled nose.

The gate opened. The courtyard was cobbled. Servants in white shirtsleeves came out of the tall gray house.

M'sieu Petit opened the carriage door, helped Sally down first, then Polly. Polly's hand was cold on Sally's, like a frantic little claw. "He's going to *hate* me—"

A man emerged onto the house's front steps. Not as big as Sally remembered him from her childhood, though still a tall man. Either she'd remembered his hair being redder or it had faded, and though the gouges of grief and sleeplessness were gone from his sharp quizzical features, she saw where their echoes lingered still.

He wore a brown coat, and had one arm in a sling, wrist tightly bandaged. Yet he slipped it out to reach down and steady Polly as he scooped her up effortlessly in his strong arms.

The next second another pair of arms went around Sally's waist from behind and Jimmy's voice said in her ear, "Who's this gorgeous lady? Can't be my sister Sally! Sally's skinny and got knock-knees—"

"I do not have knock-knees!" She whirled, striking at him as if they were children again together, laughing up into his eyes. Dark eyes—of all their mother's children, only Sally had inherited her ship-captain grandfather's turquoise-blue eyes. "You still as ugly as I remember, so you got to be Jimmy." Which was a lie. Jimmy was good-looking and he knew it.

Then Jimmy looked past her and dropped back a step, and she turned, as Mr. Jefferson came up to her, holding out his left, unbroken hand. "Sally." The soft, husky timbre of his voice brought back to her in a rush all the memories of Monticello, all the tales he'd once told her of ancient Kings. "You've grown."

You sent me away. Like a dog or a bird. But four years had passed. She'd learned that it was something all white men did.

So like the child she'd been, she peeped at him from under her eyelashes and responded meekly, "You'd have to write me up in your philosophical journals if I hadn't, Mr. Jefferson."

Something in the way his shoulders relaxed, in the old answering sparkle of his eyes, made her realize that, white man and adult though he was, he'd been as homesick as she.

He set Polly on her feet again and put his unbroken hand on his daughter's shoulder, drawing her close. "Thank you, Sally," he said. "Thank you for keeping such care of Polly, and for bringing her safely here to me."

Behind them, servants were unloading trunks from the back of the chaise: Polly's big one, and the small wicker box of Sally's few possessions. Sally was only a little conscious of her brother's glance going from her face to their master's, of the speculation in his eyes. Mostly she was aware of Mr. Jefferson, the god of her childhood, the master who wrote of freedom but kept his slaves, the ravaged face of the man unconscious in the library and the retreating beat of hooves in fog, fleeing the place he loved but could no longer endure.

With Polly's hand in his he ascended the few steps to the door of the house, and

Jimmy and Sally followed him into its shadows. Beyond the gatehouse in the avenue, someone was shouting, "We will not forever be slaves!"

Washington City
August 24, 1814

"Mrs. Madison, I cannot allow you to remain here!" Red-faced and covered with dust, Dr. Blake—Washington's stocky mayor—gestured furiously toward the parlor windows, though Dolley assumed he meant to point northeast at the Bladensburg road. "I have been in Bladensburg since dawn, digging earthworks, and I know what will happen there!"

"Have the British attacked, then?"

"That is not the issue, Mrs. Madison. They are on their way. Last night they took Upper Marlborough. The men in Bladensburg are exhausted. Their rations were lost, they'd been marching all night—"

"And the President?"

Blake shook his head. "He's there somewhere. I didn't see him. Armstrong's an imbecile—*you'd* make a better Secretary of War than he does!—giving orders now to retreat, now to advance . . . The men are untrained and there isn't a horse in the Army that's smelled blood and battle-smoke before. *They'll* break and run, if the men don't."

"I shall stay until Mr. Madison comes." Dolley folded her hands as if the dusty, exhausted man before her were any morning caller come to pay polite respects, not a messenger from the edge of battle. "I appreciate thy concern, sir, but I will not abandon the capital to an enemy, particularly one who hath not yet fired a shot at me. And I will never abandon my husband. I have a Tunisian saber on the wall of my dining-room and I am perfectly prepared to use it."

"Do you really?" inquired Sophie, coming in from the hall after Dr. Blake had left, bewildered by the obstinacy of the President's lady. "Have a Tunisian saber?"

Dolley nodded. "Patsy Jefferson gave it to me; her father got it for her in Paris." She plucked a fragment of the tea-cake Paul had brought with the refreshments for Dr. Blake and carried it to the window, where Polly had been roving back and forth on her perch for the past hour, cursing under her breath in Italian. "If thou didst know the Adamses in Paris, thou must have known Patsy and her sister there as well."

"I did, but not well. We were not intimates. To raise the money Mother and I knew we'd need in England, I worked for a time as a sick-nurse for a doctor in Yorktown. Mr. Jefferson had him up to Monticello, when Mrs. Jefferson did not seem to be recovering from her last childbirth; I stayed on to look after her. I think in her heart Patsy Jefferson always considered me a servant. And in Paris I was a paid companion to one of those disreputable old Englishwomen who hung on the fringes of salon society. Patsy was kind, of course. To those who don't get between her and her father she has great natural kindness of heart."

Dolley was silent, knowing of whom she spoke. Polly sidled over to her and curled one huge gray claw around Dolley's wrist, and with the other took the tea-cake.

"Thank you, darling," the parrot croaked.

And because Polly expected it, Dolley replied gravely, "Thou'rt welcome, Pol." Plumes of dust were rising now not just along Pennsylvania Avenue, but throughout the muddy, weedy wasteland of scattered groves and still more scattered buildings. *Dr. Blake is right,* Dolley thought, fighting against the panic that scratched within her breast like a rat behind a door. *He and I both know what will happen there, if it has not already begun.* The British were on their way. It was insanity to think that the exhausted, disorganized, starving men could stop them.

It was insanity to stay.

Sophie stepped to her side, her dark clothing like a shadow against the room's bright color, and a blinding round of light flashed from her palm as she held out her hand.

Dolley's breath caught.

She should have known, when Martha gave it to her, that it came from the French Queen. The miniature on the reverse wasn't a good one—it could have been any Frenchwoman with high-piled hair and a fantasia of ostrich-plumes—but who other than Marie Antoinette would have given a hand-mirror whose rim was studded with diamonds?

She regarded the painted face on the ivory, the long chin and sweet, pouting mouth. In 1782, this frivolous, softhearted woman couldn't have known that the powder-trail ignited at Concord Bridge was going to bring down the Bastille's walls. In 1782, Martha Washington hadn't even been the wife of the head of state: just a woman whose husband—and whose husband's cause—was the *dernier cri* of fashion in the salons of Paris.

Martha had probably sent the French Queen a letter of congratulation on the birth of her son—Dolley recalled Martha speaking of the celebrations in the new Dauphin's honor, held by the American troops at the tail-end of the winter camp on the Hudson. Martha, who at that time had just lost her own son. And because Martha's famous husband had just defeated France's enemy—or was it simply out of fellow-feeling for a woman who followed her husband to the dirt and hardship of war? Marie Antoinette had sent a gift in reply.

She's adorned / Amply that in her husband's eye looks lovely, someone had written somewhere. *The truest mirror that an honest wife / Can see her beauty in.*

Dolley turned the mirror over in her hand. *Liberté—Amitié,* the graven letters said, that most ancient of riddles: *Freedom and Friendship.* Though her faith in a truly omnipotent God precluded superstition, the echo of old beliefs still whispered in her heart, that those who'd looked into mirrors left some fragment of themselves, some echo behind within the glass. It seemed to her that she should be able to catch a glimpse of the pretty French Queen, in her diamonds and her ostrich-plumes and her fatal nimbus of impenetrable naïveté, kind-heartedly sending off this gift to the woman whose cause would transform itself into the monster that would devour the giver.

Certainly she should be able to see in it Martha's face, pale within the black of her final mourning. Or to meet within its depths Abigail's indomitable gaze.

Half to herself, she murmured, "I don't suppose either Martha or Abigail would have fled."

"No," Sophie replied. "But then, neither did the Queen who sent Martha that mirror, and these days no one calls *her* brave for not getting out when she had the chance."

Dolley looked up quickly, to meet her friend's implacable eyes.

A horse rushed by on the Avenue, appearing, then vanishing, through the dust. Voices shouted incoherently. Another gunshot cracked, followed by the frenzied barking of dogs.

Into the silence that followed, Dolley said shakily, "I don't expect even this is as bad as Paris was, in the summer of '89."

"No," said Sophie softly. "No—Even if the British sacked this city and burned it to the ground, it could not be as bad as it was in Paris, that summer of '89."

Paris
Monday, July 14, 1789

Sally woke and lay for a long time, listening in the darkness.

All was silent, but the smell of burning hung thick in the air.

Yesterday a mob had torn down and burned the wooden palisades on either side of the customs pavilions that flanked the city gate up in the *Étoile,* had stormed and sacked the pavilions themselves and routed the inspectors there. The Champs-Elysées had been jammed with carts, wagons, carriages, and terrified horses, people fleeing the town or people rushing in from the faubourgs to join in the fray. Furious, filthy men and women had rampaged among them, waving butcher-knives, clubs, make-shift pikes. Mr. Jefferson had been away at Versailles, where the newly formed National Assembly was meeting. At the first sign of trouble, M'sieu Petit had closed and barred the courtyard gates. When he'd reopened them in the evening, at Mr. Jefferson's return, the stink had been horrific, because of course every member of the mob on the way to and from the *Étoile* had used the gateways of every house on the avenue as a toilet.

Mr. Jefferson had called a meeting of the whole household in the candle-lit dining-room: servants, stableboys, his daughters, and his secretary Mr. Short. "The King's troops have surrounded the city," he said in that soft voice that everyone had to strain to hear. "But the King has pledged to General Lafayette and the National Assembly that he will not attack his own people. These are but the birth-pangs of a new government, the fire that will release the phoenix. We have no call to fear."

Sally wasn't so sure about that.

"There's every kind of rumor coming in through the kitchen, Tom," she had said to him, softly, much later in the night when he went up to bed. There was a signal between them, a Boccherini piece he would play on his violin, when all the house fell silent. Then Sally would wrap herself in a faded old brocade gown, and move like a ghost barefoot down the dark attic stair.

"Most of 'em you wonder how anyone could believe—that the King's bringing in Austrian troops, that he's going to send them in to burn the suburbs where the National Assembly has support, that he's had explosives put under the hall where the Assembly's meeting and he's going to blow the whole lot of you sky-high . . . How would he get that much powder down into the cellar with you meeting overhead?" She sat cross-legged on the end of his bed as he set aside the violin. "But all over town, people are breaking into gunsmith shops for weapons. I looked out the gate today, and a lot of those men out there had muskets."

"Good." Jefferson drew her to him, the faint shift of muscle and rib comforting through the thin layers of muslin that divided flesh from flesh. "The will to liberty must be armed, Sally, and it must show itself willing to shed blood. After all these centuries of oppression, the French people are waking up. They're remembering that they are men. It's a frightening time. But the King is a man of good heart, and stronger than the creatures who surround him. He's shown himself willing to step beyond the old ideas, and to work with the Assembly. Only barbarians fear the clear light of freedom."

For a moment the glow of the single candle shone in his eyes, as if he looked beyond that small brightness to some greater glory. Then he smiled at her, as if in her silence he read her fear.

"And this house has very stout gates. I'm known to everyone in Paris as a friend of freedom, as a regular guest, if not a participant, in the Assembly. And I'm known to the King as the Minister of his sworn ally. We have nothing to fear from either side, Sally."

He cupped her face in both hands, brushed her lips with his. "It is a glorious time to be alive." Then he slipped the nightgown down from her shoulders, and they spoke no more of the King.

A short lifetime spent at Jefferson's elbow, watching him tinker with inventions that seldom worked out in practice, had taught Sally already that Tom was an incurable optimist who tended to believe whatever he wished were true. Still, when she was with him, whether at his side in the secret stillness of his bedroom or on the opposite side of the dining-room among the other servants, it was impossible to contradict him. Impossible to pull her heart away from the power of his words and his thought.

Lying beside him in the aftermath of loving, she felt safe. Able to look, as he did, beyond the walls of the Hôtel Langeac and the veils of time, to see this beautiful fairy-tale land that had been for so long bound in the chains of the King's power and the King's friends and the all-dominating Church. To hear its people saying, at last, *There is another way to live.*

The bells of the old abbey on Montmartre Hill chimed distantly. In her attic bedroom, Sally heard the striking-clock in the hallway answer with three clear notes. In another half-hour the cocks in all the kitchen-gardens up and down the Champs-Elysées would begin to crow. Jacques the kitchen-boy would be awake soon after that, as first light stained the sky.

Then it would be too late to flee.

Sally slipped from beneath the sheets of

her narrow bed. As she shed her nightgown, found the stays and dress and chemise she'd put out last night knowing she'd have to dress in the dark, she tried not to think about what she was doing. She laced up her shoes, braided her hair by touch alone, and put on a cap. Leaving Tom's room last night, with the candle sputtering out, she had forced herself not to look back. Not to think, *That was the last time.* But as she slipped away, she did pause in the doorway of the girls' room to make out, very dimly, the blur of white that was Polly's sheets, the dark smear of the little girl's hair.

Almost as much as Tom, she would miss Polly.

She would even miss Patsy, who for nearly a year had made her life a wretched guessing-game of frozen silences, petty frustrations, uncertainty, and spite.

And she would never see her family again.

⚜

The front gates would be locked, but Sally drifted like a shadow down to the kitchen, past the cubbyhole shared by Jimmy and the kitchen-boy Jacques. There were times in the past two years that Sally had hated her brother. First, because he had slyly maneuvered to push her and their master together, then later because he had come to her to borrow—or steal, if she wouldn't lend—the money that Tom would give her, for small pleasures like gloves and shoes and fans. After Patsy came home from the convent and started keeping the household books, Tom began leaving money for Sally in a drawer of his desk, rather than buy her things as he had before.

Sometimes, she was almost certain, Jimmy got to the drawer before she did.

She moved the iron bolts of the kitchen door, slipped it open barely the eight inches that would admit her body, then closed it softly again. She paused long enough to slip her feet into the pattens that protected her shoes from the black, acid Paris mud, then tucked her small bundle of belongings more firmly under her arm. At this hour, she should be fairly safe. Even rioters had to sleep sometime.

Still she felt breathless as she walked in the hushed stillness beneath the chestnut trees. The kitchen-boy had told her yesterday that while the rioting was going on in the *Étoile,* the lawyers and merchants who'd elected the representatives to the National Assembly had declared themselves a Governing Committee, and had called for forty-eight thousand militiamen to keep order and deal with the royal troops camped in the Bois de Boulogne and the vegetable-farms around Montmartre and Rambouillet, should they attack.

A glorious time to be alive.

Everything will be all right.

Desperately, Sally hoped so. Whatever was happening in Paris, it was going to be her home henceforth.

When Mr. Jefferson had said last November that he had asked to return to the United States for a short visit, to take Patsy and Polly home, Jimmy had announced that he would not return with them. As slavery did not exist in France, he declared, he was a free man, free to go or to stay. And he chose to stay.

Jefferson had answered, with cool reasonableness, that as Jimmy was a free man he must accept a free man's responsibilities, among them not robbing the man who had brought him to France and was paying for him to be taught the skills of French cookery by which he intended to make his living. Jimmy owed it to his *former* master—

Tom's voice had gritted over the word—to return to Virginia for as long as it would take him to train a replacement there. Then he would be free to go wherever he wished.

Sally had seen that for all the calm rationality of his answer, Tom was furious.

He's a white Virginia gentleman. Sally quickened her step between the chestnut trees, the half-seen pale blocks of great houses set back from the road in their park-like grounds. *Whatever he might write, or think, or say about the Rights of Man and the injustice of slavery, what he feels is what he feels.*

It was this dichotomy, this yawning gulf between his ideals and the demands of his flesh, that had made him turn away from her, all those months.

Wanting her in spite of every inner vow he had made to himself, the promise not to be the kind of master who would force a slave-girl.

Even at fifteen, turning from girl to woman, she had seen that in his eyes.

⚜

Within a week of her arrival with Sally in Paris, Polly had gone into a convent-school.

She and Patsy would come home on Sundays, to spend the afternoon and the night in their father's house and return to the Abbaye Royale de Panthemont in the morning, and on those nights Sally would sleep in a cubicle just off the girls' bedroom. Mr. Jefferson was strict with Sally, forbidding her to go about the streets by herself. In Williamsburg, and in Richmond, she knew instinctively the kinds of places it was safe for a young girl to go, and in Williamsburg she knew, too, that any black woman, and most black men, would be her friend in a difficult situation.

Mr. Jefferson had assigned M'sieu Petit the task of teaching Sally the finer skills of service, how to clean and mend and care for fine clothing, how to pack it loosely in paper and straw to be stored in trunks in the attic til it was wanted. How to starch and iron ruffles, and how to dress hair. Miss Patty herself had taught Sally the art of fancy sewing; the little Frenchman clicked his tongue approvingly, and put her to study with Mme. Dupré, the household seamstress and laundrywoman, the only female in the masculine establishment.

But these things didn't take up all Sally's

days. When Polly went off to the convent, Sally asked, a little timidly, if she might read in the library while Mr. Jefferson was out. "Mr. Adams would let me, sir. You can write and ask him, if I ever tore or damaged anything, or didn't put it back."

To her surprise Mr. Jefferson replied, "Of course you may, Sally. Even when you were quite a little girl I remember you were always careful with books."

She hadn't thought he'd noticed.

It was his library that brought them together—his library, and Sally's unquenchable curiosity about everything and anything. She picked up kitchen-French quickly, and the slurry argot of the cab-men, street-singers, and vendors of ratbane and brooms. But Mr. Jefferson hired a French tutor for both her and Jimmy. And often in the evenings, if he wasn't invited out to dine, Mr. Jefferson would take an hour to help her read the French of good books. More than once, having left her in the library deep in Mr. Pope's *Iliad* or some article in Diderot's *Encyclopédie,* he would return late to find her still there, reading by candlelight while the rest of the house slept.

Much of the time he'd be with Mr. Short,

his secretary from Virginia who also had a room in the attic of the Hôtel Langeac, or Mr. Humphreys, another semipermanent Virginian guest. But Mr. Humphreys had his own friends among the Americans in Paris, and Mr. Short was having an affair with a society lady. On many nights Mr. Jefferson would return, a little bemused, alone. Then if Sally was still in the library he'd bring a chair over next to hers, and they'd talk about the marvels described in the *Encyclopédie,* or he'd tell her the gossip that everyone traded in the Paris salons. Sometimes he'd play his violin for her, though his broken wrist was slow to heal, and the music that gave him such joy was also now a source of pain. Sally guessed that without his daughters during the week he was lonely. For a man as gregarious as he was, there was a part of him that needed his family; that needed faces familiar to him from home.

And in a sense, she and Jimmy *were* family. She had known Mr. Jefferson since the age of two, and thought no more of being alone with him at midnight, while all the household slept, than she would have thought of staying up late talking to one of her old uncles on the cabin step of the quarters along Mulberry Row.

Jimmy, who'd started out teasing her about getting wrinkles from too much reading, sometimes looked at her with that calculating glance and said, "No, you stay up however late you want, Sal. You learn lots of things, reading."

She hadn't known what he was getting at, at first. In that first year in Paris, so enchanted had she been with that whole glittering city that she'd barely been aware of the changes in her body.

She was used to people telling her she was pretty, and used to men—both black and white—trying to steal kisses. From the age of twelve Sally had been adept at defending herself with nails and knees from would-be swains in the quarters. And like any female slave from that age up, she had learned the risky maneuvers involved in saying *No* to white men without being punished for insolence.

She was aware that she was getting taller. She knew her hips had widened, and her breasts filled out, because just before her first Christmas in France, soon after her fifteenth birthday, she'd overheard Mr. Short remark to Jefferson, "By gad, Jefferson, that girl of yours is growing into a beauty." Not long after that Jimmy had taken her aside and said, "Now, you don't let those good-for-nothing footmen down in the kitchen go sweet-talkin' you into lettin' 'em kiss you, girl," and Sally had only stared at him in disbelief.

"I ain't *that* fond of garlic," she'd retorted, and Jimmy laughed.

But he'd sobered quickly, and said, "You be gettin' more'n a tongue full of garlic, if you let 'em catch you alone. You remember, girl, you in France now. You and me, we're free here. There's no law *here* that says a black girl can't scratch a white man's face if he puts his hand up her skirt."

"And how many times *you* had *your* face scratched, brother?"

"Enough to know."

Jefferson apparently shared Jimmy's concerns. The following March—1788—when he went to Amsterdam to meet Mr. Adams and sign a treaty with the Dutch, he arranged for Sally to board with the seamstress Mme. Dupré and her husband rather than stay in the Hôtel Langeac with the other servants. Sally had romped with Mme.

Dupré's grandchildren and helped Madame and her daughter in the kitchen. At the market one morning there she had encountered Sophie Sparling, who had helped nurse poor Miss Patty in her final months. Twenty-two now, Sophie was a paid companion to a Mrs. Luckton, an English widow who lived in the nearby rue des Lesdiguères.

Things were indeed different in Paris. Here, one wasn't immersed in a world of slaves and slaveholders. She had seen in the way Mr. Jefferson spoke to her, that with her fair complexion and long, silky hair, he sometimes almost forgot that her grandmother had been African. Maybe because she knew herself to be legally free, she found herself shedding the barriers of caution that existed between slaves and masters. Here, he could no longer give her away, or send her where she didn't wish to go.

Somehow, in Paris, it didn't matter that Sophie Sparling was the white granddaughter of a tobacco-planter, and Sally Hemings the not-quite-white granddaughter of an African woman who'd been enslaved and raped. It was good to speak English to another woman who remembered Virginia's green hills. A little to Sally's surprise, Sophie seemed to think so, too.

⚜

Looking back now on those weeks at Mme. Dupré's, Sally felt a desperate longing for the simplicity she'd known then.

That's how I want to live, she thought, as she hurried down the thinning gray gloom of the Champs-Elysées. *In a little house like that, just a couple of rooms that'll be my own.*

And she shivered, though the dawning day was already scorching hot.

Around her, the city seemed eerily still. The big houses set along the fashionable avenue were dark, shutters closed tight. But as she approached the open expanse of the Place Louis XV, she could see men clustered in the wine-shops under the colonnade, muttering and waving their arms.

Saturday—the day before yesterday— men and women had poured into the huge square to protest the King's dismissal of his Finance Minister M'sieu Necker, who— everyone in the kitchen said—was the only man capable of ending the famine and financial mess that had held the country in the grip of death for a year. Cheap pamphlets—commissioned by Necker's *salonnière* wife—praised his skills, and vomited scatalogical invective on the men the King had selected to replace him.

The demonstrators had been met by a regiment of hired German soldiers, under the command of a cousin of the Queen's.

Dried blood still smeared the cobblestones, dark under a blanket of dust and drawing whirling clouds of flies.

Sally lowered her head and cut through a corner of the square, with barely a glance at the equestrian statue of a former King, now smeared with dung and garbage. Another day she would have walked through the Tuileries gardens rather than along the *quais* at the riverside, for the river stank like a sewer. But she felt uneasy about going into those aisles of hedges and trees. Men roved the streets and alleyways of Paris these days, men out of work and hungry—angry, too. With the shortages of bread, the tangled national finances that were driving more and more men out of employment, there were fewer who could pay for servants, barbers, new clothes, new shoes, food.

As she hurried along the dark *quais,* Sally

could glimpse them: long dirty hair, baggy trousers, bare legs, the wooden shoes of peasants. Some moved about the garden, others slept beneath its trees.

Everything will be all right.

She felt sick with fright.

⚜

Those days at Mme. Dupré's, those days of walking about the city with Sophie, seemed to her now like the last time that her life had been normal: that she had been herself, her *real* self. When Sophie could get away from her employer, which was seldom—Mrs. Luckton was worse than any plantation mistress—they would rove together through the gardens of the Luxembourg and the Tuileries, or wander among the exceedingly expensive shops of the Palais Royale. They'd pretended to shop for silks of the most newly fashionable hues—"flea's thigh" and "goose-turd green"—and admired the jeweled rings and watches—or whole coffee-sets or sewing-kits or travelers' writing desks of enamel and gold—at Le Petit Dunkerque.

At the cafés beneath Palais Royale's arcades, street-corner orators had denounced the King, the Austrian Queen, and the horrifying thing called The Deficit which France owed to everyone. In the evenings at Mme. Dupré's, Sally would read, sometimes the books she'd buy at the booksellers along the narrow streets, sometimes the newspapers and pamphlets that Mme. Dupré always had about the house—political, filthily scurrilous, and occasionally fascinating. On other evenings, she'd read and reread the letters Mr. Jefferson would send her, from Amsterdam, Rotterdam, Strasbourg.

Brief notes, but full of canal-locks, churches, what was being said, and worn. He knew she was eager to hear such things, of a world even wider than the one she now knew.

On the evening of the twenty-third of April he returned, and Sally walked back with Mme. Dupré on the morning of the twenty-fourth. She ran up to her attic room with her little satchel of clothes, her long hair loose upon her shoulders as it was the fashion to wear it in Paris, and had just emerged from the back stairs on her way down to the kitchen to see Jimmy, when she came face-to-face with Mr. Jefferson in the hall.

He was in his shirtsleeves, stepping from the door of his own room, and stopped as she cannoned into him. She backed away laughing, and dropped him a curtsey. He said, "Sally," as if for just a moment he was making sure that it *was* Sally, and not someone else who looked like her. A little hesitantly, he added, "It's good to see you again. I missed you."

"And I you, sir." Though he might still own her mother and her brothers and sisters as if they were so many stallions and mares, she understood, from her friendship with Sophie, what kind of life the daughters of a planter would have to look forward to, if their father were to simply free his slaves.

And because he looked weary from his journey, she added impulsively, "Thank you for writing to me, sir. It was good to get your letters."

"There were a thousand things more on that journey that I wish you could have seen." He seemed about to say something else, but then fell silent, and in silence seemed to study her face. In silence she returned his look, aware, for the first time since her childhood, of the straightness of his carriage, and the fine long-boned hands permanently stained about the fingers with ink.

He was the first to turn away. Sally walked, rather than scampered, down the back stairs to the kitchen, and through that day and the night she found her mind returning to small details of his voice and the sharp points of his shoulder-bones under the white linen of his shirt.

This awareness of Mr. Jefferson as a man, this new fascination that drew her eyes and her thoughts back to him, strengthened through the summer of '88. Sometimes she could be friends with him as she'd used to be, when on an occasional quiet evening in the library they'd talk about the canals in the Rhineland or the emissary of the pirate-monarch of Tripoli whom Jefferson had met in London. Then unexpectedly, it seemed, she would be fiercely conscious of him and of herself, and the blood would rush to her face, smothering her in confusion and heat. There were times when she felt that he must be aware of this, because he took to avoiding her. When he would return late, without Mr. Short, those hot summer nights, to find her reading in the library, he would not get the chessboard or settle down to talk, but would say only, "I think it's time you went to bed."

It grieved her, that feelings she could not help were causing him to send her away.

That summer, as the bankrupt French Treasury issued promissory notes that no one would accept and freak hailstorms lashed the countryside destroying most of the wheat-crop, another Virginian visited Paris. Thomas Mann Randolph, twenty-two, swarthy, and tall, was newly come from four years at the University of Edinburgh and Mr. Jefferson's cousin. The servants were accustomed to friends of the American Minister coming to stay for days or weeks at a time—the artist John Trumbull had remained for months. Sally's first encounter with young Mr. Randolph consisted of being seized from behind as she emerged from the back stairs into the upstairs hall, shoved against the wall, and ruthlessly kissed.

She slithered free and fled, hearing behind her Mr. Short call out jovially, where had Randolph taken himself off to? She reached the kitchen trembling, and helped herself to some of the coffee there to take the taste of the man's liquor-sodden tongue out of her mouth. "What is it, little cabbage?" inquired

Mme. Dupré, and Sally only shook her head. On any number of occasions the seamstress had expressed her contempt for masters who took advantage of their female staff, white or black. Sally knew she'd take the matter to the master of the house.

She might be a free woman now, but she'd learned in childhood that a black girl's word wouldn't be taken against a white man's in the matter of anything from stolen kisses on up to forcible rape. Mr. Jefferson was a Virginian, and Tom Randolph was his cousin, the son of one of his oldest friends. There were things that Virginians, white and black, knew about other Virginians: what they would and would not do, what they would and would not and almost *could* not speak of.

When all was said and done, it was only a kiss.

So Sally said nothing.

She was glad of her silence, seeing how Mr. Jefferson welcomed his handsome cousin, and introduced him to the salons and societies that made up his own circle of friends. When not in liquor, Tom Randolph was a quiet young man, charming and intelligent, and shared Mr. Jefferson's love of books and agriculture. When Patsy and Polly came home from the convent that Sunday, Randolph bowed over Patsy's hand and joked with her about their childhood back in Virginia, and Jefferson beamed with fatherly joy.

At sixteen, Patsy was taller than most Frenchmen—nearly six feet—and as nearly pretty as she would ever get. Her delicate complexion had been subdued to freckleless alabaster by the convent's dimness, her square face surrounded by fine ringlets of the red-gold color Sally remembered Mr. Jefferson's being. Randolph spoke to her about horses and dogs, and asked about her music. Back in the kitchen, Sally commented to Jimmy that of course Randolph was attentive: Mr. Jefferson had some eight thousand acres of Virginia land, upwards of a hundred and fifty slaves, and no son. Patsy and Polly were his only heirs.

Tom Randolph stayed for weeks, and during that time, when Mr. Jefferson and Mr. Short were away in the daytime, Sally stuck close to the kitchen. From the footmen she knew Randolph spent a number of his days sampling the prostitutes at the Palais Royale; she didn't need the other servants to tell her of the man's foul temper and occasional drunkenness. One Thursday evening in August, when Mr. Jefferson was away dining with one of his philosophical societies and, she thought, Randolph was absent also, Randolph waited in the darkness of Polly's bedroom, for Sally to pass its door. When she bit him he struck her, hard, the way a man would strike a man; tearing out of his pawing grip, she slashed at him with the candle-scissors from the bedside table, and felt the sharp upper blade rip flesh.

"Nigger bitch!" he gasped, and stumbled away from her, a black bulk huge against the shadows. "You lead me on, you give me that bitch-eyes come-hither—"

Sally said nothing, kneeling in the tangled sheets with her dress torn open to the waist, panting, praying he wouldn't come at her again for she knew his strength was too much for a second struggle. But he only spat at her and lurched out the door. Only then did she begin to shake, her weapon almost dropping from her hand. She clutched at the bedpost, then sank against it: *I mustn't faint,* she thought, *and I mustn't cry . . .*

Had he gone upstairs to his own room? *Is he waiting by the stairs? Waiting to follow me up to the attic when I leave this room? Is there no place now within this house that I'll be safe?* Her breath came in a ragged sob. *You lead me on,* he'd said—something every white man said about every slave-woman he bedded.

The creak of the doorsill and the flare of candlelight alerted her too late and she swung around, scrambled up, fumbling at the scissors.

Mr. Jefferson stood in the doorway.

It was the only time she'd seen him truly angry—

"Who did this?" He set the candle down and caught her shoulders in his strong hands, then the next second—drew her torn dress over her breasts. "Are you hurt? Sally?"

"No, sir. I—I didn't see." No Virginian, she well knew, ever believed true ill of a family member. That was just something about Virginians. *You lead me on. . . .*

Would any Virginia gentleman truly believe there was any harm in "stealing a kiss" from a black servant-girl?

"Are you sure? Because I promise you,

whoever it was will be dismissed from my service."

Not the smallest thought that it was the only other Virginia gentleman in the house.

"No, sir," she whispered. "I truly didn't see." Her eyes held his unflinching. It was even the truth. She'd known her attacker by his voice, and by the stink of the liquor on his breath.

He moved his hand as if he would touch the bruise on her face. She heard him draw in his breath. Then his eyes turned aside. "I am most sorry—and most angry—that this has happened, Sally. And I will speak to Mr. Petit, to let it be known among the servants that I *will not tolerate* members of my household being abused. You are here under my protection. I promise you, this will not happen again." He hesitated, his eyes still on her in the candlelight, in her torn dress with her hair streaming down her shoulders. "Shall I send for Mme. Dupré? She's gone home, but I will send a note. . . ."

Sally shook her head. She wanted only that the incident be over. Only that she could go to him like the child she'd once been, cling to him for comfort. "No, sir. Thank you, sir."

He left the room with swift abruptness. She heard his steps retreat down the hall, the opening and closing of his door. Later that night, lying awake, she heard, hesitant and stiff, the music of the violin.

⚜

I mustn't think about that.

Sally stopped in her tracks where the long soot-black wall of the old Louvre Palace stood above the stone embankment and the river. In the tangle of filthy streets on the other side of the Louvre, she could hear voices muttering, a man's occasional angry shout. *Already?* A sick qualm turned her cold—fright? she wondered. The stink of the river in the hot dawn? Or some other cause?

Men strode along the embankment, not the clerks and hairdressers you'd usually see this time of the morning going to work—certainly not the bakers, coming in from Gonesse, for there hadn't been bread sold in the city for weeks.

Dirty men, ragged and angry, armed as the mob had been armed yesterday, with clubs and butcher-knives. Somewhere a church bell began to ring, a wild alarm-note, waking the city to another day of fear.

If I go back to the Hôtel now, someone will have noticed I'm gone. When he comes home, he'll ask me where I was. And why I fled.

She knew instinctively he'd find some way not to let her leave. Beneath that gentle exterior he had a steely will and an iron determination to get what he wanted—to hold what he had. She'd seen that with Jimmy.

It was even worse because she couldn't imagine living without him, any more than the ocean could imagine not yearning toward the Moon. The thought of never hearing his voice again, never feeling on her flesh the touch of his hands, never tasting his mouth, turned her sick with grief.

She pushed the thoughts from her mind, and quickened her pace.

For the week between Randolph's assault and the young man's departure, Jefferson barely spoke to her. But she felt his eyes on her, whenever they were in a room together. A dozen times she felt him on the verge of speaking, of putting his hand on her shoulder. He'd be out late, most nights, but still, hours after she heard him return—heard Mr. Short go to bed, footsteps palpable through the floor of her little attic in the still of the night—she'd hear him playing. More than once she heard him open his door, but though she listened for his step on the attic's narrow stair she heard nothing. It was as if he were simply standing at its foot, looking up into the dark.

And she knew that one night he would come to her.

She saw it as clearly as if it had already happened, as if it were a memory or a dream. Almost it seemed to her she could look through the walls and see him, standing in the dark of the hall, barefoot in his nightshirt, his hair unqueued on his shoulders. On one of those dense summer nights when all the city lay waiting for the cleansing war-drums of thunder, she thought, *If I tell him No, he will go away. But then he'll send me away—back to Virginia.* Not to punish her, but so that things would not be, in his own mind, messy and awkward. How could a Virginia gentleman go on living under the same roof with a servant-girl he had tried—and failed—to bed?

Even asking her would change what lay between them, forever.

Much as he strove to transform the world, and alter how men lived their lives, in his own life he feared and hated change.

But their friendship had already changed, beyond the point where it could be pressed back into its earlier form.

He wanted her, when all his life he had despised slave-owners like his father-in-law, men who took concubines from among their bondswomen.

I am a free woman here. Back at Monticello or Eppington, Sally would already be wed, or as wed as slaves ever got. She'd be living with a man and undoubtedly carrying his child. In the markets here she'd seen girls her own age, round-bellied under the short corsets of pregnancy, and one of Mme. Dupré's sons-in-law was every bit of Mr. Jefferson's forty-six years.

And so she waited in the darkness. Not knowing what to expect, not knowing what she would say, if and when he were to come into her room, and stretch out on the narrow bed at her side.

And one night, when summer rain poured down the steep slate roofs and lightning flashed over the river, she heard the creak of his door opening below her, and the stealthy pad of naked feet on the attic stair.

⚜

The previous winter—the coldest within living memory, when the river froze solid so that food supplies couldn't come into the city and hundreds of the poor died nightly in the snow-choked streets—Sophie Sparling had parted company from her employer, owing to the Luckton equivalent of Mr. Randolph, in this case Mrs. Luckton's son. She shared a garret with three other women in rue de Vieille Monnaie, close to the Cemetery of the Holy Innocents. When Sally reached the place, the door of the old town house stood open and breathed out a stink like the halitus of Hell. Even at this hour men clustered in the wine-shop in the building's ground floor; someone inside was shouting, "It will be today, brothers! They'll march in and put the lot of us to the sword—yes, and our wives and our children, too!—because we've refused to accept one more day of being fucked in the arse by the King's ministers and the Bitch-Queen's hell-begotten friends! On the lamp-post with them, I say!

Because we have cried out against them they will murder us in our beds!"

Sally took a deep breath and ducked inside. The stair was still black with night, slippery with feces and garbage.

Sophie must still be here. She can't have gone.

She had no idea where she would go or what she would do if Sophie wasn't there.

The garret was a long bare room with half a dozen smaller leading off it. Three families lived there, the women pounding at a half-loaf of mold-gray bread with hammers, to break off pieces for the gaggle of children. One of Sophie's roommates had just come up with a jug of what was supposed to be coffee. ". . . puttin' up barricades, to slow 'em down," she was saying to the others, in her slurry Parisian French. "There's one already by the Filles de la Visitation and another in the rue du Temple. They're sayin' we're gonna march on the Invalides. There's weapons there—"

"Sally!"

Sophie Sparling stood in the doorway, holding aside the curtain that served for a door. She didn't ask what Sally was doing here, at this hour of the morning. Only held

out her hand, drew her into her own tiny
room, where two girls and a whiskery man
slept on the sagging bed. Light leaked in
from a single window, broken and stuffed
with rags. The angry ringing of the alarm-
bells, the *tocsins,* penetrated even here.

Sally said, "I think I'm with child."

⚜

Sally took a deep breath. "I haven't had my
monthly course since May; I'm going to
start showing soon. I don't want him to
know."

Sophie had worked with her surgeon father, and had been a midwife's assistant,
while she and her mother were taking
refuge with Cornwallis's troops, after her father's death. There wasn't much about the
relations between men and women that
wasn't written in those cold gray eyes.
"What do you want to do?" she asked.

"You told me, last time we talked, about
your friend Mme. de Blancheville, that's willing to help girls who're willing to work. Mr.
Jefferson's asked the Congress for leave to
take Patsy and Polly home. Then he'll come
back, he says. But that doesn't mean he'd
bring *me* back, for all what he says. And he

wouldn't bring a baby, not on a ship." Her jaw tightened, at the almost physical agony of the choice she had made. "In Virginia my baby'd be a slave."

"As would you." Sophie pointed it out bluntly.

Sally breathed a tiny snort of rueful laughter. "You're gonna think me crazy, Sophie— I know you do already. But to tell you God's truth, I really don't care whether I'm slave or I'm free, as long as I can be with him."

"You'll care when he gets tired of you."

"If you mean he'd sell me off, he won't. I know him and he won't."

"You don't know him." An abyss of bitterness echoed in Sophie's voice. "Right now he may even believe he loves you. Has he said so? I understand they generally do. At least if they're talking to white women."

"I don't know all of him, no," Sally replied quietly. "I don't think anybody does. And that doesn't matter now because I'm not going back. Not to Virginia, not to his house today or ever. I don't know the difference between thinking you love someone and really loving them, and no, he hasn't said it. I just know he won't let me stay here."

Sophie's expression was a silent reminder

of Sally's legal freedom in the Kingdom of France.

Sally shook her head. "He doesn't let go, Sophie. Not of what he sees as his. He was furious when Jimmy said he'd leave him. When poor Polly didn't want to come here, after her little sister died, he had her kidnapped, just about; tricked onto the ship. In all these years, he's never really let go of Miss Patty. It tears him up inside," she added, more quietly. "If it was just me, it would be different. But if it was just me, it wouldn't be such a problem, because he'd bring me back here next year—"

"If he still cared."

She whispered, "He'll still care. But it isn't just me."

And she knew herself well enough to know that when she was with him, she couldn't think clearly. Any more than a moth can think clearly about the amber glory of flame.

"Will you take me to your Mme. de Blancheville? And ask her to take me in?"

The din in the outer attic had grown louder, men's voices shouting now, and children crying. Then jostle and clatter as everyone left and went down the stairs. The man in the bed sat up with a grunt, ambled out into the outer room to piss in the bucket there—the few windows being too high for the purpose. "Have you eaten?" Sophie asked, and unearthed a tin box from beneath her pallet on the floor, then led Sally out to the now-empty outer attic to share her bread and what was left of the coffee.

This stuff was like eating a rock, the flour so adulterated that even soaked in coffee, it gritted on Sally's teeth. Jefferson had told Sally that the bread being sold in Paris was nearly inedible, but as American Minister—and a plantation-owner used to buying in bulk—he at least had a store of flour laid by from last summer.

"You know Mme. de Blancheville works servants hard," cautioned Sophie. "Far worse than Mr. Jefferson. You won't be allowed to go out of the house, and she'll require you to become a Catholic."

"It won't be forever. Mr. Jefferson thinks he'll get leave soon. I would have waited til just before they left, so he couldn't look for me, but I feared I'd start showing before then. He talks about what a wonderful thing it is, that the French are casting off the chains of a thousand years, but he still doesn't want his daughters here in the middle of it."

"Mr. Jefferson has always impressed me as a man who doesn't quite understand why things *can't* be the way they *should* be: why the Revolution that he considers so purifying to the human soul—God knows why, he can't have encountered some of the members of the patriot militia I did—doesn't *actually* purify the individual men who participate. Maybe he considers that it purified *his* soul and that's all he's aware of."

"He thinks men can be better than they are."

"Maybe they can." Sophie rose and collected a rather battered straw hat. "But politics won't make them so. We'd better go. If there is another riot and the King's troops do march in to break it up, I'd rather be close enough to Mme. de Blancheville's to take refuge there."

As they descended the stair, Sally said, "After he's gone I'll write to him. I'll tell him where I am, and why I left as I did. Then when he returns next year, he can do as he likes. He'll be angry," she added softly. "But I think he'll understand."

Sophie sniffed.

"As soon as the baby's born I'll start looking for something to do for my living. I can
cut and pattern dresses as well as sew. After he's gone I'll see if Mme. Dupré—our
seamstress—will take me in. I'd go to her
now but I think she'd tell him, or tell someone in the house, and it would get back to
him. She's not good at keeping her mouth
shut. And she always hated it, that a man
would be able to have women and girls as
slaves."

"It's hard to find grounds upon which to
dispute her sentiments," Sophie remarked
drily, as they reached the street. The mob
around the wine-shop was larger now, and
angrier, stirring and churning like swarming
bees. The same orator or another was still
shouting at the crowd, and men were waving pamphlets, fresh-printed and smudgy
with cheap ink. Sally glimpsed the head-
ings, ARISE! and FRIEND OF THE PEOPLE. She
shivered. This, and the mob who had
surged past the Hôtel yesterday to burn the
customs barrier, were a far cry from Tom's
sharp-featured face in candlelight as he
spoke of the National Assembly meeting in
Versailles, of the soldiers who were deserting the King's regiments in droves to join

with the men who demanded an end to royal privilege and royal inefficiency.

She'd seen pamphlets of the same sort in the kitchen at the Hôtel Langeac, and suspected it was Mme. Dupré who'd brought them in.

She was almost certain it was Mme. Dupré who'd told Patsy.

☙

All the servants knew, as servants always knew. During those first few weeks, Jefferson was discreet—with Mr. Short and various other guests in his household he could hardly be otherwise. But he quietly arranged times to meet her away from the house, to visit the gardens of the royal châteaus of Marly and St.-Cloud or to walk in the far pathways of the Bois de Boulogne, where they were unlikely to meet anyone Tom knew. Once or twice he took her, in the evenings, to the Palais Royale, masked and with her hair powdered gray, and had an artist there paint a miniature of her on ivory, to carry in a locket, out of sight of all.

They would return separately to the house, to meet again in his bedroom, behind the bolted door.

In France Sally was, to all intents and purposes, a white woman, only a little more dusky of skin than the Spaniards and Italians who carried in their veins the blood of the Levant. It was only the Virginians in the household—Mr. Short, and Patsy, and Polly—who saw her as African, and then only because they'd been brought up from childhood to look for the subtle signs.

How Tom himself saw her, Sally wasn't sure. She had heard him say to Mr. Short how abhorrent he found the mingling of the white and the African races, but they were speaking of those slave-owners who thought themselves entitled to cover any bondswoman who took their fancy. She had heard him say to several of his French guests that blacks were "inferior in the faculties of reason" to whites, but this hadn't stopped him from teaching any number of children at Monticello to read. He certainly talked to her, and always had, as if he expected her to follow his reasoning, and gave every sign of enjoying their conversations as much as he enjoyed lying in her arms.

But then, Sally suspected that if Tom were being led to the stake, he'd get wrapped up in conversation with the executioners.

Did he see her differently, she wondered, because she was nearly white? Because he'd known her from childhood? Because she and her family were halfway between the quarters and the Big House, neither white nor field-hand black?

Because she was Miss Patty's sister? Because she was "family"?

However Tom saw her—whatever they were to one another, in the enclosed and secret world of his bedroom—Sally knew that to his older daughter, she was and would always be not only a slave, but a betrayer.

She'd known the instant someone told Patsy. The silences, the spate of complaints about insolence, laziness, and imagined thefts, were unmistakable.

Jefferson would have guessed, too. But Patsy, who loved her father with a ferocious passion, would neither ask nor accuse. And it was unthinkable, for Tom to discuss with Sally the reasons for his daughter's sudden enmity. If Sally was almost white when she was alone with Tom, the moment they stepped out into the rest of the house—the moment he saw her through Patsy's eyes—she was black again, slipping from one set of rules to another, the way she herself was long used to slipping from the formal, refined speech of white folks to the language of the quarters as soon as she was with her family.

He admonished Sally gently—in Patsy's presence—to be a little more humble, a little more mindful of her duties, and like a good Virginian, Sally had murmured, "Yes, sir," and apologized to Patsy. In her father's presence there wasn't much Patsy could say, since the apology was for insolence and laziness, rather than the true crime of lying with Patsy's father—or being to him what Patsy herself could never be. When Patsy and Polly had returned to the convent, and Tom next spoke to Sally alone, he had only asked, with nebulous gentleness, that she be "patient and good."

Sally had not pressed the matter. She had known, long before the day he first told her she'd be going to Eppington with Polly, that he never let anyone talk to him about things he didn't want to talk about.

Then a week later Patsy announced that she was going to remain at the Convent of Panthemont, and take her vows as a nun.

Jefferson was livid. Like a good philosopher he waited two days to cool down, then went to the convent and withdrew both girls, hiring a tutor for young Polly—or Maria, as she was now called, the fashionable variant of Mary—and making Patsy, on the day after her seventeenth birthday, the hostess of his household.

And with his daughters under his roof, that was the end of even such small freedom as Sally and Tom once had enjoyed.

Had that been what Patsy intended all along?

⚜

The day had turned savagely hot. The tall soot-black houses and narrow streets of this most ancient portion of the city trapped the heat like a bath of tepid glue. And over all, the vengeful clanging of the church bells.

Where the rue de la Verrerie crossed the rue St.-Martin Sophie halted, hissed, "Christ Jesus!" through her teeth. Two carts had been dragged shaft-to-shaft across the rue St.-Martin. The whole of the neighborhood, it seemed, swarmed over them like ants, each man or woman adding something to the reinforcement of the wall. Timbers from houses wrecked or burned, doors, window-gratings, shutters, baskets filled with earth. Chunks of cobblestones dug up from the streets; hampers, roof-tiles, rolled-up mattresses, the ruins of a shed. Someone had broken into a wine-shop—the sign was worked into the barricade—and people passed the bottles among them as they hoisted stones and wood into place.

About thirty feet down the rue de la Verrerie another barricade was being built. A knot of the new civic militia stood by that one watching the work, muskets in their hands. Sophie remarked, "I wonder if they have the slightest idea how to load those things, let alone aim them. Let's backtrack to the rue de Diamant. They'll be barricading the bridges if we try to go by the *quais*."

"Do you think the King's troops really will march on the city today?"

Sophie cocked her head to listen, as if anything might be heard over the wrangle of the bells, the shouting around the barricade. "I think they'd better," she remarked after a moment, "if they don't want the whole city torn apart."

When the bell-ringers paused to spit on their hands, or the din diminished around those monstrous walls of cobblestone and garbage, Sally thought she could hear, far off, the crack of gunshots.

"That'll be the Invalides," Sophie told her. "I think that's where my neighbors said they were going to get guns. It's clear on the other side of the river. Let's go this way."

But there was another barricade where they came out of the tangle of medieval streets near the rue St.-Lazare. In the end they walked nearly to the priory of St.-Martin des Champs before they found a place that wasn't crowded with armed and angry rioters. By that time the distant shouting was audible over the church bells. "Do you think the King's troops have attacked?" whispered Sally.

"We'd have heard gunfire."

Even in streets where no looting was going on, everyone was out, no one was working. In other neighborhoods every window was shuttered, every door locked, like streets of the dead. It was like being outside in a storm, not knowing where lightning would hit. "Why doesn't the King do something?" Sally asked, wondering how she was going to live in this city, how she was going to get through her time, bear her child, with all this going on and maybe worse. It couldn't last, she knew—if nobody was making any money they'd all be starving, they'd have to go back to work. . . .

"The King doesn't do anything because he's waiting for the good people of France to come to their senses." The girls flattened back in the doorway of a church as a crowd of armed men jostled past. At least half of them wore the white coats of the King's troops, unbuttoned over dirty shirts and stained with wine and mud. "And because he doesn't trust his army to obey their officers. Damnation!" she added, stepping out of their shelter and moving on.

There were barricades in the rue du Temple, huge ones; it looked like the frenzied citizens were tearing down a house to build them.

Thirsty in the scorching heat and feeling slightly sick, Sally followed her friend as they tried to work their way around the mobs. The sun hammered down into the streets where for four days now neither garbage nor horse-dung had been collected. The air seemed to be a flashing river of black and silver with whirling flies. Sally stopped, gasping, in the doorway of an apartmentblock and vomited. Sophie gripped her arms to support her.

Head spinning, she leaned against the coarse stucco, wondering if she'd faint. Hoping, dizzy and sickened, that M'sieu Petit and Jimmy had barred the doors of the Hôtel Langeac tight, that everyone was safe inside . . .

"Listen!"

Sally raised her head, dark curls straggling from under her cap, sticking to her face with sweat. Gunfire. And the surging shouts of men.

"Oh, thank God. The army—"

"No. If it was regular troops they'd be firing in volleys."

Sally swallowed, the taste in her mouth indescribable. "Is that near the Place Royale?"

"Right behind it," said Sophie grimly.

People were running, when they stepped into the street again, men and women—children, too, fierce little urchins with eyes like stray cats'—clutching knives and shouting. Sally staggered, giddy. A nightmare of distant gunfire and shouting, of church bells hammering. Someone running by screeched something about the men of the faubourgs coming in, the artisans and laborers who lived around the city outside the customs-barrier. Sally caught the words "powder in the Bastille," the old royal fortress that was still used as prison and arsenal. *Had someone got word to Tom? Would he try to ride back from Versailles to be with his family?* Sally knew he'd try, prayed someone would stop him before he got caught in crossfire, when the troops finally marched in. The stink of smoke snagged her throat. Houses must be burning somewhere.

Keep him safe. Dear God, keep them all safe, even Patsy. . . .

They reached the Place Royale to find it silent, as if stricken with plague. The shops along the colonnade had been looted. Some of the brown stone town houses were locked and shuttered, barred. Others stood open, scattered trails of silverware, gowns, curtains, and broken furniture marking like blood-tracks from wounds where the rioters had gone. Exhausted, sick with terror—for Sophie was right, the Bastille lay only a street or two away and the shouting and gunshots seemed right at their elbows—Sally quickened her pace to a run. "What number?" she panted over her shoulder. "Dear God, let her open the door to us. . . ."

Sophie said, "Number fourteen." She walked more slowly. Sally paused in her flight, looked behind her impatiently, and saw the look on the older woman's narrow, pale face. Turned and looked ahead of her, at the closest broken doorway with its dribble of smashed china and spilled flour and apples. Looked up at the number, carved in its little stone shield above the door.

No, she thought, as if God had somehow made a mistake and if she pointed it out to Him, He'd rectify it. *No.*

Though it was bludgeoningly obvious what had happened, Sally had to go to the broken gateway, climb the graceful stair to the rooms above.

Blood had been shed in the drawing-room. It was splashed on the pale green wall and on the carpet. The cabinets were broken open and everything of value taken. Even the candles had been stripped from their holders. In the terrible stillness, the noise of shouting around the Bastille was hideously loud.

She looked back as Sophie came into the

room behind her. "Would you know where they'd have gone?"

Sophie shook her head. Trembling, Sally sank into a brocaded chair. "Let's check the kitchen," said Sophie reasonably, "and get something to eat. There's a fountain in the square where we can get water. Do you want to come back to my room, or try to get home?"

"Your place," Sally breathed. The thought of standing up again, of going with Sophie down to the kitchen and out to the fountain, was hideous, but even more hideous was the thought of being in that blood-splashed room alone.

There was of course not a thing to eat in the kitchen. By the state of the garbage it looked like the house had been looted yesterday, when the mobs burned the customs-barricades.

How can this be happening?

The old man who'd sold her and Tom lemonade in the Bois—was he shooting at the garrison in the Bastille, trying to get whatever gunpowder was there? Mme. Dupré's shabby son-in-law and her chubby, joking daughter—were they in the rue St.-Martin adding cobblestones to the barricade?

How was she going to live in this?

"We'd best get back." Sophie finished her inspection of the pantry stores, returned to where Sally sat at the kitchen table. The shouting nearby seemed frenzied now. It surged like the sea in a storm. There was no more shooting, but the wild baying of the mob had a deeper note to it, a savage shrieking of triumph. "It sounds like everyone's still at the Bastille. We can probably get down the rue St.-Antoine ahead of them. That way, they'll be between us and the troops, if troops ever come in."

"Do you think they will?" Sally got to her feet, shook out her skirts, so tired she felt she would die. She picked up her parcel of clean chemises and stockings, Tom's letters to her and a few books, and the silver combs he'd bought her for her hair, a parcel she'd carried through the whole of that broiling, nightmare day.

Sophie's gray eyes were like dirty ice, as if she were seeing a repeat of a bad play that had disgusted her once already. "Ever, you mean?"

Sally hadn't thought in those terms.

They crossed the Place to its handsome gatehouse, hastened down the short street that connected it with the rue St.-Antoine. They were almost at the corner when a burst of shouting enveloped them. Howls of diabolical glee rolled down the larger street like the blast of cold wind before a storm. The mob surged into view.

Army deserters, laborers, laundresses. Butchers who hadn't had meat to cut in weeks, bakers who had neither flour nor wood. Students and clerks, gunpowder and dirt making their faces as black as their coats. Housewives with a child on one hip and a pike in the other hand, hair unloosed, screaming like vicious harpies. The reek of smoke and sulfur churned in the summer air.

The men in the front row carried pikes. At first, against the hot glare of the sun, Sally thought that what was impaled on them were loaves of bread.

Then she saw they had faces.

The parcel fell from her hands and she pressed her fingers to her mouth, and it seemed to her that the entire world shifted, like one of Tom's optical experiments when he moved the lens. No food, no law, no army, no safe place to hide—no going back to what the world had been.

Those men—one of the heads still wore

the gold-embroidered hat of a garrison commander—had waked up this morning as she had, in a world where the King ruled France and things would eventually be sorted out. The eyes they'd opened this morning looked at her as the mob passed the end of the street: stared past her into a future incomprehensible, rushing like a world-consuming fireball at them all.

The mob passed, hauling with them carts and wagons filled with sacks—gunpowder or the garrison's food?—and, riding in the carts, six or seven bewildered and terrified elderly men, all the prisoners who had been kept in the old fortress's cells. Sally was afraid, when she and Sophie crept out at last, that the cobbles would be splattered with the garrison officers' blood. But even that had been swallowed up by the black Paris mud.

"Can you come with me as far as the Champs-Elysées?" she whispered to Sophie. "I have to go back. To go home. I want to go home."

⚜

It was twilight before Sally and Sophie reached the double line of chestnut trees, the handsome houses of the Champs-Elysées. There were barricades in the rue St.-Honoré, and crowds still gathered, shouting, around orators in the Place Louis XV. Sally suspected that's where the mob had taken their trophies from the Bastille: gunpowder, food, and severed heads. Wine, too. As she and Sophie made their way along those quiet fashionable streets, past the shuttered town houses, she could hear the drunken shouting.

He's got to be all right, she told herself, her anxiety growing as they passed first one house and then another silent and dark. *He was to ride out to the National Assembly today at Versailles. He wouldn't have heard about the rioting until noon or maybe later. They were all over at the Bastille on the other side of the city. . . .*

The thought of what she would do—of what they would all do—if Tom had been killed was more than she could bear.

Please, God. Please.

Beside that, the prospect of another several months in a household ruled by that bitterly silent girl who had once been her friend, of six weeks and maybe more sharing a ship's cabin with her, faded.

Please, God, don't let me find at Langeac what I found at the Place Royale. . . .

In her heart she saw the familiar courtyard strewn with shattered crockery and dropped silverware, with scarves and gloves and the broken corpses of books. Saw the rooms she knew sacked and emptied. Saw blood splashed on the library walls.

Not that. Please not that.

"Sally!"

The voice stopped her in her tracks—almost stopped the breath in her lungs. In the deepening twilight she couldn't imagine how he'd even seen her, much less recognized her.

As if she were no more than a trick of shadow, Sophie faded back into the trees and was gone.

Sally was alone when Jefferson came striding across the road to her, breaking into a run. He caught her in his arms, crushed her, as if uncertain whether to embrace her or shake her til her teeth rattled: "Are you all right? Where did you go? Why did you leave? Don't ever do that—don't *ever* go out like that. . . ."

She pulled back from him, looked up into

his face. *I'm a free woman,* she told herself. *And I can choose.*

It took all her strength to speak. "I'm going to have a baby." She saw him reel back, eyes widening at the news, all the anger going out of him for the moment. *Say it, Sally, say it*—"And I didn't want my baby born a slave."

His face changed. Blood surged up under the thin fair skin as he understood that she hadn't meant to come back. His eyes turned bleak with the same pale rage she had seen when her brother had dared to bargain with him. When Patsy had turned from him toward the Church that he hated.

An anger made greater, maybe, because he had no reply that would fit in with the ideals he had proclaimed before all the world.

She went on, "But I can't stay here in France now. The men—the mob—They killed the soldiers at the Bastille. They carried their heads down the street, and the King's army didn't do a thing. There's no bread in the city, no food—"

"And that's the only reason you came back?" He caught her face in his hand, forcing her eyes to his. The strength in his hand was enough, she felt, to break her jaw. "Because you were afraid?"

She closed her eyes, her whole body rigid and cold. "I didn't want you to stop me."

By the hoarse draw of his breath he was fighting to keep his temper, the temper of a Virginia gentleman, trained since childhood to rule his slaves and his womenfolk. The temper against which he had struggled all his life.

"Do you trust me so little, Sally?" he asked at last, and she opened her eyes to see in his not only icy anger, but grief, and guilt, and shame for his country, whose laws she feared. And still deeper, the fear of being left alone by those he cared for. "You should have told me—"

"When it comes to my child I can't trust anyone. I don't know who to trust."

His eyes turned from hers.

"You could die the day after we put foot in Virginia, Tom. And then I'd belong to Patsy—"

"Patsy doesn't know." It was one of the few times her name had been spoken between them, as if his daughter were a wife he was betraying, an adultery of the heart.

Sally said nothing. Only looked up at him with her green eyes.

"Don't leave me." His hand tightened around her hair, where it straggled down from beneath her cap. "Don't *ever* leave me." A man speaking, not a philosopher. Perhaps the closest she'd ever seen him, to the man he was inside. Not as good a man as he needed people to think he was, but a real one.

"I'll make arrangements for the child." His long hand was now cupping her cheek, his eyes, dark in the gathering darkness, looking down into hers. As if by will alone he could force her heart to return as well as her body. She saw that he wore the rough corduroy coat and boots that he'd wear to go rambling in the woods, looking for butterflies or rare plants. Later she learned that he hadn't gone into Versailles that day at all, but that the whole household had been imprisoned in the Hôtel Langeac since sunup, hearing the gunfire and the shouting across the river at the Invalides.

"I promise you our son will be a free man. I'll be coming back here next year, I'll send for you—and for him—as soon as it's safe. I swear it, Sally."

Looking up into his eyes, Sally thought, *He probably even believes that.*

"But I want you with me. I want you near me." His soft voice, husky and hesitant at the best of times, stumbled over the admission, as if he weren't used to speaking the truth about anything he felt. "I've lost too many people in my life, too many dead. People I loved, people who were the bricks and stones of my heart. One can only lose so many bricks from a wall before the wall gives way. You've always been—"

He stopped himself, as if some part deeper than conscious thought realized he was about to say words to her that no Virginia gentleman could say to a black girl. As if he were in danger of forgetting, in this darkness that smelled of drifting powder-smoke, that she *was* a black girl, and he a white man. They were both of them prisoners within their skins.

But there was a part of him that couldn't forget.

"I need to know you'll be there," he finished, stumblingly.

Like a footstool? Or a water-bottle to keep his bed warm?

Like the wife he had sworn never to take?

When he'd reach for her in the darkness, press his face to her hair, was that because he needed *her,* Sally Hemings, or just that he needed someone to fill that empty hole in his life?

Would he understand if she asked him that question?

And if he knew, would he speak a true answer?

Since the dark before dawn that morning, she felt she had aged a dozen years. Like the officers of the Bastille guard, she had opened her eyes on a world that now no longer existed.

And where else was there for her to go, but back to Virginia with him? To what acquaintance in England or Italy or Holland could the American Minister send a pregnant girl who had once been his slave, without admitting what no Virginian, much less the much-acclaimed Apostle of Liberty, would ever speak of?

"I'll be there," she said. "I promise you. Just free my children—our children—and I'll be there for you, as long as I live."

His arms closed around her, tightly, greedily, pressing her against him as he did in the secret enclave of his bedroom, that world-within-a-world which was the only place in which they could be to one another what they actually were. Having said the words, having stepped past the point of no return, Sally felt a kind of dazed relief that she wouldn't be obliged by Fate and duty to leave him. That he'd remain a part of her life, and she of his.

A voice within her was crying, *What have I done?*

But she had no answer to that.

He kissed her then, in the dark beneath the chestnut trees, and led her back across the Champs-Elysées, bloodied and filthy with the debris of yesterday's riots. His hand felt warm and strong against the small of her back.

"Did you indeed see them, when they destroyed the Bastille?" There was a wistfulness in his voice, a vibrant eagerness, as if he wished he had been there, too.

She wished he had. Maybe then he would be less ready to say, *It is a glorious time.*

Or maybe he would say it still. He was a man, and his first love was and always would be liberty. As genuine as his possessive need for her was the craving to see other men cast off the chains of tyranny, and freedom was worth more to him than his own life.

"I saw them," she said. "I heard people saying that they're tearing down its very walls, to show the King that he can no longer make them slaves."

"And I daresay to remove a potential royal cannon emplacement commanding the gate into the city," commented Jefferson, with a swift flash of practicality. "It is indeed a glorious time to be alive, Sally—but not one in which I'd wish to see my daughters embroiled. Or my son."

He kissed her again, and handed her back her parcel which he'd been carrying. Then with a businesslike air he led her to the gate of the Hôtel, and rapped at it sharply, two quick raps, then three more.

The judas slid open. Sally saw candlelight and Adrien Petit's dark eyes. Then as swiftly it shut, and the wicket beside the carriage-gate opened. "I found her," said Jefferson, and led her inside. "She went to take some things to Miss Sparling, early, before trouble could start in the streets."

As he led the way quickly across the black pit of the courtyard, the house door opened. In the dim light Patsy stood silhouetted, tall and rigid with fury, like the angel with the sword guarding the gate of a vanished paradise, as her father and Sally came up the steps.

"Sally says the mob destroyed the Bastille." Tom's eyes almost glowed in the candlelight. "The King cannot pretend, now, that things can go back as they were."

And Sally thought, *No. No one can pretend that things can go back as they were.*

Washington City
Wednesday, August 24, 1814
11:30 A.M.

"It was an ill year," said Sophie quietly, "1789."

Dolley turned the mirror over in her hand. Beyond the windows, the street was now a torrent of carts, wagons, carriages, masked in yellow dust. The silence of the morning had given way to the constant clatter of harness, the yelling of men, and the barking of dogs.

"An ill year all around," she murmured.

Pol sidled along her perch, flapped her

wings for attention and, when Dolley stretched out a hand to stroke her head, ducked into the touch like a cat. *What will happen to Pol,* wondered Dolley, *should worse come to worst?* Her mind still flinched from coming out with the words: *If the British defeat us. If the British march into Washington.*

If the city is sacked, Jemmy taken prisoner . . .

She studied, with a curious sadness, the ivory miniature on the back of the mirror. It was in 1789 that the armies had started marching again.

"We all thought it such a marvelous thing," she told Sophie. "The French rising in revolt against their King."

"You weren't there."

"No. But those who were, who saw the bloodshed, some of them saw the wider end: that Liberty should blossom in another land than ours. That year poor Martha saw her husband made President, and her hopes that she would live quietly with him and those she loved dashed. Not so great a tragedy, one would say, whose granddaughters and nieces had someone to look after them properly. Abigail would have reveled in it, save of course, that Mr. Adams was furious that he hadn't been elected Vice President unanimously, as General Washington was elected President. And so of course Abigail had to be indignant, too."

"Abigail had worries of her own that year." Sophie moved to the mantel, and took down the small clock that Mr. Jefferson had given Dolley and Jemmy at their wedding; wrapped it in one of Dolley's silver-tissue turbans as she spoke. "Troubles which she could not tell John. They were back in Braintree by then—in the finest house in town, which, she wrote me, looked much larger in her memories than it turned out to be once they tried to get all their French and English furniture into it. It was that year that it began to be clear to her that her daughter's fine husband hadn't the slightest intention of actually working for a living, being under the impression that as a Hero of the Revolution—" Her tone was as subtle and sharp as a glass splinter. "—the new government must of course provide him with a lucrative position. I think that was also the year her son Charley—one of the pair she left behind in Massachusetts—was thrown out of Harvard for a drunken prank."

"Poor Charley." A shiver of foreboding went through Dolley, at the memory of what had become of that charming, gentle, intelligent young man. "And poor Abigail."

Her own son's charming, gentle, intelligent face seemed to her, for a moment, to glance from the little mirror's depths.

Was that what invariably happened to those whose mothers set them down in what they believed was a safe place, to labor at their husbands' sides in the vineyard of Liberty?

No, she thought quickly. *Payne's case is different. My son will outgrow his bad habits. He will be all right. . . .*

Would Payne's life have been different, without the events of 1789?

She set the mirror down. "It was the year my father—" Even at the distance of two and a half decades, it was hard to understand what had happened to the man Dolley had known.

"He went bankrupt that year," she said slowly. "Dost know that it is the rule in many Meetings, that a man who cannot pay his creditors is read out of the Congregation? It broke my father. The Meeting was his life. He became lost in some inner darkness. He would not come out of his room. He would bolt the door, and Mama took to sleeping with us—Lucy and Anna and Mary and me. When John Todd offered for my hand, Mama begged me to accept him. To hesitate, and wait upon my own heart, was a luxury I could not afford. We were wed on Twelfth Night, John and I. The thirty-first anniversary of Martha Washington's marriage to the General, and a bare month before Patsy Jefferson, not even eight weeks returned from France, married her Mr. Randolph."

"And moved into Monticello with him." Sophie tucked the clock into the trunk, and packed it into place with a shawl. "To show her father she didn't need him, yet wasn't about to leave his side." She rose, shook out her somber skirts. "I'm going to go see if McGraw's anywhere in sight, with or without a vehicle. If you're going to stay here, I think it's high time we started counting how many able-bodied men we have in the house, and how many weapons."

"The day before yesterday, we had a hundred," Dolley said bitterly. "And Colonel Carberry swore upon his sword that they would stay and defend the house from the

British. I should like to think they're on their way to Bladensburg at this moment—Yes, Paul?"

The young valet had appeared again in the parlor door.

"Mrs. Madison? M'sieu Roux wants to know, will you be serving dinner this afternoon?"

"Yes, of course. Please ask M'sieu Sioussat to set the tables for forty." Dolley turned back to Sophie, who was looking at her as if at a madwoman. "Martha Washington often said to me that the whole of her task, as the Presidentress, was to *show* the country, and the world, the nature of the office of President. The nature of what we, as a republic, are and should be." Dolley sat again at the desk, where the letter she'd begun yesterday to her sister still lay unfinished beside the Queen's mirror, a fragment of normality that seemed to say, *I have not fled.*

I will not flee.

"It isn't enough to say it, she would tell me. The French spent years, during the Revolution, *saying* how things should be. One must *live* as an example. That is the reason, whatever happens, I must not flee."

Dolley looked, for a long moment, into the chilly eyes of her friend.

Then she added, "And why I must not be taken. Nor Jemmy, either."

"A challenging conundrum," murmured Sophie, "given the bravery and superb organization of the militia guarding the Bladensburg Bridge. Between counting out dessert-forks, I shall still ask M'sieu Sioussat how many guns are in the house."

"Surely the British won't—"

"I'm not thinking of the British," said Sophie quietly. "I'm thinking of looters."

She disappeared into the dark of the hall. For a long minute Dolley sat at the desk, the unfinished letter to her sister Lucy beneath her fingertips.

I am determined not to go myself until I see Mr. Madison safe . . . Disaffection stalks around us . . . My friends and acquaintances are all gone . . .

The words seemed clear one moment, gibberish the next.

And do those who remain do so only to speed our enemies' pursuit?

She plucked her tortoiseshell snuffbox from the desk-drawer, inhaled a pinch—a nasty habit, she knew, but the nicotine soothed her.

Lucy, she thought, lifting the letter and half smiling in spite of her fear at the thought of her brash and pretty blond sister. It was Lucy who had first brought her and Martha Washington together in 1793.

In the year that the world tore itself apart.

If 1789 had been an ill year for everyone, 1793 had at times had the quality of nightmare, as if the Horsemen of the Apocalypse had ridden across the land.

War, Greed, Plague . . . and Death on his pale horse, following after.

Outside the windows, above the curtain of dust, clouds had begun to thicken, and far off she heard the rumble of thunder.

It will storm, she thought, *and soak the men. . . .*

But the thunder did not stop. Not a single peal, but a heavy sustained booming, muffled by distance . . .

"Do you hear it?" Sophie reappeared, her hands full of silver plate and Dolley's shawls.

Dolley understood then, with a sudden chilling sensation beneath her breastbone, that it wasn't thunder.

"Cannon," Sophie said.

❧ 1793 ❧

MARTHA

❦

Philadelphia
Friday, July 27, 1793

Pray, dearest Aunt, do not think
worse of me, for prices of all things
remain high here and there have been
so many expenses. Would I could
hold household as you do always and
if you will but help us in our difficulty,
in future I will do so, I promise. Little
Charlie sends his love to his "dear
Nuncle" and to that I add my own,
and to you, my dearest aunt.
In deepest love and
gratitude——Your Fanny.

Martha sighed, and set the letter down. In
the yard a dog was howling, though amid

the constant din and confusion of Philadelphia that could mean anything. There were days when she felt that if she were a dog, she'd sit in the yard and howl, too.

Mount Vernon seemed a hundred thousand miles away.

It had rained that afternoon, and the brick pavement of High Street gave back a dense and humid heat. The whole of the summer had been so, wet and dispiriting. Though that had not stopped the mobs that had roved the city streets and waterfronts, either to cheer the arrival of privateers escorting captured British ships to be auctioned off, or to demand that their President declare war on England on behalf of Revolutionary France.

Since April, Martha had dreamed of being locked in a room watching a gunpowder-trail burn toward piled kegs of explosives, helpless to stop it. The situation—not only in Philadelphia, but in all the cities of the United States—was turning George's hair white. Even the War, she thought, had not been this bad.

And the man behind it—bumptious, obnoxious, and dangerous "Citizen" Édouard

Genêt—would almost certainly be at her reception tonight.

He was the Minister of France; she couldn't very well have the servants throw Genêt out. Much as she'd like to do so.

Dinner was over. In the front of the house—Robert Morris's house, which both Benedict Arnold and the British General Howe had occupied in turn—the footmen were clearing up the family dining-room. In the kitchen Uncle Hercules, Mr. Hyde, and Mrs. Hyde were in the process of getting coffee, tea, and Martha's special plum-cake ready for the guests who would begin arriving at eight. Fidas and Austin were putting fresh candles into the sconces and chandelier of the green drawing-room, while Moll made sure twelve-year-old Wash was clean, powdered, and presentable. It was astonishing how disarrayed the boy could get between six and eight o'clock.

In the office next door, Martha could hear George's light tread as he crossed from desk to window, then back again. Wary and alert as he had been at Cambridge or Valley Forge. Watching the street, over the wall of the garden. Listening for the too-familiar shouting of half-drunken sailors, singing

French songs about hanging aristocrats from the nearest lamp-post. The Americans were singing them by rote, she presumed, since most of them didn't know enough French to ask for water in that language if they were dying. Not that America had many aristocrats to hang, but anybody to whom the singers owed money would do.

But added to the mobs now were the sailors from the French fleet, in port to refit after an attempt to suppress the slave revolts that for two years had been raging in the Caribbean. Citizen Genêt had started his career as Minister Plenipotentiary by coming, not to Philadelphia to present his credentials, but to Charleston, South Carolina. There he had fitted up privateers to prey on British ships, under the French flag. They'd bring the captured ships back to Charleston and auction the cargoes to Americans, who knew no better than to fuel the growing fire of England's wrath.

For this appalling piece of meddling, Édouard Genêt had been taken to the unwashed bosoms of the working-class political clubs, the so-called "Democratic-Republican Societies" that had sprouted up in every major city, since the start, four years ago, of the Revolution in France.

Tom Jefferson—George's Secretary of State these days—insisted the clubs were necessary to educate men in the business of making decisions for themselves. Hammy Hamilton—now Secretary of the Treasury—called them "Jacobin clubs," after the most radical faction of the French National Convention. But they not only discussed politics. More and more, they noisily espoused "fraternal assistance which would expand the Empire of Liberty" (and incidentally bail France out of the dire financial effects of having declared war simultaneously on Britain, Holland, and Spain when her treasury was empty in the first place).

"Fraternal assistance" meant declaring war on Britain again, which even Martha knew the United States simply could not afford to do. When George had issued a Proclamation of Neutrality, the Republicans had followed the French pattern and begun to demonstrate. They demanded that the Proclamation—and, if necessary, the authority of the President—be set aside for the benefit of their beloved France. Genêt's presence had only served to fan the flames.

Upon the arrival of the French fleet in Philadelphia, the Revolutionary Minister had invited its sailors ashore to join the demonstrators.

The sailors had come armed.

Martha might have been completely apolitical, but she knew the situation was a bad one.

She realized she had been listening, too.

No sound from the streets, at least not of shouting or "La Marseillaise." In the long summer evenings the din of wagons hauling goods in from the docks and of the voices of passersby didn't quiet down until nearly nine. But she heard her maid's light tread in the hall outside her door, then the soft tap on the panels and the heavy rustle of velvet and silk that would be her dress for the evening: "Lady Washington?"

"Wait for me, if you would, please, Oney," she replied, and slipped Fanny's letter out of sight into a drawer and turned the key on it. "I'm just going to go up and see how Pollie is doing."

Three years ago, her granddaughters' plans to marry off their tutor Mr. Lear had finally borne fruit with the arrival of his childhood sweetheart, Pollie Long from New

Hampshire. As Tobias Lear had slipped into the role of George's secretary, so the pretty fair-haired Pollie had become Martha's. When the capital had moved from New York to Philadelphia the following year—1791—it was Tobias and Pollie who'd come ahead to make sure the Morris mansion on High Street was ready for Presidential occupancy (it hadn't been), and it was frequently the tactful, gentle Pollie who made sure that Nelly did her lessons and that bread-and-butter letters went out to the Philadelphia hostesses who entertained the President and his family at dinner.

As Martha ascended the back stair that led from the family rooms on the second floor to the offices and bedchambers of George's secretaries on the third, she heard Tobias's voice: ". . . the way the trick riders used to do in ancient Rome, I believe. He rides without saddle, standing on the horse's back, a lovely gray named Corn-planter . . ."

By the sound of it, Tobias was keeping Pollie's spirits up—and her mind off the shouting in the streets—with an account of Mr. Ricketts's celebrated circus. Pollie had fallen ill three days before, and when her fever was high, the noise of the mobs terrified her. She'd seemed a little better this afternoon, but long experience nursing the sick had taught Martha that fevers frequently shot up as evening drew on.

Her fear was confirmed when she came into the large, light bedroom, and saw Tobias's face. Pollie turned her head weakly on the pillows. "Lady Washington?"

"How are you feeling, dearest?" Though it was clear by her young friend's flushed face and restless movements that she was in pain and barely conscious of what was going on around her.

"Lincoln—?" she murmured her little son's name, and Martha took her hand reassuringly.

"Moll has taken Lincoln down to help her get Mr. Tub ready for the reception, so I imagine he'll take some dusting off before he can come up to bid you good-night." Eighteen-month-old Benjamin Lincoln Lear was a general favorite of the household. Since Pollie had taken sick, the boy'd been sleeping in Wash's room, and Wash had confided to Martha that he was glad to have a little brother to show things to.

"I'll be up after the reception, to tell you

how it all went," she promised. "In the meantime, I'll send Moll up with some cool water. I imagine that will make you feel a little better, poor sweet." Martha had already seen the dishes of rice-pudding and coddled egg, on the tray on the dresser-top, barely touched. "Mr. Lear, I'm sure the General won't *need* three secretaries at his side during the reception, so if you'd like to stay here and read to Pollie for a little . . . You'll be missed, of course, but it's entirely up to you to choose. If you want to take a little time at the reception, or just to rest, of course I'll have Oney come up."

"I'll stay here, thank you, Lady Washington." Tobias got to his feet, to walk her to the door. As they reached it he went on in a softer voice, "She ate nothing of her dinner, and when she uses the chamber-pot there are black streaks in her urine. I know that can't be right."

"I shall send Fidas with a note now, asking Dr. Rush to come first thing in the morning."

Tobias pressed her hand gratefully, and Martha hurried down the stairs in a rustle of silk dressing-gown, cursing again the necessity of appearing at a reception—and having to be polite to Citizen Genêt of all people!—when her place was with her family. With Tobias and Pollie, and poor little Lincoln; with Fanny in the house they owned in Alexandria, coping as well as she could with shaky health and new widowhood. It was no surprise poor Fanny was not doing well: Augustine's death in February had come barely six weeks after that of Fanny's father.

Those are the people who need me. Those dear ones, and poor Jacky's girls—she could hear Eliza's strident voice crying, "Thief, am I? It is *you* who seek to rob *me,* of any chance to achieve my happiness in the world!" and knew she'd be called upon to arbitrate who was going to wear Nelly's garnets to the reception.

There were times, Martha had confessed to Abigail Adams, when she felt herself to be a State prisoner, forced to watch the sufferings of her loved ones through the bars of her jail.

But George needed her, even more than they. He was a man of iron, but Martha had seen what iron looks like, after four years at the mercy of the sea. At least, in her relatively comfortable cell, she didn't have to be constantly making decisions of peace or war with a gun held to her head.

George was sixty-one years old. In eight years of leading the Continental Army to war, he had been ill only once. In his first eighteen months in the office of President he had nearly died twice, once when the capital was still in New York, of an abscess whose effects he would simply have shaken off back at Mount Vernon, when he was getting enough rest, and then of pneumonia. And despite that, Mr. Hamilton and Mr. Jefferson—whose vicious bickering in the Cabinet had made poor George's life a living Hell for four years—had both begged George to stand for a second term as President, probably because neither of them could endure the thought of the other possibly coming to power. Martha would cheerfully have assassinated them both and had the servants throw their bodies in the river.

And Jemmy Madison, too, for getting George into this mess in the first place.

And yet as she took her husband's arm, as muscular in its sheath of black velvet as that of the twenty-six-year-old militia Colonel who had led her to the preacher, thirty-four years ago, Martha had to admit to herself that for the country's sake, she was glad George had accepted a second term.

She liked John Adams, and the company of his fragile, outspoken, intimidating Abigail had been the only thing that had gotten her through any number of previous receptions. Yet she suspected that the irascible little New Englander would simply have been unable to cope with Citizen Genêt.

⚜

"They're insane! To think that with a single-house legislature the government wouldn't be torn apart by factions! These political clubs and salons they have—Girondists and Jacobins and Feuillants—all they do is keep the people in a fever—"

"—aristocrats brought it upon themselves, you know—"

"Their treasury is bankrupt! Of course they want the whole of what we owe them paid in a lump—"

Though Martha discouraged politics as a topic of conversation at her receptions, within the first twenty minutes the crowd that gathered in the green drawing-room separated along factional lines like a badly made sauce. The Senators and Congressmen who favored a French alliance and immediate war against Britain—mostly Southerners who mistrusted the strength of the new Federal government and didn't want to be taxed to pay Massachusetts's debts—clumped around Thomas Jefferson, who had been Genêt's champion from the first.

Even in the face of the news in April that the French had killed their King—with a new scientific head-chopping machine, no less!—and had auctioned off locks of his hair from the scaffold, Jefferson would hear no word against the revolutionists in France. The Spirit of Liberty must be served.

"I've seen besotted boys less obsessed with their first mistresses, than he with the French," remarked Alexander Hamilton, eyeing the tall Virginian with loathing across the double parlor. The cocky, golden-haired Headquarters aide whom George loved like a son had put on a little weight since the War, but his dazzling good looks remained. He had gone on to marry one of New York's richest heiresses, but his interest in money was more than pragmatic. Alex Hamilton was one of the few men Martha had ever met who understood how national finances actually worked. It was his proposals for a

National Bank that had put the new nation on the road to solvency.

Jefferson detested him, the Bank, and the powerful central government that was required to make Hamilton's financial proposals work. Possibly, Martha sometimes thought, this was because Thomas Jefferson was incapable of balancing so much as a household account-book.

"Tom is a man obsessed with Liberty," said John Adams. "Wherever it may take root."

"Obsession in any form is deadly," Hamilton retorted. "It blinds its victims. And personally, I would rather not have a member of our President's Cabinet listening blindly to the representative of a foreign government that has been trying since 1775 to gain a foothold in our nation's territory."

"Hammy," said Martha firmly, "this is a social occasion, and a man who enters into a political discussion out of season runs the risk of having charges of obsession leveled against himself." She tapped his elbow with her fan, and gave him her most twinkling smile.

"Lady Washington—" Hammy pointed his toe and made a profound leg. "Your wish as usual is as the Holy Writ to me." He had a voice like the god Apollo's would sound, if the deity were trying to talk a woman into bed or a man into the purchase of Bank of New York stock. "Let us confine ourselves rather to a discussion of the new Minister's utterly deplorable coat. What is it about the Rule of the People that seems to unravel all sense of sartorial propriety?"

"You shall not entrap me into slandering M. Genêt on the grounds of his taste. For all we know, coats such as he wears may be perfectly acceptable in France, as breech-clouts are among the savages of the Pacific Islands. Rather, Mr. Adams, tell me how it goes with dear Mrs. Adams. Is she feeling better? Will she be able to return to Phila-delphia next year? We have sorely missed her."

And as Mr. Adams—who despite years as a diplomat had not the smallest talent for so-cial banter—recounted the news and opin-ions that the always-entertaining Abigail had sent from Massachusetts, Martha let her eye rove over the rest of the drawing-room, as a hostess must. She picked out at once George's nephew Steptoe, the obstreperous Harriot's older brother, a handsome boy of twenty-three who'd studied enough law—barely—to get a job with the lean and rather frayed-looking Edmund Randolph, George's Attorney General.

It was due to his employment with Randolph, Martha presumed, that Steptoe was on the pro-French side of the room. Her nephew's very proper black velvet suit and powdered hair stood out among the unpowdered locks and less-formal blues and browns favored by that faction. The only other man clothed with perfect formality on that side of the room was little Aaron Burr, newly elected Senator from New York and reputedly the best trial lawyer in that city (though Hamilton also claimed that title). Martha remembered Colonel Burr from Valley Forge. He'd been one of George's aides for about ten days at Cambridge, before she'd arrived, but had left the General's household after George came into his tent one day and found the young man calmly reading the papers on George's desk.

Looking up at her towering nephew, Burr gave the impression that if he took his shoes off he'd have cloven hooves underneath. Martha saw Steptoe hand him something—a note?—which the little man slipped into an inner pocket with a nod and a conspiratorial smile.

Martha sighed. A love-note, no doubt, from some lady of one or the other's acquaintance. Burr adored his ailing wife, but that apparently didn't stop him from bedding almost as many women as Hammy did. Steptoe took his meals at the same boardinghouse as Colonel Burr, and Martha earnestly hoped the boy would have better sense than to be led into either vice or those Jacobin clubs whose views the Colonel was said to favor.

On the other hand, she was pleased to see Jefferson had arrived accompanied, not by Citizen Genêt, but by his younger daughter Maria—Mary, the girl had been christened, and only her father still called her Polly these days. A week shy of her fifteenth birthday and delicately pretty, Maria hurried across the drawing-room to clasp Nelly's hands—they'd been schoolmates in New York and here in Philadelphia—and exchange kisses of greeting, French-fashion, with Eliza and Pattie. In her wake came her cousin Jack Eppes, who was part of Jefferson's household and acted as a secretary to him.

Indeed, reflected Martha, there were a number of young people here of the next generation: Steptoe, Maria, fourteen-year-old Nelly and her sisters (Eliza still visibly smoldering over Nelly's claim on the garnets—goodness knew what had become of the pearls that Martha had bought for her at the same time), and Mr. Adams's youngest son, twenty-one-year-old Tommy, plumpish and amiable and newly fledged as a lawyer. All following in the footsteps of their errant parents, making their lives the best way they could.

It is the next generation, thought Martha, *who'll have to pick up the pieces if we go to war, either with England or, God help us, with France on England's behalf.* It was for them that George had issued his Proclamation of Neutrality, and neither England nor France seemed to understand the meaning of the word: *He who is not with me is against me.*

"But don't you see, the French will help us clear the British out of the Great Lakes forts!" Pennsylvania Governor Mifflin's voice carried over the subdued chatter as footmen, liveried in white and scarlet, came in to light the candles. "They've refused for

years to live up to the treaty terms that demand them to leave—"

"And you think having the forts in the
hands of those lunatics in Paris is going to
be an improvement?" countered Robert
Morris. "It's all very well for the French to
swear they'll be our allies, but considering
they can't even keep their own people from
murdering one another I doubt they'd be
much help to us if the British came back."

Across the room, Washington signaled
Steptoe with a glance and the two of them
moved in on the trouble-spot. Before they
could reach the Governor and the merchant,
however, the drawing-room doors swung
open and Citizen Genêt stood framed in
them, clothed, not in the long-tailed coat and
knee-breeches of polite society, but in
trousers, top-boots, and a coat of such military cut as to give the impression of a uniform. A young man—thirty—of medium
height, he was, Martha supposed, good-
looking enough, except his skin was bad, his
teeth worse, and his manners more deplorable than either.

"Citizen Washington!" Édouard Genêt had
a voice trained to cut through the hubbub of
gatherings and, presumably, frenzied mobs.

Martha saw George's eyes open wide in startlement at this completely undiplomatic form of address, and, at his elbow, saw Jefferson wince. She could almost feel sorry for the man. He had spent the past three months praising Genêt and trying to smooth over the feelings of those he'd offended— and trying to mediate between the Cabinet, the Congress, and Genêt's increasingly threatening demands.

"You have toyed with me, avoided me, and set your face against the obligations of your country long enough!" Genêt cried, striding forward. "I must and will speak to you, and remind you of your duty—and your country's duty—not only to the nation to which you owe your liberty, but to Liberty Herself."

Stunned silence fell on the room. Jefferson, looking as if he were about to become prey to one of his worst migraines, started to move toward Genêt, but Washington raised his hand. His face wore that calm, stony expression that was worse, Martha knew, than shouting rage.

"Please come into my study, Monsieur Genêt," he said in his most even voice. "I'm sure we will be more comfortable there than among all these people."

Martha thought for a moment that Genêt would stand his ground—the Frenchman looked like he'd have preferred to make a speech in front of an audience rather than have a private interview—but since he was about to get the conversation he'd demanded he couldn't very well complain that he didn't like the venue. As James opened the door for them to the private quarters at the rear of the house, George bowed to the room and said, "If the company will please excuse me."

In the silence, the quiet closing of the door was like a gunshot. Martha suspected that every person there, had he or she been alone, would immediately have rushed to the study door and put an ear to the keyhole.

She knew she would have.

Instead, she signaled Nelly with her eye, calling her like a general beating commands to troops with a drum in battle. Picked out others she could trust in the room—the lovely Ann Bingham, at twenty-nine Philadelphia's most prominent hostess; Hamilton's graceful wife Betsey; Helena Pennington, the wife of one of the wealthiest Quaker merchants; Elizabeth Drinker, virtual queen of Philadelphia's Quaker society; Elizabeth Powel and Maria Morris and others who ruled the city's society. Whether their husbands were pro-French or pro-British, these ladies knew, exactly and instinctively, what they had to do, what any woman of proper upbringing would do in a like situation in her own drawing-room: break up the political claques before the entire gathering degenerated into a shouting-match.

Beside her, Adams had turned bright pink with fury and Hamilton's blue eyes fairly snapped. "Did you see Jefferson's face? I swear the man is in the pay of the French!"

"Nonsense, Hammy, if Tom were in the pay of the French he wouldn't be in debt." Martha laid a gently restraining hand upon the golden man's elbow. "Now tell me honestly, do you really think when the year 1800 rolls around, there will be *any* buildings in the new Federal City for us to occupy? Or will poor Mrs. Adams—" She turned with a smile to her husband's Vice President, "—be obliged to hold her receptions in a tent?"

Hammy looked as if he were about to rail at her: How could she possibly speculate about domestic architecture when Philadelphia stood on the brink of erupting into flaming riot with an invading force of French sailors? But furious as he was—and Hammy had a vicious temper—the Secretary of the Treasury knew better than to shout at any lady at a reception, much less the wife of the man who had been his Commander in Chief for almost twenty years.

"I'm sure it won't come to that, Lady Washington," he replied, with a steely rictus of a smile. "The rest of us may be dwelling in tents, but I'm sure the Senate will organize a barn-raising, as they do on the Ohio frontier." And he inclined his head to his lovely Betsey, who appeared at his side to take his arm.

Martha had lived on a plantation long enough to know that the best way to keep a bull from charging is to bring his favorite cow into his line of sight. She turned her attention to Adams. The room was quieting down, though no one left. After some twenty minutes the inner door opened again and George returned, escorting Édouard Genêt with every appearance of cordiality through the room—unobtrusively permitting him to talk to no one—and to the head of the stairs. There, after a firm handshake, the footmen took over and saw him out.

Within minutes, Jefferson, Jack Eppes, and Maria made their good-nights. Jefferson was pale and looked ill. "And why shouldn't he?" demanded Hamilton snidely. "He's been urging everyone in the Cabinet for weeks to give Genêt money to fund a French expedition against Canada and Louisiana." He spoke loudly enough to make certain Jefferson heard. Martha saw the Secretary of State's back stiffen, as he paused in the doorway, but Jefferson didn't turn back.

In his wake, Aaron Burr and young Steptoe Washington departed together, heads close in soft-voiced talk.

⚜

Martha didn't learn the content of the conversation with Genêt until late the following day, and by that time, she had other matters to worry about. After the reception was over and Oney had undressed her, locked up her jewels, and brushed the powder from her hair, she spent most of the night sitting up with Pollie. She, the maid, and Tobias took it turn and turn about, to sponge the sick woman's body with cool water, or as cool as they could manage from the well. By morning Pollie seemed to rest a little easier, but there were times when she barely seemed to recognize those around her. Just after full daylight Dr. Rush arrived and bled her. It didn't seem to relieve the fever, but she did sink into sleep.

Martha would have liked to do the same.

Every woman who had been at the reception, however, came to call, and Martha got all the political clamor she—and they—had succeeded in quashing the previous evening. This morning, at least, she was spared red faces, foul language, and the danger of anyone calling anyone out. "It isn't as if M'sieu Genêt doesn't know any better," sniffed Lucy Knox, the Secretary of War's stout, outspoken wife. "Ann Bingham tells me his father was the head of the Bureau of Translations under the King, and his sister a lady-in-waiting to the poor Queen."

"I was barely able to shut my eyes all night," gasped Eliza, "for sheer terror through the dark hours . . ."

"You certainly gave a good impression of being able to," said Nelly imperturbably.

"You snore. Will you have sweet cakes, Mrs. Knox, or bread and butter?"

"I do not snore!"

"I hear you through the wall."

"Mrs. Washington." James the footman appeared in the doorway, imposing in his livery and snowy powdered wig. *He's coming up on his six months,* thought Martha, in a combination of annoyance and regret. Due to Pennsylvania's law that any slave dwelling there would be declared free after six months, she found herself obliged to send each of the servants back to Mount Vernon periodically on a variety of trumped-up errands. It played havoc with her house-keeping and irritated her at a deeper level, that the laws of property would be one way in one state, and different in another. Wasn't that what the new Constitution was supposed to fix? It was particularly maddening because she didn't want to be living in Philadelphia in the first place. The British had never paid them for slaves they'd carried off during the Revolution, either.

"Yes, James, what is it?"

The footman stepped close—which in itself told her there was some sort of problem that would need sorting out—and held out his salver to her. The single card on its polished surface read, *Mrs. John Todd.* "Two ladies are here asking to see you, ma'am. A Mrs. Todd, and a Mrs. Payne." His face was absolutely immobile and his voice without inflection.

Something was definitely amiss.

"Eliza, dearest, would you take over for me?" Martha asked. "I shall see Mrs. Payne and Mrs. Todd in the dining-room, James." Even with all the additions she and George had requested to the red-brick mansion, there still wasn't really enough room for their extended family, especially when Pattie and Eliza came to visit.

The question of tea for the newcomers would, of course, be decided when she ascertained who they were. It wasn't only rioters bent on demanding war with France who came to the door of the red-brick house on High Street. As had been the case at Mount Vernon, old soldiers who had served with George would sometimes appear, or visitors from other towns whom Martha had never seen in her life.

Martha seated herself at the family dining-room's small table and folded her hands. A moment later James ushered in a tall, powerfully built woman in the rusty black of home-dyed mourning: cotton chintz in the cut of a respectable working-woman's dress. Behind her, the young woman who was clearly her daughter—and taller still—was also in mourning, though her gown was more fashionably cut and of far better fabric. The black must have been hellish in the morning's heat, but it complemented the younger woman's porcelain-fair complexion and jewel-blue eyes, and the sable curls neatly confined under a plain cap. Certainly the softer modern lines suited her extremely advanced state of pregnancy.

More advanced, Martha judged, than was proper for a woman to be walking abroad, unless the matter were quite serious indeed.

"Mrs. Washington." The older woman held out her hand. Properly gloved, Martha saw, though the glove was worn and mended, and, like the dress, home-dyed black. It left smudges on Martha's lace mitt. "I am Mrs. Payne; please excuse me, that I have no card." A Virginian, by her soft drawn-out vowels, and well-bred. "My daughter, Mrs. John Todd, the wife of a lawyer of this town."

"I see thee stare in amazement, Mrs.

Washington," added Mrs. Todd, with a fleeting sparkle in her blue eyes. "But if there can be Quaker generals, surely there can be Quaker lawyers."

And Martha smiled back, though Mrs. Payne's lips tightened at her daughter's wit. Tightened resignedly, as if in losing battle against an incurably spritely nature. The mother went on, "For two years now I have operated a boardinghouse on Third Street; a number of gentlemen of the Congress have rooms there, and many more take their meals with us. Among them is thy nephew, Mr. Steptoe Washington. 'Twas there that he came to know my daughter Lucy."

Martha shut her eyes. It was an opening line straight out of a romantic novel, the kind that involved some calculating harpy—frequently a boardinghouse landlady—turning up on the doorstep of a silly young man's wealthy family crying the seduction and rape of her daughter.

Yet one look at Mrs. Payne's lined face and grief-filled eyes told Martha this was no entangling madame out for a wealthy family's hush-money.

"What's happened?" she asked gently. "How far has it gone? And James," she added, raising her voice slightly, "please bring tea for myself and my guests."

When the servant left, Mrs. Payne silently handed Martha a note.

Dearest Mother, said the rather unformed hand. *By the time thou readst this I shall be far from home, and a married woman.*

"My daughter is fifteen," said Mrs. Payne. "We found her bed empty this morning. This note was on the sideboard as we cleared up after breakfast."

Into Martha's mind snapped at once the image of her nephew, handing a note to little Aaron Burr. Of the two men leaving together, almost furtively, in the wake of Jefferson's departure. "Is Senator Burr one of your guests?"

Mrs. Payne seemed startled at the guess. "He is so indeed, and a good friend of our family. Colonel Burr is one of the few men I've met who doth share my opinion on the education of young women."

And how many other notes, Martha wondered, suddenly effervescent with wrath, *has the Senator carried between my nephew and his landlady's daughter?*

She leaned across the table and took Mrs. Payne's hands. Hard hands, beneath the glove-leather, probably work-calloused the way Abigail Adams's were by years of lye soap. "Mrs. Payne," she said, "I promise you, you have nothing to fear. Steptoe is a harebrained boy, but he's no seducer. His word is his bond."

Which wasn't entirely true, at least as far as his gambling debts were concerned. But in this case George would jolly well see to it that Steptoe's word *was* his bond, even if it did mean bringing another underaged child—and the daughter of Aaron Burr's landlady at that!—into the family, as Jacky had long ago done.

"If he has promised marriage to your daughter, he will indeed hold to it."

At this Mrs. Payne turned her face aside and wept. Disengaging her hands, she rose quickly and hurried from the room, leaving Martha disconcerted.

The pretty Mrs. Todd rose, as if to follow her, then turned back. "Mrs. Washington, I thank thee, more than I can say, and my mother, too. I know thy nephew's a well-meaning boy—I am often at Mama's house, and know many of her guests. 'Tis not that Mama is ungrateful, to thee or to the President, for whatever thou canst do on Lucy's behalf. But Mama—She is a good member of the Congregation of Friends, and hath spent her life trying to lead us in the path of righteousness. And for marrying outside the Congregation, Lucy will be 'read out,' ejected from the Meeting and from all the Society. In saving her daughter's honor, my mother hath lost her child, and I my sister."

She held out a gloved hand to Martha: black kid, newer than her mother's, and leaving no mark where it touched. "Nevertheless I thank thee, ma'am. And though I see in thine eyes that thou hast thy doubts—as who would not, for Steptoe *is* but a boy—I can at least promise thee, that thou wilt have for thy niece one of the sweetest jewels that ever God made."

⚜

When the two ladies had gone Martha returned to her drawing-room, excused herself to the ladies there, and drew Nelly aside. "I need you to come with me to your cousin Steptoe's lodgings—and not a word to the others, please. We'll take Richmond with us, I think. Goodness knows, after last night, what sort of trouble may be brewing in the streets."

But as they walked the three or four blocks to Steptoe's lodgings the streets were quiet, though men clustered around the doors of the taverns favored by the Democratic-Republicans, and angry voices could be heard inside. When George had refused to pay the French the whole of America's war debt to fund an invasion of Spanish Louisiana, broadsides had begun appearing. They called the American people to rise against Washington's "despotism"— to overthrow it, if necessary, in the cause of a liberty that only a strong alliance with France could provide. *The freedom of this country is not secure,* trumpeted the *Columbian Gazetteer, until that of France is placed beyond the reach of accident.*

God only knew where it would end. It was said that the French Queen was in one of the most wretched prisons of Paris now, awaiting execution. The whole world, it seemed, stood on the brink of flames.

At Steptoe's lodgings, the landlord informed them that young Mr. Washington had departed early that morning. He would be gone some weeks, he had said. No, he hadn't said where.

"Harewood," said Martha grimly, as she,

Nelly, and Richmond retraced their steps back toward High Street. Harewood Plantation—originally owned by George's younger brother Sam whose death back in 1782 had thrown the care of Steptoe, Lawrence, and Harriot onto George in the first place—lay in the western part of Virginia, in the Shenandoah Valley. It was a week by carriage. "When your grandpapa returns we'll see about sending a messenger. Not Mr. Lear," she added, her face clouding. Since Dr. Rush had left, Martha had been upstairs to Pollie's room two or three times, and found the girl whispering with fever, even in her sleep.

"Will Pollie be all right?" asked Nelly. Walking at Martha's side in her schoolgirlish white muslin, she had already, Martha reflected, the demeanor of a young woman. And then, more softly, "Will *everything* be all right, Grandmama?"

Martha tried to remember the things that had troubled and frightened her when she was fourteen. Her father's constant worries about his debts to British factors and whether the tobacco-crop would cover them; the never-ending fear of a slave uprising, or of individual slave vengeances. The fact that, at fourteen, she was being fitted with the corsets and dresses of woman-hood with an eye to finding her a husband.

Nothing like the new and uncertain world Nelly faced.

"There have been many times in my life," she answered, "when I've wondered if things would be all right. When your grand-papa rode away to the Congress for the first time, and ran the risk of being hanged as a traitor to the King. And later, every summer during the War, when I'd hear of this battle or that, or that dreadful winter at Valley Forge when the Army was deserting a regi-ment at a time."

When Patcy died, and all the world was darkness . . .

"And things all *did* work out, you know," she went on briskly. "For better or for worse, spring always came after winter. I suspect it will again this year."

"You're right, Grandmama." Nelly took a deep breath, and straightened her shoul-ders. In a very grown-up voice she added, "One must keep these things in due propor-tion."

They turned the corner onto High Street, and behind them, Martha could hear the voices of the French sailors, shouting around the taverns: *"Vive la Liberté!"* and the smashing of glass.

⚜

When they reentered the house, with the thick heat of afternoon stifling in the high-ceilinged hall, Martha's first question of James was, "How is Mrs. Lear?" and then, before she even removed her bonnet, "Is the President home yet?"

"Mrs. Lear's no better, ma'am, but no worse I don't think." The footman's eyes flickered nervously as he spoke, as if he had heard some kitchen rumor—about the rioting? about Pollie's sickness?—from other slaves. "The President come in a few minutes ago. He's up in his study."

George's study was part of the private area of the house, divided off from the rest as their bedroom and dressing-room were at Mount Vernon. Since his days as a retired Hero of the Revolution, they had learned that this was the only way in which he could ever get anything done.

"Patsie." He stood as she came in, then bent his tall height to bestow a kiss on her cheek.

"Did you speak to Mr. Jefferson?"

He nodded. "I found him in his office, with M. Genêt, who seemed to be repeating to him all he had said to me last night. Which was, in effect, that the Proclamation of Neutrality annulled the most sacred treaty with the French people, by which they'd sworn to defend us and which they had honorably kept."

Martha had suspected as much, but George had been far too angry last night before bed to give her details.

"I suspect he was trying to pump Tom for information about my plans," George went on, seating himself again at his desk and drawing Martha down to sit on his knee. The office's curtains were shut, in an effort to keep in some of last night's fugitive cool. In the shadowed corners of the room Martha could hear the whine of mosquitoes, which hovered in brown clouds around every puddle and rain-barrel in the city.

"When Genêt was gone, Tom offered to resign."

"He's been offering to do that," remarked Martha tartly, "since he himself stepped off the boat from France."

"This time I accepted." George rubbed a

big hand over his eyes. Every time Martha had waked last night, she'd seen him awake, sitting by the tight-shuttered window, or visible only as the wan ghost of a single candle's light reflected through the door of his study.

Yet he'd been up as usual in the gluey half-dark before dawn, when through the window the first sounds of milk-carts rattled up from the street and the clank of the well-chain sounded in the yard.

"I don't believe for a moment the rumors that Tom's in French pay, any more than I believe the ones that Mr. Hamilton sells information to the English. Yet Jefferson knows Genêt has gone too far. I have asked him to stay on until the end of the year, since he is the man most knowledgeable about the French, and he has agreed. And I've called a meeting of the Cabinet for tomorrow. We will draft a formal letter to Danton asking for Genêt's recall. A letter of which I will *not* inform M. Genêt," George added quietly, "until just before the Congress adjourns in September, lest one of his pet privateers should accidentally sink the vessel carrying it, somewhere on the high seas."

"So what will happen?"

"That remains to be seen. But as I told M. Genêt, neither I nor the Congress will be dictated to by the politics of any nation under Heaven." He was silent for a moment, gazing into the gloom of the study, and the sharp blade of light where the curtains fell imperfectly together. Then his arm tightened around her waist, as if for reassurance that whatever his Secretary of State might do and however badly the nation to which he had given his life might fracture, Martha at least was there, as she had been through all the years of the War.

"A trying morning," he said. "I trust you passed a more pleasant one?"

"Well," said Martha slowly, "not precisely."

⚜

The following morning, the French fleet sailed. For New York, it was said, to refit and reprovision. It was also said, in the newspapers favorable to Washington, Hamilton, and a British alliance, that their intention was to divide, and use New York as a base from which to attack Spanish Florida and Louisiana, and British Canada.

Only a fool would fail to see that it was

against New York that the British would counterattack, with the largest and strongest Navy in the world.

The United States had not a single ship.

The same day—muggy, hot, and whining with mosquitoes—Martha ordered the light town-carriage harnessed, and, accompanied by Nelly, was driven down High Street, past the old brown-brick steeple of the former State House where the Congress now met, to the pleasant brick house on Walnut Street where the lawyer John Todd lived with his wife.

"I do thank thee for coming." Dolley Todd rose from her chair in the neat little parlor—what was locally called a "tea-room"—and held out her hands to Martha as the girl who'd met them at the door showed her and Nelly in. Though fairer and more delicately made than Mrs. Todd, the girl had the same porcelain complexion and tip-tilted eyes. And because, like Mrs. Todd, she, too, wore black, Martha guessed that it was their father who was lately dead. "My mother thanks thee for thy trouble, and for the honor of thy coming. I know 'tis not a usual thing, for the wife of the President to pay calls. Yet Mama sends her regrets, that she is not able to meet thee here. Please excuse her," the younger woman went on, her blue eyes filled with compassion and concern. "This matter of Lucy hath grieved her deeply. Too deeply, I think, for her to speak to anyone just now. Indeed, she hath said to me, more than once, that my sister is to her as one dead."

Dolley Todd led Martha to one of the room's comfortable chairs, upholstered in straw-colored dornick; though plain, as all Quaker dwellings were supposed to be and frequently weren't, the room radiated simple comfort and exquisite taste. Muslin curtains were hung over the book-case against the city's summer dust, and also mitigated the glare and heat of the windows. The tea-pot and cups that the young girl—"My dearest sister Anna," Mrs. Todd introduced her with a smile—brought in were blue-and-white China-ware, and the tea, first-class.

While Anna drew Nelly into quiet conversation on the other side of the room, Mrs. Todd poured out tea for herself and her older guest: "Hast thou heard anything, of thy nephew and Lucy, Lady Washington?"

Martha nodded. "The President sent another of his nephews in pursuit of them. We did manage to find the minister who performed the ceremony, so you can at least reassure your dear mama that a ceremony *was* performed."

"I had no doubt that it had been," replied Dolley softly. "As I said yesterday, I have met young Mr. Washington at Mama's, and I knew well before thou said it, that he is no seducer—at least not of an *innocent* girl," she added, with a wry twinkle of regret with which Martha heartily concurred.

As for roving young matrons or ladies of a certain class, well, thought Martha, *that might be a different story.* Of course she couldn't say so, but meeting Dolley's eye, didn't think she needed to.

She began to like this young woman tremendously.

" 'Minister,' thou sayst," went on Dolley after a moment. "Not a Quaker, then?" and Martha shook her head.

"Anglican. But perfectly respectable—"

"Oh, yes, yes of course!" Dolley hastened to agree. "And yet, to the Meeting, a 'hireling priest,' as they say." And she fell silent, caught as her mother was, between her faith and her love. "We are taught—we girls—that we must wed within the Congregation, or if we wed outside of it, as my mother did, we must bring our husbands to the fold." Her half-bemused smile tugged at the corner of her mouth, as if in spite of her grief something irrepressible inside her couldn't help catching a glimpse of the joy of life. "I think we may agree that this is, in the case of young Mr. Washington, unlikely in the extreme."

Martha said slowly, "I understand—at least, I should like to *think* I understand your mother's feelings: I should be most upset for instance if Nelly took it into her head one day to marry a Mohammedan, though I assume there are good men and bad in every faith. Yet I have lost a daughter myself. And though I would never say as much to your mother, it is one thing to declare 'She is dead to me' because she's left the Church or the house, and another for that child, that daughter, to actually *be* dead. There is . . . no coming back from that."

"No," whispered Dolley, and laid a hand, in an almost protective gesture, on her belly where her own child slept. "No, I know that."

"You were fortunate to have found a man

you loved within the Congregation," said Martha after a moment.

The lovely blue glance touched hers for a moment, then ducked away. "Aye," Dolley said. "For five years poor John courted me faithfully. He is a good man."

Did Mr. John Todd, like Dolley's mother, purse up his lips at his wife's bubbling humor or admonish her on the stylish cut of her gowns? Would he, like the widowed Mrs. Payne, refuse to admit the erring Lucy to his house, when and if she returned to Philadelphia? *He is a good man* is a very different statement from, *I love him,* though it was clear that this beautiful, sparkling woman was a loving wife. But the light of joy shone from her face only when she touched her belly again, and smiled at the thought of the baby there.

"When will he be born?" asked Martha, who could never see a baby or a child without a pang of envy, a surge of joy.

"*She,* if it please thee!" And both women laughed. "Mother, and John, and Anna—" She nodded with a smile at her sister, "—talk as if 'tis inscribed in gold somewhere that I'll birth another boy. But since I know the child I bear is matchlessly perfect . . ." She gestured like a tragedienne at the exaggeration, ". . . it *cannot* be a son, for I have already borne the most perfect son the world has ever seen, at least for nigh onto eighteen hundred years. Although," she added with a sigh, "Mama would have it that I do little Payne no good by telling him so. And perhaps she is right."

The news that there was another child in the house had its usual effect on Martha, and little Payne Todd, seventeen months old, was immediately sent for, accompanied by the fourth Payne sister, a bright-eyed twelve-year-old named Mary. It was wonderful to spend an hour with a toddler, and this one seemed to have inherited all his mother's considerable charm. Soon Martha found herself calling Dolley "dearest" and slipping into the Quaker "thee" and "thine," and Nelly, Anna, and Mary gave up trying to carry on ladylike conversation and got out a game of Fox and Geese, at which Anna beat Martha and everyone else soundly.

"It feels like months since I've laughed so much," remarked Martha, as Dolley walked her down the stairs. "It reminds me of how much I miss Mount Vernon, and my niece and her little boy, and quiet evenings out on the piazza instead of holding court every Friday night."

Dolley's eyebrows shot up. "I've not spoken to a woman in Philadelphia who hath not said thy receptions are marvelous."

"Thank you, my dear." Martha tucked up a strand of hair under her cap, which little Payne's happy fingers had dislodged. "I'm glad people think so, for I *do* like to do a good job of work. And it *is* my work, you know, the way it's your mother's work to make sure all those poor Senators and Congressmen who're away from their wives get a decent dinner."

Dolley nodded, her sunny face thoughtful as she opened the door onto Walnut Street. "Rather like the man who dresses the stage at the theater, in fact. People don't see just the actor who speaks, but the whole of the stage, though I don't think but one in a hundred doth realize 'tis so. They'll listen differently to—and think differently of—a speech if 'tis said on a wild heath or a battlefield, than if it's spoken in a drawing-room with dirty curtains."

"Exactly!" This young woman was the first person, Martha reflected, who understood, other than George. Even Nelly—at the moment bidding farewell to Anna and Mary on the flagway beside the carriage, and kneeling to kiss little Payne. Though she strove to be a good organizer, Nelly regarded their task as a social one rather than political. It was something every man's wife, in good society, must do.

But in the eyes of this Quaker lawyer's wife, Martha saw something else: the comprehension of how a political theme must be played—and constantly improvised—in a social key.

"It is my work to make the President look his best. It is my work to make those Spanish and Danish lords go away from the mansion saying, *He may not have been born a King, but the office—and the nation—has a dignity that I must respect.* To make Congressmen say, *Here is a man of worth, whose words are not only important, but true.* And you can't get people to say things like that by telling them so, because people frequently *don't* believe things they're told—except by those *dreadful* newspapers! People must be *shown,* in order to believe things in their hearts."

"What a marvelous task." Dolley's eyes were shining.

Martha was about to retort, *YOU try getting a roomful of politicians to stop arguing
when a scoundrel like Citizen Genêt walks in
and insults your husband,* but she didn't.

"Yes," she said softly. "Yes, it is."

"And one no man could do."

Their eyes sparkled in mutual complicity,
and impulsively, Martha clasped her tall
hostess's hands.

"Steptoe and Lucy will be welcome guests
in my home whenever they come to
Philadelphia, you know." Austin helped her
into the cream-colored carriage. His livery
and powdered wig, and the fineness of the
chestnut horses, were yet another unspoken message, for all the town to see. "I shall
send you a note, shall I, when they're in
town? Perhaps Mr. Todd might be prevailed
upon to dine?"

"I doubt John would," replied Dolley. "He
hath a most conscientious regard for the
opinion of the Congregation." But her blue
eyes warmed at the thought of a venue in
which she might see her sister again, away
from the censure of the disappointed family.
"He can have no objection to my paying a
morning-call, though."

"Then you shall pay as many morning-calls as you please. And please bring little Payne, and his new *sister,* as well." As Austin clucked to the horses, Martha looked back to see Mrs. Todd in her black dress on the step, holding Payne by the hand, her sisters flanking her, and everyone waving as if they'd all been friends for years.

She would have to write Lucy a note at Harewood, thought Martha, and ask the new bride to come soon. And she needed also to write to poor Fanny, not only sending her the money she'd asked for, but reassuring and advising her. She felt a pang of regret that Dolley Todd would in all probability not be able to visit until after her confinement. It would be good to have babies in the house again.

But before Martha's letters were even sent, all things had changed, and even the deadly antics of Citizen Genêt came to seem like those of an ill-mannered child banging on a pot.

Two days after Martha's visit to Dolley, Pollie Lear died.

And within days, other people, rich and poor, black and white, began to die, all over the town.

The fever summer had begun.

ABIGAIL

⌒ঔ

Boston, Massachusetts
Thursday, September 27, 1793

"And you have had no word from your father?" Abigail knew that if Johnny had, the first words out of his mouth when she came into his dark little office on Queen Street would have been, *I've had word from Pa . . .*

But she couldn't keep from asking.

The news from Philadelphia had been simply too terrifying.

Yellow fever, the whites called it. Blacks, who had seen it in the Caribbean, spoke of *vomito negro,* or of Bronze John.

Thirty people were dying a day.

"None save that Congress had adjourned, and that he would start for home within two days. It was but a note, dated the eleventh."

Her son spoke brusquely over his shoulder as he cleared the books from his desk and put his few papers into drawers. John was habitually neat, and Abigail had inculcated into all three of her sons the need for order and system in all their endeavors. Johnny was the only one upon whom her efforts seemed to have made a lasting impression, though according to John, Tommy—who had just begun his law practice in Philadelphia—was getting better about it.

Charley, at twenty-four a lawyer in New York, sweet and charming as he was, was hopeless. He always claimed he followed a system of his own.

Her boys. Men now in a world that was turning out very differently from that which she and John had imagined, in the days of the War.

When had things begun to go wrong?

"Father did not say whether he meant to return in Tommy's company or not." Johnny fetched his coat from the cupboard. Though the day was unseasonably hot—on her way through the streets from wily Cousin Sam's house near the Common, Abigail had seen more than one gentleman (if such they could be called) in shirtsleeves outside the coffee-houses and taverns—since the age of ten she'd never seen her eldest son leave so much as his bedroom less than properly dressed.

Indeed a son to be proud of, she decided as she watched him. His old nickname "Hercules" suited him more now as his body settled into a burly strength. As John had done, Johnny had begun his public service, writing for the *Columbian Centennial* a series of scathing rebuttals when Thomas Jefferson had endorsed Tom Paine's *The Rights of Man* with an introduction bemoaning "the political heresies that have sprung up among us." It was quite clear that Jefferson meant her husband's criticism of the way the French were conducting their Revolution, and his evasive apology had come far too late to prevent his supporters—who assumed that John had written the rebuttals himself—from jumping in with their own libelous replies.

Yet as she took Johnny's arm to walk back to Sam's house on Winter Street, Abigail couldn't help seeing the sag of a much older man beginning in her son's shoulders. Though only twenty-six, Johnny had a shuttered look to his eyes, like a house whose inhabitants have gone away, or withdrawn to its innermost rooms.

He didn't look that way in France.

His old easy cheerfulness had vanished. *It's because of the factions that have split this country, ever since the fighting began in France.*

That conflict, growing like a cancer as John had predicted that it would, was enough to trouble anyone's rest, even before the French had declared war on everyone around them and started trying to drag America into it to save their own unwashed necks. In Paris, Johnny had spent at least two evenings a week at Jefferson's Hôtel, and had looked on the Virginian as a sort of exotic uncle.

To watch the man he'd respected—the man he thought he knew—become a supporter of the crew of murderers now in charge of France must be as difficult for her son as Abigail knew it was for her husband. Sometimes it seemed to her that she had never really known Jefferson. That the Jefferson she had known had been . . . What? A dissimulation? A mask?

But she knew how deeply John felt betrayed.

The newspapers that supported Jefferson's faction had begun to claim that John Adams must be a supporter of monarchy and an enemy of freedom. Abigail had grown used to this kind of thing from the Tory press in London. To see this slime being thrown at John by his own people filled her with rage.

And so it must Johnny.

The cobbles underfoot were treacherous—she caught her son's strong arm for support. Wrath for his country's sake had to be what ate at his heart. His secretive gloom couldn't, certainly, have anything to do with that silly girl he'd fallen in love with, just after he'd finished his legal studies. Completely aside from the fact that the girl was only fifteen, Johnny had been in no financial position to take on a bride: Abigail wasn't about to permit a repeat of Nabby's difficulties. Faced with her objections—and John's—Johnny had renounced his Miss Frazer, and had settled down to politics and work.

"Did Father write to you before he left?" he asked, in his abrupt way.

"I've had nothing since last we spoke." Which had been ten days ago, when Johnny

had ridden down for Sunday dinner in Braintree—although the northern part of the
town, where John and Abigail had settled
upon their return from France, was now
called Quincy, in honor of Abigail's grandfather who had helped found it. "He said that
he, and everyone else in the government,
had removed from Philadelphia to Germantown, on account of the yellow fever."

She shuddered, remembering the women
who'd made her Philadelphia receptions
so entertaining: Ann Bingham and Eliza
Drinker, Eliza Powel and Harriet Manigault
and Betsey Hamilton. Educated women,
well-read and well-informed. Most of them
had the means to flee the city, but how far
would the disease spread inland from the
wharves where the newspapers said that it
had started?

"Nothing about Tommy?"

Abigail shook her head. Tommy had been
sharing quarters with his father in the house
of Mr. Otis, the Secretary of the Senate, but
when John had fled, like everyone else, to
Germantown, his letter hadn't said whether
Tommy had gone with him, taken up residence elsewhere, or remained in Philadelphia. Since the plague had only begun to

take hold then it probably had not seemed important.

Now long lists of the dead were being published, so many there were not men enough to bury them, nor carts to haul away the bodies. The mansion at Bush Hill, the Boston paper said, "formerly the home of Vice President Adams and his wife"—a drafty, horrible place it had been in the winter of 1790, its fourteen fireplaces beggaring them just to keep from freezing—had now been converted to a plague hospital. Though not in general fanciful, Abigail had had a hideous vision of John being taken there, dying in the place where he had once been honored. The town was empty. Even the church bells had been stilled to avoid panicking the remaining population. The ships at the wharves stood silent, their crews dead or deserted.

Her hand closed tight over Johnny's arm as they walked along the bricks of Queen Street—only these days it was the upper half of State Street—toward the Common. They passed Brattle Street: The house still stood where her daughter Susanna had been born and had so quickly died. Their feet trod the same bricks over which she and Nabby had raced at the sound of gunfire, to see the snow of King Street all splashed with blood.

Boston had changed. After the noisy grandeur of London and the stinking glamor of Paris, it would always seem small. The streets were as narrow as those of Paris, though they smelled, like everything else in the town, of fish as well as wood smoke and privies. The buildings cramped shoulder-to-shoulder, soot-darkened wood, the tiny panes of window-glass a memory of England's rules about what could be imported and what couldn't. The tin horns of fishmongers, the iron wheels of carriages, the muffled thump of workmen's hammers in cobblers' and cabinetmakers' and silversmiths' shops reechoed through those twisty streets, and the tap of passersby on the cobbles, their voices mingling with tavern dinner-bells.

But since the new Constitution had gone into effect—since the various states had begun pulling together instead of in whatever direction each chose—Abigail had seen the town's wharves rebuilt, that had been pulled apart for firewood during the siege. New houses were being constructed on the high ground north of the Common, and up toward Barton's Point.

In Boston, reflected Abigail, one didn't see beggars in every alleyway, as there had been in London and Paris. Or boys who should have been in school sweeping horse-droppings from the pavement in the hopes that someone would throw them a halfpenny so they might eat that day. Trade—with both England and France—was slowly getting back on its feet. Small manu-factories were growing in spite of England's efforts to undersell local competition, new farms were springing up along the frontiers.

And all of this—all that we have accom-plished—will be swept away again, if we go to war.

She felt the implacable heat of rage rise through her, at those—like Thomas Jeffer-son, who once had been her friend—whose passion for faction was pulling the country apart.

⚜

Cousin Sam's house stood on Winter Street, a gloomy three-story structure that had at one time been painted yellow and was long overdue for a freshening-up. For years he'd hung on to the moldering pile of the family home on Purchase Street, though after the damage done to it by the British occupation he'd never had the money to get it put right. The Revolution was pretty much the only thing Sam had ever turned his hand to that had succeeded. He was as bad about keeping track of money as Jefferson was.

And as deluded in his enthusiasm for France.

But much as Abigail distrusted Sam, it was difficult not to like the bright-eyed gentleman who met her at the door with a smiling embrace and a kiss on both cheeks. "My dear, you're as beautiful as ever you were. So glad to see you in better health these days."

"Abigail, dearest!" Bess Adams slipped around her husband, took Abigail's hand. "It's good to see you in town at last. Louisa's in the kitchen with Hannah and the children"—Sam's daughter by his first marriage and her family shared the house with them—"and I've made Sam swear a Bible oath to leave off politics for the duration of dinner. We are family," she went on, sliding a plump arm around Abigail's waist and leading her down the passageway to the kitchen. "And I'm sure, worried as you must be about John and Tommy, that the last thing you need is a lot of wrangling over the roast."

As Bess had promised, Abigail's niece Louisa was in the kitchen. But instead of Hannah Adams Wells and Sam's grandchildren, with that dark-haired, pretty young woman was a young man in shirtsleeves, whose raven hair fell in a rakish curl over black brows that flared back like a bird's wings. He held the coffee-caddy while Louisa set the mill on the table. He was saying something to her, quietly and intently, and both looked around at once as Bess and Abigail entered the room.

"Now, Louisa, don't you be listening to a single thing Mr. Boyne has to say to you," warned Bess, with a good-natured shake of her finger. "Abigail, this is Sam's clerk, Mr. Boyne. Mr. Michael Boyne, Mrs. Adams."

"A pleasure and an honor, ma'am." If his name hadn't announced his origins, his sliding Irish vowels did so as he bowed. "I've read your husband's work with interest; my employer didn't lie when he said his cousin had read everything under the sun and had it all at his fingertips." He glanced at Louisa, catching the young woman's eye, and added, "He didn't lie either, when he said Mr. John Adams had done his posterity the favor of marrying into the handsomest family in the state."

Bess stooped to the hearth and swept the coals from the top of the Dutch oven. "I told you not to listen to a word he said." She lifted the lid and the rich odor of duck and molasses billowed into the air like the music of trumpets.

Sam's Bible oath held good for about ten minutes, which wasn't bad, for Adamses. During that ten minutes, Abigail related to Sam and Bess, to Hannah and her husband Captain Wells, the contents of John's most recent letter from Philadelphia, which was the reason she'd accepted Bess's invitation to dine. Despite their political differences— and despite John's occasional jealousy, during the War years, when in Paris people would lose interest in him the moment they realized he wasn't *the* Mr. Adams—Sam and John loved one another like brothers. Sam had gathered every fragment of news from Philadelphia that he could, though it was little enough.

"I've heard that the young wife of the President's secretary died of the fever—one of the first cases, I believe," he told Abigail. "Mr. Hamilton and his wife were both taken ill, though Mr. Hamilton, being from the West Indies himself, treated himself and her with cool infusions, and stayed away from doctors. Never a bad idea," Sam added with a chuckle, though his only son, who had died soon after the War, had been a surgeon in Washington's Army.

"You don't think Mr. Hancock has the fever?" asked Bess, genuinely concerned. "He's not been well all summer."

The dapper little ex-tea-smuggler had beaten Sam for Governor of the State of Massachusetts every year for the past seven years, to Sam's bitter chagrin. In 1789 Sam had been elected lieutenant governor, and his friends in the legislature had gotten together and pushed through a bill attaching a salary of five hundred pounds to the post, so that Sam would have something to live on.

"The Hancocks have a summer place in Braintree—Quincy," Louisa corrected herself with a fleeting smile that reminded Abigail heartbreakingly of Louisa's father, her scapegrace brother William, when he was young. "It's mostly dropsy, Mrs. Hancock says, and he gets so tired so easily, for all that he's only a few years younger than Uncle John."

Shortly before they'd sailed from England in '88, Abigail had gotten word of her brother William's death, and of the fact that William had left his wife and daughters penniless.

Will hadn't been a bad man, Abigail insisted. Just a very foolish one, given to drink and bad company. During her years in Europe, she and sister Mary had had a code between them: If a letter concerned Will, Mary would put a special mark on the outside of it, to warn Abigail not to open it until she was alone. She would usually speak to John later about it, but it was understood in the family that matters concerning Will were not for unguarded public consumption.

In sixteen-year-old Louisa—whom Abigail had not seen since her good-bye party at Cousin Isaac's, when the girl had been twelve—Abigail had found the company she so painfully missed, now that Nabby and Colonel Smith were living near New York. In some ways more satisfactory than Nabby, much as Abigail loved and missed her daughter: Louisa was quicker-witted and more outspoken, without Nabby's silent withdrawals.

Without, also, the unspoken anger at a husband who had turned out to be worse than useless.

"They're saying that in Philadelphia, the worst of the fever is always along the water-front," put in Sam's daughter Hannah. "Wasn't it that some ships had unloaded sacks of rotten coffee from the West Indies, and it was the fumes from those, piled along the wharves, that engendered the plague?"

"And I've heard it said," provided her husband, "that it was the refugees from Saint-Domingue that brought it in."

"Refugees. Or the sailors from the French fleet that was in Philadelphia when it began," growled Johnny.

The young clerk Mr. Boyne snapped to attention like a dog at an alien step. "That's precisely the sort of tale that the Federalists are putting about in their tame newspapers, to stir up hatred against the French."

So much for Bible oaths.

"You think Americans with their nation's

good at heart need to be 'stirred up' to mistrust an invading force that seeks to overthrow the government by riots?" demanded Johnny. "The way they've already overthrown half a dozen of their own?"

Sam set down his spoon. "As much as you Federalists seem to think that Americans need to be 'stirred up' by outsiders, to take up arms in the cause of Liberty, both abroad and at home."

"If it *were* Liberty that is being practiced in France, I shouldn't have any objection," interposed Abigail calmly. "But there is a line between the cause of Liberty intelligently pursued, and the chaos that leaves men open to the manipulation of demagoguery, and I hope we all know on which side of the line the massacre of innocent people falls."

The remainder of the meal reminded Abigail a great deal of those arguments that had taken place around the kitchen table of her old house on Queen Street, with brilliant, passionate Joseph Warren arguing for the necessity of organizing the colonies, and James Otis rising from his seat and spreading his arms in the firelight as if he would embrace all the sleeping earth, speaking of his vision of a world where every man would be free.

But Joseph Warren's bullet-torn body had been carried from the field at Breed's Hill, Abigail remembered as Briesler drove her and Louisa home along the shores of the bay. How would the government now be different, had he lived to contribute his intelligence to the nation for which he'd given the last blood in his heart?

When she closed her eyes it seemed to her that she could still smell the gunpowder, the sea, and the heavy green perfume of cut hay as she sat with eight-year-old Johnny on top of Penn's Hill watching that battle: pale gun-flashes flickering through the smoke and flame of Charles Town's burning houses.

And James Otis, so mad that he had sometimes had to be confined, had rushed into that same battle with a borrowed musket and emerged unscathed, only to be claimed within months by the demons within his mind. He had died, Abigail recalled, exactly as he would have requested God to take him: struck by lightning, while watching a summer storm, only months before the end of the War.

How would the world have been different, had his mind remained clear?

Had John—and Tom Jefferson for that matter—been here, and not in Europe, when the Constitution was forged?

Would the country now be facing the twin devils of faction and violence, that were dragging the United States toward a firestorm of fratricidal war?

She looked at Louisa, who had been quiet since they had left Cousin Sam's house. The girl's face was weary and a little sad in the luminous glow of the long summer twilight. If Abigail herself hadn't been so genuinely frightened at the prospect of the pro-French party precipitating the kind of rioting that was tearing France apart, she would have enjoyed the intellectual swordplay over dinner. Even as angry as she was at Sam for his blind disregard of the facts, she felt alive as she hadn't in over a year.

She loved Stonyfield Farm, loved having her family around her. But she missed the steely sparkle of Philadelphia politics, the clash of educated minds. She missed the aroma of power, of being part of the destiny of the young nation that was her life.

John's life, too, since first they were wed.

Dear God, don't let it be too late, she prayed. *Bring me back to John's side, if it is Your will. He needs me at his side—he WILL need me at his side, if he's to rule this country after President Washington steps down.* The two men who were as brothers to him— Tom Jefferson and Cousin Sam—were deceived into the camp of his enemies. It was only upon his family, upon herself and Johnny, that he could rely.

If he was not already dead, in a mass grave somewhere in Philadelphia. *Vitaque mancipio, nulli datur, omnibus usu,* the Roman Lucretius had said: *Life is only lent to us to use, not given.* As the lights of Quincy gleamed ahead of them, a comforting daffodil-yellow against the matte silhouette of hills and trees, Abigail thought despairingly, *But don't take him away NOW! The country needs him, desperately.*

I need him.

Desperately.

Half her life, it seemed to her, she'd been waiting to hear whether John were alive or dead. At forty-nine, Abigail was old enough to know that she could survive his death, if God so willed it. She just couldn't imagine how.

"It's still light," Louisa remarked. "Shall we walk over to Uncle Peter's before bed, and tell Gran how we found Cousin Sam?" John's brother Peter now lived in the old wooden house on the Plymouth road where Abigail and John had raised their children during the War. His family included Granny Susie, at ninety-four still brisk and lively after a second widowhood.

Briesler turned the chaise from the sea-road, inland toward the house that Royall Tyler had once planned to buy for Nabby, in the days when that long-vanished young rake had meant to make her his bride.

And now it is ours. Politics and faction weren't the only things that turned out differently than Abigail had expected.

While still in England, John and Abigail had bought the house and its acres. Though not nearly as big as Abigail had remembered it after five years abroad, John was pleased with it. "It is but the farm of a patriot," he had said, and had named the place Stonyfield. Abigail had planted beside the path two white rosebushes that she'd brought from England, and in the garden a lilac tree.

"It sounds a good idea," agreed Abigail.

An evening walk in her niece's company was certainly an improvement on lying awake yet another sweltering night, wondering if she would ever see John again.

Yet when Briesler drove the chaise in from the road, and helped aunt and niece down, Abigail stopped short, looking up at the house.

Wondering why the dog Caesar hadn't dashed out to greet them. Wondering what was different.

Too many windows lit.

One of them the window of John's study.

She felt as if someone could read a book by the light that bloomed instantly from her heart. Without a word she broke from Louisa and Briesler and almost ran up the path, up the steps to the door. He must have heard the carriage-wheels because he was running down the stairs as she burst into the hall, and they clung laughing, rocking in one another's arms with shaggy little white-nosed Caesar dashing happy circles around their feet. It was dark as a grave in the hall and all Abigail could see of John for that first moment was the blur of shirt-sleeve, stockings, and face; she knew she must have been no more than a silhouette.

It didn't matter. They would have known each other in the darkness of Death.

"Is Tommy with you?" Louisa asked, something Abigail realized she should have asked as well, and surely would, when the incandescent wave of gratitude for John released its grip.

"I hoped to find him here." John's voice was grave. Abigail stepped back, cold sickness clutching again at her heart. "He was to leave Philadelphia the same day I left Germantown, and meet me on the road. When I didn't encounter him, I didn't know whether to wait a day at Trenton, or hasten my horse."

"If anything had happened to him," Louisa pointed out, leading the way down the hall to Abigail's parlor, "someone would have written us here, you know."

Another man would have spared his wife's fears by agreeing, whatever he knew or privately thought. John being John, he only shook his head and said, "You don't know how it is in Philadelphia, Louisa—or at least how it was when I left there two weeks ago. The corpse-gatherers sometimes don't even stay to identify those they find. I doubt now I could even write to enquire at his lodgings, for there is no one who would take the letter to that accursed town. Nor anyone there alive to receive it."

⚜

Her dearest Tommy.

Long after John drifted to sleep at her side, Abigail lay in the darkness, listening to the singing of the night-birds.

Thinking about her son. Her gentle, affable Tommy.

He hadn't seemed any the worse for being left behind when they had departed for England, under the charge of her sister Betsey. Although perhaps too fond of a third glass of wine, of all her sons he seemed the steadiest, without Johnny's tormented air of being unable to fit in anywhere, and without Charley's—Her mind ducked away from her suspicion of what might be at the root of Charley's problems, and substituted, *Without Charley's lightness of mind, as well as of heart.*

Though now that Charley was practicing law he seemed much steadier and more mature. So everything might very well be all right.

But as the thought went through her mind

she couldn't put aside the recollection of her brother Will, handsome like Charley and with Charley's questing intelligence.

They deserved more of us.

Yet another thing that hadn't turned out as planned.

Five years of entertaining on a scale that even approximated that of the noblemen who comprised most of the diplomatic corps in England and France had driven John into debt. Five years abroad had been five years that neither John nor Abigail had been able to work the farm into a paying proposition. Like the Smith side of the family, Tommy had wanted to be a merchant when he'd emerged from Harvard. But John had simply been unable to provide his youngest son the money to make his start.

In law, at least, a man could get a start with no tools but his mind and his books.

Would Charley have found a vocation that called to his quick mind and restless heart, had there been some other one available?

On his way through New York to Philadelphia last April, John had visited Charley in the city, and had called on Nabby and Colonel Smith in that isolated stone house in the woods of Long Island. At least

Colonel Smith appeared, at long last, to be solvent, to such a degree that John had worried about what Jefferson's tame news-papers would say of him if his daughter and her husband continued to swan about the city in brand-new finery and a coach-and-four. Abigail agreed that it looked bad, with the country on the verge of war, for the daughter and son-in-law of the Vice Presi-dent to be so obviously rich, but her heart couldn't avoid a whisper of relief.

Only the autumn before that, 1791, on her way from Philadelphia to Braintree, Abigail had been struck with a rheumatic fever, and had lain for nearly six weeks at Nabby's, head aching, joints burning as if she had been racked, listening to the newest baby crying and her two undisciplined grand-sons—Willie and Little Johnnie—shouting at one another, and wishing she could die.

There had been no servants in her daugh-ter's house and sometimes, almost no food. Colonel Smith was gone most days and sometimes overnight, and Nabby was very shut-mouthed about what the family was living on. The Colonel's mother occasionally came over or sent one of her giggling, pretty daughters to help with the cooking or look after the children—apparently nobody bothered with cleaning—and acknowledged that "The dibs ain't in tune just now," meaning that the family was almost destitute. "But the Colonel, he's a knowing one," she added, and tapped the side of her nose with an expression that was supposed to be wise. "My son's always got some speculation going. You'll see."

On that visit Abigail had seen about as much as she wanted to. She shuddered to think of her grandchildren being raised among that tribe.

It was partly the thought of being taken ill on the road again—of finding herself an enforced guest for who knew how many weeks in that household filled with fictions, pipe-dreams, and promises that turned out to be lies—that decided Abigail not to attempt to travel to Philadelphia last winter, nor again this year.

She realized she, too, had changed, from the woman who'd thrown herself like a dove into the wind to cross the ocean, to be with the man she loved.

John was safe, at least now, at least so far. She turned her head on the pillow, imagining from long familiarity, the pugnacious nose, the sensual lips, every wrinkle and line of his cheeks.

It was her children who were becoming lost to her, body and heart.

⚜

Through those long weeks of late summer, Abigail dreamed, again and again, of wandering through the silent streets of Philadelphia, looking for Tommy. The streets were always as she knew them: the neat grid so beloved of the city's Quaker founders and so different from Boston's twisting alleys. Sometimes in her dreams the streets were empty, the bricks dotted with dead cats, dead rats, dead birds. In other dreams, they were crowded, and she kept meeting people she knew: Ann Bingham, Martha Washington, her father in his black coat and white clerical bands, the pretty Mme. de Lafayette who had been so kind to her in Paris. All of them were dead, with the faint green rime of grave-mold on their faces. When she'd ask them, "Have you seen my son Tommy?" they would only point.

Then she'd wake and lie in the heat, sweating and praying while John slept at her side.

"At least the yellow fever's dispersed the mobs," John told her, the morning after his arrival. "Even those who haven't money to flee avoid human contact, and walk for safety down the center of the street. If Citizen Genêt can get as many as five men to attend a Jacobin club meeting, I shall be very much surprised."

As Johnny had said, the sailors of the French fleet were widely blamed for bringing in the fever in the first place. To the further chagrin of the troublemaking French Minister, a large number of those same French sailors, when informed of plans to sail out of New York against Canada and Louisiana, mutinied, burned Genêt's house, got on their ships again, and set sail for France. Abigail hoped uncharitably they'd carry the yellow fever to Paris as a souvenir. Before President Washington left the Germantown house where he was staying, he informed the French Minister that he had sent a request for his recall.

"Whatever instructions Genêt had from his government," remarked John, as they strolled along the green shade of the orchard rows, "they won't be happy that he's made himself this unpopular—if indeed they're still alive by this time."

From his pocket he took the folded sheets of the *New York Advertiser.* "A Correspondent" reported from Paris that after six weeks of intermittent riots and uprisings, the Girondist faction had been expelled from the National Convention, Danton had been ousted from his position on the Committee of Public Safety, and a man named Maximilien Robespierre had taken his place. "Genêt is a Girondist," John told Abigail. "A number of Girondists, including Genêt's chief, have been arrested. One could almost feel sorry for the man."

"One could," retorted Abigail acidly, "were one not paying attention to what damage is happening in *this* country as a result of his activities."

She turned her face from him, looked out through the pale gray columns of the apple trees, toward the open pastureland and the stream beyond. Across the road the voices of the hired men drifted as they swung their scythes at the curing yellow wheat-stalks; John had promised to join them no later than noon. At breakfast, though clearly still weary from his journey, Abigail had thought he already looked more relaxed, as if antic-ipating the joy of having a scythe in his hands again, and sweat on his face.

It seemed almost incongruous, to be stand-ing here knee-deep in orchard grass, she in the faded apron she'd put on to work in the dairy and he in his smock and his braided straw hat, discussing the deadly wranglings of the so-called French government.

Yet why not? It was as it should be, that a farmer and his wife would understand the meaning of these things. That a farmer and his wife would make the decisions that would affect the whole of the country.

That was the world they had seen, beyond the smoke of the War. The world they had striven to found.

"Tom Jefferson's an intelligent man," she said, frustrated, as they walked back toward the house, Caesar trotting, arthritic but game, at their heels. "How can he not see what happens, when factions and parties develop? How can he go on saying that this divisiveness is of any benefit to anyone? We won our freedom by acting *together,* John. The Sons of Liberty, and the people of Boston, took their direction from a small group of men who knew all the facts, who had been educated and took time to study the matter. Now all is anarchy, with the newspapers spilling out the most horrible lies! You remember what the press was in France! Printing filth about anyone they didn't agree with, only to whip on the mobs, as rags like the *Aurora* and the *Examiner* whip them on now." Her voice shook with anger.

John regarded her for a moment with watchful eyes. Then he put his arms around her, and said gently, "We've found our way through this so far, dearest Portia. We'll make it safe to harbor. Now tell me, if you will, how Cousin Sam looked, and all his family, and what's been happening in Boston. I take it there's no sign there yet of the fever?"

So they spoke of other things. But all through the day, as Abigail returned to the kitchen and the dairy, fed her finches (this latest pair she'd named Anthony and Cleopatra) and settled down to the task of sorting through John's laundry for mending, washing, replacing, her mind kept going back to its anger, as if anger were easier to deal with than her fear for the Republic, and dread for Tommy's sake.

As the day lengthened into a week, and the week into another, she found it was the same. Whenever there wasn't anything else to occupy her, the fear would return. And in the wake of dread that her son was dead would come anger at Tom Jefferson, or annoyance at the French and the Irish, who were just as vocal about wanting a war with Britain, for obvious reasons of their own. Boston was filled with both.

Fortunately, it was the busiest time of year on the farm, and there was much to occupy Abigail's mind and time. The corn was brought in, husked, cribbed; the wheat harvested, winnowed, taken to the mill; apples to be picked, cider pressed. There were work-crews to feed, Peter and his men helping John, or John and his men going down the road to Peter's, or both going to the neighbors. Peter's wife Mary, and Abigail's sister, and old Granny Susie would come, to sew and bake and make cheeses.

These summers were and always had been Abigail's greatest joy. It was as if God had given them to her, like a certain number of gold pieces, as reward for those weeks of being seasick or terrified or exhausted from feeding all those refugees at the time of the Boston siege.

But always she was listening for the sound

of hooves. For a message from Tommy, or, worse, from some stranger *about* Tommy. John walked into town daily to check the post, and the newspapers that he brought back were appalling. A hundred people a day were dying in Philadelphia now. In France, the Committee of Public Safety had seized the reins of government: The Republic, Robespierre explained, was the hope of mankind, and if it disappeared, tyranny would prevail forever. Thus it was necessary to preserve Liberty by temporarily suppressing it. Neither he nor anyone else specified for how long.

Émigrés were flooding into Boston and New York, bearing news of the Terror. Abigail tried in vain to learn whether the friends she'd made in Paris, who had made her welcome in their homes, had gotten out: the Duc de la Rochefoucauld, and the lovely Mme. de Lafayette.

Even Thomas Jefferson, she thought in disgust, could not ignore what was happening there now.

Or maybe he could.

Twice, to Abigail's annoyance, Sam's clerk, young Mr. Boyne, rode out to the farm, with messages for John that contained nothing about Tommy nor about much of anything else. It was only on the third occasion, when Louisa shyly suggested that Mr. Boyne be asked to remain for dinner, that Abigail began to suspect that the young man was the one inventing correspondence for his employer to send.

When Sam drove out to visit, the Monday that the church bells tolled through Massachusetts for the death of John Hancock, Boyne came with him. Cousin Sam—Hancock's partner since the days the pair had conspired to turn Boston Harbor into a teapot and thirteen separate colonies into a single self-governing nation—followed the funeral wagon on foot as far as he was able. Afterwards he, his clerk, and his son-in-law Tom Wells came to Stonyfield Farm to dine.

John was the first to raise his wineglass and say, "To his Excellency the Governor," and Abigail saw a tear glisten in Sam's bright gray eye.

How many of the men who made France's Revolution, she wondered, watching Johnny step around the table to shake Sam's hand, would end their lives quietly governing their home territories, surrounded by their families, growing grizzled and chubby in peace? Lafayette had been outlawed and had had to flee his own country; he would be killed if he returned. Had M'sieu Danton been permitted to go home to his wife, if he had a wife, after he'd been ousted from power? Would M'sieu Robespierre live to quiet old age?

Somehow, Abigail didn't think so. She wondered what made the difference. Sam had, by all accounts, been a troublemaker and an intriguer in Congress, but nobody had hustled him to prison and beheaded him in the public square.

Of course, if Jefferson and his faction take over, she reflected, *who knows?* Few of the men who'd started the Revolution—Sam, Mr. Hancock, Patrick Henry—had real power in this new nation.

She looked around for Louisa, and seeing her place empty, rose to fetch the corn pudding herself. The pro-French newspapers were already full of talk of making Jefferson the next President, though it was clearly John's right to take the office after Washington stepped down. *Faction again,* she thought, crossing the yard to the summer kitchen, her long skirt rustling in the deep grass. It infuriated her, not only that John might be deprived of the due he had earned, but to know how much that public humiliation would hurt him. *Faction and interest, and refusing to follow the best interests of the country!*

In the kitchen, Louisa and Mr. Boyne stood, the young woman with her head bowed, the clerk clasping both of her hands. Neither heard Abigail's step on the gravel until too late; Louisa looked around, startled, and stepped back hastily at the sight of her aunt's icy eye. Abigail said, "Please get the cream and some more butter from the spring house, if you will, dear," in her most deadly tone, and brushed past Boyne without a glance or a word.

With her usual quiet speed, Louisa hurried down the path to the branch, while Abigail loaded a tray with cake, pudding, and the molasses pitcher. Mr. Boyne took a pace toward her and said, "Mrs. Adams, I can explain," and she fixed him with a glacial regard.

"Oh, I'm sure you can," she replied in a friendly voice that could have cut glass. "But you needn't."

Color flooded up under the thin Irish skin. He turned and strode from the little building; the sinking summer sunlight flashed like a blackbird's wing on his hair. He didn't return across the yard to the house; instead, he disappeared through the gates onto the road.

"You didn't need to send him away, Aunt Abigail," Louisa said, standing in the kitchen doorway. There was anger as well as sadness in her voice.

"I didn't," Abigail answered serenely. "The young gentleman seems to have a regrettably Irish temper, and a great deal of pride."

"The same might be said of Uncle John," Louisa said. For all that she had lived with her aunt as a dependent for five years, Louisa was no subservient poor relation.

Abigail smiled. "It can indeed." She studied her niece's pretty face, with its sharp Smith nose, its dark intelligent eyes. There was something to her after all of Nabby's closed expression, as if growing up in the tensions and uncertainties of Will's disorderly household were not so very different from growing up under threat of the British guns.

More quietly, she went on, "But what cannot be said of your uncle John is that he would see harm done to his country for the sake of party politics. Mr. Boyne is a Jacobin. The last thing your uncle needs right now is an enemy on his own hearthstone."

"Because a man disagrees politically doesn't mean he is a wicked man. Or that he is an enemy. Or that he would make a bad husband."

"Any man adhering to the faction that would split the government of this country—that would turn it into the chaos of disunion that we see in France—is by definition your uncle's enemy," replied Abigail. "As he is mine."

In the silence that followed, Abigail wondered how far things had gone, between Sam's clerk and her niece. As far as a kiss? A surreptitious walk in the orchard one evening when he'd come out with a "message" for John? A betrothal?

Betrayal stirred in her, like coals waked to life around her heart. Louisa had lived under her roof, fed and clothed and educated as if she were the daughter Abigail so dearly missed—the daughter she feared she had lost forever. The young woman had frequently quoted, laughing, the words of Beatrice in *Much Ado About Nothing: I would rather hear my dog bark at a crow than hear a man swear he loved me.*

Recalling her own brisk disavowals, Abigail had waited in amusement to see her young companion encounter the passion and joy of love.

But a Jacobin! Abigail felt as disappointed, as betrayed, as if she'd found her niece with her hand in the family cash box.

And an Irishman, who had no stake in the country to which he'd fled! Who understood only what he was told in those scabrous rags like the *Aurora,* who wanted to see the bloody French version of revolution spread across the world, so that those who hadn't worked for their fortunes could take away from those who had.

Such a man would only bring her unhappiness, thought Abigail. *And in its wake, chaos in the family.*

"I'm sorry, dearest."

Louisa took a deep breath. "They'll be waiting for us in the house, Aunt," she said.

⚜

After supper, Abigail lingered at the table to talk of the state of the country with Cousin Sam, John, and Johnny over coffee. It was then that John spoke to his son once again about entering the diplomatic corps. "I thought it a waste of your experiences and skills, when you left France to go to Harvard," he told Johnny. "But I knew also that you wanted to go. But to simply remain a lawyer in Boston, with your knowledge of Paris, St. Petersburg, and Holland!"

Johnny said, rather stiffly, "I felt that I needed what Harvard could teach me."

"And you were like to die there of melancholia within a year," Abigail pointed out.

"We are, God help us, a provincial nation, a nation of 'colonists,' most of whom have never left their native shores," John went on. "That includes the men who now must cope with negotiations in Europe. God knows when I went to Paris I was provincial enough. Your knowledge of both Dutch and French puts you ahead of five sixths of the men Washington has made ministers, never mind that you've been there and know how the people live."

"I've been there," replied Johnny grimly, "and I have no desire to return. I am content here."

"Content?" erupted his father, turning bright pink as he always did when frustrated. "I was pretty content, too, to remain at home with your mother and let Massachusetts look after itself as best it might. But I didn't!"

"Nonsense, John." Sam accepted the sugar-dish from Abigail's hand with his easy smile. "You'd have died of chagrin if you hadn't been elected to the Continental Congress, even had you been married to Cleopatra—who would certainly have suffered in comparison," he added gallantly, "to your charming Portia."

"Your country needs you, Johnny," insisted John. "It already has plenty of lawyers."

"Most of whom can't make a living," added Sam, and Johnny's cheekbones reddened. Though Sam didn't know it, work for new-fledged lawyers in Boston was so short that John and Abigail had been providing their eldest son with a stipend to keep going, with the argument that he was John's lawyer.

"It is your choice, of course, Son," added John grudgingly. But in his voice Abigail heard his thought. For him, as for her, there had never been the question of any other choice. One answered the call of one's country first. One defended its rights, and all other things came secondarily. Farm, family, wishes, husbands, wives.

Only so could the country remain strong.

Only when Sam departed did Michael Boyne appear out of nowhere, to climb into the chaise at his side. John and Abigail waved them out of sight as they turned onto the road back to town. Over the rich green countryside, the church bells still tolled for the death of John Hancock, the man who'd stepped up to be the first to sign the declaration of the country's independence. The first to publicly defy the King.

Louisa had gone into the house.

⚜

A week later a letter reached them from New Jersey.

It was from Tommy. He'd gotten out of Philadelphia all right and tight, he wrote, but was now perilously short of cash. Might they send him some?

SALLY

∽

Monticello Plantation
Albemarle County, Virginia
Wednesday, October 23, 1793

"I love you, Sally. I could ask no greater happiness in this life, than to be your husband. Will you be my wife?"

The tall man before her bent his head, pressed his lips to her hand. Sun-dapple through the yellowing leaves of the mulberry trees flashed in Sally's eyes, warmed the tear she felt trail down her cheek.

It was good, to have a friend.

She whispered, "Thank you, Lam," and Lamentation Hawkin raised his head, saw his answer in her eyes. "That's one of the nicest things anyone has ever said to me. But you know I can't accept."

The Charlottesville carter moved his head

a little, glancing back up the hill at the two-story red-brick house. "Because of him? Or because of me?"

"Because of *me.*" Sally wrapped her other hand around the one that Lam still held, smiled up at him. He was one of the ugliest men she'd ever seen, and had the kindest eyes. She wished very much that she loved him, and wondered if that would make a difference to her answer.

Probably not.

"You know I'd take your boy—"

"I know. It isn't that." Although it was, partly. Sally knew to the marrow of her bones that Thomas Jefferson, no matter what his current feelings about the woman he had once loved, would never allow his four-year-old son to be raised by a black man.

Particularly not one who lived in a town not five miles away.

Lam was silent. Not asking, *Has he taken you back?* Not asking, *Are you still thinking he will?*

"May I still call you my friend, Lam?"

Warmth kindled in his eyes as he brought her hand up to his lips again. His fingers were strong enough to bend an iron pot-hook. "To the end of time, girl," he said.

As he walked away down Mulberry Row toward the stable-yard where he'd left his wagon, Sally sat again on the bench where he'd come upon her, beside the wash-house door. Almost no one was around, the carpentry-shop silent, the dairy empty, the cleared ground where Mr. Jefferson was having a small nail-factory built deserted. Tobacco harvest was nearly done. Every spare hand, male and female, was down at the curing-barns, sorting and tying the leaves to dry. Only around the kitchen, a hundred feet away on the other side of the Row, was there activity, her brothers Jimmy and Pip getting dinner together for the family at the Big House.

"Papa, do come!" Patsy's strong firm alto, drifting clearly down from the unkempt lawn behind the house on the hill's crest, could still raise the hairs on the back of Sally's neck. "It's the cunningest thing! Little Annie's decided she's ready to ride Bergère, and poor Bergère isn't sure what to make of it."

Bergère was the shaggy-coated sheepdog Patsy had begged her father to buy for her, just before their return from France.

Sally picked up the chemise she'd been working on, rolled the tiny hem of its ruffle between expert fingers. Tom was back from the tobacco-barns, then, she thought: Dinner would be soon. She could picture him striding across the ragged grass to Patsy and little Annie, his head thrown back and his smile like the dazzle of the sun.

Once Pip and Burwell carried the dishes across to the house, it would be safe for her to slip in and distribute the garments she'd been working on all morning: Maria's chemises, Mr. Jefferson's shirts, M'sieu Petit's waistcoat with its new buttons, all to be packed in their trunks for departure. She could be in and out without fear of meeting anyone.

And the day after tomorrow, they'd be gone.

"They dyin' in Philadelphia." Betty Hemings's quiet voice spoke at Sally's elbow, and her mother stepped around the corner of the washhouse, with an armload of newly ironed shirts. "Sixty, seventy people a day, the newspaper said."

There were masters who would whip the

possessor of any newspaper they found in the quarters, but Thomas Jefferson wasn't one of them. Her mother's news was no news to Sally.

"Takes two weeks to get to Philadelphia." Sally measured out thread from the spool and snipped it with the little scissors Abigail Adams had given her in London, six years ago. "First frost'll come by then. That always kills the fever, Lam says."

Patsy's voice lifted again, rejoicing in her tiny daughter. *Even Socrates might ride on a stick with her without being ridiculous,* Jefferson had said of his first grandchild's sunny charm.

She heard her mother's skirts rustle, smelled the mingled pungence of soap and starch in her clothes as she sat at her side. Glancing sidelong at the older woman, she saw her mother, too, watching the kitchen door, in her case because she'd promised to lend Pip a hand in getting the dinner ready for serving. Two years younger than Jimmy, Pip had been chosen to act as his assistant and to learn from him all the skills of Parisian cooking, before Jimmy could get his papers as a free man. Jimmy was still in charge, but today was one of "Jimmy's days," as everyone said around the quarters. Meaning that Jimmy had started drinking earlier than usual.

"Lam's a good man, Sally. And you don't have to go down live with him seven days a week. If you ask, Mr. Jefferson will give you your freedom, and you can stay here a few days a week to look after Little Tom, til he's old enough to be left. Mr. Jefferson made no trouble over Mary going."

Sally's half-sister Mary—daughter of that Wayles slave who'd also fathered Martin the butler, and their sister Bett—had been leased to Tom's friend Colonel Bell in Charlottesville while the family was in France. By the time the family returned, she'd had two children by him, in addition to the two she'd borne earlier at Monticello. Last year when Bell had offered to buy Mary—and Mary had added her request to his—Jefferson had complied, and had included the two Bell children in the bargain.

Would Tom "make no trouble," she wondered, if she asked him leave to marry another man?

Patsy would see to it that he didn't.

"And if you want to talk to him, now's the time to do it." Betty's face, still beautiful in her fifties, was grave, her dark eyes wise with the wisdom of a woman who has survived and kept her family together against staggering odds. "They leaving Friday, and he might not be back for a year. A lot can happen in a year, first frost or no. Mr. Jefferson's daddy died when he was a younger man than Mr. Jefferson is today. You think he's got it in writing anywhere, that you and Little Tom's to go free? You really want to end up bein' sold off by Mr. Randolph, to settle Mr. Jefferson's debts? You and Little Tom both?"

Sally said nothing. The French lawn of Maria's chemise lay like silk over her fingers, thin enough to show through it the warm café-au-lait of her flesh.

Paris seemed like a thousand years ago. Except for Little Tom, with his sharp Jefferson features and red hair, those years could have been something Sally had dreamed, no more real than the fairy-tales she and Polly used to tell each other at night.

Except for Little Tom, and the deep-smoldering pain that never left her heart.

☙

The voyage back from France in 1789 had been a nightmare.

Jefferson had taken two tiny cabins on the *Clermont,* one for himself with a pallet for Jimmy, one for the girls and the extremely pregnant sheepdog Bergère. Departure had been delayed for two weeks due to storms, though once on the sea the voyage was fast, if rough. Sally kept herself bundled up in the damp cold of the autumn sea, and stayed out of sight of the other passengers when she could. Patsy—almost certainly at Jefferson's request—had subtly conspired in the pretense that her maid was suffering nothing more than *mal de mer.* It was no more than could be expected of any good Virginia lady faced with the mortification of a serving-maid who'd found herself pregnant, no matter who by.

But in private, Sally could have cut the atmosphere in the little cabin with a knife.

Between morning sickness, being kept out of sight, and the daunting logistics of proximity, there was of course no question of seeing more of Tom than a couple of friendly words exchanged, and Patsy made sure she never left her father's side. Only her resolution that she would somehow, some way, find the means to return to France with him in the spring—surely the King would have put down the rioting by then—enabled Sally to get through the journey without flinging herself over the side from sheer wretchedness.

The first thing that greeted them when they reached Norfolk, Virginia, was the froth of rumor that the new President, General Washington, would ask Mr. Jefferson to be his Secretary of State.

Sally didn't need to ask what that would mean. A Virginian might take his mulatto mistress to France with him, and establish her discreetly in rented rooms somewhere near his Hôtel. No Virginian would bring a colored woman to the nation's capital where his neighbors and their families were going to live.

Not even a man who spoke and wrote so eloquently of—and truly believed in, Sally knew—striking out into the unknown territory of the future, rather than living in bondage to the past.

Sally had long ago guessed that though Tom could be a poor judge of people—especially people who professed the same ideals as his—he had an almost womanly perception of the unspoken currents of gossip and public opinion: how they spread and mutated and dyed people's thought. For all his idealism, he knew what things a gentleman simply could not do, if he wished to marry his daughters into respectable families.

⚜

The washhouse stood downslope from the Big House, part of the long row of cabins and workshops shaded by mulberry trees that Jefferson had planted when first he'd come to the mountain twenty-two years before. Sally remembered how little and thin the trees had been in her childhood, and how bare and raw the cabins had looked. For three years now Sally had waked every morning to the sound of the birds in their branches. That daily beauty had gone far toward soothing the hurt of betrayal, and had helped her put her anger in its place.

A gaggle of children dashed around the coal-house. She glimpsed Davy and Kit and Jenny's Lew, Aunty Isabel's Aggy and Eddy, Molly's Bart and Cannda, and dashing along in the rear Little Tom, three and a half years old, a toddler still but long-legged like a baby gazelle. The sight of him brought a smile to her face. If she had lost Tom, Little Tom's presence in her life more than made up for it.

Would I go through all that again, to know I'd have my boy at the end of it?

Yes, a thousand times.

And like any slave-woman who sees her child, she felt the chill on her heart.

Promises are cheap, especially a man's promises made four years ago, to a woman he has ceased to love.

Her mother's voice was soft as she rose. "You still have the chance to do what few of us ever get to do," she said. "Little Tom—well, Mr. Jefferson's gonna do about him whatever he's gonna do, and there's nuthin' you can say that'll change it. And you know, even should harm befall her daddy, Miss Patsy got too much regard for what the neighbors would say to sell him off. But as for you—you'd be a fool not to take the chance to go."

Halfway up the slope from Mulberry Row to the hilltop, the door of the kitchen opened in the bottom floor of the little brick pavilion that had been the first dwelling on top of the mountain, the tiny house to which Tom Jefferson, in the long-ago days before the War, had brought Miss Patty as his bride. Pip stepped out, looking harassed. Jimmy must be sliding from idly talkative to argumentative.

"You better go, Mama. I'll get these done before dark." She patted the folded stack of garments.

She was a fool, Sally thought, as she began to work an eyelet, not to take Lam up on his offer. Lam had been free for ten years, and owned his own livery stable in Charlottesville. He'd been making it his business to seek her out, to talk with her, every time he came up to the mountain since Jefferson had departed last September, presumably when word got around that Jefferson hadn't lain with Sally on that home visit, either. At thirty-five he was steady, gentle, no genius but reasonably well educated, didn't drink, and—a big plus, though Sally was a little embarrassed to put it in so many words—had good teeth and sweet breath.

I'm twenty years old, she thought, looking in the direction of the stable, where her son and his friends had vanished. *What am I waiting for?*

But the answer to that question was a shadow at which she did not wish to look.

⚜

Patsy Jefferson had chosen the day Sally bore her child, to run hand in hand with Tom Randolph to her father and announce that they were engaged.

"I could not ask a better husband for my girl," Jefferson had said, sitting on the foot of Sally's bed in her mother's cabin beside the washhouse, on a snowy January day in 1790, less than two months after the *Clermont* had deposited them on American shores. "I suppose every father rejoices to see his child happily wed. Yet I shall miss her desperately. Patsy tells me their attraction is of long standing, though I confess that wasn't my impression in Paris."

A frown briefly pulled together his reddish eyebrows—at remembered kitchen-rumor about Randolph's expeditions to the Palais Royale?—but with a slight shake of his head he dismissed the thought, and leaned across to tweak back the wrappings from the face of the infant in Sally's arms. "I am— glad of her happiness, though," he added, as if forcing himself to speak the sentiment he knew he should feel. "She's denied it, but I have felt that Patsy was . . . unhappy. At leaving France, perhaps."

So that was where he'd been all day, reflected Sally. Drinking toasts and making plans with old Tom Randolph in the parlor, while Sally clung grimly to her mother's hands, tried to breathe her way through the waves of labor-pains. While the child she'd carried in her womb back across the Atlantic struggled to be born.

The one thing that Patsy would have known absolutely would keep her father from Sally's side.

The Randolphs were neighbors as well as cousins. Tom had grown up with old Tom Randolph, whose plantation of Edgehill lay an hour's brisk walk from Monticello along the river road. The Randolphs had been among the first to visit when the family had returned to Monticello, two days before Christmas after a leisurely journey from Norfolk via Eppington, Richmond, and Charlottesville.

After all her years away Sally had nearly wept with joy to see the mountain again, that magical, beautiful world of her childhood. The slaves with whom she'd grown up, her family and Aunty Isabel, Tom's groom Jupiter and Mose the Blacksmith and all the others, had rejoiced just as much at their master's return, for the simple reason that Jefferson was one of the better masters in the state and no plantation runs well under an overseer's hand. They'd unhitched the team and dragged the carriage up the mountain themselves, laughing in the frigid twilight.

The following day Tom Randolph had ridden over and begun to court the girl he'd played with as a child, the girl he'd met again in France two summers before. The girl who would be heiress to several thousand acres and the slaves to work them.

And though Patsy had bubbled to everyone about how glad she was to be back in Virginia, Sally knew, from weeks of living in the close confines of ship and coach, that beneath her cheerfulness the older girl was still as furious, as jealous, as hurt as she'd been when she'd announced she was going to become a nun. (*And I notice,* Sally remembered Sophie Sparling commenting back in Paris, *Patsy seems to have recovered from her yearning for Catholicism quite quickly—Have you ever seen her pray the Rosary? Or eschew worldly dresses?* In spite of her hurt, Sally had laughed.)

Taking the first husband who asked her,

Sally supposed, was as effective a way of leaving her father's house as taking the veil.

You left me for a designing black wench— now I'll leave YOU. See how you like THAT.

The goal was the same: the pain in Tom's eyes, at the thought of losing his daughter.

Sally could have slapped Patsy—if it hadn't been unthinkable to do so—for hurting him. For sliding a poisoned knife into his most vulnerable spot, his unhealed dread of losing those he loved.

Because she couldn't say any of this—because in her weaker moments she told herself such spiteful malice couldn't be true— Sally said only, "She had many friends in France." As she pressed her cheek against her infant son's, past Jefferson's shoulder she met her mother's eyes. Saw Betty Hemings's mouth twist in a soundless commentary of exasperation at her master's naïveté.

⚓

Looking back on the scene from three and a half years later—sitting in comfort beneath a tree, stitching at the hem of Maria's chemise less than ten yards from the bed where she'd lain that night—Sally could only shake her head at the fierce love she'd felt then for Tom.

He deserves all the pain Patsy or anyone else can hand him.

But her own pain at the memory was so great that her needle stilled and she had to close her eyes again, willing herself not to cry.

⚜

"They'll be married in February," Jefferson went on, and wonderingly brushed Little Tom's hand, where the baby lay wrapped at Sally's side. "I shall have to leave soon after that, if I'm to be in New York for the opening of Congress. Will you be all right here?"

And his eyes, from being focused beyond her upon what he perceived as his daughter's joy, suddenly returned to the present, to her, and to his newborn son. Most white gentlemen, Sally was very well aware, didn't think of their sons by slave-women in even remotely the same terms as they thought of even their white bastards, let alone the true-born children of their wedded wives.

She searched Tom's face, Tom's eyes—the eyes whose shape was already printed in Little Tom's bone structure—for some clue to his thoughts. It wasn't for her to say, *This is our son; child of our mingled flesh. Child of our love.*

They were in Virginia now. He was her master again. Even in two months, she'd seen how it had changed him, to be back in a land where slavery was accepted as normal and where blacks were calmly regarded as being lazy, malicious, and slightly dim-witted.

What had seemed possible in France now stood revealed to her as a naïve and preposterous dream. The simple friendship of a child with the clever and kindly philosopher who was master of the house had dissolved into the unnerving complexities of black and white, slave and master, woman and man.

Would it change him still further in the years to come, to be surrounded by all his neighbors who tupped their slave-women as casually as they pissed?

Her mother, she knew, would have told her, he'd never been *un*changed. He'd always been just like his neighbors. That was how white men were. His nephew Peter Carr was regularly towsing her sister Critta and at least two other girls in the quarters: Critta had already borne his child. Peter's brother Sam was acquiring the same reputation.

And why did it bother her anyway? She had Tom's promise that their son would be free.

"I'll be well," she told him softly. "Shall I write you in cipher, and tell you how he is? 'The tree you planted grows tall.' "

And he'd smiled. "I'd like that."

Because her mother was there, he didn't kiss her. Only cupped Little Tom's tiny head in his white hand, and smiled down at Sally. His expression was impossible to read in the firelight. "I'll be back tomorrow," he said. "Now I must leave; they're waiting for me up at the house."

Cold air bellied into the little cabin as he slipped out the door. She heard him singing in Italian as he climbed the top of the hill, and the crunch of his boots in the snow.

⚜

He hadn't come back, of course. Stitching in the autumn sunlight, Sally shook her head at herself. How could she have been so stupid as to believe a white man's word?

And those few moments when she did encounter him again, "they" were *always* "waiting for me up at the house."

Once news of Patsy's engagement got out, friends, neighbors, and relatives had poured into Monticello for the wedding, which had been held a month later. Even before that, from the moment Jefferson had realized there was going to *be* a wedding at Monticello, there'd been a thousand things to do, completely aside from the new crop of tobacco-seedlings to be prepared. Typically—a situation so thoroughly Tom-like—when they'd arrived at Monticello, half the rooms had been in the same unfinished state in which he'd left them, six years before.

Sally had grown up watching her master continually start building and remodeling and redecorating projects that either misfired or were suspended due to lack of money or Jefferson leaving for Philadelphia or Richmond. Poor Miss Patty—and Aunt Carr who had succeeded her as housekeeper—had been driven half crazy by having furniture shifted around to make room for this or that change in the walls or the floor, and in two years at the Hôtel Langeac Sally had seen doors plastered over and cut in more efficient places in the walls, round windows put in, and ordinary beds replaced by space-saving beds in wall-niches.

So of course, faced with the prospect of all the Randolphs and Carrs and Eppeses in Virginia arriving, rooms that had been roughly finished off with a coat of paint so the girls could be moved in suddenly had to be emptied, replastered, new curtains made . . .

Between the birth of Sally's son, and Jefferson's departure on the first of March, six days after the wedding, Sally was able to speak to him exactly four times, one of those at the wedding itself.

It was the night after the wedding that her sister Critta had broken the news to her. "You know when they get back from their weddin'-trip, Miss Patsy an' Mr. Randolph gonna be comin' back here to stay?"

"Here?" Sally's stomach twisted with shock. She was sitting in her mother's cabin, nursing Little Tom and listening to the din of festivities all along Mulberry Row. Now and then, drifting down from the house, the sweet skirl of Jefferson's violin came to her, as the scent of dried flowers echoed the sun's remembered warmth.

She felt as if the floor had dropped from beneath her. Looking up into her sister's eyes she couldn't even ask, *Is it true?* She knew it was.

"Mr. Jefferson asked her to, specially." Critta, a few years older and like Sally light-complected and pretty, regarded her with enigmatic eyes. "Mr. Randolph don't get along with his papa, over to Edgehill. But his papa's been ill, and needs him to look after the place. And if Mr. Jefferson going to New York, he'll need someone here to look after this place, too."

There was an undertone of satisfaction in Critta's voice, a kind of pleased spite. Sally had heard the echo of it all her life, when people spoke to her mother or to any of her siblings. The whole Hemings clan were set slightly apart, as left-handed members of the family who were in line to receive special favors; slaves who would be the last to be sold in bad times.

And when the master of any plantation took a woman, it set her apart still more, even from her family. As if she had sold herself, to put herself ahead of them.

Maybe it was only because Sally had their master's promise that her son would be a free man, while Critta's boy Jamey—Peter Carr's son or not—could be sold like a blood-horse or a dog.

She wanted to reach out to Critta, to say, *Don't turn against me!*

But Critta would only deny that she felt anything of the kind.

And Tom of course didn't see what the problem was, in the few minutes he was able to snatch, to speak to Sally before he left for New York. "Patsy was in charge of my household for a year in Paris, and you got along quite well," he said, conveniently forgetting the occasions when his daughter's needling criticism and cutting remarks had reduced Sally to tears. And seeing the look in Sally's eyes, he took her hands. "She doesn't know, Sally—"

He glanced over his shoulder as if to make sure they were unobserved, though there wasn't much place for spies in a one-room cabin ten feet by fourteen. "And there's no reason she ever has to know. You won't be doing maid's work until the summer . . ." His eyes warmed as he glanced down at Little Tom, asleep on Sally's cot and folded thick in his quilts. "I'll be back before then."

But before he returned in September, Patsy was with child.

Jefferson had given Randolph and Patsy a thousand acres of his land as a plantation called Varina, and—because land was worthless without them—a hundred and twenty-five slaves. But the lowland climate of Varina was too humid for Patsy's health. And just before Jefferson's return, Tom Randolph's fifty-year-old father had suddenly married a girl Sally's age, who had let it be known that neither Randolph nor Patsy—nor, for that matter, Randolph's sisters Nancy and Virginia—were welcome in her home.

So Patsy and her husband returned to Monticello to live.

⚜

Above her on the hillside, Sally saw Pip and her sister Bett's son Burwell emerge from the kitchen with big wicker trays of Queensware vessels in hand. The savory odors of sugared pumpkin and roasted chicken drifted down to her as she folded up shirts and chemises, climbed the slope of the hill, the long grass rustling against her skirt. Even though she was still Maria's maid when her charge was in residence, Sally had mastered the technique of coming silently, doing her work quickly, and departing like a shadow. It wasn't only Tom and Patsy she sought to avoid, but Patsy's husband: Two days ago word had gone around the quarters that Tom Randolph had had his wife's sixteen-year-old maid Lacey in the linen room.

So much for keeping your menfolks away from the help.

There were also Peter and Sam, and Jack Eppes, who was also part of the household these days. All had so far kept their distance from Sally, even as Tom Randolph did, as if she still bore Jefferson's mark upon her flesh.

But she'd felt them watch her. Knew they speculated among themselves about whether the master of Monticello was done with her or not.

To avoid the family, when they were at dinner—when she knew Tom was with them—she made it a habit to slip into the house through the floor-length window of Tom's "cabinet," the little half-octagon office that opened off his bedroom. Laying his folded shirts on the bed, Sally had to shake her head and smile.

Tom would always act just like Tom.

Every horizontal surface in both cabinet and bedroom was stacked with books, far more than could fit into the three trunks he'd allotted himself for the trip. From a lifetime of acquaintance, Sally knew he'd be awake until almost dawn Friday—the day of his departure—trying to figure out which to take and which he could bear to leave behind. Even then, he'd be sure to send for them within days of arrival in Philadelphia. Upstairs in the library the situation would be even worse.

All that first year he'd been gone, in spite of Patsy's enmity and the demands of new motherhood and the apprehension about encountering Tom Randolph or one of the Carr brothers, Sally had sometimes made the time to steal into the cabinet and try to make some order out of the chaos there. She knew better than to even try going into the library.

Once she'd found in his desk the smashed pieces of the miniature he'd had painted of her in Paris—did he really think Patsy didn't know? Before he'd left, she'd returned to him the letters he'd written her on his travels in Europe, fearing that if she kept them in her mother's cabin, they'd fall into Patsy's hands.

She had written him twice: *The tree you planted grows tall—*

He had never replied.

When at the end of a year he came home—for barely six weeks at the time of the tobacco harvest, the busiest of the year—Patsy had made sure she was always at his side.

His daughter would cling to him like a lover, take him for walks in the garden that was his deepest delight. Patsy had been four months gone with child by then and frightened that like her mother she would be harmed by the birth. She had played that card for all it was worth, making sure she was at her father's elbow the first time he and Sally saw one another after his return, and where possible, every time after that.

With an infant to look after—an infant who officially did not exist—Sally had been unable to fight her.

He was my friend, she thought as she laid down the shirts, stood for a moment looking around her at the cabinet and the bedroom beyond. Virtually no one in the quarters, including the other members of her family, accepted that it was possible for a white to truly be a black's friend, especially where the one was the master of the other.

It seemed to her now that they were right.

The shame of feeling what she had felt—what she still felt—kept her silent, apart from those with whom she lived as she was apart from the folks in the Big House.

As she had always, it seemed to her now, been apart. Neither of one world nor the other.

His violin lay on the desk, with the folders of his music and the little iron dumbbell that he was still forced to use, to strengthen the stiff and damaged tendons of his mis-set right wrist. On the chair were two intricately wrought pedometers he'd purchased in Paris, to measure how far he walked; on the floor all around, stacks of newspapers and correspondence, of charts and notebooks, keeping track of everything: When did peas first sprout and how long from that sprouting did it take them to be table-ready? On what date did the first redbuds bloom in the woods? Temperature and barometric pressure for every day, wind direction and speed—details of the physical world that entranced him, details that did not change or leave him as human beings changed and left. Among the papers lay a palm-sized hunk of gray flint, in which the coiled shapes of strange shells seemed to be molded, life transformed into stone.

As she slipped into the hall she heard Tom Randolph's loud voice grate from the dining-room: "Everyone knows that the Bank is just Hamilton's way of making money for his speculator friends." He sounded sober still, but angry. That anger had smoldered in him since April when Patsy had testified, in open court in Culpeper County, that in her estimation his sister Nancy had indeed gotten pregnant by the husband of his sister Judith. News of that particular scandal had percolated around the quarters like an infestation of bedbugs since the winter before, when Randolph's sister had, it was said, either aborted her brother-in-law's baby or given birth to a child whom her paramour had then murdered and left on the woodpile: Tom Randolph had been brooding and drinking over the disgrace ever since.

Jefferson's reply—scarcely audible, like a summer breeze whispering through the treetops—was, as always in dealing with his son-in-law, friendly, as if no scandal or difficulty existed: ". . . not simply a matter of States' debts. The Bank means that only bankers can understand the country's finances—that the purse-strings of everyone in the country will be held by the central government . . ."

Patsy was encouraging her husband to go into politics—Sally suspected as a way of supporting her father. A gift to him that only she could give.

But then, after years of watching Patsy manipulate her father the way her father manipulated his own political constituents, Sally would have suspected her of anything.

⚜

When Tom had returned from New York in September of '90, he had been his usual genial self, greeting Sally with the same embrace and kiss he gave Betty Hemings, Critta, Bett, and Thenia. What more could he do, with Patsy standing by? His eyes had met Sally's once, and had looked swiftly aside from the withdrawn hurt in them at those unanswered letters, those twelve long months of sewing for his daughter and living under her orders. And before he could look back, Patsy had taken his arm and said, "Now you must come down to visit Iris, she's just had a child, too. . . ."

The following day his younger daughter Maria had arrived from Eppington. A few hours behind her had appeared Aunt Marks, Tom's silly younger sister, and after her the withered little Mr. Madison, and then two touring Frenchmen with letters of introduction from the Philosophical Society in Paris.

For six weeks, during the height of the tobacco harvest, there had been no moment for the master to find a few spare minutes to walk down to Mulberry Row unaccompanied or unwaited-for. Nor had he made the attempt. She had waited for a word from him, for even an enquiry as to how Little Tom did. None had come. It must be tiredness, she told herself, or the press of business, that made him leave the room, on those rare instances when she'd stolen a minute to try to speak to him alone. That brought that withdrawn expression in his face, when their eyes fleetingly met.

Through forty long evenings, when he returned late from the tobacco-fields to find his company still sitting outdoors taking the coolness in the starry dark, he would sit up and talk with them, sometimes past midnight—Sally would hear their voices drifting down the hill. Afterwards no sound of the violin sang from the dark of the Big House.

What had happened to change his mind?

And after that, he was gone for another year.

⚜

He'll be gone again on Friday.

If I want to marry Lam Hawkin—if I want to ask for my freedom before he goes back to Philadelphia—now is the time.

"I don't see why Mr. Hamilton's opinions should make any difference anymore," came young Jack Eppes's voice, as Sally returned from Maria's room. "He's retired, hasn't he?"

In the parlor, Miss Patty's old parrot Shadwell screeched at one of the maids.

China and cutlery clinked as the dining-room dumbwaiter lifted dishes up from the pantry below. Jimmy liked to impress the other servants by telling how the dumbwaiter had been invented by the lascivious old King Louis XV so that servants couldn't spy on his orgies where all the rich old nobles and their gorgeous mistresses sat naked around the table, but Sally knew that the only true part of that tale was "so that servants couldn't spy."

"And a good thing, too," put in kindly Aunt Carr. "You never speak to that man when he doesn't give you a headache, dearest. Honestly, when you arrived in September I was truly worried for you, Tom."

Betty's remark about the age at which Tom's father had died flitted again through Sally's mind as she stepped through the rear door of the house and hurried down the hill to the sanctuary of Mulberry Row. Upon his return to Monticello, Tom had indeed looked ill, too thin. His hair had definitely begun to gray, and he did not sing as he rode out or walked about the house. He looked like he'd had a headache for months.

Sally could guess why.

At the same time the newspapers began to write of the yellow fever in Philadelphia, news had reached them, even here at Monticello, of what was happening to the French Revolution that Tom had hailed with such triumph shining in his eyes. The guillotine had been set up near the gates of the Tuileries gardens: It would have been visible from the front gate of the Hôtel Langeac.

Tom had come to Monticello for two months last year, and six weeks the year before, and on those visits he'd looked tired beyond computation, but healthy. Now he had the look of a man being torn to pieces inside.

The memory returned, of the letters she'd taken such pains to send him secretly, to which he had never replied; of the chilly politeness with which he turned away even her glance, much less any chance at speech; of Patsy's remarks to guests that Sally had gotten herself with child by one of the French grooms in Paris. *Let him die of it,* Sally thought. *He is not the only one who has been betrayed.*

But he would not speak to her. Nor could she bring up that or any other subject to him.

He will never be other than he is. She carried soiled garments from the bedchambers back into the square stone washhouse, with its two big iron cauldrons, its smell of ashes and soap. *And things will never be other than they are.*

Her mother was right. She could do nothing to remove Little Tom from Monticello—

certainly not to a town where everyone would recognize him as Jefferson's son. But she could get away herself, from a situation that was intolerable.

Last week Jimmy had cornered Sally in the cabin she shared with their mother. "What you up to, girl?" he'd demanded roughly. "You foolin' away your chances, and gonna end up with nuthin'."

"I haven't been offered a chance so far to fool away," Sally had retorted, "in case you ain't been watching." The encounter had been late in the evening. Jimmy's shirt smelled of cheap rum under the sweat.

Jimmy grabbed her by the arm and shook her, his voice hoarse with the fury that seemed never to have left him, since they'd sailed for home. "You waitin' for him to send you a bouquet? Write you a love-letter in French maybe?" Up to the night before departure he'd spoken of staying in France, had tried to talk Sally into remaining with him. What would have become of them—of Little Tom—if she had? "You be waitin' for him in his bed when he quit jabberin' with his folks some night, he give you all the chances you want."

"I'm not his whore!" Sally jerked at her arm

and her brother's hand tightened hard. "You think I'm like those girls in the Palais Royale, the ones who'd stand on chairs with their skirts pulled up to their waists, showin' what they got to passersby?"

Jimmy dragged her face close to his, so that she could see the gleam of the dying hearth like streaks of gold in his eyes. "You his slave, girl. You was a free woman in France and you came back here to be his slave. You his whore."

If she slapped him, Sally knew he'd strike her back. Drunk, he'd struck her before. So she twisted her arm and turned her body, the way she'd learned to do when the footmen in Paris would grab for her, and slithered free of his grip. Her arm smarted so she knew already it would bruise up bad. She had to bite back the words on her lips: *If I'm his whore, what does that make you?*

But she knew they were the words that Jimmy would have said to himself, if he hadn't drowned them in rum.

So she only whispered, "Go to bed, Jimmy." And retreated into the hot dark of the cabin.

⚜

I was a free woman in France. She emerged from the washhouse, to the speckled afternoon shade. The bruise left by Jimmy's hand still hurt. *And I came back here with him, knowing I'd be his slave.*

But even if he had changed his mind about wanting her, he was a man who wouldn't let go.

Who would never let any man have what had once been his.

But I'm not his whore.

If what she wanted was his body between her thighs and those little sums of money he'd used to leave for her in his desk drawer—the money Jimmy wanted to get his hands on—then yes, she could simply slip through his cabinet window and be waiting for him, naked, on his bed tonight. And she was sure he'd be delighted to bull her and send her on her way with a friendly slap on the flank and a little present in the morning, because—no matter what they said to their friends and in public print about the amalgamation of whites with blacks—men didn't turn *anything* down when offered.

But it wasn't what she wanted.

She knew that what she wanted was no

longer possible: to read in his library, to talk far into the night, to play backgammon and chess after he'd come back late from one of his dinners, to drive out with him to the old palace at Marly or to walk under the trees of the forest at St.-Cloud. It wasn't possible in Virginia. It wasn't possible with an adult Patsy. It wasn't possible with Little Tom.

If she wanted sex and upkeep, there was Lam—and safety, too. And she wouldn't have to deal with Patsy.

Or with the satisfied pity in her sister Critta's eyes.

But there was a word for trading sex for upkeep, even with Little Tom's safety thrown in. Those girls standing on the chairs in the Palais Royale with their skirts pulled up to their waists probably had children to feed, too.

Outside the washhouse, children's voices called her name. Not joyful now but scared—badly scared. She stepped quickly to the door as they swarmed around her, Eddy and Aggy, Bart and Cannda, all those children too young to be put to work yet: round faces, wide frantic eyes, brown legs sticking out under faded calico shirttails. Danny, the oldest at nine, carried Little Tom on his hip like a baby, Little Tom clutching his right hand in his left, his face ashy with shock.

"Tom got snake-bit," Eddy whispered, terrified, and four-year-old Aggy wailed, "He ain't gonna die, is he?"

Panic struck Sally like a single cold arrow going into her heart. *Dear God, not Tom and Little Tom, too!* But to say so would only scare them worse, so Sally took a deep breath and said, "No, he isn't gonna die," and held out her arms. "What'd the snake look like? Did he have any red on him?"

She sat on the bench beside the door where she'd been sewing, Little Tom clinging to her, face buried in her bosom. Davy said, "No red, ma'am," and looked around at the others for confirmation. "It was black and shiny like oil."

"And ten feet long!"

"And he had yellow on his belly, and black spots."

"And I bet he bit you by the corncrib, when you went stickin' your hand in through the slats." Almost faint with relief, Sally turned Little Tom's hand to the light, to show up the small horseshoe of tiny punctures in the creamy skin. As a child, she'd explored every foot of the woods on the mountain, and between them her mother and Mr. Jefferson had conveyed to her all their considerable woodcraft.

"See that?" she went on, gesturing the children close. "When it looks like that, it means the snake wasn't poison, and there's nothing to fret about—except that you, little man, are damn lucky it wasn't a rat that bit you, instead of a king snake who was just tryin' to catch up on his sleep. A poison snake'll leave two marks, like that—" And she pressed with the tip of her little scissors, not breaking the skin but leaving two pink indentations on the back of her son's wrist.

The children gazed, fascinated, logging the information for further use. Little Tom's tears vanished, and he turned his wrist over, studying it.

"Then do we got to cut a X with a knife," asked Bart excitedly, "and suck out his blood?"

"Then you got to come to *me*," replied Sally firmly, "and *I'll* do whatever cuttin' an' suckin's to be done around here—*after* I wear the lot of you out with a cornstalk for goin' playin' where you got no business to be. You hear?"

They all murmured, "Yes'm," but they knew Sally was just as bad as they were, for wandering among the trees and seeing what she could see under every rock and hollow stump.

As the other children dashed off, Sally led her son into the washhouse, and scrubbed the wound with a fingerful of soft-soap and a little rainwater dippered from the barrel. Monticello's breath-taking prospect and mountaintop magic meant that there was no well and no spring convenient to the house. Another oversight, smiled Sally wryly, blindingly typical of Tom.

He would always strive for what ought to be, and then scurry around trying to make it work, like championing the Rights of Man in a world where no one could afford to give up owning slaves.

"That wasn't a poison snake?" asked Little Tom softly, his hazel eyes still worried. "Eddy said I was going to die."

"Well, Eddy was scared." Sally led her son out to the bench and held him against her. "You can't believe everything people say, 'specially when they get scared. Then people say things they don't mean, and some-times they try to scare other people, to make themselves feel better."

Like Jimmy, she thought: bitter with being still back in Virginia and obliged to do work before he could leave. For all his talk, he hadn't had the nerve to simply disappear into the terrifying Paris of '89, either.

Like Patsy, in the face of her husband's sullen mutterings about how she'd betrayed his family honor. In the face of her own choice to wed, and her need to have her father be what she thought he should be.

Sally held the boy against her, feeling those small shoulders, like the shoulders of a kitten. Marveling in the compact warmth of him, and the silkiness of his red hair against her cheek.

Whenever Patsy handed a chemise or a tucker back to her with a tart remark about paying a *little* more attention to the work she was *supposed* to be doing—whenever Tom Randolph would stroke her arm and whisper that he knew how much she wanted "it"—Sally would remember the ragged shouting of the mob, and the blood spattered on the cobblestones of the rue St.-Antoine. *At least I kept him out of that.*

Only last week she'd come on Maria weeping over a letter that told of the death of Sister Himmisdal, the nun who'd taught her Christian doctrine at the convent-school. The old woman had been guillotined in front of a howling mob. Sally wondered what Tom had had to say to his daughters about that.

She pressed her cheek to Little Tom's hair, and tightened her hug.

"You all right?" she asked, letting him go.

The boy nodded. "Eddy threw Aggy's dolly in the corncrib," he explained. "Aggy was scared to get it."

"Aggy was smart," said Sally, and kissed him. "But that was very brave of you, and very good to help her. Next time use a stick, though, all right?"

His face brightened. "All right."

She took the bitten hand, kissed the little horseshoe of harmless pin-pricks that were already beginning to fade. "All better, sug-arbaby?"

"All better, Mama."

She smiled after him, watching him run through the long grass after his friends. He was almost old enough to begin teaching him his letters, she thought, settling back on the bench. His memory was good. He could repeat back any of the hundreds of stories that got told every night in the quarters, when the work was done for the day: tales of wise rabbits and ugly stupid foxes, and of High John the Conqueror who always was able to outsmart the whites, and of little boys who went on magical journeys with their talking dogs.

Yet another reason to remain at Monticello—not, she knew, that she'd have a choice. To make sure Little Tom *did* get some instruction. It was a good bet Patsy wouldn't give him any.

She sighed, and turned her head—

—and saw Tom Jefferson standing where the hillside crested beside the kitchen, his shoulder against a poplar tree, outlined by the twilight sky.

⚜

Her eyes met his across the distance. She thought about getting up and walking back to her mother's cabin, but knew already that she wouldn't.

His shoes swished in the long grass as he came down the hill. Dinner with his family was about the only time of day he wasn't in riding-boots. Sally found she was holding her breath. Bracing, not only for the bleak chill she'd seen so often in his eyes, but for the sound of Patsy's voice, calling to him from the house.

"What happened?" he asked when he got close, and nodded in the direction of the stables where Little Tom had disappeared.

For one flash of time, the sound of his voice obliterated the years, and she remembered how it had been, to be friends with this man.

She exhaled, made herself let go of her own dread of another silent battle with Patsy, another wordless round of her anger and his coldness. He sounded like he was forcing himself to speak as he'd used to, but that, at least, was something. She replied, "He put his hand in the corncrib and got bit by a snake. I remembered what you told me about the teeth-marks—" She held out her hand and traced on the mound of her thumb where Little Tom's wound had been. "It sounds like a king snake. Eddy said it was ten feet long but I suspect that isn't the case."

Tom's eyebrows shot up and his whole face relaxed. "If it is I shall have to trap it

and write it up for the benefit of those natu-
ralists who claim American species are
smaller and degenerate—though I think I'd
prefer it should go on living in the corncrib
and eating rats. Is he all right?"

"Scared."

"Good Lord, I should think so. The first
time I was bitten I was convinced I'd swell
up and die in agony. My father—"

"Papa?" called Patsy's voice from the
house.

Sally felt her face freeze. She'd known the
moment was too good to last. "You'd better
go."

"Do you wish me to?" His voice, too, had
gone cold.

"Papa?"

She'd appear over the edge of the hill in a
moment. Sally looked up into his eyes.

Tom took her arm and led her into the
washhouse, and closed the door.

But having done so he didn't speak. For
some moments they only stood, inches
apart, in the big stuffy chamber with its smells
of soiled linens and damp stone and soap.
Then he asked, "Is it true you're going to
marry Lam Hawkin?"

Her heart raced, as if he had opened a door for her.

But a door to where?

"Who told you that?"

"You know what plantations are like for gossip. Is it true?"

Now is the time. He'll never be other than he is. I made a wrong choice once. . . .

Slowly, she said, "I ran away from you once, sir. When I came back, you were angry that I hadn't trusted you. I promised you then that I would always be here. No, I'm not going to marry Lam Hawkin, or anyone else."

Stillness again, and the chitter of birds as they nested in the eaves for the night. A dog barked: Bergère, or Bagwell the cowman's one-eyed herd-dog, driving the cows in for milking. The magical peace of Monticello.

Tom asked, in a voice that sounded much more like his own, "Why didn't you answer my letters?"

Her shock must have showed in her face, for his own eyes widened. To her own astonishment she kept her voice calm. "Did you get mine?"

"I got two. I answered both."

And the next moment, as fury rose

through her like a heat, she saw his own cheekbones darken with the flush of blood as he, too, realized what had happened to his replies.

Of course, she thought, he'd enclosed them in letters to Patsy. Even had he not, any messenger would have laid them on the table in the front hall. It would never have occurred to him to send his messages to her via a slave. Not if Patsy "didn't know."

Levelly, knowing that words once spoken can never be taken back, Sally said, "Yours must have gone astray. When I didn't hear from you, I thought—" She stumbled a little. She took a deep breath, and went on. "I thought you had changed your mind."

His eyes flickered back to hers, filled with that bleak wariness she'd seen in them these past three years, and she couldn't keep the edge from her tone as she asked, "What else did you hear about me?"

She didn't add, *And from whom?* and she didn't need to. She saw the muscles of his jaw clench and felt the anger that stiffened the whole of his body: anger at her for implying that his daughter knew and had deliberately lied; sick disgust at the impossible position of being trapped between two women; outrage at the circumstance that put him, a white master, in the position of owing an apology to a slave. Wishing—she could see it in his eyes—that he could simply walk away and go back to being what Patsy wanted him to be.

"Nothing to signify. Idle gossip only."

Sally became aware that she was trembling with anger. Had Tom really believed that having a touch of African blood in her veins, she would casually betray him, as she guessed that Patsy had implied? That she would take a lover—or several lovers—in the quarters, men whom Tom couldn't even challenge because the subject was not one to be discussed?

Of course he did. Weren't blacks more amorous than whites? Didn't every white man in Virginia—including Tom—keep saying how they were slaves to their own passions? "Born under the sign of Venus" and incapable of anything more than "animal eagerness"?

It wouldn't have needed more than one or two sidelong comments to put that bleak distaste for her in his eyes. To give Patsy her victory. To "save him from himself."

If Patsy had been of her own color—*And I*

am damn near almost of hers!—Sally would have stormed out of the washhouse and torn out every handful of her rival's hair. The fact that she couldn't silenced her, stilled her, and in that stillness she was forced to look at Tom again, and see disgust and outrage ebb and alter, and his chill steely anger shift.

"Next time you hear something, sir," Sally told him, "ask me yourself."

"Papa?" They heard Patsy's skirts swish as she passed the washhouse door on her way down to the half-dug terraces of what would be the new vegetable gardens on the lower slopes of the hill. Tom's eyes moved a little, as if they followed her. As if, hearing his daughter's receding steps, he were putting together a thousand fragments of irrefutable and unacceptable truths, to form a conclusion that he could not face.

Sally added, more quietly, "Ask me and I will tell you the truth, whatever it is."

"I know that." He held out his hands to her. "I will. I promise."

After a long moment she reached out and took them.

"I've missed you, Sally."

Even when I was right down the hill and

you were poking around the gardens with your daughter?

But she knew that she would never rival Patsy in his heart.

She sighed, letting go of something within her, although she couldn't tell whether it was the future or the past. "And I you, Tom. I'm sorry if I did wrong—"

"It wasn't your doing. I should not have believed . . . rumor. I will not do so again. Forgive me."

Sally only nodded, and let him draw her against him. The nature of what lay between them, she thought, existed beyond the bounds of words. His kiss was gentle, the kiss of a friend, but the touch of their lips was like flame thrown onto oil, and his arms tightened crushingly around her. It was nearly dark before they spoke again, as they lay together on the damp brick floor of the washhouse, panting in the tangled disorder of half-shed garments. She whispered, "When will you be back?"

"In January."

She sat up, her hair hanging like a dark mermaid's around her shoulders, her body feeling queerly shaky with the aftermath of passion: aching, exultant, yet longing to weep.

"I'm going to risk sounding like those ladies in the Palais Royale and ask, would you have time before you go to ask Mr. Randolph to get another cabin built for me, while you're away? I wanted to ask you before—"

"It's my fault." He put his palm to her cheek, then stood, and helped her to her feet. "And I am sorry, Sally, more than I can say. I will see to your cabin myself." He straightened his clothes, looked around for the black velvet ribbon with which his long hair had been tied. Sally found it for him, gathered up her own disheveled curls under her cap again.

"I'm coming back to stay, Sally," he said softly, and looking around at him, startled, she saw in his eyes a bitter and beaten weariness. It was as if, she realized, the prospect of returning to Philadelphia even for two more months was more than he could endure.

"I can't—" He almost visibly stopped himself from the admission, *I can't take it anymore.* "I can't sleep at night. I find I'm barely able to take pleasure in reading, nor in conversation, since everything in Philadelphia concerns politics these days, and half of everything men speak is lies, or half-truths twisted by ignorance or malice."

He hesitated on the words, as if at the reminder of gossip and lies closer to home, then shook his head.

"I've done everything I can to keep this country from being dragged back into despotism stronger and more subtle than the King's. I feel as if I'm shouting into a windstorm. And in return I've been reviled, and betrayed by all in whom I've placed my trust." He fell silent a moment, then added quietly, "All except you, it seems.

"I've never been good at brangling and quarreling, and it seems to me that there is only that, twenty-four hours out of every day. I'm not that strong, Sally. For three years now I've been tilting at windmills, and have been well and truly beaten by them. I don't know what else to do."

She touched his hand. "Does your family know?"

"I told them this afternoon, at dinner. I only want to come home, Sally. To be with those I love, to wake each morning with nothing more important to occupy me than the progress of my garden, and the observation of the clouds."

Don't we all? thought Sally wearily. *Don't we all.* She knew it was Patsy, Maria, his sister, and his granddaughter he was thinking about, when he said, *those I love.*

"There's a lot of knights out there in the world," she said after a time. "Enough to keep the windmills at bay. I'm glad you'll be home."

"And I," he answered softly, "that you'll be here to come back to."

⚜

Sally's mother gave her a long look when she joined her family, gathered in the candle-glow of the cabin steps. Little Tom clung to her skirts and wanted to know where she'd been, for it was the first time she hadn't been at supper, or somewhere that he could find her, in the evening.

Jimmy watched her narrowly, but after supper Betty Hemings sent her sons on their way before Jimmy could corner Sally with questions. "Too many people in this family pokin' into what don't concern 'em," she said.

What Betty Hemings didn't know about

other people trying to manipulate a woman's relationship for their own profit, Sally reflected, could probably be written on the back of a button and still leave room there for the Lord's Prayer.

All she said to Sally was, "You want me to tell Lam?"

It would be all over the quarters by midnight, thought Sally with a sigh, and up to the Big House with breakfast in the morning—unless Patsy's maid Lacey thought twice about mentioning to her mistress who was tupping whom in that household.

"No." She dipped the cups into the bucket of hot scrub-water on the hearth, mopped them briskly with the rag. Like other things in the Hemings household, they were finer than the gourds or hand-fashioned clay used by the field-hands: salt-glaze stoneware that had been the original dishes up at the Big House. "There's too many people as it is, not saying what they need to say to the person they need to say it to."

She tucked Little Tom into his low trucklebed and told him a story about Mr. King Snake in the corncrib, and how he'd bit the Giant Hand that came busting into his house whilst he was taking a nap. The night was warm, but fall had definitely come to the mountain. When she went out to sit on the step again, there was only the crying of crickets in the woods, and the hoot of hunting owls.

Her body ached, between her thighs, from the unaccustomed movements of lovemaking, and she had a bruise on her shoulder from the bricks of the washhouse floor. A kind of languid peace filled her, as she pulled off her cap, shook out her hair, and combed it with the silver comb that she kept locked in her chest beneath the bed. Lam had said to her that afternoon that he was coming up tomorrow, with salt and coffee and sugar, and nail-rod iron for the new construction Jefferson planned. She would have to speak to him then.

Tell him there was no chance of her changing her mind, soon or ever.

You foolin' away your chances, Jimmy had accused.

But which chances had she been fooling away?

And was she still?

She ran her hands through her long hair, curly and silky as a white woman's, gathering it back into a wavy knot. *I love you,* Lam had said.

And Tom, as usual, nothing at all. To him words were weapons, and the palette with which he painted dreams.

And in any case words shifted their meanings, depending on the race of the speaker and the one to whom they were said. Does *I need you* really mean *I need someone*?

Was it his heart that needed her, or only his prick?

She knew what any woman on the place would have answered to that, yet in three years, there were easier solutions to *that* problem than the one he chose. Because she was a Hemings, and not, in his eyes, truly black? Because she was familiar, trusted, a friend since childhood—because he knew he could dominate her?

Because she had known him from her childhood, had seen everything that had gone into making him the man he was?

With Tom, one could only speculate—she wondered if Patsy had any clearer idea of her father's heart than she had. And oddly, she felt a regret that they could not talk as they had when they were children. She would genuinely have liked to compare notes with the one other woman who knew him well.

But in love with him and out of love with him didn't seem to matter to the deeper attachment of her heart, nor did her awareness of his faults. They were—and would always be—a part of one another's lives, completely aside from whatever he might tell himself about his feelings for her, if he told himself anything at all.

He might simply tell himself—or his little friend Mr. Madison, who these days seemed closest to his heart—that a man needed an occasional "bout" with a woman for the sake of his health, and a clean, healthy country slave-woman was certainly preferable to whatever was available on the pavements of Philadelphia.

Yet in her heart she knew it was more than that. And she suspected that whatever her mother might say, Tom probably didn't understand it any more than she did.

Light and sweet, above the crying of the crickets the whisper of a violin drifted down from the house, playing Boccherini in the dark.

DOLLEY

⚭

Gray's Ferry, Pennsylvania
Thursday, October 24, 1793

A child was crying in her nightmare.

I must wake up, Dolley thought. *I must wake up and save Payne.*

The British are coming and we have to flee to the woods.

No, that's wrong, she thought. *It's Willie who's crying. Baby Willie.*

The infant's red face returned to her, fever-flushed, the little withered scrap of body that looked so much like that of a newborn kitten.

It's just a little summer fever, she told her mother, as she wrung out the damp cloth, over and over again. Sponged the delicate skin that seemed to bag so horribly over bones more fragile than a bird's. *Just a little summer fever. If we can keep him cool, we'll be fine.*

The stone cottage John had rented on the banks of the Schuylkill had a good, deep well behind it. The water came up so cold, even in the sticky October heat, that she had to settle it out in a pan, so it wouldn't be too cold for poor little Willie's flesh.

How could she feel so passionate a love for someone whose face she'd first seen only seven weeks ago?

In her nightmare she sat beside the infant's cot, in the small chamber her mother had laid claim to when first they'd come to Gray's Ferry. But the sounds she heard through the window were the sounds of Philadelphia, in those last weeks before Willie's birth: the endless tolling of the church bells, the jolt of wagons on the cobbles of the street as families hurried from the town to seek refuge from the fever in the countryside. The creak of the dead-carts, and the voices of the black drivers calling, "Bring out yo' dead!"

⚜

Dolley's eyes snapped open.

Morning light streamed in at the wide-flung window, the hot air already rank with the musky scents of the country.

Would the heat never break?

She sat up, and was at once swamped by a wave of dizzy weakness. She clutched at the bedpost. *Don't lie down,* she told herself. *If you lie down, you'll fall asleep again, and Willie needs you. Payne needs you.*

She took deep breaths.

As she'd dreamed, she saw she was indeed in the stone house at Gray's Ferry that John had rented for them when the fever began to spread beyond the waterfront.

So that part at least hadn't been a dream. Birds twittered in the trees outside the window. Somewhere close a dog barked, clear as a bell in the stillness of the morning. Dolley's head ached from too little sleep, but the autumn scent of turning leaves and clear water revived her. It woke in her heart the echo of pleasure-parties when all the young people of the Meeting would drive here to walk in these green woods by the river, away from Philadelphia's oppressive heat. In those days she'd strolled past this house a hundred times with barely a glance.

She wondered now, a little superstitiously,

how she could not have felt a shudder of dread.

By the time the fever spread inland, Dolley had been too close to her time to be moved. John had rented the cottage at Gray's Ferry to take her and the children to the moment she could travel.

For some minutes Dolley sat, trying to recruit her strength. Listening to the birds and hearing in her mind, as if it spilled through from her dreams, the tolling bells and the creak of the carts collecting the dead. In her nostrils the spice of autumn leaves, the swoony sweetness of hay, turned to the sulfur reek of the barrels of tar that had been burned in yards and on street corners to cleanse the fever miasma said to hang like an unseen vapor in the air. When, in her final week of pregnancy, Sarah Parker and Lizzie Collins came calling, they carried lengths of tarred rope in their hands, believing that some quality of the tar itself, rather than the smoke of its burning, would keep the fever at bay.

Aaron Burr—completely unrepentant about slipping love-notes from Steptoe to Lucy—wrote her from Germantown, *I have entertained myself in the Senate Chamber by devising a catalogue of the talismans clutched by my colleagues in the hope of frightening the Grim Reaper: six lengths of tarred rope, eight handkerchiefs soaked with camphor and four with vinegar, and one peeled onion. The smell is as you may imagine.*

He also sent her a copy of *Tom Jones,* which made the concluding days of August easier to bear, though she had to hide the book from her mother. "Libertine" or not (as John disapprovingly described Burr), it was hard to stay angry at the diminutive Colonel for long, particularly after the joy she read between the lines of Lucy's first letter from Harewood Plantation.

And as September brought the death-count to sixty and more a day, even John had to agree with her that it was better that Lucy was somewhere safe, even if it did mean she was married to an Outsider.

"We shall leave just as soon as Dr. Kuhn says thou'rt strong enough after the baby's birth," John had promised, gripping Dolley's hand. "The air is better, up in the hills. There is no fever there."

⚜

Listening hard, Dolley heard the murmur of voices elsewhere in the house, and the creak of her mother's stride on the planks of the hall. Then Anna's voice saying something about water. Anna and Mary, and her eleven-year-old brother Johnnie had all come out with them to Gray's Ferry. Dolley closed her eyes, thanking God again that like Lucy, they were away from the horrors of the plague-stricken town.

Though she'd been hale and lively while carrying Payne, eighteen months ago, Dolley had been exhausted by the final weeks of her second pregnancy. Willie's birth had seemed endless, draining every atom of strength from her as she clung to her husband's hands. As that night wore on she had wept with weakness, pain, and a fear that she had never known while birthing Payne. Then in the long nightmare of the ordeal's aftermath, suffocating in the heat and listening to her child's feeble cries, she had whispered to her mother to leave her, to go out to Gray's Ferry and not to wait for her. To save themselves, save Payne, save little Willie who was clearly sickly himself.

Before she was even well, she recalled, she had crept from bed to sit holding her frail tiny son in her arms. Nights and afternoons blurred into one long half-dream.

Willie had seemed a little better when they removed to Gray's Ferry, for the family cow could get good fresh grass out here and her milk was better: To Dolley's mingled sadness and relief, her own milk had dried.

But he hadn't put on weight as a baby should. And last week, his bouts of fever had returned. Dolley had sat up with him last night and the night before, til the hot lamplight swam before her eyes and the whine of the single mosquito in the room had seemed like the drawn-out note of a hellish violin. She didn't know what time it had been, when her mother had forced her to go to bed.

Her hands trembled as she reached across to where her wrapper lay on the bed. Just standing up made her pant. *Has John come back?* she wondered, as she gathered up her long black braid into a loose knot at her nape. *And is Willie silent because he's sleeping at last, or because . . .?*

She pushed the terror away and crossed to the door, only to have it open as she reached it: Anna, her gray dress and white apron water-spotted, a pitcher in her hands. "Sister—!" She was clearly as startled as Dolley had been. "Art well?"

Dolley nodded. "Willie—?"

"Sleeps." Anna's voice cracked a little on the word.

A truth, but not the whole truth.

Without a word Dolley brushed past her, hastened down the hall.

The house at Gray's Ferry was a simple one, built of stone, its plastered walls whitewashed rather than painted. The large room on the east was hers and John's, with a truckle-bed for Payne. At her mother's insistence, they'd set up Willie's cradle in her mother's cubicle next door, so that Dolley could rest—as if anyone could rest, reflected Dolley, too weary even to feel annoyed, with the sound of her child crying, and the constant frightening shuffle of comings and goings that brought her out of bed a hundred times a day to ask, *Doth he better?*

The cradle stood near the window, where the light was best. Her mother sat on the edge of the bed beside it, a basin near her feet and on a tray a pile of rags. Molly Payne was working steadily, mechanically, as she and Dolley had worked all last night and the nights before, wringing the rags out in the water, and gently laying them on the little body. From the doorway Dolley could hear what she had not, in her own room next door: the faint, sobbing whimper of an infant too exhausted to make any other sound.

Molly looked up. She was crying as she worked, without breaking the movement of what she did and without making a noise. Dolley came to her side. From downstairs in the parlor she heard Payne's shrill voice, insisting, "Mama!" and Mary, with artificial brightness, "Now, sugarplum, thy mama is laid down on her bed. Dost not want the hobbyhorse?"

"Want Mama *now*!"

Payne had made no secret that the acquisition of a tiny brother—and one who did nothing but cry—was not an acceptable exchange for a mother who no longer had the time to play with, fuss over, or sing to him. Through her illness and fatigue, Dolley had always made time in the evenings to play with Payne before she slept. It was not her son's fault that his world had turned topsy-turvy.

Molly got to her feet, crossed to close the bedroom door against the high-pitched insistent protests. Dolley lifted tiny William Temple Todd from the damp mattress on which he lay, sat with him on the edge of her mother's bed. She didn't need to touch him to know he was burning with fever. He was bone-thin, unable since yesterday to swallow either gruel or milk. She wrapped him in the crib's sheet and held him against her shoulder, rocking him gently, knowing in her heart that it was time to say good-bye to her son.

"No word yet from John?"

"Nothing. Mrs. Ridgley tells me that none come or go from Philadelphia now, and that it is like a city of the dead."

Dolley shivered, trying to imagine any situation worse than the one she had seen there nearly four weeks ago. At John's request she had returned briefly to Philadelphia, to witness his ailing father's will. She shivered at the recollection of the empty streets, of the choking miasma of burning tar, sulfur smudges, waste and garbage left in streets because there was no one to cart them away. She had never warmed to her father-in-law, whom she considered too quick with his schoolmaster's rod—one reason, she suspected, for John's profound gentleness with Payne. But she carried enough of the love she had felt for her own father to understand John's deep love for the stern Todd senior, and his stubborn loyalty when the old man had fallen ill.

After the will was signed, both she and John had tried to talk John's mother into taking refuge with them in Gray's Ferry. She would not leave her sick husband's side. Nor would John desert his father, despite Dolley's pleas. As her closely shrouded carriage had rolled through the streets once more, the rattle of its wheels in the deathly silence had sounded to her like the echo of pursuit.

That visit was the last time she'd seen John. Nearly a week after that, a letter had reached them from John's brother James, who had taken his family even farther into the Pennsylvania countryside. His first letter to Dolley had gone astray. With this, his second, came the news that Todd senior was dying; that John's clerk Isaac Heston, who had been left to look after their Walnut Street house, was dead. After agonized days of waiting, word came from John: His father had died; his mother lay dying.

No one knew why one man sickened and died, and another survived. Through the leaden heat of the summer's end, all had discussed endlessly what caused the disease, and by what means it was transmitted. The formidable Mrs. Drinker recommended Duffy's Elixir mixed with vinegar, while Dr. Rush prescribed mercury purges, "heroic" bloodletting, and blisters to draw forth the evil humors. Sometimes a man would greet his friends hale and healthy in the morning, and be carried to his grave before the sun was down. Others lingered for weeks, until the black blood flowed out of their mouths and their souls flickered away like candles going out. Sometimes those who worked among the sick took ill themselves, as Dr. Rush had. Others came away unscathed. Still others, who kept themselves to their homes and walked only down the centers of the streets, died in their isolation.

⚜

Dolley laid her baby back into his crib, tenderly peeled off the damp rags from his flesh and began again the process of wringing them out in cool water, rewrapping those sticklike arms and legs. Willie's eyes were glimmering slits, his face grotesque from the flesh he'd lost. "Thou shouldst be back in bed, child," said her mother softly, and Dolley only shook her head.

"Thou must be weary thyself, Mama."

" 'Tis naught I haven't seen before."

Dolley glanced across at her, remembering the three little babies between her brother Isaac and sister Lucy, born in those first years after they had returned to Virginia from the woods of North Carolina where Dolley's earliest memories lay. She couldn't imagine going through this three times.

My son, she thought, caressing the baby's cheek. *John's son.*

⚜

She thought she'd known the depth and breadth of John Todd before they had gone before the Congregation to be approved to partner one another. She had known the steady capacity for affection that made up for his lack of humor, had appreciated the gentle tolerance of others that went hand in hand with his own stringent adherence to the principles of their faith. Though she usually had to explain to him why she laughed at jests or at the foibles of their friends, he would always smile and join in her mirth. After her father's erratic rages, John's phlegmatic nature had been a welcome relief. And if she'd felt no passion for him, she took great pleasure in his undemanding company.

Yet for weeks before and after their marriage she had been plagued with dreams of being lost in the woods, of having strayed down the wrong path, wandering farther and farther from the place she truly wanted to get to. Waking, she had never felt the smallest doubt about the strength of her husband's love for her. But the dreams persisted, ceasing only after she found herself with child.

The boundless, exalted delight that radiated from John Todd from the moment he saw his baby son had taken Dolley completely by surprise. John loved Payne to adoration, carrying him about the streets, buying him trinkets and toys with joyful abandon. As if Payne were a new sun whose light showed John the world in unsuspected colors. Where once John would have said, *Thou canst wear only one ribbon at a time,* he began to surprise her with little gifts. *He hath such joy in a rattle or a ball,* John would say, smiling, *that I think, "My Dolley would have such joy, too."*

He had completely refused to join in the guessing-games played by Dolley and her sisters, about whether her second child would be Little William or Little Mary. Instead he would say, *Since the foundations of Time, God hath known who it were best to send to us. Who are we to guess at His intent?*

How can I write to him, Dolley wondered, stroking the hot, wrinkled skin that felt like the most fragile silk, *and tell him that his son is dead?* Closing her eyes, she saw John standing at her bedside in the flickering glow of the candles, with her mother and the midwife smiling in the background as he rocked Willie in his arms for the first time, and wept with joy.

⚜

A wild flurry of stomping in the hall. The door slammed open. "Want Mama *now!*" As Payne flung himself at Dolley, grabbing and dragging the skirts of her wrapper as if by main force he could pull her downstairs, Mary's voice could be heard in the staircase muttering, "Drat the boy—!"

"Mama, *now!*" pleaded Payne, bursting into tears as Molly tried to seize him. "Want Papa! Want Mama! Want Limberjack!" Limberjack was the wooden stick-puppet whose continuing adventures Dolley would illustrate for Payne at bedtime. As Molly tried to pull him away, Payne began to scream, the frantic wailing of one whose secure golden world has shattered into an incomprehensible exile of loved ones too long absent, and explanations that meant nothing except that he was neglected, rejected by those whose idol he had once been.

As Payne, still screaming, grabbed at Dolley's hands, Willie began to wail, too, the thin feeble protest of inexpressible pain.

"Here," said Dolley, seeing her mother's face cloud with anger. "Here, I'll take him." Payne clutched at her neck, grabbed handfuls of her hair, wrapped his short chubby legs around her waist as she lifted him despite her mother's protest. Payne was sobbing something that could have been either *Mama* or *Papa.* He refused to release her, as Mary tried to take him.

"Now, Payne, thy mama shouldn't be picking thee up, thou'rt grown too big—"

"It's all right." Dolley cast a quick look back over her shoulder, at the wet, crimson, sobbing little bundle of Willie now gathered in her mother's arms. "I'll be back directly."

By her mother's dark glance she could tell

Molly didn't believe the older child would turn his mother loose anytime soon.

But Dolley understood. Payne and John had shared a secret world, from the moment Payne was born, a pact of absolute unquestioning mutual adoration. John had been Payne's world, as Payne was John's.

And John was not here.

To a boy twenty months old, four weeks is eternity.

As it was, Dolley reflected, to a woman of twenty-five.

⚜

John had written that old Mother Amy, who had remained behind to watch over the now-deserted boardinghouse, would come to help him nurse his mother, and did the cooking and washing while John made forays through the stricken city for either money that was owed him by law clients, or food to buy with the little that he had.

As fewer and fewer would take produce into the city, bands of looters raided abandoned houses for the contents of their storerooms. Ships at the wharves, whose crews had died or fled, provided rations of stolen rum. Flour, potatoes, and oatmeal could be bought, but for frightening sums. Dolley heard rumors of families trading silver or clothing for a few pounds of corn.

John's last message had been a brief note, saying that his mother had died, and that he was going to gather up what money he could and return to them.

That had been ten days ago.

"Limberjack," whimpered Payne pitifully, tugging on Dolley's shoulders as she sat with him beside the cold downstairs hearth. So Mary fetched Limberjack from the corner where Payne had flung him in a temper, and Dolley forced cheer back into her voice as she recounted the wooden puppet's adventures. Fortunately she was widely read: Limberjack had already encountered Cyclopes, battled infuriated Lilliputians, defeated giants cleverly disguised as windmills, and rescued any number of princesses from threats shamelessly gleaned from Greek myth and King Arthur—Payne listened in open-mouthed delight. But every time Dolley would attempt to finish and go back upstairs, he clung to her and wept afresh, and she had not the heart to push him away.

"I'll see how he's doing," Mary would whisper, and scurry upstairs. Thunder boomed heavily in the distance, and instead of bringing coolness the air grew muggy and thick as treacle. Payne followed Dolley upstairs and stood jealous guard in the hallway while she washed her face and dressed. Waited, clinging to her skirt, with ill-concealed tears in his eyes as she visited Willie again, and began at once to weep and fret for his dinner.

"I shall have to go up and lie down again," said Dolley, as she sat once more with Payne after dinner. Payne, too, was exhausted. Still he clung to her hand, his mouth turning stubbornly down.

"And I shall have to go back to thy brother," she added, as firmly as she could. "Willie is littler than thee, Payne, and needs his mama more." Before Willie's birth, John had carefully explained to Payne that another little soul was standing beside the gates of Heaven, eagerly waiting God's signal to fly to earth and join their family, to be Payne's dear brother or sister. Payne had smiled and hugged him, and had seemed to accept. But then, Payne would accept anything, from John.

"Thou'rt all but a man." She smiled, and patted his golden curls. " 'Tis for a man to possess himself of patience. Dost not wish to play with thy aunt Anna?"

A tear slid from the huge blue eye. "Mama—"

Shadow winked past the window, gone before Dolley could turn her head. She heard the splat and thud in the muddy gravel outside, as if something had fallen; got to her feet and started to cross to the door. Someone knocked, flat hard sounds as if struck not with the knuckles but with an open hand.

Someone ill.

Some sojourner from the city.

Her stride lengthened on the stone-flagged floor: *He will have a letter from John . . .*

Her visitor was John.

In that first instant Dolley thought, *Why do I think it's John? That isn't John's face—*

In that first instant, Dolley wondered if she had slipped into sleep again, and if this was a nightmare, where no one looked like they did in waking life.

The face of the man was a stranger's, gaunt instead of squarely plump, stubbled with a week's worth of beard. The skin was ghastly orange-yellow where it could be seen at all under the streaks of mud and rain-thinned black vomit. He'd vomited on his clothing. The rainwater spread the horror; flecks of it clung to his chapped lips.

From a skeletal face, blue eyes stared at her. John's eyes. Begging her to recognize him.

Dolley caught him as his knees buckled, dragged him inside. Payne ran forward, crying "Papa!" and stopped abruptly, the horror hitting him like a club. Dolley called out, "Mama! Get some water, quick. Get Mama—"

Through his clothes John's body radiated heat like a smoldering log. His face, pressed to her bare throat, seemed to scorch the skin. Dolley whispered, "Oh, dear God," as they sank together to the floor before the open door, the tail-end of the afternoon rain spattering in around them.

John whispered, "Dolley," and fumbled for her hands.

She caught them, pressed them to her breast. Footsteps shook the enclosed wooden staircase and she felt rather than saw her mother and Anna come running out; heard her mother say, "Open the bedroom door," meaning the door of the downstairs "best bedroom" where guests would sleep.

Anna raced to obey; young Johnnie came dashing in, face pallid with shock. "Get him to the bed," said her mother, and Dolley whispered, "No," as John's body convulsed in her arms, his fingers crushing her hands.

Black vomit began to flow out of his mouth again, not in spasms, but like a dirty stream. Around it he whispered, "Payne?"

"He is well," answered Dolley. And because she knew it didn't matter, she added, "Willie also." The stench was absolutely appalling. Dolley gathered John's head to her shoulder, as she had only minutes ago held Payne's.

"Dolley," he said again, or something she assumed was her name. Then he convulsed again, writhing and striking, his elbow ramming her belly, the strength of his arm nearly breaking her back. To hold him away would only expose her to more injury and she wouldn't throw him aside to flop like a dying fish on the floor. Instead, she closed her arms tight and held on, with all the strength of a farm-girl who has done the work of the slaves her father freed.

It felt like minutes but couldn't have been more than a few seconds. Then he seemed to slither down, his weight like the weight of a sack half filled with corn.

How long Dolley sat on the wet stone of the floor, her husband's body cradled in her arms, she never afterwards knew. It felt like hours—it actually could not have been more than a few minutes. When her mother tried to make her stand she pulled away from her hand, tightened her hold around John's chest, unable to speak, or cry, or make a sound.

At last her mother got her to her feet, and led her from the room.

Washington City
August 24, 1814

"I sometimes wonder what I would have been, had John not died." Dolley raised her head from her half-written letter as Sophie came back into the parlor, a trio of silver compote-bowls in her hands. From the dining-room next door the muted rustle of tablecloths, the tiny chink of porcelain being set in its place, made a whispered through-line to the dim counterpoint of cannon and the jangle of fleeing wagons and running feet.

Dolley's heart was beating hard, but oddly, remembering John's death gave her a sense of calm.

After John had died, she had gone into the kitchen, stripped out of her fouled dress, washed her face, put on something else that her mother brought her—to this day she couldn't remember what it was—and went out, first to comfort the howling, terrified Payne, then to wash her husband's body.

A few hours after that, just before sunset, Willie died.

She understood then that even the worst days contained only twenty-four hours. One did what one had to do to get through them, and afterwards, one slept.

"I venture to guess, a respectable Philadelphia matron and a—" Sophie visibly stopped herself from adding something. *Probably,* Dolley guessed, *the queen of the Quakers for miles around.* Even after all these years, that was the single regret that stung. "A doting grandmother—and in fairly short order, knowing Payne," Sophie finished, with a wry twist to her mouth. Dolley rolled her eyes. Jemmy had already been obliged to get Payne out of several scrapes with girls.

"John could have kept Payne on the straight and narrow road, if any could," she agreed after a moment. "That he hath some-times strayed is not Jemmy's failing, but my own. And I hear he doth well, in Ghent with Mr. Adams's son." This wasn't entirely true, but if Sophie had heard rumor of the swathe Payne was cutting through Dutch diplomatic society—and the gambling-hells of Amster-dam—she didn't show it.

As she returned to her letter, Dolley won-dered: Would Payne have been different, had she done as her mother had urged her to do? If she had limited herself to being the wife John had wanted her to be, even after his death?

Instead of being herself?

Philadelphia, 1794
Winter and Spring

The hard cold of November ended the yel-low fever in Philadelphia. The winter was a bitter one. The river froze, further crippling sea-commerce already disrupted by the summer's riots and plague. The whole city seemed to be in mourning, numbed by grief and shock.

"Everyone I know hath lost members of their families," Dolley said to Lady Washington, when she and her mother called at the Morris mansion to thank the older woman for her note of condolence. "Going to Meeting for the first time, 'twas hard not to weep, seeing so many clothed in black. So many empty seats."

Lady Washington set down her cup, and leaned across to take Dolley's hands. She, too, wore the sable of mourning.

"Doth Master Lincoln well, in New Hampshire with his granny?" Dolley asked.

And the plump little lady smiled. "Yes. Mary Lear and I have been writing all the summer, and have concluded that we must actually be sisters, our thoughts are so much akin. She is of the opinion—as am I—that it would do the city of Philadelphia much good, if instead of keeping all the theaters and assembly-rooms closed, some kind of public amusements could be available. I don't mean Roman orgies or revel-routs through the streets, of course—"

"I should give a great deal to see Alexander Hamilton in a toga," remarked Dolley thoughtfully, at which her mother looked shocked.

Lady Washington suppressed a delighted giggle with the greatest of difficulty. "My dear, so would he. But it would be a good thing, I think, for people to get out of their homes a bit." She cocked a bright brown eye up at Dolley and added, "And that means you, dear, when you're feeling up to it. Will you be removing back to Walnut Street?"

"I think so, yes." The thought of reentering the big brick house on Fourth and Walnut felt strange to her. The thought of sleeping in the big bed alone, without John.

On the other side of the drawing-room, beside the hearth's cheerful blaze, her mother and her sister Lucy—a startlingly stylish Lucy in a rose-pink polonaise dress and a Norwich silk shawl that had to have cost several pounds—were chatting with the Custis girls about the sale of the boardinghouse and the removal of Molly Payne and her two youngest children to Steptoe Washington's plantation.

"Anna will be staying with me, to help look after Payne," Dolley told Lady Washington. "And as we have *finally* gotten my father-in-law's estate probated, I am able now to hire a cook and a maid-of-all-work." While Dolley was still in the first shock of bereavement in Gray's Ferry, John's brother James had gone into Philadelphia and collected all the papers and receipt-books, not only from the house of Todd senior, but from John's office in the Walnut Street house as well. To Dolley's repeated requests for the papers—since she knew very well that under her father-in-law's will she stood to inherit some six hundred pounds, plus whatever John had left her—James sent a little housekeeping money and the suggestion that she apply to the Meeting for support.

"I trust all things have worked out well?"

"Well, there is much yet to be done—" *Like making James hand over John's papers,* thought Dolley, though she couldn't say so at tea. "But Mr. Wilkins, a friend of my husband's in the Congregation and a lawyer himself, hath offered me his services."

"Will that answer?" Nelly Custis joined them from where she and Mary had been feeding bits of plum-cake to Payne. Like her grandmother, Nelly wore the muted grays and blacks of half-mourning for young Pollie, who had been so integral a member of their household; a sharp contrast to the dramatically funereal garb affected by her older sister Eliza. "For a member of the Congregation to handle the affairs of another in the Congregation, who might have to collect from still others in the Congregation?"

Lady Washington frowned at this talk of business, but Dolley replied cheerfully, "There are those in the Congregation, of course, who might find it inappropriate." *And who might side with James and frown on even the suggestion of a lawsuit.* "But Colonel Burr—who as thou knowst was one of my mother's boarders last year—hath also offered his assistance. So I do not think there shall be any difficulty."

"Not with legal matters, at least," agreed Lady Washington darkly. She glanced across at Lucy, as if Burr had seduced her himself instead of playing Cupid for her nephew Steptoe.

"When I see how happy Lucy is, ma'am, I

cannot find it in my heart to hold the Colonel's role in their romance against him." Dolley smiled.

"Well, no." Lady Washington sounded unwilling even to credit the New York Senator with inadvertent good. "But you watch out for Colonel Burr, Dolley—if I may call thee Dolley? Oh, dear, now you've got me saying 'thee' and 'thou.' He is a rake, and a man who knows how to make himself *fatally* attractive to women."

"I don't imagine a man *could* be a rake— at least not a very successful one—who did not," pointed out Dolley, and squeezed Lady Washington's plump, black-mitted hand again. "Do not trouble thyself, ma'am. I know Colonel Burr too well to be taken in by his ways. And indeed, it seems to me now that it will be enough, for me to look after my Payne and Anna, and to . . . to live in quiet. I do not think I shall marry again."

"Oh, you will, my dear," predicted Martha wisely. "You will."

⚓

Dolley wasn't so sure of that. It was, of course, expected that every widow would remarry, if for nothing else than to provide a guardian to her children, though from re-marks Nelly Custis let drop about her mother's morose and reclusive second hus-band, some guardians were more effective than others.

The truth was that she enjoyed being a widow.

She missed John. In those first few weeks of December, back in their home on Walnut Street, there were days when she could only sit beside her bedroom fire, gazing out the window at the falling snow. But the dazed, uprooted confusion she saw in the eyes of Lady Washington's dear friend Mrs. Powel—widowed also by the fever—was strange to her, and a little frightening.

"No, Elizabeth has taken her husband's death very hard, poor darling," Lady Wash-ington agreed, when, after another of Martha's "at-home mornings" Dolley re-mained to help her and Nelly wash up the good china. "When my Daniel died—Mr. Custis . . ." Her brown eyes lost a little of their bright focus, gazing back across the gap of years. "I was . . . I was shocked, of course, and devastated—I had nearly lost our son Jacky to fever, only weeks before—

But I never felt that the world itself had ended."

She glanced up at Dolley—who stood nearly a head taller than she—and in her face Dolley saw the shadow of the future. "I don't think . . ." she began, and hesitated to even speak of it. In a tiny voice very unlike her own usual briskness, she said, "I am not sure that I could survive losing the General."

The pain in her eyes, the dread of a grief greater than she knew herself able to bear, and the aching love, caught Dolley's throat, so that she put her arm around her friend's shoulders, wet hand and all, and declared, "And I am very sure he could not survive the loss of thee, ma'am. Which presents a terrible conundrum, doth it not? So thou must take care to predecease him, and steel thyself to look down from Heaven and see him falling prey to the wiles of Kitty Burke, or Georgina Morris—" She named two of the most intently marriage-minded belles in Philadelphia society, and Martha, surprised into laughter, gave her a schoolgirl shove and went back to drying cups.

But Dolley understood. With John's death, she had no feeling that the world had ended. She only felt deeply confused, and for many nights the old dream returned to her, of having taken the wrong road and being unable to find her way back.

"For Heaven's sake, Mrs. Todd, rearrange the furniture," Aaron Burr advised, when he came in February to help her draft yet another demand that James surrender John's papers to her for probate. "Every widow I've ever met says it's the quickest way to lay ghosts. Paint the rooms, if you can spare the time—in a month you won't have an unscheduled week to do it in—and buy yourself new dishes."

He'd been holding Payne on his knee while the boy examined his watch and fob, but when the servant-girl came in with the tea things, Payne leaped down—watch in hand—to show it off to her, and Dolley met Burr's eyes. "Thinkst thus I will forget him?" she asked softly.

"Nothing of the kind." The dark eyes looking across into her own were kindly, their perpetual ironic amusement muted by the recollection of griefs of his own. "My Theodosia says—" And his voice, beautiful as cut black velvet, hesitated over the name of the wife he never ceased, despite his many infidelities, to adore. "Theodosia says, and I believe her to be correct, that while one doesn't always remember, one never forgets."

Privately, Dolley wondered how much remembrance Theodosia Burr gave to *her* first husband, a British officer during the Revolution, whom she had enthusiastically betrayed with Burr for some time before his death. Then she shook herself inwardly for the judgment. Theodosia Burr was ill—dying, Dolley suspected, though Burr remained at least outwardly optimistic. The poor woman would no doubt be remembering the first husband whom she was so shortly to meet.

⚜

And rather to her surprise, Dolley found that rearranging the furniture, and having the tea-room painted a sprightly yellow, did in fact dispel a degree of her grief. What her mother would have said about it, she wasn't sure: It occurred to her that perhaps in selling the boardinghouse, and taking Lucy's invitation to return with her to Harewood to live, her mother had been dispelling the brooding ghost *she* had lived with for two years.

In any event, Dolley bought new dishes, too, and began to entertain her friends in the tea-room: not simply the ladies of the Meeting, but more and more frequently the ladies whom she met at Lady Washington's.

Even with young Wash away at school, Lady Washington had her hands full, and often asked Dolley to assist her at her "at-home mornings" between eleven and twelve. Eliza and Pattie Custis were still in residence, having a "season" in Philadelphia, but they, like their younger sister Nelly, were as often as not on an outing with their friends, as life slowly stirred back into the city. Moreover, Dolley guessed that the older two girls were less than completely useful socially. Shy Pattie was aglow with her first serious courtship. Eliza—who as the older of the two considered it her right to be married first—consequently swung from tragic airs to petulant rages.

So Dolley stepped in to assist, and found herself in the company of women whom she had only previously glimpsed from afar: the brilliant Ann Bingham and her remarkable sisters; the elegant Maria Morris; sweet-tempered Betsey Hamilton, and the fascinating Harriet Manigault. Though few of the members of Congress brought their wives to Philadelphia—particularly not after the yellow fever—Lady Washington's callers also included émigré ladies from France, the wives and daughters of exiles in flight from the Terror, who brought with them fearful stories of events in Paris, and the news of the execution of the French Queen, the beautiful and doomed Marie Antoinette.

"I've always been sorry I never met her," Martha confided once. "She sent me a present, I'm told—which of course those dreadful British intercepted and sold . . . Still, it was a kind thought. Mr. Jefferson despised her, and said she brought all her troubles down on herself, but no one deserves such a fate."

Dolley, since girlhood an avid reader of newspapers, was quick to flesh out her knowledge of world events by listening. Always good with faces and details, she slipped easily into the role of conversation-starter. And because she was genuinely interested in people, she found herself receiving cards of invitation to houses where, as merely the wife of a Quaker lawyer, she would never have had cause to visit: the astonishing Bingham mansion with its curving staircase and its wallpapers of brilliant red, yellow, and blue; the Chew mansion, graceful with age.

This meant new clothes, and under the Presidentress's careful eye she passed quickly into the grays and silvers of second mourning, touched up with enough black that she did not look dull. Fourteen-year-old Anna, who always accompanied her, wore the pale pinks and gauzy whites of a young lady in her first season, and rather to Dolley's amusement began to be seriously flirted with by the younger attachés of the various legations, and by occasional diplomats, bankers, and unmarried Congressmen.

There was a great deal to talk about, as winter passed into spring.

Repercussions of the Proclamation of Neutrality still shook the country and the world. England declared that it would enforce its blockade against France by confiscating French cargoes even when they were carried by American ships, and hundreds of vessels were seized in the West Indies, which were America's largest customers for corn and wheat. And since the cargoes were sold to the profit of the Crown, very few of them were judged to be not French. As long as they were stopping American ships anyway, the British captains generally helped themselves to whatever crewmembers they thought they could get away with, claiming the men were "British deserters."

Technically, Dolley supposed they were right. Any American had, in 1776, "deserted" the British Crown.

And without a Navy—or sufficient money to build one—there wasn't a solitary thing America could do about the situation.

Nor, implied a good many merchants, should the solution involve naval power. France was the enemy, not England. The bulk of American trade was with England, and the French had lost whatever rights they had to American aid when they'd turned themselves into a howling mob of bloodthirsty atheists. At this point in any discussion, Dolley usually sallied in to shift the conversation either to provable facts like how the fighting in Europe was actually going, or to a less volatile aspect of the situation such as where the émigrés were settling and how they were making their livings, or, with luck, to a complete change of topic.

She found she could distract almost any Virginian by a well-placed query about either horses or land speculation in the Ohio Valley. Even this last was tricky, with the British garrisons still occupying forts on the Great Lakes. These garrisons deliberately exacerbated Indian grievances against American settlers, playing hob with speculators' efforts to get people to buy Western lands.

But between winter and spring of 1794, Dolley estimated she learned the bloodlines of every horse south of the Potomac and at least fifty percent of the mules.

⚜

And the pain of remembering John lessened. It would return sharply sometimes, after she had kissed Anna good-night and sung a little to Payne, as the child drifted to sleep holding her hand. Sometimes when she would pass the stairway that led to John's office, she would glance down, looking for the smudge of lamplight there, fully knowing there would be only darkness. When she lay in bed, she would call to mind what it had been like, to feel John's warm bulk beside her, to smell the scent of his flesh and his hair and his clean-laundered nightshirt. What it had been like to know that if she put out her hand, she'd feel the round firm curve of his back.

It was Payne who brought him back to her, mostly. For months, when Payne was unhappy or uncomfortable or when his will was crossed, her son would strike at her and shriek, "Papa! Want *Papa!*" and then turn away in floods of tears, as if he saw again his last terrible vision of Papa, thrashing out his life on the floor of that stone cottage at Gray's Ferry. At times like that, there was nothing Dolley would refuse him.

In time, these tantrums grew fewer. In time, Payne slept the night through, and he swiftly learned that his ready charm would win him attention and praise from his mother's new friends. Payne especially adored Aaron Burr, who on his legal visits was never too busy or too preoccupied to listen to the boy's concerns, to answer his questions or tell him a story. Burr was the only person, besides Dolley, who "did Limberjack *right.*"

But the light of Payne's life had somehow been extinguished. He clung to Dolley in a passion of disoriented grief, but Dolley was aware that he was always looking past her, always hoping that that dirty, yellow-faced man who had sunk down limp in his mama's arms hadn't really been Papa.

That one day his real papa would come back.

But for Dolley, it was as if she stood on a wharf watching John at the rail of a ship. And the winds took the sails very quickly, bearing John out of sight.

And with John's departure—and that of her mother—she was free for the first time in her life to be herself.

⚜

The note was a short one.

> *My dear Mrs. Todd,*
>
> *My esteemed friend and colleague, Mr. James Madison of Orange County, Virginia, has asked me to introduce him to you. Shall you be home this evening after six?*
> > *Ever sincerely,*
> > *Col. A. Burr.*

James Madison!
Dolley lowered the note to her desk.

The Great Little Madison, he was called—and she remembered those brilliant blue eyes, the tired premature lines and graying hair of the slender gentleman in black velvet, who had kept her from falling off the step of Mrs. House's boardinghouse the day General Washington had ridden into Philadelphia for the Convention, seven years ago.

James Madison wanted to meet her!

She realized her heart was pounding hard.

She had read almost everything Madison had written—either under his own name or a variety of pseudonyms—in newspapers and pamphlets protesting such issues as the corruptibility of the National Bank, and the perils of placing too much power with the President, even a President as honest as Washington. As always, logic, cogency, and clarity impressed her—and at heart, Dolley never quite trusted Alexander Hamilton's thrust to make the Presidency stronger than the Congress.

She had too strong an impression that Hamilton intended to occupy that strengthened Presidency himself.

But because Washington loved his former Secretary of the Treasury as a son, James

Madison was seldom a guest at Lady Washington's receptions, and almost never at those given by ardent Federalists. Dolley had always heard his name spoken with respect, even by men who pointed out that most of the Republicans who objected to friendship with England (like Madison) were Virginians who owed huge sums of money to British merchants (like Madison).

Burr liked him.

Dolley wrote two notes, one directed to Burr, saying that of course he must bring his friend to dinner that afternoon at four, if they had no other engagement, and the second to Lizzie Collins.

> *Dear friend, thou must come to me.*
> *Aaron Burr says that "the Great little*
> *Madison" has asked to be brought*
> *to see me this evening.*

⚜

Having first encountered President Washington in the dining-room of the Executive Mansion while she was helping Martha wash up the good china (he'd offered to help dry), Dolley felt perfectly at ease with most members of the government. As a

Quaker, she had been taught from tiniest childhood to disregard worldly titles, and to see all men and women equally as the blessed and fallible children of God. She'd already met many Senators and Congressmen at her mother's boardinghouse at suppertime, or at least had overheard details of their personal lives discussed by their colleagues. It was disconcerting to be introduced at a Presidential levee to a man whom she'd heard wore women's clothing when he attended the theater.

But she found herself worrying, uncharacteristically, what she'd say to Mr. Madison. "Colonel Burr saith he is the most brilliant of the Republicans." She passed a hairpin back over her shoulder to Anna, who was coaxing Dolley's raven curls into a fashionable *style à la Méduse,* and met her eyes in the mirror. "Which he must be, for Colonel Burr to admit anyone is more brilliant than himself. Mr. Madison will think I'm a goose."

"If Mr. Madison has asked Colonel Burr to introduce him to thee," pointed out Anna pragmatically, "he isn't coming here to pick out flaws." Her hands rested on Dolley's shoulders, white, plump, and unfashionably broad above the stiff restriction of corset.

"He's just another gentleman who's going to make a little bit of a fool of himself."

"Colonel Burr come to dinner?" Payne appeared in the doorway behind Anna; Dolley turned in her chair.

"He is. But I promise thee, he shan't come up to visit thee if thou give cause for one single problem during dinner—and he surely shall, if thou'rt patient and good."

The boy climbed confidingly into Dolley's lap, unimpressed with the threat. "I be good." He picked up from the dressing-table the gold locket and chain John had given her, put it around his own neck and admired the effect in the mirror, then turned back to seek his mother's approval. "Mama, thou'lt marry Colonel Burr?"

Lately he'd begun asking that question about several of the gentlemen who called to take Dolley and Anna to the theater, or to assemblies, or even walking along Chestnut Street now that the weather was fine again. Usually they'd call in company with friends of Dolley's—William Wilkins the lawyer generally enlisted the Drinkers, and more than once theater parties had been made up including Lady Washington's three granddaughters with assorted bachelor Congressmen. Dolley supposed it meant that Payne had accepted that his own father wasn't coming back, but couldn't be sure.

"I cannot marry Colonel Burr, my love, because Colonel Burr is already married to someone else." She smiled as she said it, but her heart pinched her. Only the week before, when he'd paid her a morning visit at one of her own "at-homes," Burr had quietly confided his despair over his wife's eroding health. He had had a letter that day from his daughter—"my two Theos," he called them—and he'd apologized immediately for letting personal concerns intrude.

It's all right, Dolley had said.

Burr had looked away. *For years now I've had to prepare myself for what I should do without her,* he'd said. It was the first time she'd seen the Senator's self-possessed confidence broken, like a duelist driven weaponless to the wall. *I still haven't succeeded.*

"Besides," she added, removing the necklace from Payne's throat, "even were he a bachelor, Colonel Burr is not of the Congregation. I could not marry him."

Payne looked crestfallen. Had he had a bigger vocabulary, reflected Dolley with a sigh, he'd have tried to argue the point, for he was very fond of the catlike little Senator.

She had Anna lace her into her mulberry silk dress—one of the new ones Martha had urged her to have made, when she began to emerge from mourning—and laced Anna into a complementary white, with a long cherry-colored sash. She privately suspected neither her mother nor John would have approved, but when she and Anna came into the tea-room, Lizzie exclaimed, "Oh, famous!" at the sight of the rich silk. "Richard—Mr. Lee," she amended hastily, "—said he hath seen thee in red at Mrs. Morris's. He said how much it became thee—"

"Richard?" Dolley's eyebrows went up, and her friend colored. "Not Mr. Lee of the Congress?" She had introduced Lizzie to Virginia Congressman Richard Lee. Lee had been very taken with her friend, but Lizzie, at twenty-six, was notorious in the Congregation for her unsusceptible heart.

"Mr. Lee is a perfectly rational gentleman, and a pleasure to converse with." Lizzie opened her fan.

It occurred to Dolley that at her last several at-home mornings, Richard Lee *had* made it a point to call . . . and had spent a good deal of time in conversation with the quiet Lizzie.

"And," went on Lizzie, "he tells me that the great scandal at Mrs. Morris's—dost remember the French émigré bishop, M'sieu Talleyrand? The tall one who looks so strange? They say he was seen walking down Chestnut Street with his mistress, a woman of color, as if this were Paris or Lisbon!"

"Oh, I've seen her!" gasped Anna. "Getting out of her carriage, and she was wearing one of the new Grecian gowns from Paris, like an ancient statue, they say, and no petticoat under it, nor corset either!"

"Ma'am." The servant-girl appeared in the tea-room doorway. "Colonel Burr is here, with Mr. Madison." And she held out her silver tray bearing two white cards.

⚜

Looking back across the years from her desk in the oval parlor—the dim thunder of the guns crackling in the capital city's heavy air—Dolley still smiled, remembering Jemmy as a stranger.

She had remembered Mr. Madison was small, from that first fleeting encounter on the steps of the boarding establishment, and had taken care to wear flat slippers instead of her white silk shoes with their raised French heels. Standing in the doorway of the tea-room, James Madison was indeed an inch shorter than Burr, who frequently claimed he was exactly Dolley's height and flattered himself when he did so. Though Burr had said they'd been up at Princeton together, Jemmy Madison was five years older than Burr and looked three times that. At forty-three, his hair was nearly white: unpowdered, the way the Republicans were wearing it now, but braided back in an old-fashioned queue and tied with a black velvet ribbon.

Burr—and Lady Washington—called this man a kingmaker: unimpressive himself, Madison certainly had an unerring eye for charismatic men who could draw the loyalty of both thinking men and the mob. Eliza Custis described him as "a dried-up apple-doll," though he lacked an apple-doll's roundness: It was a lifetime of uncertain health which had left him with a labyrinth of fine-pleated wrinkles around his eyes, his mouth, his cheekbones.

His bright blue eyes were still a lifetime younger than his face.

⚜

"I trust after last summer, every man in the Congress hath his bags packed and one foot out the door already, the moment Mr. Adams's gavel comes down for the final time?"

Madison's dry smile altered the whole of his narrow face. "Alas, Mrs. Todd, I've never yet been in any city that wasn't foul in the summer. New York was just as bad. My friend Mr. Jefferson tells me that Paris was unspeakable even before they started chopping off each other's heads there, and on the authority of classical writers, ancient Rome was the worst of all. I am forced to assume that the gods intended government to be a winter affair only."

Dolley understood at once why Burr and Jemmy were friends. Both had the same dry wit, the same lively sense of humor, the same extraordinary erudition. Like Burr, Madison had an outlook of amused irony on the world, without Burr's cynical edge. Like Burr, Madison was brilliant, but unlike him, he had, over the years, kept his ideals—

Talking to the pair of them was like learning to juggle comets.

After they left, Dolley lay for a long time awake, trying to read by candlelight and instead reliving bits of the evening's laughter.

⚓

Almost from that first evening, she knew Jemmy was interested in her. She knew, too, that if he asked her to be his wife, she'd say yes, without a second's hesitation.

That fact in itself filled her with alarm.

The pestering, recurring dreams about taking the wrong road, the nagging sense that her true destiny—her true self—lay elsewhere, if only she could find it . . . The deep-felt alteration that had consumed her thoughts during her earlier courtship: when sometimes it had been *Yes, I do love John,* and sometimes only, *He is a dear man and a dear friend BUT . . .*

These were as absent as clouds on a clear morning in summer.

The morning after their first dinner, Jemmy sent her a note asking her and Anna to be part of a small theater party he was making up. The three lines filled her with as much exultation as if he'd asked her to fly with him to some distant corner of the earth. She found herself blushing when Anna mentioned the dinner—and the theater party—to Mrs. Drinker, and that good-natured Quaker matron raised her brows . . . as well she might, reflected Dolley.

The other thing that Jemmy Madison and Aaron Burr had in common was that neither one was a Quaker.

And most of Dolley's closest friends still were.

She recalled her mother's tears, when she'd found Lucy's elopement note. Remembered how Molly Payne had sat on the bench in the meeting-house, weeping with a face like stone, when Lucy had been "read out" of the Congregation. Walking home afterwards, she had murmured to Dolley, "I have lost my daughter, and all of her children as well."

And yet, thought Dolley, her mother was with Lucy now, looking after her daughter as she prepared for the birth of the first of those children. Molly Payne had written her, inviting her to Harewood that summer. Dolley had already found an émigré Frenchman willing to rent the Walnut Street house with all its furniture until the first of November.

How utterly had the world changed, since the morning they had gone to Lady Washington's with that note!

The child about whom she'd laughed with Martha, born and already dead.

John dead.

And herself, lying awake at night, secretly wondering what it would be like, to have Jemmy Madison lying at her side. Knowing she should feel shame, and feeling none.

She found herself examining John's old map of Virginia, to see how far Harewood lay from Orange County, where Jemmy would go the moment Congress adjourned in June.

"Art thou engaged to James Madison?" Martha Washington asked. The last of the morning callers had just departed and Martha's pretty green-and-white parlor was quiet. Dolley started and flushed like a schoolgirl. The President's closest supporters—fat Secretary Knox and lean-and-hungry Secretary Pickering—regarded Jemmy as both enemy and apostate for supporting Jefferson and the French.

She murmured, "No, ma'am."

Martha left her chair—which did tend to give her the aspect of a diminutive queen on a throne—and came in a rustle of stiff silver taffeta to sit on the couch beside her. "Dearest, don't be ashamed. You should be proud. All of us are—Nelly and the General and myself, I mean. And pleased, too, if it's true, because for all his fondness for those horrible ministers the French keep sending over—and doesn't the latest one look *just* like a weasel?—Mr. Madison is a dear friend. And we've all been so hoping he would find a wonderful woman and fall in love, and she with him. Has that happened?

"Austin, dear," she added, as one of the liveried servants opened the door through to the dining-room, "please bring a little more tea for Mrs. Todd and myself. . . . *Such* a nuisance," she added with a sigh. "We're going to have to send most of the servants back to Mount Vernon when the General goes to visit next week, but we ourselves must remain in Germantown, because of this horrible ship business with the British. *Has* Mr. Madison found a lady who'll love him as he truly deserves to be loved?"

Dolley folded up her fan, held it closed for a time, looking down at it in her yellow silk lap.

John had given her that fan, she suddenly

recalled. The pierced sandalwood was her favorite; it was the first present he'd surprised her with, after he'd discovered the joys of buying things not because his wife or his son needed them, but solely for their pleasure and his.

"Maybe not as he deserves to be, ma'am," said Dolley slowly. "I *did* try to make John a good wife. I know I tried his patience sorely, about things like the cost of running a household, and what I spend on dresses, and not spanking Payne. And now I'm thinking of marriage, and poor John hasn't been gone but seven months, completely aside from the fact that he'd be horrified at my wedding a man outside of the Congregation. I feel like I want to write him a letter somehow, apologizing, or explaining . . . But I don't even know what I'd say."

Beyond the window, the tulip tree flourished its pink blooms. When first she'd admired it, Dolley recalled, it had almost been done with its season. She had spoken about its lavish beauty to John.

Not even a single cycle of its flowering had passed by.

"Well, dear," said Martha gently, "perhaps you might think what *John* would write to *you.* If he were—Oh, if he were about to be sent on a voyage to Tasmania or China, or the Moon, and it was a condition of the voyage that he would never, ever come back, nor be able to write to you ever again. Do you think he would write, before he left, *I want you to be loyal and lonely? I'd rather you weren't* too *happy? Please let Payne grow up without a father?* Our vows of marriage are until Death comes between us—but only until then."

For a long time, Dolley did not answer. Then she asked softly, "How long was it after Mr. Custis died, that thee knew thou wanted to marry the General?"

"Eight months."

Their eyes met. At another time, in another context, Dolley knew they both would have laughed.

"And yet I very much loved Daniel. There are many sorts of love, Dolley. Do you think John, who is now able to talk daily with the Inventor of all love, doesn't understand this?"

Dolley shook her head.

"And I've never subscribed to the belief that each of us is capable of truly loving only one other person in our lives. Thank you, Austin." Martha smiled at the servant who brought in the fresh tea. "Or is it just that you're worried what the members of the Congregation will say, who knew and loved John?"

Her glance was so knowing that this time Dolley did laugh. "Nay, I know what they shall say. And it shall have naught to do with loving or not loving John, but only that Mr. Madison is an Outsider. I shall lose many friends for it."

"Perhaps not as many as you think, dear." Martha held out the dish of tea-cakes: Dolley shook her head. "And for the rest . . . friends do have a way of coming back to us, the ones who truly have our good at heart. And as the Arabs say, *The dogs bark, but the caravan passes on.* Would you rather be a village dog in the middle of the desert somewhere, or bound for some marvelous city bearing all the treasure of the world?"

When she returned home that afternoon, Dolley packed up her mourning dresses and had Anna help her carry them to the attic. They both made silly jokes and laughed a great deal, like schoolgirls playing truant, having a wonderful time yet nervous about the inevitable repercussions. Between her own preparations for renting out the house and visiting Harewood, and lending a hand in Martha's packing-up of the Presidential Mansion in order to move out to Germantown before the fever could return, there was a great deal of dust raised, and when Dolley came down with an eye infection she couldn't avoid the superstitious reflection that she was being "punished where she had sinned."

For Love, said the ancient Romans, was a disease transmitted first through the eye.

"Nonsense," declared Burr, when he called to take his leave of her early in June. "In that case, you'd have been stricken with heart-disease." And he raised her hand to his lips.

The lines settled deeply around his eyes gave the lie to the light jesting tone of his voice. Against the black of his coat his face looked pale and tired, but to Dolley's words of condolence, he only shook his head. "She was ill for so many years, almost since first I knew her. I know she became very tired of it."

Dolley said softly, "Of course," squeezed his hand, and dropped the subject at once.

"Mark my words," said Mrs. Drinker darkly, when Burr departed and the others who had come to pay a morning-visit that day gathered around Dolley. "He shall have that poor woman's place filled with one of those *hussies* he frequents before Congress reconvenes in the fall." And the formidable Quaker dame glanced sidelong at Dolley, as if she'd have quizzed her on her own plans for spousal replacement had not others been in the room.

As Dolley looked around the cozy parlor she felt a pang of impending loss. Not only of Lizzie and Lizzie's family and Mrs. Powel and the others in the Congregation, but of the life she had known in Philadelphia, the life and the friends she cherished.

Jemmy had spoken often of his father's plantation of Montpelier, in the mountains behind Charlottesville. *Within a squirrel's jump of Heaven,* he said—if your idea of Heaven was sweet wooded mountains, climbing to the Virginia sky, and seeing mostly your own family and your own slaves, day in and day out. Having grown up in the Virginia countryside, Dolley knew that one reason everyone in Virginia was considered so hospitable was that to have *anyone* new come by was an occasion to be celebrated and prolonged.

Lady Washington might pine for the peace of Mount Vernon, but Dolley knew in her heart that she was a city creature. From the moment she had come to Philadelphia at the age of fifteen, she had wanted to live nowhere else. It was true that Jemmy couldn't imagine not being involved in government, but as an elected official there was no guarantee how long he'd have that option. How could she get from day to day, she wondered, without the lending library, the theater, the lively conversation of a wide circle of friends?

But how could she get from day to day without Jemmy at her side?

"You look pensive, Mrs. Todd." Mr. Wilkins took advantage of a general discussion of life at Harewood Plantation to speak quietly, and Dolley smiled apologetically, and shook her head.

"Only regretting God's scandalous oversight in not giving us the ability to see into the future."

⚜

"And, Lizzie, I felt like a hypocrite, not to speak to him," sighed Dolley, as she later walked her friend downstairs to the door. "He hath been so good to me, helping with old Mr. Todd's will. But I haven't even truly made up my own mind." Behind them on the stairway, her mother laughed over something

Mrs. Collins said, and from the tea-room she heard Anna's voice, and Payne's demanding why Colonel Burr had gone.

"Hast thou not?" Lizzie turned in the shadows by the front door. The vestibule at the bottom of the stair was darker than Dolley remembered it, since she kept the door to John's office closed. Even now, with the room a jumble of packing-boxes of books—which James Todd, drat him, would have sold if she hadn't stopped him—Dolley found that passing its door filled her with sadness. "Is it that— please forgive me prying, Dolley!—is there something about Mr. Madison that makes thee draw back? Or that he is an Outsider?"

"Nothing so elevated, I'm afraid." Dolley threw her arms out in a helpless shrug. "It's just that . . . Now I'm used to it, I rather enjoy living as I do."

Lizzie laughed, and hugged her. "I'm glad," she whispered, "that it isn't being read out of the Meeting that stops thee, I mean . . . for I think . . . I'm afraid . . . Dolley, I think I shall be read out myself!"

"Richard Lee?" Dolley asked.

Lizzie nodded. "Mother doesn't know yet, but I'm to meet him in New York—"

"Richard Lee of Virginia!"

Her friend nodded again.

"Oh, famous!" Dolley sighed, and flung her arms around her friend. "Then even if we're both to be a scandal and a hissing in the Congregation, and everyone rolls their eyes and cries, *Elizabeth LEE, alas!* at least we shall be neighbors!"

⚜

Three months later, it was to Lizzie Lee that Dolley wrote—from Harewood Plantation, with Lucy's laughter coming from downstairs at one of Jemmy's jokes, and Payne howling because he wasn't the center of attention, and the brash loud voice of Steptoe's sister Harriot proclaiming a wedding-toast—and signed herself:
Dolley Madison, alas!

Washington City
Wednesday, August 24, 1814
3:00 P.M.

Dolley Madison, alas!
"When all was said and done, yours was one of the better marriages that took place

around then," Sophie remarked, as she and Dolley wedged the last of the silver service into the trunk. "Not terribly long after that, Charley Adams married yet another of the egregious Smith clan, his brother-in-law's sister Sarah. Abigail was spitting bloody nails over it, the letter she wrote to me."

Dolley rose, shook out her skirts, and walked back to the desk for another pinch of snuff. Though the sky was clouded over, still the southern window's brightness turned the surface of the Queen's mirror to a round of burning light.

I've always been sorry I never met her, Martha had said.

The last Queen before the inevitable Revolution. The victim of what revolution could become. Yet she had had the frame engraved: *Liberté—Amitié.* In those days everyone had been so trusting about what *Liberté* would bring.

Sophie eased the trunk-lid down, calculating what else might fit, then opened it again. "We'd best wrap that up carefully. What next, do you think?"

"The drawing-room winter curtains," said Dolley promptly. "They're in the attic, I'm pleased to say; I have my mother's good teaching to bless, that I got the room in summer dress right after Congress rose. Now is *not* the time I should care to wrestle a hundredweight of red velvet down from the windows on a fifteen-foot ladder."

"Mrs. Madison, what on earth are you still doing here?" Mr. Carroll—youngish, hawk-faced, the son of one of the wealthiest land-holders in Maryland and a frequent dinner-guest—entered the room. Her sister Anna's husband, Congressman Richard Cutts, was at his side. Both were rumpled, dusty, and exhausted; Dolley hoped they'd put their horses somewhere out of sight. "Cutts tells me—"

Dolley drew herself up and hastily slipped both snuffbox and mirror into the desk-drawer. "Mr. Carroll, I know how much respect *I* would have, for a leader who fled at the mere sound of cannon—or for one whose wife so little respected his courage or the courage of the men behind him." She turned toward the window with calm she was far from feeling, and pretended to scan the distance under her palm. "I see no trace of British grenadiers as of yet. By the sound of the guns, I collect the battle is not yet over."

Even as she spoke the words, her heart sank within her. The constant crashing of the guns had diminished, about half an hour ago, to intermittent booms and the broken spatter of musket-fire. Among the fugitives on Pennsylvania Avenue, she now saw that many wore militia uniforms, filthy and torn, some of them, and some bearing the blood and powder-blackening of battle.

Deserters in retreat. Their Army had fallen apart on the field.

Summer soldiers and sunshine patriots, she thought bitterly, recalling those who had sworn on their swords to remain in her defense.

Untrained men, Dr. Blake had said—was it only this morning?

Jim Monroe is with him, she tried to comfort herself. *He was a soldier. He shall get Jemmy out of there before there's real danger. . . .*

But in her heart she guessed Jemmy wouldn't run.

Like herself—like General Washington before him—Jemmy understood what a leader could and could not be seen to do.

Carroll gestured impatiently. "Ma'am, you know they cannot hope to win."

Dolley turned back. "If I recall correctly, that is what was said about General Washington and his forces." And more quietly she added, "I will not go without my husband."

Both men opened their mouths to argue and both fell silent at the sudden crash of hooves on the drive. Dolley ran to one window and saw Sukey leaning from another upstairs, but the rider had already rushed inside, leaving only a bay horse, trembling and foaming with exhaustion, before the front steps. "Sophie, get one of the servants to bring that horse to the—"

Footfalls in the hall, booted feet, running. The next second Jemmy's manservant Jamie Smith strode in, face, shirt, jacket streaked and matted with dust and sweat. He gasped, "Clear out, ma'am! You got to clear out!" and thrust a slip of sweaty paper into her hand.

Run for your life or be taken prisoner by the British.

In pencil. In Jemmy's neat hand.

Her eyes met Jamie's and the young man said hastily, "He's all right, ma'am, he's well. But General Armstrong ordered a retreat—"

Cutts cried, "Devil take it!" and Carroll ex-

claimed something considerably less refined.

"Now you *shall* go!" he added, making a
move as if he would have seized Dolley by
the arm and frog-marched her to the door,
had he not remembered who and where
they were.

Dolley saw Paul Jennings in the hall beyond the doorway, hurrying to the dining-
room with a tray-full of dessert-dishes,
called, "Paul, put those down, we have to
get out. Bring a screwdriver, please, and the
stepladder to the drawing-room—"

"A *screwdriver*?" Carroll looked ready to
explode. "What in the name of—?"

But Dolley slipped past him and hurried
into the hall.

"Gentlemen, I do not propose to be led in
triumph down the streets of London, but
neither do I propose to let President Washington's picture be carried there like a plac-
ard on a stick to have mud thrown at it by the
populace." Looking through the door of the
big dining-room opposite her, she was
struck for a moment by its look of normalcy,
the square tables that Jefferson had brought
dressed in their white damask like ladies
ready for a ball. The blue-sprigged china

that Jefferson had ordered from France, the glitter of silver.

The thought crossed through her mind, *This is the last time I'll see this room this way, ready for company.*

The last time I shall see the drawing-room, she thought, as she led the men into that graceful salon. From the wall, in the filtered buttery glow from the muslin-curtained windows, the General's face had a calm look, as if he knew he had delegated authority well. So many times, Martha had repeated Washington's words, that he relied upon her more than on any of his subordinates, to guard his back.

Not in battle, to be sure, but in those covert wars more conclusive than open violence; the battles for opinion and goodwill.

George had trusted Martha—as Jemmy had trusted Dolley, all these years—to handle the greater and more delicate task of sustaining the goodwill that long-ago battles had won.

She took a breath, looked up at the portrait, dominating the room just as his presence had dominated every gathering, the moment he came into it. It came to her with a sinking dread just exactly how enormous the painting was. In its gilded frame it was over five feet wide and eight feet tall, and so heavy it was screwed to the paneling rather than hung by wires.

Jemmy had talked the General into coming out of retirement twenty-seven years ago. Had shattered the peace her dear friend Martha had so treasured. Had, Dolley knew, shortened the General's life.

Would that tall, quiet gentleman who'd ridden into Philadelphia that day have agreed to Jemmy's proposal, had he known what the strain of office would cost him? Dolley suspected he would.

She owed it to her friend, to get his picture away safe.

"This is madness!" Carroll almost shouted, as Dolley helped Paul position the ladder beside the portrait.

We'll never get it down, she thought despairingly. *And if we do, we'll never get it safe into the carriage.*

How close are they? The noise of vehicles, horses, fleeing foot-traffic along Pennsylvania Avenue prevented her from hearing whether the guns were still firing, whether the sound of British drums could yet be heard. Panic closed her throat, made it difficult to breathe. How many of Jemmy's forces had fled? How many remained around him, between the invading Army and the town?

How hard would those fight, if they saw all around them their comrades break and flee?

Above her, Paul fumbled and scratched at the screws in the frame, and Carroll snarled, "Forget the picture, madame! You must come away!"

"Yes, Dolley, please!" Cutts pressed his hands on her shoulders and Dolley tightened her grip warningly on the stepladder.

They had a point, she supposed. Neither was willing to brand himself a coward by leaving a woman—and a friend and the President's wife to boot—in the path of a vengeful Army. But if caught, they would be in considerably more physical danger than she.

With the dust, the heat, the noise, how could she tell when the last possible moment was?

And yet, as she had said to Sophie, there were things that could not be left behind. Not only for the sake of the future, but for the sake of those who'd passed them along in trust.

"Paul, get M'sieu Sioussat and Mr. McGraw and get an ax from the garden shed," she commanded, astonished at how calm she sounded. "We shall have to break the frame."

"Mrs. Madison—!" protested Carroll, and other voices called from the hallway, "Mrs. Madison!"

French John came in, with a tall gentleman Dolley had never seen before, and—of all people—a Quaker shipowner named Jacob Barker whom Dolley had first met in her days at the Philadelphia Meeting. "Mrs. Madison," said Barker, sweeping off his rather dusty hat. "Pardon us for coming in on thee thus unannounced—"

"Mr. Barker, if I knew thee better I should fall upon thy neck in hysterics," said Dolley, and Barker returned a quick grin.

"Robert dePeyster, of New York, madame— he saith he's a good friend of Secretary Monroe. We're staying at Blodgett's Hotel—"

"We were, if they don't burn it down," added dePeyster morosely, and stepped aside as the gardener came in, carrying the kindling-ax.

"—and we came to see if thee stood in need of assistance."

Quakers never said things like *Thank God,* but it was as close as Dolley ever came to it. "Hast a cart that we might take?" she asked urgently. "A horse as well, though we could use that poor beast Jamie rode here from the battle—"

"There's that old nag of Blodgett's back at the hotel, that nobody can catch. And the cart he fetches groceries in—"

"Canst bring it?"

"Ma'am." DePeyster snapped her a military salute and strode out the door; Barker came to help steady the portrait as French John began chopping at the gilt wood frame. Sophie returned with a pitcher of cider and a couple of crystal goblets; she poured one out and stood sipping, her shoulder against the corner of the mantel-piece, watching the scene with narrowed eyes.

What part of her past, of her heart, Dolley wondered, had *Sophie* left behind, in that burning plantation-house in Virginia?

After a moment the dressmaker poured a second goblet and brought it to Dolley, who had stepped back as the portrait was eased down.

"And where will you be taking Mrs. Madison?" she asked Carroll casually. "To Bellevue?" Carroll's father owned most of the land in and around Capitol Hill; his mansion in Georgetown was justly renowned as one of the most beautiful in the countryside.

"If she'll come."

Dolley picked up one of the knives Sophie had been in the process of wrapping to pack. "Can we cut it out and roll it up? We cannot let them take it—we should destroy it rather ourselves."

"You shall destroy it, madame, if you roll it up," said French John calmly, and took the knife from her hand. "The brushwork would never survive. I think it can be loosely laid over the top of a load, with the corners weighted. I shall see to it."

While French John was delicately cutting the canvas free of its stretcher—and Mr. Carroll was pacing furiously in and out, looking through every window he could toward Bladensburg—dePeyster returned, miraculously with the promised cart. The sky was darkening now toward storm, and strange, flickering winds blew the stench of gunpowder through the open windows. Dolley realized she had begun to tremble.

Jemmy will come, she told herself. *I know he will.*

Yet how could she stay and put everyone else in peril?

She looked up and saw Sophie's eyes on her, calculating and icy.

French John and Barker lifted the canvas, carried it toward the door. *I'm forgetting something,* thought Dolley, as Carroll steered her firmly toward the door. *I know I am . . .* She balked, turning back.

"Mrs. Madison, please!"

Dolley, her heart pounding, nodded. "Paul, please have Joe bring the carriage."

Something important. Something that people will one day want, and miss. Like recollection of something we dreamed in childhood, that frightened us, or inspired us, or filled us with understanding or joy.

But all she could remember to say was, "M'sieu Sioussat, please see to it that the food prepared for dinner, and the cider and wine, be given to any of the soldiers who come past."

"I shall do it, madame, but please—"

"And please see that Pol goes to the French Minister's house. They'll look after her there, and I don't think the British will burn it."

"I shall see it done, madame," promised the steward, "but please, go!"

I should wait for Jemmy. He'll be here soon, I know he will. . . .

As the men hustled her into the hall, Sophie said quietly, "It might be a good idea to take some silver with you in the carriage, in case you become separated from the cart."

Dolley halted, their eyes meeting.

More softly, for her ears only, Sophie added, "Had we had hard silver when *we* were burned from *our* home, my mother and I, we might have fared better than we did."

"I'll be going to friends."

"That's what my mother thought."

Dolley broke away, strode into the dining-room to scoop as many forks and spoons as she could fit into her reticule. "Canst ride in the front with Joe and Sukey, Sophie? All the Cabinet papers are on the other seats."

"I shall be staying here. Don't worry about me," her friend added, as Dolley froze at the foot of the front step, looked back in alarm. "I scarcely think they're going to torch the town."

Richard Cutts thrust Dolley up into the

carriage, clanking reticule and all. Closed the door.

"I shall tell Mr. Madison to look for you at Bellevue, shall I?" asked Sophie, from the mansion's steps.

"Mrs. Hallam, we cannot allow you—" Cutts protested, but Sophie made a gesture like shooing flies.

"Get Mrs. Madison away. I can look after myself."

Or knowst thou someone in Cockburn's force, who shalt look after thee? Dolley turned, watching the enigmatic dark figure on the mansion's steps as the overloaded carriage jolted into motion. French John and Jacob Barker were gently draping General Washington's portrait across the top of the grocery-cart as Dolley lost sight of them. For a few minutes more, the white walls of the mansion were visible to her over Mr. Jefferson's screen of young poplar trees.

Fourteen years, thought Dolley, fighting to keep panic from her heart. She fumbled in her reticule for her snuffbox. *I saw this house fourteen years ago . . . .*

With Lady Washington's mirror, she realized in shocked dismay, *in my hand!*

She half turned in the carriage's crowded

seat, seeing herself sweep snuffbox and mirror together into the desk-drawer as Mr. Carroll entered shouting . . . *If I call out to have us turn back, Joe will pretend he can't hear me.*

Such was the din of traces rattling, hooves pounding, other carriages, carts, fleeing riders, and cursing barrow-pushers all clogging Pennsylvania Avenue in a solid wall of dust, his deafness might not be sham. And even if he did hear, the crowd forced them on.

She twisted back around, looking at the roofline of the big sandstone house, visible still. Her hand closed, recalling the small solid shape of the Queen's mirror, as it had been that evening she'd seen the house like this beyond the trees.

Recalling, too, the grief and fear of that season of uncertainty. It seemed to her, that year, that everything she had witnessed since 1776—everything Jemmy, and General Washington, and Jefferson, and Mr. Adams had worked for—was shattering to pieces around them.

Dust swallowed the big house. In her heart she knew she'd never see it again.

❧ 1800 ❧

DOLLEY

᳁

Edgehill Plantation
Albemarle County, Virginia
Sunday, April 6, 1800

"Mrs. Madison?"

At the sound of the voice, Dolley looked around, and to her great surprise recognized Sally Hemings standing beside the garden gate.

"Please forgive my being so bold, ma'am, but might I have a few words with you?" The young woman—Dolley guessed her age at not quite thirty—stood just on the other side of the white wooden palings that separated Patsy Jefferson Randolph's beloved beds of tulips and azalea from the still-greater beauty of the spring woods. With her turquoise-green eyes, and the morning's mistiness still clinging to the gray-barked trees around her, she looked rather like a spirit in a tale who cannot cross cold iron, ready to evaporate when the day grew bright.

"Of course, dear." Dolley cast a quick glance back toward the frame house where Thomas Randolph's butler was just emerging from the back door, a wicker tray of breakfast leftovers in hand. With Patsy going into her fourth day of a devastating migraine, Dolley hoped somebody would remember to round up eight-year-old Payne and seven-year-old Jeff Randolph for lessons before they disappeared into the woods. Patsy ruled her household with a kid-gloved hand of iron and when she had a headache, everything tended to slither fairly speedily into rack and ruin.

On the other hand, Dolley had never expected to see Sally Hemings set foot on Patsy's property. Whatever had brought the young slave here, it had to be important.

Dolley folded her shawl more closely around her shoulders and stepped out through the garden gate. For all her years in Philadelphia, she had slipped quickly back into the Virginia habit of thinking: It was almost without awareness that she made sure she and Sally couldn't be seen from the house.

"Is all well at Monticello?" Even as she said the words she thought, *If anything happened to Jefferson, word would come here, or to Jemmy, first. . . .*

"Yes, ma'am, quite well." Sally had a pleasing soft alto whose gentle refinement had impressed Dolley, on the few occasions she'd heard her speak. Since she'd first visited Monticello with Jemmy in 1795, she'd seen the beautiful maidservant any number of times, and had easily believed her own maid, Sukey's, matter-of-fact gossip: *She Mr. Jefferson's woman, you know.* Had believed it even before she'd observed that Patsy Randolph never spoke of or to Sally and looked through her as if she were a pane of glass. This didn't happen often, because Sally was unobtrusively never in the same room with Patsy if she could help it.

And Jefferson, like every other Virginia planter Dolley had ever met, appeared to notice none of these interactions.

Dolley may have been a Quaker, but her Coles cousins down in Hanover County hadn't been, and she'd learned everything there was to know about concubinage by the time she was ten.

Like most of the concubines Dolley had

seen over the past five years—and Sukey could point out every one for six counties around—Sally was very light-skinned, and well dressed even for a maid at Monticello, where the house-servants were clothed as well as many Philadelphia artisans. In Spanish cities like New Orleans or Mobile, according to Aaron Burr, such a woman would have been a free courtesan, kept by her protector with an establishment of her own. It was only in the United States that there existed no place for such a woman.

"I'm not sure whether this is any of my business, ma'am," Sally went on softly, "or to whom I should speak of it. But it touches Mr. Jefferson; I believe he may need to know."

Dolley said, "Go on."

The young woman was silent for a moment, as if arranging her thoughts. Though her green muslin dress was reasonably new and had clearly been made for her, not handed down from someone else, she wore no jewelry beyond a thin gold chain around her neck. Considering the way other women in her position were sometimes decked, this spoke well for either Jefferson's taste or her own. It impressed Dolley, too, that she was matter-of-fact, as if she knew Dolley knew perfectly well who she was, but was neither bold nor coy about it.

It was a fact, that was all.

"Have you heard Mr. Jefferson speak of a gentleman named Mr. Callendar, ma'am? Mr. James Callendar?"

Dolley felt her lips compress at the name. Only the system that required every person of color to speak of any white man as a "gentleman"—usually on pain of a beating—could have given Callendar that title, as far as Dolley was concerned.

"I'm acquainted with him," she replied evenly. "He's the editor of the *Richmond Enquirer.*" She didn't add that upon the few occasions she had met James Callendar, she always wanted to go wash afterwards.

Sally's eyes flickered to her face, then away. She kept her voice neutral, as any slave learned to, when speaking about any white. "Yes, ma'am. And I know he's a friend of Mr. Jefferson, and that his newspaper supports him. But my niece Betsie, who lives near Richmond—at Eppington, you know—"

Dolley nodded. Tom Jefferson's younger daughter had married her handsome cousin Jack Eppes three years ago—Dolley had come to Monticello for the wedding. She recalled Jemmy telling her that Jefferson had given the newlyweds a number of slaves, as part of the dowry. Betsie Hemings must have been one of them.

"Betsie's told me that Mr. Callendar has been asking questions around town, about Mr. Jefferson. Questions about scandal and rumor." Her troubled glance touched Dolley's again. "There was a woman, the wife of one of Mr. Jefferson's friends, that Mr. Jefferson fell in love with when he was young . . . that kind of thing. Scandal that's really nobody's business. Things everybody knows about everybody, that get passed around among the colored and the poor whites, and talked of in the taverns."

"In that case I believe Mr. Callendar must hear a great deal of it," said Dolley drily. Across the younger woman's face, quick wry appreciation of the comment flitted, instantly sponged away.

"As you say, ma'am. Betsie—my niece—says she hears from the potboys there that Mr. Callendar is always asking where and when, when the talk touches Mr. Jefferson. Then he buys men extra drinks to get them talking more. I don't know what Mr. Callendar is up to, but I've seen the kind of thing he writes. I think Mr. Jefferson ought to know what's going on."

Dolley never swore herself, but at times like this she understood why someone would want to. A number of Jemmy's favorite expressions passed through her mind.

"I know it isn't my place to speak against a white man, ma'am, nor to pass along gossip," concluded Sally. "But I know Mr. Madison is working to make Mr. Jefferson the President, writing to the newspapers and meeting with men in the legislature. The kind of rumor Mr. Callendar is asking about isn't anything that will be helpful, if it goes beyond Virginia."

Again their eyes met, and this time they held. Dolley knew exactly the first rumor James Callendar would have heard upon his arrival in Richmond eighteen months ago: the same one Sukey had first whispered into her ear. *She Mr. Jefferson's woman. . . .*

Sukey had spoken without innuendo or judgment, merely as a piece of information that her mistress would need in adapting to the household. She'd used the same tone to remark that Aunt Carr had a room up on the attic floor, and that there'd been another sister, Miss Elizabeth, who'd been not right in her head and had died in a snowstorm many years ago. In Virginia—in the whole of the South—concubinage and its more casual variations were simply part of the landscape, like mosquitoes in summer, although among slave-owners it was considered extremely bad form to talk about it.

For a man looking to discredit a political opponent, particularly in the North, it was a smutty treasure-house of innuendo.

And the logical defense against it would be to send the woman away.

Dolley said quietly, "Thank you, Sally. It will most likely come to nothing, for Mr. Callendar is after all one of Mr. Jefferson's most loyal supporters. But thou'rt quite right to be concerned for his reputation, and thou art quite right in letting him know what thou hast heard. I'll write to him this evening, since I don't believe he'll be back until the end of May." She'd heard from Sukey that Sally Hemings could write, but whether it would be safe for a slave to write to her master—particularly in the vicious political climate of the approaching election—was another matter. She added, "I will keep to myself that thou wert the one who told me."

"Thank you, ma'am. I do appreciate that. I hope Mrs. Randolph is better? Shep said that she was bad enough that you'd been sent for, to help with the household." Shep was one of the slaves who worked in Jefferson's nail-factory on Monticello. "I hope she's feeling more herself?"

"She was a little better this morning," said Dolley. "I thank thee for asking. Migraines usually pass off quite suddenly, don't they? 'Tis hoped she'll feel better today."

"Yes, ma'am." Sally curtseyed. "I am sorry to have disturbed you, ma'am, and if I may I'll leave you to get back to your family."

"Of course. My thanks again."

For a time Dolley stood watching as the other woman retreated along one of the narrow foot-traces that threaded through the woods behind the Edgehill home-place, her green muslin dress flickering in and out of the thin-leafed pale trees.

⚜

In the carriage on the way back to Montpelier later that day, Dolley turned them over in her mind: Sally, and Tom Jefferson; James Callendar, and the election that would take place at the end of the year.

The election that would—it was hoped—peacefully alter the growing strength of the central government into something the States were willing to live with, before the dominance of the one and the independence of the others led again to violence.

Only Jefferson, Jemmy said, had the stature, and the popularity, to draw the votes of both the North and an increasingly angry South. Having avidly read every newspaper she could get her hands on for three years, Dolley had to agree with her husband. The thought of a vicious little scandalmonger like Callendar turning against Jefferson at this stage made her shiver, as if a rat had run across her flesh.

⚜

It was in Philadelphia in 1796, Jemmy's last year in Congress, that Dolley had first encountered James Callendar.

That was the year General Washington—to Martha's unspeakable relief—had announced that he would not seek a third term as President. That he would at last go home to Mount Vernon to stay.

It was the year that the new nation had held its first true election, between candidates who held radically different opinions about how the nation should be governed and with whom it should ally itself.

It was the year when every newspaper in the country—pro-Jefferson or pro-Adams—had felt called upon to vomit every reason, real or fancied, political or personal, hysterical or merely scurrilous, for voters to elect their perceived Savior and reject the man whom they felt to be the Antichrist.

And the most vivid and copious producer of this verbal sewage was James Thompson Callendar.

Four years previously—the year of Payne's birth, when Dolley had been no more than a good Quaker bride—newspapers had backed Jefferson or Alexander Hamilton in another round of mud-slinging, with Jefferson referred to as an "intriguing incendiary," a "concealed voluptuary," and "the promoter of national disunion, national insignificance, public disorder, and discredit." Dolley had read with interest Jemmy's clearheaded defense of Jefferson, and that written by the third of the loyal Virginia triumvirate, quiet, tactful, perpetually rumpled Jim Monroe, who was now Governor of the State. Rather less creditably, Jefferson's clerk in the State

Department, Phillip Freneau, in his newly founded paper the *National Gazette,* had attacked both John Adams and Hamilton, the one as an "unprincipled libeler" and the other as "not only a monarchist, but for a monarchy bottomed on corruption."

By 1796, Maximilien Robespierre had perished on his own guillotine and the revolutionary National Assembly in France had been crushed by the five-man Directorate. In the United States, with the Presidency at stake, the war of political libel began in earnest.

It is all-important to our country that Washington's successor shall be a safe man. But it is far less important who . . . may be named . . . than that it shall not be Jefferson.

He was an atheist, a puppet of France, inept, indecisive, a foe of Washington and of the Union. Jeers were written of his flight from the British forces during the Revolution that had first occupied Richmond, then almost trapped him at Monticello.

Not to be outdone, the pro-Jefferson *Philadelphia Aurora* crowned Adams "His Rotundity," and declared him unfit to lead the country, the "champion of kings, ranks, and titles." It warned that he was scheming to transform the Presidency into a hereditary monarchy in order to pass it along to his son. Jefferson, concluded the paper proudly, had only daughters.

Dolley, who by that time had met nearly everyone concerned, could only imagine what Abigail Adams would have said to *that* piece of reasoning.

She remembered Callendar from Philadelphia that winter, a dark-haired Scotsman with a head that seemed too large for his body and an indefinable air of physical crookedness about him. He'd been standing near the fireplace during one of the receptions at the house she and Jemmy had rented from Jim Monroe on Spruce Street, railing about the injustices of tyrants who sought to chain not only the body, but the mind, and the minds of children down to the tenth generation, in a harsh wild voice like that of an Old Testament prophet.

"Jefferson's wisdom is the hope of our nation," he had pronounced, and coming close, Dolley had been struck by the rankness of his body, and the thick odor of Jemmy's best port on his breath. "The sweetness of Xenophon and the force of Polybius, information without parade, eloquence without effort. How can any hear Thomas Jefferson and remain unmoved?"

⚜

And he was right, Dolley reflected, watching Payne trot importantly alongside the carriage on his pony, his gold hair catching the patchy brilliance of the April sun. But there was some people's praise that reflected as badly on their object as outright insults, and James Callendar was one of those people.

"Watch me, Mama!" Payne kicked his mount into a canter, effortlessly cleared a fallen tree-trunk near the road, and flourished his hat to his mother's applause.

"I've jumped him over fences, too," the boy said, trotting back to the carriage. "Jeff and I, we took out Annie's horse back at Edgehill, and there wasn't any trouble. I'm big enough to have a horse of my own, not a pony. Annie's only a few months older than me, and she has a horse. You have to tell Papa I'm big enough."

Dolley pretended to frown in concentration. "I'm to tell thy papa thou'rt big enough to be a horse-thief? Well, all right . . ."

He crowed with laughter, and swiped the air with his riding-whip. "You know what I mean!" And cantered ahead to jump the little creek, singing as he rode.

Fair as Dolley's sister Lucy, and with the promise of Lucy's good looks and their father's height, Payne had slipped easily into the role of a planter's son. Maybe too easily, Dolley thought. John Todd had believed devoutly in education, not simply because his own father was a schoolmaster but because he saw learning as the gateway to an honorable career. And Jemmy, of course, was one of the most erudite men in Virginia.

But from the moment Payne had realized that his stepfather was a wealthy planter, with ten thousand acres and over a hundred slaves at his beck and call, he seemed to have understood that the issue of his future livelihood was already taken care of. And as the years had passed and Dolley had realized, first with disbelief and then with an agony of regret, that Jemmy's seed could find no root in her womb, it had become harder and harder for her to discipline Payne, or to endure his sullen wretchedness on those few occasions when his will was thwarted. During one of those miserable battles of will when he was five—Dolley recalled it was over his first pony—he had sobbed, *You wish I'd died so you could marry Papa!* Papa being Jemmy. The words, and the way he'd turned from her, had gone like a knife-blade into her heart.

In all other things, Dolley believed herself to be fairly rational: firm with the slaves, since there was no keeping house unless one learned to be firm; tactful with her tribe of new sisters-in-law; adept at balancing the demands of running a plantation household against the constant stream of Virginia hospitality and her own need for a quiet hour now and then.

But with Payne she was helpless.

It was a good thing, she reflected, that the boy was so good-hearted. She had been less concerned during the first two years of her marriage, when she and Jemmy had wintered in Philadelphia every year for the sessions of Congress. Payne had had his familiar friends around him. Only in the summers had they returned to the relative isolation of Montpelier, where Payne's only company was the children of either slaveholders or slaves.

But in 1797, so many things had changed.

⚜

The vicious Presidential election of 1796 had gone to Adams by three electoral votes.

And because the Constitution had been written before the emergence of distinct political parties—not to mention before such events as the bloody Revolution in France and England's ruthless decision to seize American ships, cargoes, and seamen— Thomas Jefferson had emerged from retirement to become Vice President to his former friend, whose political views were now in direct opposition to his own. ("One can't think of everything," Jemmy had sighed.)

But the country's unofficial Vice President—the man who privately gave orders to, and received privileged information from, the new President's Cabinet—was Alexander Hamilton. A man who had never been elected to any office in his life.

Standing in the crowd of Philadelphians outside Congress Hall on a chilly March day in 1797, Dolley had watched Jefferson go up to take office as president of the Senate, tall and lanky in a long-tailed blue coat. And she'd smiled a little, remembering him two years earlier, when Jemmy had first brought her to Monticello. Untidy and eccentric-looking in the old clothes he wore while gardening, he strode down the front steps— that was before he'd started tearing the house apart—with his hands held out to greet his old friend. "Jemmy! I do hope you know what you've let yourself in for, my dear Mrs. Madison," he'd added in his soft voice, bowing over her hand. "When you marry a Virginian, you marry his entire family *and* his friends—"

"—And their horses and dogs and Negroes—" Jemmy added with his dry smile.

"—in season and out, bed and board—"

"My dear Mr. Jefferson," Dolley drew herself up with an air of assumed haughtiness and a twinkle in her eyes. "I see you mistake me for a Philadelphian. I happen to *be* a Virginian, born and raised. There is nothing about the feeding and housing of two dozen strangers at five minutes' notice that I hadn't mastered before the age of twelve."

His eyes widened with pleasure. Instantly, it was as if they'd known one another for years. "Really? What county?"

"Hanover, if you please."

"Good Lord! There are some quite remarkable remains of a Pamunkey Indian village on the banks of—"

"Mrs. Madison," interposed Jemmy patiently, "please permit me to introduce my friend Mr. Jefferson. Mr. Jefferson, my wife.

And I warn you, Dolley, that if you encourage Tom with the smallest query about the Indians, or fossil mammoths, or what varieties of alfalfa best grow in these mountains, you shall be kept awake until dawn with the natural history of the entire region."

Two years after that meeting, moving through the crowd around Congress Hall, Jefferson had looked grave and collected, Dolley thought, and a little grim. The Federalists were strong in the Senate, and feelings were running so high about whether to ally with a domineering Britain or revolutionary France that there had been outbreaks of mob violence.

Even so, she thought, as she watched George Washington cross the State House yard, kingly in black velvet, with stout little gray-clad Mr. Adams bobbing in his wake, she had been aware that she was seeing something that no one in the world had ever seen before: the ruler of a nation quietly handing off power to his successor, then returning home to private life.

"No severed heads—no daggers in the dark—no rioting in the streets," she murmured to Anna, who stood at her side. "No blood on the steps of the throne—no more fuss, really, than taking over as vestryman of the parish. Flat dull, in fact," she added with a laugh. "Canst think of another time in history, when the transfer of rulership from one man to another did not involve someone dying?"

At her elbow, the black-clothed widow Sophie Hallam responded with a wintry smile. "We do indeed witness a remarkable event. Yet I'm sure that somewhere, Dolley, someone has died for it."

⚜

Sophie had returned to Philadelphia in time to attend that same Christmas reception of 1796 at which Dolley had first encountered James Callendar. Across the very crowded double-parlor, the black and gray of second mourning had caught Dolley's eye, striking in a room filled with women determined to show off their best. As she approached, Dolley saw the woman was in conversation with Aaron Burr—who stood several inches shorter—and coming close heard her voice, a wry alto like smoke and honey: "One must allow it's an effective way to raise money: If your people are too poor to tax, send your army on a looting-expedition across the border into your neighbor's territory."

Bonaparte. Dolley identified the topic of conversation at once and with an inner sigh. Since the Directorate of France had begun sending its troops into Italy, very little else was being talked about.

And the next instant, identified the voice. "Sophie!"

The woman in gray turned, her cool sardonic smile melting into an expression of genuine pleasure. "Dearest!" The two women clasped hands, then, impulsively, embraced. "My mother always vowed you should marry a planter! She would be pleased to see herself proved right."

Dolley's eye flickered over the exquisitely fashionable somberness of her friend's dress, and she bit back her query, *And how is thy dear mother . . .?* Sophie seemed to read both her unspoken words and her instantaneous afterthought, and added, more quietly, "She would have been pleased to see you looking so well, too, Dolley. She always said you were the best of my friends."

That time, the past tense was unmistakable.

"I'm sorry."

Sophie shook her head, though her features tightened momentarily with some unsaid and bitter reflection. "In many ways I miss her more than I miss Mr. Hallam—who was a good husband, as husbands go. . . ." She waved away his specter dismissively, and smiled her sidelong smile. "I am a mere dressmaker these days, but as we live in a democracy now, both Colonel Burr and Lady Washington assured me there would be no objection to my accompanying him here."

"Mrs. *Hallam*? Art *thou* the Mrs. Hallam whose needlework Lady Washington doth praise so highly? She hath said she knew thee as a child—"

"And so she did. My father consulted with her on her own health and her daughter Patcy's, when she'd bring her into Williamsburg. I owe Lady Washington a good deal."

And Dolley thought, as Aaron Burr turned aside to bow over Maria Morris's hand, that the diminutive Senator gave Sophie a curious, speculative look.

After years of wondering, Dolley had learned almost by chance from Tom Jefferson that her friend had made it to Cornwallis's camp at Yorktown, and that she had done nursing for a Yorktown doctor in the final year of the War. Later, Patsy Jefferson Randolph had spoken of meeting Sophie again in Paris. Dolley learned that Sophie and her mother had taken ship with the departing British troops in 1783, and that her mother had died on the voyage. Hence, Sophie remarked with brittle lightness, her stint as a paid companion to an Englishwoman in Paris when all Hell was about to break loose. But how she had gotten out of Paris, who Mr. Hallam had been, and how and why Sophie had returned to Philadelphia to take up life as a seamstress, she would not say.

Because of her friendship with Martha Washington, and because of her undeniable good breeding and wit as well as her skill at cutting a gown, Sophie Hallam rapidly made herself a fixture in Philadelphia society. She knew everyone and everything, and was welcome in both Federalist and Republican circles. For she had early issued her own Proclamation of Neutrality, she claimed, in imitation of the President's: listening to any gossip and never passing a word of it along.

Which was odd, Dolley thought, in a

woman whom she recalled as being sharply outspoken in her loyalty, long ago, to the Crown.

⚜

Certainly Sophie's letters had enlivened the next few years.

Only weeks before John Todd's death, Jemmy's brother Ambrose had died back at Montpelier. Each summer after that, when Jemmy and Dolley had returned to the plantation, it had been to find more tasks undone, more bills unsettled, more finances entangled by debt and poor management as old Colonel Madison grew less and less able to ride his own acres daily the way he once had. Thus it was that when Virginians gathered to elect their representatives to the Fifth Congress, Jemmy stepped aside. For the first time since the Revolution, he returned to private life.

Watching the sunlight on the flanks of the carriage-team, on Payne's gold hair as the boy galloped his pony into the green stillness of the wooded hills, Dolley was still hard-put to piece together how the country had come, so swiftly, from that point—that astonishingly peaceful hand-over of power from Washington to Adams—to the very verge of darkness that threatened to undo everything Jemmy, and Tom, and Mr. Adams himself had fought for.

Tyranny masquerading as the necessary actions of reasonable men, the way it now did in France.

⚜

Even as a permanent resident at Montpelier, of course, Jemmy was never completely detached from politics. He would always, Dolley reflected wryly, be a kingmaker at heart.

Sophie, and Lizzie Collins, and Aaron Burr kept them up on the gossip of the capital, sending them clippings from newspapers and, as Sophie phrased it, reports on the gales in various tea-pots around town. It was Sophie who sent them the tracts published by James Callendar entitled *The History of the United States for the Year 1796,* which detailed Alexander Hamilton's 1792 affair with a certain Mrs. Maria Reynolds, whose husband was involved in speculation with Hamilton's Treasury funds to the tune of thirty thousand dollars. *So much correspondence could not refer exclusively to wenching,* Callendar wrote of the letters which he claimed Hamilton had helped Mrs. Reynolds forge. *No man of sense can believe that it did.*

Hamilton, livid, had challenged Jim Monroe to a duel on the grounds that Monroe, to whom Mrs. Reynolds's husband had sent proof of the affair in an effort at blackmail back in '92, had, after four years, passed along the details to Callendar. After words like "liar" and "scoundrel" had been exchanged, the two opponents had been talked out of bloodshed by Aaron Burr. Instead, Hamilton published a confession in the *Gazette of the United States: The charge against me is a connection with one James Reynolds for purposes of improper pecuniary speculation,* he wrote. *My real crime is an amorous connection with his wife.*

Alexander Hamilton, who had already retired as Secretary of the Treasury, never held public office again, which as far as Dolley was concerned was just as well. Sophie noted—goodness knew what her sources were—that when Hamilton's books were examined, his assistant (a cousin of his wife) was found to be $238,000 short.

Sophie related all this with a kind of relish,

as if profoundly entertained by the murderous infighting of men who had begun their careers as traitors to the King. "The Constitution gives your friend every right to laugh at us to our faces," sighed Jemmy, as he laid down the letter that contained the *Gazette* confession. "God help this country, if she could not say of us whatever she wished."

⚜

But Jefferson's letters were first disquieting, and then frightening. In May of 1797, in response to the treaty Washington had negotiated with England, France started seizing American ships and cargoes. The new President Adams sent a delegation to Paris to iron things out, and mortally offended his Vice President and half the Congress by requesting "measures of defense."

Adams's Cabinet consisted mainly of men hand-picked by Hamilton, and the second President found himself surrounded by pro-British New England merchants and bankers. No doubt remembering Jefferson's championship of Citizen Genêt, Adams shut his Vice President out of nearly every aspect of the government. By November of that year, with

Bonaparte preparing, it was said, to conquer Switzerland and then invade England, anti-French hysteria had reached dangerous proportions.

By January of '98 feelings in Congress were running so high that the Honorable Representative of Vermont (Republican) crossed the floor of the House chamber to spit in the face of the Honorable Representative of Connecticut (Federalist). This in turn led to a brawl on the floor with a cane and some fire-tongs as weapons. ("Not," wrote Sophie, who'd been in the gallery, "the Congress's finest hour.")

By the following April, when word came to Philadelphia that French Foreign Minister Tallyrand had refused to receive the American envoys unless they lent France twelve million dollars and gave the Foreign Minister himself a further quarter million as a "sweetener," anti-French mobs were storming the streets of Philadelphia, and the country was clamoring for war.

In June, a Naturalization Act was passed. Effectively blocking the citizenship of émigrés from both France and Ireland, it was followed, a week later, by the Aliens Act, which permitted the President to summarily banish any foreigner he personally deemed a threat (for instance, Jefferson's staunch supporter Albert Gallatin).

And in the blazing heat of July, the Sedition Act was passed, forbidding any newspaper to print attacks on the President—in direct disregard of the Constitution.

٭

"It is a reign of witches," declared Jefferson softly, as he paced the darkness of Montpelier's pillared porch in the heat of a July night in 1798. He'd arrived after a day of blistering sun; Dolley, sitting at Jemmy's side, had heard in the throb of the cicadas, smelled in the damp thick air, the coming of storm. "Because one Frenchman is dishonest, and another is greedy, they seek to go to war with the only nation strong enough to counterbalance England's desire to swallow us up, to transform us back into her colonies again. To hold us not in chains of iron this time but of gold. It is enough to give you a fever."

July 2, 1798. Twenty-two years to the day, Dolley remembered, since the Congress had voted to declare independence.

Bitter years. Since taking up his office

again, Jefferson had been spending as little time in Philadelphia as he could manage, coming home from the capital in early July and not returning until December. During those long summers and falls he was in and out of Montpelier, and Jemmy and Dolley would go to stay with him at Monticello, where the older man seemed to take refuge from his savage frustration in the remodeling of the Big House: Dolley hoped by the time they went for their next stay there would at least be a roof.

So preoccupied had their friend been with what was happening in Philadelphia, she wasn't certain he'd notice whether he was sleeping under the stars or not.

"Now Adams has called for an army, to fight the French—Does he *really* believe that Bonaparte will invade our shores? They've even got Washington to come out of retirement to lead it—"

Dolley had wondered what Martha had had to say to that.

"—which of course he is too old to do. So he's demanded that Hamilton—*Hamilton!*—be his second in command: in effect, the generalissimo in the field."

She asked, *"Can* the President ask the Congress to set aside the Constitution?"

"He certainly has," replied Jemmy, grimly.

And Jefferson whispered fiercely, "Who's to stop him? With a standing army in the field, they've made the President into a sort of elective King, and the State Representatives his subjects, not his partners in rule. Adams tells them what he wishes, and they do it—which I understood was the entire reason we fought in '76."

In the dark that followed the lightning, Dolley could sense his eyes meeting Jemmy's. "I think it is for the States, don't you, to tell Adams that he's overstepped his bounds? It is *we* who made the Constitution, *we*—the *States*—who agreed to give up our individual liberties and enter into the Union. It is up to us, to abrogate the laws which violate it."

More silence followed, broken only by the rumble of thunder on the mountains, and, some minutes later, the patter of the rain. The house behind them was dark, that long house of yellow brick whose southern half—completely separated from the north end where Jemmy, Dolley, Payne, and Anna lived—still housed the Old Colonel and Mother Madison, Jemmy's sister Fanny, and, since March, his brother Ambrose's orphaned daughter Nell.

The house that seemed some days so profoundly peaceful, and some nights, as if it were isolated from the world by the endless miles of the sea.

Jemmy said at last, "I think you're right, Tom. And I think we must speak further of this. *Speak,*" he added quietly, "not write. Nor commit a word to paper, until we are ready for the States to draft resolutions to that effect. For if we appear to be urging the adoption of such resolutions, that would set the States in opposition to the Congress, I think that you and I, my friend, would find ourselves in danger of prosecution. For conspiracy, certainly. And I would not put it past Hamilton, to bring a charge against us of treason."

⚜

As the carriage emerged from the trees at the foot of Montpelier's long hill, Dolley saw at once that something was going on. Every window in the house was illuminated, and even at that distance she could see far more people than usual moving about the porch.

Her mind still on that July night twenty-one months ago—the legislatures of both Virginia and Kentucky had adopted resolutions declaring that the central government of the United States could not assume powers not specifically granted by the Constitution (such as arresting people for making rude comments about the President's rather ample bottom)—Dolley felt an instant's surge of panic at the sight. She rose in the carriage and called out, "Payne, *no!*" as the boy spurred his pony off into the gloom.

Anna, who had sat quietly at her side through most of the drive from Edgehill, looked up at her in surprise. "What's wrong, dear? It just looks like company."

A great deal of company, thought Dolley, her heart racing. And at an hour when everyone should have been indoors.

Jemmy stood waiting for her in the shadows of the porch. His sister Fanny was beside him, and with her her fiancé Dr. Rose: Both Jemmy and Fanny, Dolley saw at once, were clothed in black. "Who is it?" she demanded, as Jemmy stepped forward to hand her down from the carriage. "Not thy father—?"

Jemmy shook his head. "Francis," he answered.

It took Dolley a moment to register who they knew named Francis. "Thy brother Francis?" Past his shoulder she could see through the door of the south parlor—the parlor of the Old Colonel's section of the double house—a coffin resting on a black-draped table.

"He was driving back from Gordonsville yesterday evening," said Jemmy. "His horse took fright at something just where the road goes through the woods near the old tobacco-barn."

Dolley shuddered—having one's horse bolt when pulling a vehicle was far more dangerous than when under saddle—but privately she wondered if brother Francis had been sober.

"I sent a man to you with word this morn-ing—"

"We would have missed him, if he rode cross-country." Dolley looked around her, glimpsing the figures hurrying about in the half-gloom: Jemmy's sister Sarah Macon from Somerset Plantation, and several children of their neighbor, Tom Barbour, plus brother Will's black valet and at least two servants she didn't recognize. "Shall Susannah and Francis's children stay here the night, then, for the funeral?"

Francis, two years younger than his brother Jemmy, had been a quarrelsome man, self-pitying and inclined to drink. There had been trouble between him and his father over the boundary of the land the Old Colonel had given him when he'd married, back before the War, and everyone in the family had taken sides. As a result, the only times Dolley had seen him had been at the Old Colonel's New Year's parties. No wonder it had taken her a moment to recognize his name.

But family was family. And in Virginia, family was all. So Dolley caught Payne—his grave face telling her that he'd already heard the news from the grooms—and made sure he knew he'd be sharing his attic room with several small boy cousins: "And if I hear one peep out of the lot of you, sirrah, I shall know who to send out to sleep in the barn."

Payne laughed—since they both knew Dolley would no more have made good on the threat than she'd have thrown him down the well—and kissed her: "Will Aunt Patsy and Uncle Randolph be coming tomorrow, then? I can take Thundercloud and ride back with a message—"

Dolley suspected Payne's offer had more to do with the drama of galloping a full-sized horse over hill and dale than it did with any real concern for Jefferson's daughter.

"The messenger will have got there by this time."

Everyone for five counties around would be coming for the funeral, Dolley knew, which meant a visit to the kitchen would be in order at once. No wonder the place had the air of a kicked anthill.

For several hours after that Dolley was on her feet, supervising preparations far into the night for what she knew would be an exceedingly long and trying day tomorrow. Starting early in the morning, Dolley knew the entire county would be on hand to condole them in their loss.

The women would bring pies and spoon bread, rolls and butter and thick pots of greens, but the sheer logistics of dinner and hospitality would outstrip those helpful contributions, not to speak of finding sleeping-space for fifty guests tomorrow night, along with their grooms, valets, and maids. Dolley consulted with Hannah the cook, counted up chickens in the runs, turkeys, ducks, eggs on hand and likely to be gathered at this season of the year, hams and sausages in the smokehouse, tea and coffee and sug- arloaves, and calculated when the baking needed to be started for bread, beans, mo- lasses pies. She drafted the plantation cooper and carpenter to the job of carrying additional water and wood, made sure Joe in the stables would have more helpers than usual to deal with the guests' horses, ascer- tained that there were sheets, blankets, and pallets clean, aired, and ready to be laid down everywhere in the house there was room for them at the end of the day tomor- row. She made lists on her ivory house- keeping tablets and ticked them off in pencil: *money for the preacher. Letter to Jefferson. Lend Buster to Susannah*—her new-widowed sister-in-law would certainly need the extra help.

She tried not to reflect that it was charac- teristic of Francis to die in the height of the tobacco-planting season, when no one had help to spare.

Between all that she slipped back into the house and up the stairs to the guest-room, to make sure her sister-in-law was comfortable, and sat talking quietly until the widow had cried herself out, and whispered she thought she could sleep now. Dolley felt again the ache of grief for poor tiny Willie, like a heated nail driven into her soul.

And not for Willie alone. For her oldest brother Walter, lost at sea the year the War ended. For her brothers William and Isaac, both dead just after her marriage to Jemmy. No wonder she treasured Payne so!

The kitchen was in turmoil, when she stopped there to heat cocoa for old Mother Madison. Whatever Francis's peccadilloes, the old lady had still lost a son. Dolley entered her mother-in-law's little parlor to find Mother Madison dozing in her chair beside the fire, a shawl around her knees and another laid over her like a blanket. Huddled in her chair, she looked more like the withered mummy of a child than a living woman.

As silently as she could, Dolley set the pewter chocolate-pot where it would stay warm by the heat of the hearth. From behind the Old Colonel's closed door she could hear the murmur of the old man's voice, hoarse and strong for all his years.

As soon as whoever was with him should leave, she decided, she would gently wake her mother-in-law and help her to bed. On her way in she'd heard the little wall-clock in the hall strike, and knew it was close to midnight. The big brick house was growing still at last.

From the corner of the desk she took a battered copy of *A New System of Agriculture, or, A Speedy Way to Grow Rich,* and concentrated her mind on the four-course system and Tull's Drill, and the advantages of rapeseed cakes over pigeon-dung as a fertilizer. On the other side of the door the Old Colonel's voice droned on. Words rose above the murmur like fragments of rock above a churning sea: "—have the lot of them on my hands as well as Ambrose's lands now—" "—put you in charge—" (*He must be talking to Jemmy,* she thought.) "You're the only one who knows how to work, the only one who knows how much work it takes—"

As the Old Colonel had grown feebler, his proud spirit had grown more autocratic, and his hold on the acres that had been his since his father's death, when he himself was a boy of nine, more unyielding. The Virginia Piedmont was his world, the only world he cared about; his neighbors, his family, and his slaves, the only people who mattered to him.

The words "debt" and "damned stupid overseers" cut in, over the softer murmur of Jemmy's replies: "Won't see it fooled away like that idiot Randolph's—"

Jemmy must have made some further protestation, because the old man suddenly shouted, "Damn it, boy, you *owe* me!"

Dolley's glance shot quickly to her mother-in-law, but the old woman did not stir.

"And you owe your family! Your brother Will's as poor a farmer as you could find in this county! I need you, more than Tom Jefferson or your damn Congress does! This land needs you! What gives you the right to turn your back on us?"

I should leave, thought Dolley. *This isn't my business.*

"Get out, then! Go to your damned Philadelphia, if that's what matters to you. But you have your head on wrong way round, boy! And your heart as well."

"Father—"

"The world crawls with politicos, Jemmy, like meat with maggots. And every one of 'em will put you in the street next week, if they take a dislike to the cut of your coat, without a word of thanks for all you've given to them. It's only family that matters, Son. Family and the land. And if you believe different, for all those books you read, you're the damnedest fool in Christendom and I pity you from the bottom of my heart."

⚜

"It isn't that Father doesn't understand," said Jemmy quietly, when at last he and Dolley were together in their bedroom, and the door was shut upon the world. He unlaced her—Sukey having long since been sent to bed—and sat on the bed behind her, to brush out her hair. The fire whispered in the grate. Outside the window, the mountain silence lay oceans deep.

"He does understand," Jemmy told her. "He's been sheriff and magistrate in this county, has watched Virginia go through war and revolution. He knows perfectly well that those who would make a despotism of our country must be stopped. He simply doesn't think it's more important than keeping Montpelier running as well as it's always run."

"No, and I understand his point." Dolley

rose, and went to the dresser to pour water from ewer to basin, to wash from her face the dust of the road that afternoon. She had not, she realized, even changed her dress, much less had anything resembling supper. "Even had he not been—been pushed to reflect upon his mortality, by the death of a son. He hath seen the way people behave, in politics. In truth I can't even completely blame Mr. Adams, for wanting to make it illegal to call him names in the press when he's doing what he feels to be his best."

She was silent for a moment, recalling the peppery New Englander who'd come to one of her dinners back in Philadelphia: the towering erudition and the kindly questions asked about Payne and her mother. "*Will* Jefferson go against Mr. Adams again, for the Presidency?" she asked. "For if he does—I was told something today that disquieted me very much."

Jemmy listened gravely to Dolley's account of what she'd heard that morning beside Patsy Randolph's garden gate. When she had finished he said, "Right now Callendar has a bigger target for his spleen. But he hates injustice more than he hates the mighty. It may be he is gathering material to blackmail Tom with—and certainly we must write and warn Tom at once. But it may also be that he gathers it to confront him with what he perceives as hypocrisy."

Dolley opened her mouth to say, *And is it not hypocrisy?*

Is accepting from thee the gift of a woman as a wedding-present? Is keeping *such a woman, so as not to offend thy dear good parents or upset thy political standing among thy neighbors?*

How long would it be, she wondered, before Payne began asking for a slave of his own?

Tom Jefferson is right, when he speaks of slavery as corrupting all it touches. And she asked herself, not for the first time, if she had not done Payne a terrible disservice, in marrying a slaveholder. In bringing her son here to Virginia to grow up in an atmosphere that she sensed was dangerous, even to those who meant well.

Yet from the first evening she'd spent in Jemmy's company she could conceive of living with no one else.

The Great Little Madison, tired and shivering in his scuffed brown velvet wrapper, as he always shivered when he was tired. His long white hair hanging to his shoulders, he paced to the window, where the white rainbow of stars burned above the trees.

"Tom must run for President, Dolley," said Jemmy wearily. "He is the only one with the stature for it. He is the one whose name everyone knows."

Just as everyone knew Washington's name, thirteen years before, Dolley thought. When the country was falling apart and someone had to be found to hold up as a beacon of personal loyalty, to draw men's approval to the Constitution.

Poor Martha. She recalled her friend's reserve when she and Jemmy had driven down to Mount Vernon only a few months ago, on a visit of condolence after the old General's death. Martha understood—and had known how her husband loved and respected Jemmy's judgment. But despite Martha's exquisite manners, the strain had shown through.

"Tom must run against John Adams, and he must win." In the fire's sinking glow Jemmy's pale, wrinkled face was as intent as Dolley had ever seen it. "They will eviscerate the Constitution—Hamilton, and the men around him who think that freedom of speech applies only to speech *they* deem appropriate, and freedom of ideas only to what they consider proper and safe. They have already begun the process.

"Hamilton—and the bankers and merchants who would make up his court—would have this country be like the other nations of Europe, nations ruled by the 'right sort of men,' who are 'right' because they're like themselves. But this is a country that isn't like the nations of Europe, and has never been. It isn't despotism only that I fear, Dolley. I fear the dissolution of the Union that will inevitably follow. Men like my father—and Jefferson, if you put a pistol to his head—would choose Liberty over unity. And no single state is strong enough to withstand conquest, by England from Canada or France from the Caribbean or Spain from Louisiana and Mexico. We were lucky to have won through the first time.

"This country is more fragile than men think, my beloved. And both its strength and its weakness lie in the hearts of its citizens. Jefferson must win. And if he wins, it is you and I who must go with him—not to Philadelphia, but to this new capital they've built—to make certain that the government does not fall victim to a clique of the wealthy again."

His hands closed over hers, but his gaze turned back to the window, and to the mountain night beyond. In the profound stillness, a hunting owl hooted in the woods, where even in darkness the dogwood shone white, like drifts of snow.

Within a squirrel's jump of Heaven.

A retirement I dote on, Jefferson had described his mountaintop world, *living like an antediluvian patriarch among my children and grandchildren, and tilling my soil. I cherish tranquility. . . .*

And little enough he hath had lately of that, Dolley reflected, recalling the things the newspapers had called him. It crossed her mind to hope that Sally took good care of him.

"I had thought I could finish, and come home when Father needed me," Jemmy said. "I see now that isn't true. Maybe none of us can finish, ever."

"Nonsense." Dolley tightened her grip on his hand, which was smaller than her own, and smiled up into his eyes. "If Mr. Jefferson is correct, and the genius of humankind doth fling forth the truth in its consensus, then the coming generation shall engender minds every bit as great as his or thine. They will take the load of the sky from off thy shoulders, when it shall be time to do so."

But her heart lifted at the thought of returning to the center of government again, wherever that center would be.

Jemmy chuckled. "Then let us hold up the sky for them, my darling, til they're grown."

SALLY

֎

Monticello Plantation
Albemarle County, Virginia
Sunday, June 1, 1800

"I think she's resting easier." Sally wrung out the rag with hands aching from the action repeated most of the night, then laid the cloth over tiny Mollie's brow. Mollie's mother Jenny watched her anxiously, a sturdily built young woman with round Ibo features: A decade younger than Sally, she looked a decade older, from hard work and child-bearing.

"Is it scarlet fever?"

Sally nodded. "See how she's scratching at herself? Tomorrow she'll be out in a rash." After almost three years, Sally could speak of the symptoms dispassionately. "I'll tell them up at the Big House." She nodded toward the pallet in the corner where her friend's older children, aged five and three, watched the activity around the family's communal bed with solemn eyes. "Mr. Jefferson's gonna ask you to keep them separate from the other children, but myself, I think it's too late. They're all gonna be down with it. He'll send Aunty Isabel to come look after Mollie when it gets light."

Jenny nodded, and whispered her thanks. With haying starting there was no chance she'd be released to stay with her children, and her husband had been hired off down to Charlottesville to do carpentry. Both women knew the old nurse could be trusted to look after the sick baby as if Mollie were her own.

Scarlet fever. Sally's jaw tightened at the recollection as she stepped from the cabin's dim glow into the chilly dark outside. It had been two and a half years since the death of her daughter from the disease. It still felt like yesterday.

She stopped in the blackness among the trees, fighting tears as she always did when tiny Harriet's face returned to her mind, and that saved her. The next instant she heard a man whisper, "That you?" and from the shadows another reply, " 's me."

And Sally froze. She saw the flickers of tiny flame—burning sticks of pitch-pine that were the candles of the poor—coming from half a dozen directions.

The chestnut trees were a meeting-point because they stood on the back-side of the mountain, out of sight of the Big House but close to the slave-cabins that dotted the wooded slope. Mostly it was lovers who'd meet there, or children out on midnight expeditions to charm away warts or hunt for buried treasure. The trees were a part of the complex geography of trails and landmarks invisible to the whites, even to Tom, who was sharper than most at woodcraft. They were also the meeting-point for the kind of illicit trade that went on at every plantation, where backwoods traders would creep close to exchange rum or bird-shot or fish-hooks for such small items as could be "lifted" from the laundry or the pantry: cured tobacco-leaves, iron from the nail-factory, one of the master's fine linen shirts. Her brother Jimmy had excelled at this: Jefferson property appropriating Jefferson property.

For an instant, seeing the tiny flames assembling by the trees, Sally wondered if Jimmy had come back. If, for all his great talk of seeking his fortune in Europe, after four years of freedom he'd come down to this: being a trader in pilfered goods.

The next instant she knew it couldn't be so. There were too many assembling, for it to be merely a secret transaction.

A preacher?

But if a preacher had been expected, Sally knew she, or her mother, would have been told. And a preacher would have come earlier in the evening, not in this dead hour between midnight and cockcrow.

The voices were too quiet, the rhythm wrong. A single voice would murmur, barely audible under the rattle of june-beetles and cicadas in the trees. Then men would reply, and fall quickly silent. And that single voice would go on.

Sally stood like a startled animal, invisible within the shadows, until the men dispersed. Then she remained where she'd been, concealed in the thickets until she was sure every one of those men was safely in his cabin again, and not likely to see her slipping through the trees. And when she moved on, she was trembling.

She didn't know what was going on, but she had her suspicions. And those suspicions kept her lying awake in her cabin, listening to the soft breathing of her two sleeping sons, until every bird upon the mountain started up their morning song, and the sky grew light.

⚜

When she heard the voices of the carpenters on the way up to the Big House, Sally rose and waked Young Tom. The boy was beginning his apprenticeship to David in the plantation carpentry shop. He had his father's manual deftness, and a young man riding into some small settlement in western New York or Pennsylvania with a carpenter's skills would always be able to make a living. Both Young Tom and his two-year-old brother Beverly had the fair skin and Caucasian features that would let them pass easily for white, no questions asked.

Little Harriet had been the same. Tom had agreed with Sally that great care would be taken, to teach the little girl proper manners and speech. When she was old enough,

Harriet would leave Monticello. She would enter the home of one of the many families of French émigrés whom Tom knew in Philadelphia, to be introduced to the town as a white young lady. These days there were hundreds such, many of them Tom's friends from his days in Paris who would be delighted to adopt and educate their distinguished friend's "orphaned ward."

Then one icy December morning in 1797, little Harriet had waked up crying with a sore throat and a crimson flush to her skin that faded under the pressure of a thumb, and immediately flooded back. Tom couldn't linger, if he was to reach the capital in time to open Congress—he was Vice President to Mr. Adams by that time, and fighting to keep the United States from being completely reabsorbed by the political power of England. Not long after his departure, Harriet died.

Knowing that Bev played with Jenny's children, Sally scooped her younger son out of his cot while Young Tom was washing, carried him to the light of the door. As she'd feared, he looked flushed and feverish, and complained that his throat hurt. She put the toddler back to bed and poked up the fire, filled the kettle with water for a willow-bark tisane, struggling to keep the panic out of her heart. Everyone had been sick in the quarters, that winter Harriet had taken the fever. The little girl's health had never been good, even before she took sick.

Sally stopped at her mother's cabin, and told her of Bev's sickness, on her way up to the Big House to tidy Tom's quarters while the family was at breakfast. Her mind was full of the boy as she climbed the hill. Tom was leaving tomorrow for Richmond for James Callendar's trial, and as usual hadn't even begun to pack. Callendar's arrest under the Sedition Act, charged with speaking against the President, made her profoundly uneasy, as if she'd felt the ground shift beneath her feet.

Among the papers on Tom's desk, she had seen a few days ago the rough-printed proof-sheets of the book for which Callendar had been arrested, *The Prospect Before Us: That strange compound of ignorance and ferocity, of deceit and weakness,* the pamphlet had called that ferocious red-faced little New Englander whose gruff kindness Sally still recalled with gratitude. *A hideous hermaphroditical character which has neither the force and firmness of a man, nor the gentleness and sensibility of a woman . . . The reign of Mr. Adams has hitherto been one continued tempest of malignant passions . . . The historian . . . will ask why the United States degrades themselves to the choice of a wretch whose soul came blasted from the hand of nature. . . .*

More than enough, she guessed, to be used as evidence of conspiracy, should the proof-sheets be found in Jefferson's possession. Particularly with men already suspicious of Tom's involvement in the attempts of the States to strike down the Sedition Act. Somewhere in his room, she knew, was the newly printed book itself.

Since Patsy and her family were visiting that week, Sally slipped quietly up the hill and through the tangle of scaffolding that enclosed the front of the house, to enter as usual through the cabinet's long window. As she did so, she noticed the workmen, who should have been sliding floor-planks through the unfinished windows of what would be Mr. Jefferson's new first-floor library, grouped quietly talking with a black man whom Sally vaguely recognized—one of Mr. Crinn's yardmen from Charlottesville?

Before she came near enough to hear, or

even to see clearly who the stranger might be, the men broke apart.

But watching the stranger stroll off down the hill to the stables, Sally saw that as soon as he thought he was out of sight of the house, he turned aside, and broke into a trot toward the woods.

Sally felt the workmen's eyes on her, as she ducked under the scaffolding and into the house.

Because they'd been idling in talk with the stranger?

She didn't think so.

This was something different.

Her hair prickled a little on her scalp.

The cabinet, and the bedroom beyond, were jammed with boxes, crates, trunks, and piles of books removed from the library three years ago when the roof had been torn off to alter the second floor. Tom had plans to raise a dome, like a Roman temple: Betting in the quarters on the completion-date ran all the way from next summer to the first notes of the Final Trumpet. The new library would be an extension of the cabinet, enlarging the island of privacy that was Tom's *sanctum sanctorum.* Here, no one was permitted without an express invitation—except Sally herself.

Sally noted, as she entered, that the floor was filmed with construction dust and sawdust yet again; she'd been sweeping four times a day for months. Tom's trunk and portmanteau lay beside the bed, and on top of the inevitable stack of books to be packed lay Callendar's proof-sheets. As she removed them to the desk, the words caught her eye in the slatted light of the window jalousies: *Repulsive pedant. Gross hypocrite. One of the most egregious fools upon the continent.*

Was that truly what Mr. Jefferson wanted to have said, about the man who had once been his friend?

The bedroom door opened. "It's outrageous," said Tom, sliding his shoulders out of his coat and crossing the bedroom to the cabinet where Sally knelt before a stack of books. "Peter's just ridden in with word from Richmond. They're going to try Callendar before Sam Chase, of all people. Why don't they just send him to stand before Parliament in England while they're about it? Sam Chase would have made Washington King, if he could have."

Sally drew the printed book of *The Prospect Before Us* from the stack, rose to her feet, and held it out. "It'll be easier to explain than proof-sheets, if one of the inn servants takes it into his head to see what you've got in your luggage."

Tom's eyes widened, then narrowed and turned cold: "You have a good point, I regret to say. I'll be staying with Mr. Monroe, but that doesn't make it less likely that we'll be spied upon, if word gets about that I'm in town." He laid the book down on the bed. The lines of strain that had faded during the three quiet years of his retirement were back, deeply and permanently, around his eyes and mouth.

"Will you speak on his behalf?" She kept her voice neutral: The mere thought of Callendar made her skin crawl.

Tom shook his head. "It's unlikely I shall even show myself in the courtroom. I just don't want to be three days' journey away, should anything *. . . untoward . . .* develop at the trial." He went to his desk, picked up the little bran-stuffed pillow he would rest his elbow on when he read, and the small iron dumbbell that he still had to use, to exercise the stiffened tendons of his right wrist. Even after thirteen years, there were nights when he could not sleep from the pain.

"Are you expecting something *unto-ward*?" Sally asked quietly.

"I don't know." He tucked dumbbell, pillow, and seditious book into a corner of the trunk. "Despite Mr. Adams's orders that it disband, there is still a standing army of ten thousand men in New England. And Hamilton's still in command of it. He's up there now."

"I thought that was all finished last year."

"It is." His voice had a grim edge. "He's now offered to take *his* army and use it to conquer Mexico, so that we should have New Orleans as an American city—and so that Alex Hamilton should have a hero's glory and a path back to power, now that Washington is gone."

He made the motions of sorting through the books piled on the bed, but Sally could see his eyes were absent, his mind barely registering the titles, his thoughts bitter and far away.

On Mr. Adams? The friend with whom he'd worked and laughed and conversed?

By whose Sedition Act Tom could very well be convicted as a traitor?

On the election in November, and his hopes to wrest control of the central government away from those who would make its rule negate the local right of each State to determine its own needs?

On the galling failure of France's Revolution? He had been ill during the last months of the Terror in France, had barely glanced at the newspapers that spoke of bloody mob-rule and a corrupt Directorate. For three years after that, while he quietly watched the trees and the clouds on his mountaintop, the French had gulped one another down like Roman triumvirs until the last man standing had conspired to hand the country over to Bonaparte.

She remembered his face in the candlelight of the Hôtel Langeac: *It is a glorious time to be alive.*

Then he sighed, and shook himself out of his reverie. "Well, if they want to crush Callendar, they'll find themselves publicly turning their backs upon the Constitution before the whole of the country. Richmond is as full as it can hold, of men from all over Virginia. Prominent men, men of property and power.

If we cannot win, we can at least hold Hamilton and his party up for all to see, and force them to admit that their aim is to ignore the fundamental right of every man to say what he wishes, to print what his conscience dictates. With the election coming, it could not be better timed. I only regret that it's Callendar who will suffer."

"He's dangerous," cautioned Sally softly, and Tom looked surprised and a little hurt.

"Am I a despot, too, now, to go about distrusting my own supporters? Were I President, I would have to defend James Callendar's Constitutional right to print about me whatever he chose. *Whatever* it might be," he added more gently, smiling down into her eyes. "Mrs. Madison gave me your warning—it *was* you, was it not?—and I thank you for your concern for me. But Mr. Callendar, though the man is personally reprehensible, is a friend of Liberty. He will not turn against us."

Sally heard in that phrase, *friend of Liberty,* the kind of self-evident magic that seemed to have such power over people's minds, and knew better than to press the issue. In many ways, Tom had no sense at all.

"Patsy and Mr. Randolph will be here in

my absence," he went on. "Will you be all right?" Meaning, *Is there anything in that area that I need to know about?* Though there seldom was, and Sally was well aware that Tom didn't really want to know.

"Thank you, yes," she replied, as she always did.

Her sister Critta had recently said to her, with a touch of exasperation in her voice, *Why don't you just tell her you're layin' with Peter Carr instead of her daddy? That's all she really wants to hear. Make your eyes all soft an' ask, kind of breathless, "Miss Patsy, do you know when . . . when* Mr. Carr *gonna be back here next?"* Critta had put on her most simpleminded expression and crooned the name of Tom's nephew—the father of her own son and the source of innumerable trinkets and presents—with exaggerated adoration. *Is that so difficult?*

Sally felt her back-teeth clench at the memory. *I may be a concubine,* she thought, *but I'm not a whore.*

Instead she told Tom, "Please tell Mrs. Randolph that some of the children have come down with scarlet fever—"

Tom startled, eyes widening with concern.

"I think Bev may be sickening for it, but it

doesn't look to be bad just yet. I'm going to let Aunty Isabel know. I'll write and let you know, how Bev goes on."

❦

She left him to his packing, and returned to her son, whose face was already beginning to show the flush of fever. Through the remainder of the day she had little thought to spare, either for Callendar, or for the election that had become the focus for Tom's considerable energy for the past eighteen months, or for the curious, ambient tension that she could feel slowly coiling its way like a poisoned mist among the cabins that dotted Monticello's hillside.

After dinner Tom slipped away from the house and came down to the quarters, to sit for a time beside Bev's bed, holding his son's hand and anxiously studying his face. When the children were well, Sally reflected, as she tied up bundles of herbs to dry, Tom treated them with the same friendly affection with which he treated all the children in the quarters. Plantation gossip being what it was, he could do nothing else. But Harriet's death had shaken him, more than he would ever express. In his face tonight she saw his anxiety, and when he spoke to her—the soft-voiced commonplaces of treatment, of herbs and symptoms—she thought she heard sadness and guilt there as well.

They had been united as partners for a dozen years—as long as his marriage to Miss Patty. If the desperation of her first love for him had not survived the years, it had settled into an acceptance of him, and a deep-rooted affection.

He would never be other than he was. He would never understand the rage she'd felt, four years ago, when M'sieu Petit quietly informed her that Tom had mortgaged all his slaves to obtain money to rebuild the Big House along modern architectural principles: "I'll be able to purchase the mortgages back within a few years, with profits from the new nail-factory," Tom had assured her when she'd confronted him. "In any case I would not include you, or any of your family. It is only a businessman's way of raising money. It's done all the time."

Did Patsy know her father had just promised her patrimony to someone else if he couldn't pay his debts? If he broke his neck taking old Silveret over a fence some day on the mountain, Patsy and Maria would be left with nothing.

But Sally knew, that even without that mortgage, if he broke his neck some afternoon on the mountain, it would make little difference whether her family went to Tom Randolph or to some bank in Richmond. They'd all end up sold and scattered.

By the same token, Tom would never believe that Patsy knew that he was the father of Sally's children. He would always need to know that he stood first in Patsy's heart—as she stood first in his. And though he was aware of the many afternoons Tom Randolph spent drinking himself quarrelsome in the Eagle Tavern in Charlottesville, was aware of the young man's black moods and mercurial temper, he persisted in thinking well of his son-in-law, or at least saying that he did.

He was who he was. He never said he loved her and probably, she reflected wryly, never even thought of their relationship in those terms. But she knew he needed her. As much as the physical desire that was still as warm between them as ever, was his need to know, when he was away, that she would be there when he returned to his home.

He needed to know that he was loved.

He kept even yet the slim bundle of his letters to her, that he'd written on his travels to Rotterdam and The Hague. Sometimes she'd find them slipped behind a clock or under a book, hidden when Patsy interrupted him. He treasured those memories still.

He rose now from where he sat at the side of the cot, went to clasp Sally's hands briefly—briefly, because Young Tom was there, sitting beside the hearth-fire with a copy of the *Richmond Enquirer* angled to the glow. Even before their own son they kept a distance, lest talk go around that couldn't be denied. Very softly he asked, "Shall I send Ursula or Isabel down to help you tonight? He doesn't seem badly off—"

"It's early days yet."

"I shall leave it to your judgment, then, Sally. As we pass through Charlottesville tomorrow I'll ask Dr. Burns to come see Bev and Mollie. Patsy will be sending me messages—please, you write me, too."

As they stepped outside into the darkness he kissed her: "Get some sleep if you can.

I'm afraid you'll need it." Then he strode away up the hill toward the Big House, too preoccupied by his thoughts—of Bev? Of Alexander Hamilton's plots and machinations? Of James Callendar? Of the election?—to whistle or sing.

If he becomes President, thought Sally, *he will be in Philadelphia more—or in that new Federal City on the Potomac.* As Mr. Adams's Vice President, he'd spent as little time in the capital as he could, and Patsy and Randolph had lived a good part of the time on their own plantation at Varina. *If he becomes President, will they be back here as they used to, ten months of the year?*

The thought, though annoying, didn't bother her as it once had.

She had done as she'd meant to do: had guaranteed freedom for her children, which was more than her mother had been able to accomplish.

Surely, she thought as she turned back into the dim warm glow of her cabin, that should be enough.

⚜

Tom left as soon as it was light enough to see the road down the mountain. He'd knelt in his riding-clothes to kiss bright-haired Annie and burly Jeff, and Sam and Peter Carr hugged their mother breathless and pretended they hadn't had two of the younger spinning-maids up to their room last night. Patsy held baby Cornelia in her arms, and stood alone half-hidden in the dark of the scaffolding that covered the front of the house; three-year-old Ellen was sickening for a cold, and had remained indoors. Tom Randolph seemed silent and awkward as his father-in-law shook his hand.

Then Tom swung into Silveret's saddle— he never took the carriage when he could ride—and rode out at a frisky hand-gallop, raising his hat to his family. As he passed Sally, in the misty twilight where the road curved down the mountain, he touched the brim again, in salute.

Then he was gone.

Along Mulberry Row, and in the cabins that dotted the woods on the back-side of the mountain, all the cocks had commenced their second crowing. In less than an hour the carpenters would be starting their hammering, the white craftsmen Tom had hired commencing the more exacting labor of plastering the new rooms. The whole mountain smelled of the smoke of breakfast-fires. As Sally descended to her cabin she saw that the door of the joiner's shed stood open.

Her first thought was *Mr. Dinsmore's up early. . . .* Which was totally uncharacteristic of the young Irishman who'd come to do the fine carpentry within the house.

Her second, *Why is there no lantern-light inside?* was still half-formed in her head when a shadow appeared in the doorway, a huge hand reached out and caught her wrist. Sally's hand was coming back to claw, her breath dragging into her lungs to scream, when she saw in the chilly dawn light that it was Lam Hawkin.

He swept her into the joiner's shed with a violence that pulled her off her feet, shut the door, not with a kick, but with soundless swift care.

"I can't stay." His fingers were already pressed to her lips. "And I can't be seen here—"

"You're a free man, Lam." Sally pushed his hand away. "Who you runnin' from?"

"I don't know. And what I tell you, you must swear to keep to yourself, for your own sake and your boys'. Or they'll be after you, too, Sally, to keep you silent."

In his eyes she saw everything: the lights bobbing through the darkness to the trees, the way the carpenters had looked at her yesterday. The strange black man disappearing fast in the direction of the woods.

Who? died on her lips and even her breath felt stilled for a moment, as if she'd been slammed against a wall.

Then she whispered, "Is it a revolt?"

Lam nodded.

And she remembered: It was what the French King had asked, when someone told him about the rioters seizing the Bastille. *Is it a revolt?* The messenger had replied, *No, sire, a revolution.*

A terrible complex shiver went through her, born of a thousand memories. She felt cold, as if, the grannies said, a goose had walked across her grave. *A revolution.*

She whispered, "Sam and Peter Carr were down in Richmond two days ago, they hadn't heard—"

"It ain't started yet. I don't know when it will start. Soon, I think, before the tobacco harvest. It's big, Sally, and it's organized like an army, with scouts and spies and re-

cruiters. And it's spreadin'. They got lieu-
tenants workin' in secret, in Henrico County,
an' Hanover, an' Caroline, an' Louisa Counties. They got secret workshops makin' bullets, hammerin' plow-iron into pikes. They
gonna take Richmond, they say, an' make a
kingdom of black men, where none are
slaves to none. Just like Toussaint did in
Saint-Domingue, nine years ago."

"An' kill the whites?" Sally remembered
the torrent of panic that had swept Virginia,
just after her own return from France, at the
news that in the wake of the French Revolution, the slaves in the French sugar-island of
Saint-Domingue—who outnumbered the
whites on the island ten to one—had risen
in revolt. They had slaughtered not only the
whites, but the free colored caste of artisans, slaveholders, shopkeepers there. Two
French fleets had been defeated there so
far. The blacks were still free.

Lam's eyes shifted. "Some of 'em. I hear
there's some they won't, those they feel are
on their side and will help."

She felt the half-truth through her skin but
said nothing. No man who owned slaves, no
matter what he'd written about equality and

freedom, would be considered *on their side.* Nor would his family.

"Sally, I took a chance comin' here to warn you. Because I trust you. And I don't want to see you hurt, or your boys hurt. I don't know when it'll happen, but when it does, I'll come here, me an' my girls." Lam had married the year after Sally had returned to Tom, the cook-girl of a Charlottesville lawyer. He'd bought their two daughters as they were born, and had saved up about half the two hundred dollars it would take to free his wife, when she'd died last year. "We'll go back into the mountains, until it all blows past, for better or for worse. But you gotta be ready to go. We may not have more'n a few minutes to spare. Food, money—all the money you can gather. We gonna need it. An' you cannot tell, Sally. Not your family, not anyone. Swear to me that."

He had risked his life, to come up here and tell her. If rebellion was being planned, the community of the unfree would—and could—strike swiftly at a potential talebearer. And no white sheriff would even investigate a black man's unexplained death.

She whispered, "I swear." Then: "But if you honestly think a rebellion's going to succeed, you're mad. You really think a—a *kingdom of black men* can stand here in Virginia? That any white will help 'em? The whites got militia, Lam. They got an army up north of ten thousand—"

"That's exactly what people said when your Mr. Jefferson an' his friends all spit in the face of the British," Lam said harshly. "You don't hear anyone goin' around these days sayin' how stupid *that* was." He was silent for a moment. Then he asked, "Whose side you on, Sally?"

She pulled her arm sharply away from his grip. "I am on my children's side."

"And your children look white enough to pass for white boys. Or to be killed in mistake for 'em, if killin' starts."

Sally knew he spoke the truth. But for years she'd heard Tom talk of the Saint-Domingue rebellion, as he'd talk to her about almost anything that was on his mind at bedtime, in the world-within-a-world that was his room. He talked the way he made music, to clarify his mind, and from things he had said, it was perfectly clear to Sally that the only reason the blacks in Saint-Domingue were still free was because Saint-Domingue was an island, and the French were too busy fighting everyone in Europe to spare an invasion force of sufficient strength.

But in Saint-Domingue, the rebelling slaves had murdered white—and free colored—children along with adults.

"I'm not sayin' these people is smart or dumb, Sally. And I'm not sayin' what their chances are. I'm only sayin' they're comin'. It could be soon. It could be *damn* soon."

Richmond is as full as it can hold, she heard Tom say, *of men from all over Virginia. Prominent men, men of property and power. . . .*

If they was smart, thought Sally dizzily, *NOW would be the time to strike. An attack now would buy 'em time.*

And she felt in her heart the slow hot blaze of anger, at the thought of the men and women she'd known in Eppington and Williamsburg, who had been sold away from their families or seen their wives, their husbands, their children sold away.

Who had seen their daughters or their wives or their sisters raped or seduced— who lived daily with the knowledge that any white man *could* molest them with nothing more to fear than his neighbors saying, *Tsk.*

Who lived hourly with the awareness of men sizing them up, as Tom Randolph and Peter Carr and Jack Eppes sized her up each time she walked past.

Serve them right.

For the unavoidable and unquestioned fact that one day the children Young Tom and Bev played with were *all* going to be sold away from their families and friends, sent to places where they knew no one; and when they were grown, they'd see their children taken away and sold in turn.

For the sheer *unthinkability* that a white man would or could feel genuine love for her—unthinkable even by the white man himself.

Serve them right, if it was a thousand times worse.

Outside the window, she heard Young Tom whistling as he came back from the kitchen. Like his father, he was always singing, and Tom had even begun, in his casual way, to teach him to play the fiddle. She said softly, "You better go. The men'll be up at the Big House soon and they'll see you if you stay. I swear I'll be ready, and I swear I'll tell no one. Thank you, Lam," she added, as he clapped on his hat, and opened the shed door a crack to make sure the coast was clear. "More than I can say, thank you. You're a good man."

He brought the door shut again, regarded her in the gloom. "And you're a good woman, Sally. I just wish you were as happy as you deserve to be."

She returned a crooked smile. "We're all as happy as we deserve to be, Lam. God bless you. I'll see you soon."

"That you will, girl." His eyes grew hard. "That you will."

⚜

Bev's fever-flush had spread over his face and body. His throat, when she carried him to the cabin's window to look, was fiercely inflamed. Young Tom was sitting on the edge of the bed with a dish of leftovers from the Big House breakfast, his sharp face worried: "He didn't eat anything last night, Mama, and now he won't have anything either."

"There grits there, sugarbaby? Mix 'em up with a lot of milk, and pour some honey in. I bet he'll take a little of that."

Between them, Young Tom and Sally got the toddler to eat a little, and to drink the bitter willow-bark tea against the fever. When Young Tom had gone back up to the Big House, Sally carried her younger boy over to her mother's cabin, where Betsie told her that Jenny's Mollie was worse that morning, and Minerva's youngest two were showing symptoms as well. Despite all this, and between Sally's own tasks at the Big House of keeping Tom's room in order and feeding his three mockingbirds in their cages, she made the time during that day to discreetly scout hiding-places and exit-routes in the woods that could be used *that night,* if necessary: hiding-places that would accommodate both herself and a three-year-old boy. Young Tom, she knew, was clever enough to escape on his own and rejoin them later.

She came back from one of these scouting expeditions to find both Jeff and Annie Randolph at Betty's cabin, with another jug of milk pilfered from the kitchen, and some extra blankets. "We heard some of the pickaninnies were sick, ma'am," explained Annie, glancing worriedly from Betty Hemings's face to Sally's, and back. Since Patsy couldn't very well order her children to shun Sally without an explanation, the golden-haired nine-year-old and her brother had never been told to keep away from her: Like the white children of most plantations, they played with the slave-children and ran in and out of the cabins as cheerfully as if they lived there. "Will they be all right?"

"We're praying so, sugarbaby," replied Sally, and smiled down at the girl: Tom's granddaughter, even if she was Patsy's child. Only a year older than Maria had been, when Sally and she had set sail for France. Unlike Jeff, she hadn't yet grown bossy around the slave-children; she would hold the babies with the same grave care that a few years ago she'd devoted to her dolls, practicing to be a mama herself.

Even Jeff seemed cowed in the presence of sickness. To Betty he murmured, "They gonna die?" and he sounded both scared and grieved. He added, stumbling a little on the words, "My baby sister got sick and died. The first Ellen, not Ellen now." Jeff had been not quite three years old when that fragile little girl had succumbed.

As she watched Tom's two oldest grandchildren dart back up the slope toward the brick mansion in its tangled cocoon of scaffolding, Sally seemed to hear in her mind the distant clamor of bells ringing the tocsin, of rough voices singing *Ça Ira.*

She shivered, although the afternoon was warm.

⚜

That night Sally dreamed of fire. Dreamed that Paris was burning, that the flames leaped over the customs-barrier and kindled the faubourgs beyond it, and the woods and fields beyond that, fields of tobacco and sugar. The blaze was spreading, and would soon consume the world. Sick with panic, she crouched in the shadow of a wall on the rue St.-Antoine watching the baying mob surge closer and closer, and in the lead walked a woman she knew was her grandmother, the proud black African woman who'd been raped by a sea-captain while on her way to the New World in chains. She carried a torch in one hand, and a pike in the other, and impaled on the pike was the head of Thomas Jefferson.

Sally woke with a gasp, lay in the darkness staring in the direction where she knew the window lay, half expecting to see the shutters limned by flame in the dark.

But the hot, thick night was still. The only

sound she heard was the drumming of the cicadas, the skreek of the crickets, and Young Tom's deep, even breath.

☙

Nearly every slave conspiracy Sally had heard of had ended up betrayed by someone on the inside, some slave who'd gone running to his master with all the details. As a child Sally had sniffed with contempt at such craven treachery; and because she had loved Tom and Patsy and Polly and Miss Patty, it had never crossed her mind that one day vengeance might come knocking on *their* door.

Now she understood how people could be good and well-meaning—even shocked by the evils of the society of which they were a part—and still deserve retribution for the part they had played.

Now she understood how a man or woman could betray the freedom of all, for the sake of an oppressor who had been gentle and kind.

It is a glorious time to be alive, Tom had said in France, his eyes shining in the candlelight, but he'd still made preparations to get his daughters out of the bloody path of the juggernaut.

In the days that followed, Sally was careful to go about her business, and avoid any show that she was listening more carefully to half-heard conversations. She'd always kept money cached in the rafters of the cabin where Jimmy wasn't likely to find it, money Tom gave her for little luxuries for her children, like Young Tom's secondhand fiddle. Now she began to conceal food there as well.

In this she was aided by the fact that nothing at Monticello was quite normal during that time.

Bev's sickness was soon seen to be mild: he cried and scratched, but he always seemed to know who and where he was. But in the Big House, Patsy's daughter Ellen was very sick indeed.

Sally found herself plotting out routes of flight—plotting out hiding places—suitable not for one woman with a three-year-old, but two women with not only toddlers but a baby. For she understood, almost without conscious decision, that if she got Tom's grandchildren to safety, she would have to spirit Patsy away as well.

It wasn't just that Tom would expect nothing less of her.

When faced with the thought of rebelling

slaves overrunning Monticello—coming up from Charlottesville or across the river from Edgehill, crazy as the men and women of Paris had been crazy—she simply could not leave Patsy to her own devices.

⚓

Any slaves who worked for Tom Randolph, Sally guessed, *would* be crazy with rage if a revolution sparked to life, and out for blood. Though Randolph was careful not to get a reputation in the neighborhood as a harsh master or a cruel one, he had qualities that were almost worse. He was careless with money and in debt—Tom had on several occasions had to lend his son-in-law money—and he was unpredictable.

Sally didn't know a slave on Monticello who didn't dread the day when Tom Randolph would become their owner.

As the hot June days of haying and corn-harvest advanced, Randolph came seldom to Monticello. His son Jeff, the only child in the Big House not sick, would sometimes sit on the dismantled pillars of the front porch for hours, waiting for him, and twice had to be stopped from going over to Edgehill, to see if he was there. Sally found herself worrying at the thought of that eight-year-old, son and grandson of slave-owners, walking by himself through the woods along the river's edge.

It would serve them right, she told herself again.

And maybe it would.

She cached a length of rope at the back of the cupboard in the little girls' nursery, knowing that if the house were to be set on fire, the narrow stairway—which Tom claimed was so modern and heat-saving and which every servant who had to carry things up and down it despised—would turn into a lethal chimney.

If it came to flight—if it came to a rebellion—the house, with walls and windows already breached by construction, would be no refuge. They might have only minutes to escape. And as she passed the door of the nursery in the darkness of the night, Sally would look through and see Patsy sitting quietly beside Cornelia's cradle or little Ellen's bed. And at the sight of her, she'd feel a sick despair.

⚜

Standing in the dark of the upstairs hall, Sally considered her old friend—her old enemy—in the soft glow of the single apple-seed of light shed by the *veilleuse* on the nursery dressing-table. Clothed in her wrapper of rust-colored brocade, her red hair braided down her back, Patsy had never looked plainer, her long face lined with weariness and her mouth bracketed by gouges of temper and disappointment too long held in rigid check.

It was the face she never showed her father—never showed anyone. Like Tom, who had molded his daughter into the image of what he thought a woman should be, Patsy was determined to be unfailingly cheerful and polite to all.

She and Randolph had quarreled that morning, over yet another dunning letter from one of his creditors; his shouting could be heard down on Mulberry Row. He had slammed out of the house, ridden off like a madman leaving the overseers in charge of the harvest. He had not returned for dinner.

Now—and it was nearly midnight—Patsy looked as if she had a headache as savage as any that so frequently felled her father. As Sally watched, Patsy reached down to stroke the matted hair from Ellen's forehead—as Sally herself had stroked Bev's earlier that evening—and drew back her hand, lest she wake the child. Then her whole body shivered, shaking, as if she were being racked with silent, tearless sobs.

Quietly, Sally withdrew. She descended the narrow twist of stair with the practiced care of one who has studied for years to come and go undetected. She passed like a shadow from the house and down the hill, to her own cabin where Bev dozed fitfully alone, Young Tom having gone to his grand-mother's to sleep. Sally bent over her child, then returned to the hearth and gathered up the ingredients for the "headache tea" she so often made for Tom: catnip, betony, va-lerian, and rue, which he said the Indians had showed his father.

Well it isn't forbidden for me to come into her Sacred Presence, reflected Sally.

The Big House was dark, save for the dim light visible in the nursery window. But as Sally stepped through Tom's cabinet win-dow, she heard Patsy's voice downstairs in the high-ceilinged, half-finished room that would one day (Tom said) be the entry hall, low and reasonable as it always was. . . .

"That isn't what I said—"

"It's what you thought! It's what you goddam think every time you see me here! You'd be happy if I took my sorry carcass out of your life so you could turn my children over to Papa for good, like you did before!"

"You know you were ill—"

"I know more than you about it, woman! You *wish* I was ill! You *wish* I was goddam *dead* so you could come back here to Papa!"

From the doorway of Tom's bedroom Sally could see their shadows in the light of a branch of candles, huge grotesque shapes looming over the half-plastered walls, the unfinished gallery. "That isn't true—"

Randolph struck her, a backhand blow that knocked her to her knees. Though Patsy was a towering woman, her husband was built like an oak tree. "Don't you goddam tell me what's true, you sneaking bitch! All you wanted was to give your precious Papa grandchildren and you didn't care whose spunk you made 'em with!" He stepped close to her and she cowered—

Patsy, thought Sally, shocked and sick. *Patsy cowering.*

Cowering like a woman who's been beaten before.

He caught her by the hair so that she cried out, twisted her head to force her to look into his face. For a moment they remained frozen thus, a huge shadow and a crumpled pale shape. Then with a strangled groan he shoved her back against the wall, and disappeared into the passageway. Sally heard him collide with a wall, and then the crash of his body on the floor.

In the nursery, Cornelia and Ellen began to wail.

Patsy lay where she'd fallen, trembling with soundless sobs as she had before, but Sally knew in her bones that the only thing needed to complete the wretched agony of her humiliation, would be the knowledge that Sally had seen it.

The only dignity she had left was secrecy.

Like a swift shadow, Sally ascended the stair, set the tea-pot down on the nursery table, went to the cradle, and gathered Cornelia in her arms. "It's all right, sugarbaby," she murmured. "Nothing to be afraid of." Holding the baby with one arm, she brushed Ellen's cheek with the backs of her fingers.

"Mama," Ellen whispered.

Grizzle the dog crept to Sally's feet, glad that a human had come to take charge.

"Your mama be up soon, or your aunt Carr." Not that Aunt Carr, who didn't believe in getting involved in "unpleasantness," would emerge from her room before morning.

On the other side of the little room Annie turned her face on her pillow, whispered, "What happened, Sally?"

"Your papa got mad at one of the grooms, that didn't put his horse away right," Sally replied. "That's all, sweetheart." She gently laid Cornelia back down, wrung out another rag and wiped the baby's face with it. It was impossible to distinguish much about the rash in the nursery's near-dark, but she thought Cornelia's fever seemed less, no more than what Bev's had been yesterday. The little girl had grown quiet with the touch of careful hands.

Tom's granddaughters. Her own kin. *And if they weren't,* thought Sally despairingly, *could I really stand aside and watch even the children of total strangers killed, for what their parents did?*

Ellen whimpered, "Mama," again, and Sally said, "Your mama's on her way, baby."

She thought she heard the creak of a footfall in the hall, and Grizzle raised her head and thumped her tail eagerly. But looking toward the door, Sally saw only darkness. It was ten minutes before Grizzle thumped her tail again, and this time Sally saw the moving firefly of a candle there, and a moment later, materializing in its glow, Patsy's haggard face. She'd re-braided her hair and her eyes looked swollen, as if she'd been crying.

Sally got at once to her feet, curtseyed, said, "Ma'am," and made to go. Patsy stepped in front of her, her face cold and hard as carved bone. Weary, as if Sally were one more rock in the load of rocks that she was forced to carry to her grave.

Yet she made her voice low and pleasant as she said, "Thank you, Sally. I appreciate your taking over."

"Ma'am." Sally curtseyed again, as if she'd never played with this person when they both were children; as if Patsy had never taught her to read, or let her into her father's library in quest of books. Then, because of that unspoken past: "I made you some tea, ma'am; a tisane I should say, that's supposed to be good for headaches."

Patsy's breath drew in, blew out in a sigh like the sigh of the dying. She whispered again, "Thank you," in a voice that made it very clear that the tea was going to be poured out the window the minute Sally was out of the room.

"Ma'am," said Sally quietly, "if you'd like, I'll stay with them tonight, so you can get some sleep. I think Miss Cornelia's fever's less."

Patsy turned immediately to feel her daughter's forehead; Sally saw her wide, flat shoulders relax. "I think you're right. Thank God." She closed her eyes for an instant, though her hand pressed briefly to her mouth as if she would hide from Sally even its momentary tremor. "Thank you very much for your concern, Sally, but I shall be all right here." And as she turned back her eyes said, *Anything, rather than accept a favor from the hand of my father's whore.*

Sally wanted to shake her. Wanted to shout at her, *Can't you see that you and I can't go on living this way?*

He needs us both.

Why don't you admit the truth? We're both going to be in his life for a long time.

But Sally knew, as surely as she knew her

own name, that if she said those words, even now alone in the deep of the night, Patsy would simply gaze at her with those chilly eyes and change the subject, exquisitely polite and stone-deaf.

Like her father, when there was something he didn't want to hear.

Sally curtseyed again, and turned away with a sense of despair. She was the betrayer, the seductress. The succubus who had lured the father Patsy adored away from his true nature, into the disgrace of being a man who bedded his slaves.

And beyond that, Patsy could not see and would not look.

Sally thought, *Dammit.* Took a deep breath, and turned back in the doorway. "Miss Patsy?"

Patsy straightened up from Ellen's bed, face stiff with distaste. "What is it now?"

"Miss Patsy." Sally injected a note of what she hoped sounded like shyness into her voice. "You wouldn't know whether—whether Mr. Peter is coming back with Mr. Jefferson, would you?"

As disgusted as she was at herself for this piece of play-acting, Sally was astonished to see that it worked exactly as Critta had

said it would. For one moment Patsy regarded her with a startlement—an expression of enlightenment—that was almost
comical. "Mr. Peter *Carr*?"

"Yes, ma'am." Sally dropped her eyes,
and for good measure twisted her apron a
little in her hands. And as she lifted her gaze
again to the other woman's face, she saw
there a look of such dawning relief that it
struck her to the heart with a sense of shock
and pain.

Did she truly need the illusion *that much*?

Had her spite, her cold talebearing, come
from pain that desperate?

Critta had been right. The only thing in the
world Patsy had wanted to hear was that
her father was not the father of Sally's children.

"I—I had no idea—"

Whether she simply didn't want to think
about the issue of Young Tom, or whether she
clutched at the belief that Tom's Casanova
nephew had succeeded his uncle in Sally's
life, Sally didn't know and never afterwards
found out. But the frozen enmity in Patsy's
voice dissolved like mist in the sunlight.

She was once more, in her own eyes, the
only woman in her father's life, and Sally

was shaken by a sense almost of shame as she saw how the reprieve from unhappiness altered the white woman's face. It was like watching a woman drinking water, who has stumbled for days in the desert.

"Please don't speak of it, ma'am. Not to Mr. Peter—please not to your father. Your father's been so good to me."

"Of course," promised Patsy, with an eager sincerity that reminded Sally achingly of their vanished days of mutual innocence. For all her coldness and spite, Sally knew that when she gave her word about something, Patsy Randolph would keep it. "I thought—Of course. Never a word." She drew a deep breath, as if bands of iron had snapped from off her chest for the first time in twelve years, and the freedom to breathe left her dizzy.

They stood in silence for a few moments in the darkened nursery, the breathing of Patsy's children soft around them, the house and the mountain sunk in night as if at the bottom of the sea.

⚜

Tom returned a few days after that, fuming at the result of Callendar's trial. Judge Chase had interrupted, disallowed, and overruled the journalist's defense attorneys until all three of them had walked out of the court-room in disgust. Callendar had not even been given a chance to speak. He had been convicted, heavily fined, and sentenced to prison for the duration of the Sedition Act's existence, whether that should be nine months—until Adams was out of office—or nearly five years.

"Every newspaper in the country shall carry it." Tom's voice was both enraged and exultant. "Madison's already writing for the papers in New York, in Philadelphia, in Charleston. No man who loves his country can ignore what's being done now. When the vote comes, they must surely be driven from office—or the country itself will be destroyed!"

But destruction lay closer than the election, ran deeper than any Sedition Act. It was averted only through the inexplicable machinations of Fate.

On the night of the thirtieth of August, a thunderstorm of unprecedented violence inundated Richmond, swelling Virginia's rivers to impassable floods and washing out bridges for miles. The following day, two

Richmond slaves cracked—as Sally had sworn her own resolve would not crack—and went to their masters with the information that on the previous night, despite the downpour, a band of armed slaves had assembled at the rendezvous point, ready to attack under the command of a slave named Gabriel Prosser.

Because of the rain, Prosser had reset the date of the uprising—which comprised almost eleven hundred armed and organized rebel slaves—for the following night, the thirty-first.

But by the following night, Governor Monroe had militia patrols out sweeping the roads. Within days, almost thirty of the leaders had been taken.

⚜

"Did you know?" Tom asked.

Sally didn't answer. The sharp golden half-light of autumn, slanting through the jalousies of the cabinet's windows, laid bright slits across his sharp features. In his eyes Sally saw the shaken look of a man who has stood near a tree in a lightning-storm, only to see God's hammer rend the living thing to pieces a yard from his elbow.

Was it the nearness of their escape that frightened him? she wondered. The fact that he and all his friends had barely avoided being overrun and slain, as the aristocrats of France had been murdered? The fact that while he and his lanky friend Governor Monroe and clever little Mr. Madison had all been scheming about the balance of local rule with the power of the Congress, black men whose labor they all took for granted had been making plans of their own?

Or was it the awareness that he, and they, and his daughters, and his friends' families, all stood unmasked in the eyes of the country as the oppressors, the exact equivalent of those French aristocrats who had "brought it on themselves"?

Sally folded her hands and answered calmly, "No."

His eyes met hers. *I think you're lying, Sally.*

And hers replied, *Better a liar than a coward, Tom.*

Both knew that the words could never be said. That to speak them would end the friendship that, flawed as it was, was still a source of comfort to them both.

And Sally had known for a long time, that he would not and could not be other than he was, no matter what was said.

It was he who looked aside.

⚜

The rebel slave Gabriel Prosser was hanged on the tenth of October. Rumors went around the quarters for weeks beforehand, of slaveholders demanding that the forty or so men condemned with him be "made an example of" by mass executions, or burning alive. Tom Randolph's cousin (and brother-in-law) John, newly elected to Congress, had written, *The accused have exhibited a spirit, which must deluge the Southern country in blood:* and many had demanded vengeance accordingly.

While tidying Tom's cabinet, Sally found a letter from Governor Monroe, asking Tom's advice. Pinned to it was a note containing Prosser's reply to the question asked in court, of why he had conspired to revolt.

I have nothing more to offer than what General Washington would have had to offer, had he been taken by the British and put to trial by them. I have adventured, endeav-

oring to obtain the liberty of my countrymen, and am a witness to their cause.

After a little further search among the papers, Sally found Tom's polygraph copy of his reply.

The world at large will forever condemn us if we indulge a principle of revenge, or go beyond absolute necessity. They cannot lose sight of the rights of the two parties, and of the unsuccessful one.

Later, Lam Hawkin told her that on Tom's recommendation, ten of the accused had been reprieved, and their death sentence commuted to banishment.

Not a spectacular change of heart, Sally reflected. But like her decision to help Patsy and her children, what he could do without betraying his own. And more than one might expect, of a man who sought the Presidency, a month before the election in the South.

ABIGAIL

❦

East Chester, New York
Friday, November 7, 1800

In Weymouth, nearly half a century ago—
in those bright quaint times when it never
occurred to anyone that one day there
wouldn't be a King—there had been a man
named Goslin who'd been the Town Drunk.
Abigail's earliest recollections of him included seeing him work now and then, casual labor like digging ditches or splitting
shakes, always followed by a spree in
Arnold's Tavern and a stagger through the
streets, singing at the top of his lungs. She,
Mary, and Betsey had always fled him, at
their mother's orders. But Abigail, being the
Original Eve of curiosity, had watched from
a distance the man's innumerable argu-

ments with his long-suffering, snaggle-haired wife. Nobody knew what they lived on or why she'd married him, but through the years Abigail had seen him work less and less; until he became a dirty, whiskered, trembling automaton, stinking of his own urine, glimpsed sitting in a ditch or under a tree, engaged in rambling conversations with people who weren't there.

She'd often wondered about his wife. It had never occurred to her to even think about his mother.

Until now.

⚜

The carriage lurched heavily as it turned through the break in the fence, and despite Jack Briesler's careful driving its wheels slithered into ruts deep in mud. The jolt of the springs made Abigail feel as if every bone in her body were being broken with hammers.

Even that didn't hurt as bad as the pain in her heart.

Oh, Charley. Oh, my beautiful boy.

When an infatuated Charley had begged his parents for permission to marry Colonel Smith's spritely sister in the summer of

1794, both of them—John from Philadelphia, Abigail from the farm in Quincy—had written back immediately, begging him to wait. They'd both had a pretty good idea, by then, of the financial status of the Smith family. Charley had regretfully agreed that his parents were right, and said yes, he would wait.

And had married Sarah Smith within weeks of his letter.

To Abigail, the stone house seemed even more isolated now under snow than it had been when she'd been trapped there, ill in the fall of '91. The yard was a perfect soup-pit of muck, crisscrossed with ruts around the low stone curb of the well. As Briesler maneuvered the carriage as close as he could to the farmhouse door, Nabby appeared: Nabby grown heavy, silent, and gray-faced in her not-quite-clean blue dress. The woman beside her, under a thick shawl, wore a much-patched caraco jacket that Abigail recognized as one she had herself purchased in London fifteen years ago, and passed on to Nabby.

"Mama Adams," the woman said, wading through the mud and holding out one chilblained hand. She still retained some of the Colonel's charm, some of the dark, lively beauty Abigail had seen in her on her first visit to Nabby here back in '89.

With the other arm, Charley's wife held a child on her hip, a black-haired girl of two. A four-year-old in a dress made up from the fabric of one of Nabby's London gowns clung to her skirt, looking from her mother to Abigail with brown eyes heartbreakingly like Charley's. The mother's eyes had the wrung-out look of someone who has been weeping, on and off, for weeks.

Abigail was familiar with it. She had only to turn her head, and see its echo in Nabby's tired face.

"Sarah," she greeted her daughter-in-law, and mentally thanked God she'd remembered to bring the highest pair of shoe-pattens she possessed. As she got out of the coach, the tall iron cleats sank in the mud like stilts.

"Thank you for coming," Sarah whispered, and tears began to track from her eyes. She led Abigail through the farmhouse, to the small lean-to built off the kitchen.

The lean-to was bitterly cold. In a way it was a fortunate circumstance, reflected that critical little voice in the back of Abigail's mind that never left her, not even in her worst moments of shock, of pity, of grief. Had the room been warm, the stink would have knocked one down.

Sarah had clearly done her best to keep Charley clean, and it was a task clearly beyond her.

Oh, my beautiful boy.

Abigail pressed her hand briefly to her mouth, then went to Charley's bedside while Nabby gently led the two little girls from the room.

How did it come to this? How could it come to this?

Charley's face was so swollen she hardly recognized him. His puffy hands groped and picked at the stained coverlet. She remembered Nabby writing her—that summer when she and the Colonel had been living like royalty in New York on the proceeds of the Colonel's "investments"—that Charley and Sarah were wildly happy together, and that she thought that marriage to her husband's young sister would settle her brother down.

Apparently that had lasted about as long as the Colonel's latest fortune. By December of that year—1794—Nabby had been alone again, pregnant again, and frantically trying to find money to live on. Again.

And Charley . . .

"Ma?" he whispered, and fumbled for her hand. His breath almost made her gag.

"I'm here, Son."

"I'm sorry." Alcohol—recent and abused for years—slurred his words. " 'S the las' time, I swear you 's the las' time. I'll sober up now, I'll . . . pull myself together. Not fair to Sarah . . ."

Abigail had to bite back the urge to snap at him that it wasn't fair to his daughters, either, not to mention his father. Her jaw ached with the unsaid words and she managed, "I know you will, dear." *Hypocrisy,* she thought, furious at herself. *You tell him a lie, forgive him, and he'll only go on getting himself like this. . . .*

But no words of hers—no tears, no pleas of Sarah or Nabby or anyone else—had ever kept him from drinking.

And she knew, looking down into his face, that it no longer mattered. She knew she was seeing her son for the last time.

It occurred to her that she hadn't seen the real Charley, that smiling boy who only wanted to be with his friends in his own home with his family around him, for many years.

He was crying now, a drunkard's easy tears. "I'll make you proud, Ma. Make Pa proud. He wasn't ever proud of me."

"Now, that's not true!" protested Abigail sharply. "When you went to Harvard—"

"Got thrown out," sobbed Charley bitterly—for dashing nude across the snowy Yard, to be exact, Abigail recalled, with a flash of exasperation. An exercise neither he nor his friends could possibly have performed sober. "Couldn't finish," he went on tearfully. "Couldn't stay in Holland with Pa. Johnny stayed. Pa's so proud of Johnny, goin' to Russia an' Berlin an' Spain."

And while Johnny had been making John proud, Charley had borrowed, invested, and lost all of Johnny's savings: just in time for Johnny to be a pauper when he married, in London, a girl Abigail feared was spoilt and pampered.

"I remember what you tol' me, Ma, how it was the chance for us to learn French an' meet important people. An' I wasted it."

Tears flooded Abigail's eyes at the recollection of the inn-yard in the gray port-town of Beverly, where poor little Charley had fetched up after five months on the high seas. *Too exquisite a sensibility for Europe,* John had said in his letter, and had consigned his eleven-year-old son to home-bound American friends. It was all he could have done at the time—there was no question of John abandoning negotiations for the Dutch loan that had kept Washington's troops in powder—and Charley hadn't seemed a penny the worse at the time. He'd spoken of being stranded in Spain, and of finding himself stuck on a ship whose drunkard of a captain couldn't find his way out of the North Sea, as a sort of astonishing lark.

But the fact remained that John had sent him away, while Johnny had done his duty and stayed.

And Johnny, after a wretched attempt to set himself up as a lawyer in the already lawyer-infested Boston, had gone back to Europe as George Washington's Minister to Holland only weeks before Charley had married Sarah.

"I wasted it all," Charley mumbled, his bloated fingers slacking, picking at the coverlet. "Nuthin' I could do, could make him proud. Forgive me, Ma. Forgive me."

Forgive me, Ma. The words sliced at Abigail's heart. Her brother Will had always pleaded for forgiveness after his binges, or when he'd come back to Braintree during the War, penniless and with rumors of counterfeiting and swindling trailing him like flies after stale meat. And their mother always had forgiven him, and always had given him money, even during that last year of her life, when the British had been bottled up in Boston and their raiding-parties were burning farms, and prices were so high that there was no sugar or coffee or medicine to be had in the town.

Dying, that dreadful autumn of '75, Abigail's mother had neither smiled nor wept, but she had whispered her son's name again and again, with love and sorrow in her voice. She had had three daughters, but only one son, and he the youngest, her baby boy. And he, of course, had been nowhere around.

Had Will looked as Charley did now, before he died?

But somehow the memory of her anger at her mother, like a cold stone dropped into boiling water, turned her own anger to pity as she finally understood. Whatever she'd felt about Charley's sins—against her and John, against his wife and daughters in their patched dresses—he was dying now. And he was her son. The child who'd played on the sanded floor of their kitchen back on Queen Street in Boston, listening to the British drums on the Common. The child who'd chirped up gamely in the face of a British raid, "We'll *kill* 'em, Ma!"

She put her arms around his shoulders, laid her face against his chest. "My darling, what's done is done. I love you. I, and your father, have always loved you."

He was just thirty years old.

She knew that later she'd be angry at him again, furious at the weakness that had led him to throw away everything she and John, Sarah and Johnny and Tommy and Nabby, had given him. Knew that before she left this place—and she planned to flee as soon as she could—she'd be back to pacing, to demanding of Nabby and Louisa, *How could he?* But the tears she shed were tears of love and of untainted grief.

She knew when she journeyed south again, to that brand-new Federal City on the Potomac that people were already starting to call Washington City, she'd be taking

Charley's little Susie with her as well as Nabby's red-haired Caroline. Permanently, she hoped, the way she'd taken Louisa.

The world was cruel to the daughters of wastrels.

Mount Vernon Plantation
Wednesday, December 3, 1800

"I have tried not to—to take blame upon myself," she said, some weeks later, to Martha Washington. "My brother—Louisa's father . . ." And she lowered her voice with a glance across the Blue Parlor at the little group on the sofa near the fireplace, ". . . was—was weak that way."

Louisa, now twenty-seven, was relating to the other two women beside her how Abigail had dealt with the Quincy neighbors who'd objected to Jamey Prince, their free black servant, attending school with *their* precious sons. Martha's dear Nelly—who could not possibly, Abigail reflected, be twenty-one years old and a mother herself now!—was laughing and shaking her head. On Louisa's other side Sophie Sparling—now the Widow

Hallam—merely looked amused, as if such hypocrisy were to be expected of those who'd rebelled against the King.

"And I've often wondered," she went on quietly, turning back to meet Martha's troubled gaze. "*Was* there something amiss in the way my parents raised my brother? Was there something they could have done, or failed to do, to turn him from drink and ill company?"

Martha set down her cup, and laid one plump black-mitted hand on Abigail's. "You cannot think that, dearest," she said softly. In her eyes Abigail saw pain that was the twin of her own, perfect comprehension of shared grief and shared doubt. In the footsore aftermath of innumerable teas and levees in Philadelphia when they'd shared the duty of sociable small-talk with each and every guest, Martha had spoken often of her own concerns about the disordered household in which her granddaughters were growing up: a pattern that clearly seemed to be repeating itself now in Eliza's.

And if the current condition of Mount Vernon was any indication, Abigail reflected, there wasn't much to be said about young Wash Custis, either.

Would any of the long-dead Jacky Custis's children have been different—happier or more capable of finding happiness—had the matriarch of the family chosen to rule the family instead of follow her husband and her heart?

"Men, and women, become what they become." In the frame of Martha's cap—black gauze, as all her clothing was of deepest mourning for the General, who had not yet been a year in his brick-lined tomb—her pale plump face and white hair were a pretty echo of the woman Abigail had first met that chaotic winter in Cambridge almost twenty-five years before.

"We can help them—guide them—but their own basic natures *will* emerge. And when all is said, I think we have little to do with it. I wish it weren't that way," she added with a sigh, and a glance toward the parlor door. "But I suspect that it is."

Though it was almost noon, young Wash Custis—it had taken Abigail a moment to recognize the tall young man who'd answered the door—still loitered in the paneled hall, talking horses with Nelly's cousin-husband. Little as Abigail approved of slave-labor plantations, she'd had enough conversations in Paris with Tom Jefferson to know that unless the planter himself—*not* simply an overseer—rode his acres and checked everyone's work, work would not get done.

And by the look of it, a great deal of work was not being done at Mount Vernon.

Or had it always been this unkempt?

When her carriage from the Federal City had topped the little rise before Mount Vernon, Abigail's first thought had been that same sense of completion that she'd experienced on seeing Westminster Abbey for the first time, or Notre Dame de Paris: *So this is what it actually looks like.*

Martha had described the long white "mansion house" to her many times, as they sat stiffly side by side, smiling as guests were presented, but it was good to see her friend's home at last.

The place of which President Washington had spoken with such profound love. The place to which he and Martha had so longed to return.

Now, at last, he was finally here to stay.

And, Abigail suspected, Martha as well.

Unscythed grass grew rank in what had to have been the bowling green Martha had spoken about. Weeds choked the little oval of lawn before the door. Even two weeks in the Federal City had served to inform Abigail that in addition to not talking about things they didn't want to talk about, Southerners as a rule seemed to have far lower standards of tidiness than Abigail was used to. Conditions prevailing in the kitchen of the Presidential mansion—not to mention in the potholed, muddy gravel-dump that surrounded it—made her wonder what Monticello was really like.

Was it as untidy as this, and Jefferson simply hadn't noticed?

Or were the dilapidated buildings she saw here, the peeling paint and broken window-panes, simply the measure of Martha's grief?

Wash Custis had answered the door because when Jamey Prince—that same free colored servant to whose education the neighbors had so objected—had knocked, no slave could be found to admit Abigail. "Likely they're in the kitchen, or playing cards in the tack-room," Wash had grumbled. "I'll catch 'em a lick for it!"

Nelly, Abigail had noticed, was the one

who'd hurried away to bring more hot water for the tea and meringues from the kitchen.

"Since the General died," Martha apologized now as Nelly rose again and rustled from the room, "it seems that nothing gets done around here anymore. I know I ought to keep the servants at their work, but it somehow seems more trouble than it's worth.

"He freed them, you know," she went on, her dark eyes filling with tears. "*Freed* them! I can't *imagine* what he was thinking."

Startled, Abigail said, "He never . . . I mean, he would not have left you without servants, surely!"

"But he *did*! His will said they were to be freed at my death—his own Negroes, of course, not those belonging to the Custis estate. But Wash thinks—" She lowered her voice, and glanced around her in the way Abigail had seen all slave-owners glance, for fear of eavesdroppers in their own houses. "Well, especially with the rumors of an uprising this past summer. Wash thinks that perhaps it would be . . . be *safer . . .* if they were all freed next year."

Abigail's eyes widened at the implications of this and she traded a startled glance with

Louisa. But Martha's thoughts had already returned to her friend's pain, as if it was the most ordinary thing in the world, to fear members of one's own household.

"Truly," she said in her gentle voice, "there is nothing for which you need reproach yourself, dear. I've never been as dutiful toward our country as you have, but I knew the General needed me, every bit as much as I needed him. And John needs you, not just to know that you're keeping things safe at home, but by his side. Men—even the strongest men—need someone's hand to hold in the middle of the night, bless them. We made our choices. And your Charley, poor boy, made his."

Abigail was silent. Nelly returned, carrying a green-and-cream French tea-pot with more hot water from the spirit-lamp in the pantry. She was clothed like her grand-mother in sable crape that left black smudges on the faded blue woodwork of the West Parlor. Though the pretty, dark-haired young woman was married now and a mother herself—and, Abigail guessed with a shrewd glance at her figure, getting ready for a second child sometime next sum-mer—she still seemed very much the precocious schoolgirl who had poured tea at the receptions in the Morris mansion. The favorite granddaughter still, rather than any man's adult wife.

Nelly, too, it appeared, had made her choice.

"You treated them all alike," Martha reminded Abigail. "Now Johnny is Minister to Prussia and may be President himself one day. Had your children grown up with a mother whose heart and mind were elsewhere—or in a country that had just *lost* a war with England—would they have been better off?"

Abigail whispered, suddenly wretched, "I don't know."

"No one knows, dearest," said Martha. "We go where our hearts command us, in the faith that it is God who formed our hearts."

⚜

Before they left, Abigail took from her pocket, and pressed into Martha's hand, the small box that had been waiting for her at the President's House when she had arrived the day before yesterday: "What is it?" Martha asked, astonished. And then, "Oh,

how beautiful!" as she took from the wrappings the small bright circle of a gold-
framed mirror, and the cold, tiny fire of diamonds winked in the pale sunlight.

"It's something that belongs to you,"
replied Abigail, smiling at the pleasure in her
friend's eyes. "And has rightfully belonged
to you for eighteen years now."

Martha looked up, surprised, from trying
to read the engraving traced on the rim. Abigail's eyes hadn't been good enough to de-
cipher it without her spectacles, either,
but she knew it said *Liberté—Amitié.* "Dear
Heavens, not the Queen's gift, after all this
time?" And she turned it over, to look at the
ostrich-plumed portrait on the back.

"A part of it, I believe—Sophie believes,"
Abigail added. "She sent it to me, to ask
what should be done with it: Did it rightly
belong to you, or to the nation? She came
by it from a New York friend—" Privately,
Abigail suspected Aaron Burr . . . and suspected that he and Mrs. Hallam were rather
more than friends. "—and would have
thought nothing of it, she says. But when
she was in Paris she was friends with that
little slave nursemaid of Mr. Jefferson's—a
dear good-hearted girl but never about

when you needed her—and they still correspond."

For a moment Martha looked as if she had something to say on the subject of anyone so foolish as to teach a slave to read, but then, as if recalling Mr. Jefferson's known eccentricity, did not.

Which was just as well, thought Abigail. She went on, "Apparently the girl reminded her that they'd seen *nécessaires de voyage* of the kind at a shop in the Palais Royale— with night-lights, combs, that sort of thing— and that the proprietor had boasted of crafting the one the poor Queen sent to you in some kind of lavish casket in 1782. She ordered it set with her portrait surrounded by diamonds, he said, and engraved: *Liberté— Amitié.* And I do think this must have come from it, wherever the other bits have gone."

Martha turned it again, the gold sparkling in the firelight. In a moment, thought Abigail, she'd call Nelly and Louisa over to admire it. But for an instant longer the old woman held it to herself, looking into its depths as if within them she could see 1782 again: the General alive, her niece Fanny alive, the French Queen herself and so many others still alive. Charley safely home from Europe and happy again with his family. The bloody consequences of Revolution and the bitter exhaustion of dreams shattered still wool unspun on Fate's distaff. A year when "happily ever after" was still in sight.

"As you weren't the Presidentress in 1782," Abigail went on, "I don't see how this can belong to the nation. It was simply a gift from one woman to another."

From the last Queen of a kingdom that no longer existed, she thought, to the first hostess—the first consort—of a nation that, in 1782, had yet to be born.

"So all things do come in time to where they're meant to be," Martha murmured. "No matter what happens to us in the meantime. Thank you, dear. I'll keep this, and look at it whenever I need to remember."

⚜

"Is she all right?" Abigail asked Sophie, as the widow's black driver helped her into Abigail's carriage.

"As well as can be expected." Years, matrimony, and bereavement didn't seem to have changed Sophie much. She appeared little altered from her days of advising Abigail on the purchase of inexpensive ambassadorial china in Paris. Those cool eyes still regarded the world—or at least the United States—with amused derision. "She took the General's death very hard. And since those years when the capital was in New York she's never been really well."

"Who among us has?" Abigail drew her own thick collection of black shawls and cloaks more tightly about her narrow shoulders. "I swear there was something in the air of that city that gave everyone who lived there an ague. I've certainly never gotten over it."

For a moment an elusive expression flickered on Sophie's face: Abigail almost had the impression she was about to say, *Served the traitors right.* But she said instead, "I doubt this new 'Federal City' will prove more healthily situated. My father always said these Potomac lowlands bred fevers. I suppose it's well enough now, when every house is at least half a mile from its nearest neighbor and there's room for air to circulate. But how it will answer in the future, to have built a city for the enrichment of Southern land-speculators, remains to be seen."

"Had they not," replied Abigail, "the government would even yet be at a standstill while they squabbled over payment of the Virginians' debts to the English—I think that's how the deal was worked."

"It is how all such deals are worked," answered Sophie, with her sidelong cynical smile. "I suppose the placement of the Parthenon in Athens had something to do with which Archon's brother-in-law owned the land it was to stand on."

As they crossed the ferry to Georgetown the wind blew up with a bitter chill, though the day remained clear and bright. Abigail shivered, and Louisa pulled up the lap-robe more closely around her. The gray stone houses of the little tobacco-port looked bleak among the bare trees. Beyond the new wooden bridge the woods closed in, the carriage-team floundering in the soupy ruts. "On our way here we were lost for two days, trying to find our nation's capital," remarked Abigail drily. "I shall suggest to Mr. Adams that funds be asked from Congress for signposts."

"One must admit, though, it's a beautiful situation for a city." Louisa folded her gloved hands. "And it is indeed a new thing in the history of the world, to have a capital city purpose-built for a new nation, instead of taking history's hand-me-downs. There is much to be said for that. I expect," she added, as the carriage emerged from the brown-and-silver shadows of the woods, "it will be beautiful in spring."

Beside the little clump of buildings that housed the State Department's seven employees, their driver paused to rest the team. Brushy pastures foraged by cows stretched before them. Here and there buildings rose, inconsequential in the open wilderness, like toys set down and forgotten by giant children. "That's Mr. Moore's farm, there among the trees," pointed out Sophie. "He's a more reliable source of produce than the markets, if you get on his good side. And General Washington's friend Mr. Tayloe has just finished a quite handsome town house, and is now waiting for the town to arrive."

"I count myself lucky the plastering and painting were actually finished in the President's House before John arrived last month," remarked Abigail, as the driver clucked the horses into motion. "We keep all twelve fireplaces going, and that helps, though God only knows how we're to afford to heat the place when winter really sets in. And instead of a grand front staircase, we have a lovely cavern in the front hall, no doors in half the rooms, and not a bell in the house. I suppose its unfinished state simply means Mr. Jefferson will have less to tear down before he starts to make changes."

She couldn't keep the bitterness from her voice. Only days after John had gotten on the road for the Federal City in October, someone had brought her Alexander Hamilton's newly printed pamphlet, *A Letter from Alexander Hamilton, Concerning the Public Conduct and Character of John Adams.*

Long usage had partially inured her to the spectacle of her husband being called doddering, fat, monarchist, and insane by the people for whose freedom he had broken himself—and sacrificed his own happiness and that of his family—the whole of his life. But coming from a man of his own party— from the man whom many Federalists looked up to as the true leader of America— Abigail knew this meant John's almost certain defeat in the upcoming contest for President.

Almost certainly, the victor would be Jefferson. And with Jefferson would come the mob-rule that Abigail had feared since the days of Citizen Genêt's street-riots.

"And the irony of it is," she sighed, as the horses stopped again so that Sophie could get into her own chaise near the corner of a dilapidated country graveyard, "for all that wretched little man's venom about John being incompetent, a treaty with France has finally been signed."

"It's official, then?" Sophie raised her brows. "I'd heard it printed in the newspapers, but—"

"It's official," said Abigail. "First Consul Bonaparte drank a toast to our envoys and dismissed the riots in our streets and the seizures of our ships as a 'family quarrel' which will not be repeated. No family of mine."

"No," murmured Sophie as she descended from the carriage. "And one wonders what England will have to say on the subject."

" 'Sufficient unto the day,' " replied Abigail wisely, " 'are the troubles thereof.' "

⚜

The Mansion bestowed by the country upon its executive stood isolated in a wagon-rutted field, surrounded by heaped stone, building debris, and weeds. Smoke trailed from its chimneys but Abigail wasn't fooled: It would be cold as a tomb inside. At least, she thought, trying to rub the ache of rheumatism from her shoulder, she wouldn't be expected to put on many entertainments in the great half-finished pile. At the far end of the brushy two-mile vista of what was pompously referred to as Pennsylvania Avenue, she guessed rather than actually saw the movement around the tiny pale bulk of the Capitol. Electors gathering, to cast their States' votes for the new President.

George Washington had had two terms, and would have been elected for a third if he'd chosen to stand.

John was being pushed out after one—and that one achieved by only three votes, for which the Democratic-Republicans had never ceased to mock him.

After all he had done—after all *they* had done, he and she together—the young nation was destroying itself, as France had destroyed itself. The taste of despair was wormwood in her mouth.

She climbed the rattletrap wooden stair that bridged the sunken areaway which let light into the kitchens. The oval reception hall was, as usual, jammed with men—many of whom had clearly neither bathed nor had their shirts washed since the days of Royal governors. Though everyone was fairly sure that John had lost the election, many still hoped for government jobs. Beyond the oval chamber, the Mansion's central hall was gloomy and the stink of wet plaster overrode even the riper petitioners. She'd have to have the oil-lamps lit. In addition to being clammy, drafty, and without any means of summoning servants bar shouting, the Executive Mansion was also immense, a statement of Presidential majesty. Such furniture as they'd shipped down from Quincy huddled, lost, in those enormous rooms.

The house had been built for a man of George Washington's wealth (or Martha's, if truth be told). It would, Abigail estimated, take thirty servants to run the place, counting the stable help.

She and John had six, and would be paying Sophie Hallam's cook a dollar a week to come on Mondays and help with the laundry. With the weather inclement, she and Esther had been hanging the clothes to dry in the huge unfinished "audience room" at the east end of the house. The bedsheets smelled of paint, but the room was drafty enough that there should be little danger of mold.

She made her way to the winding servants' stairway that was the sole route to the upper floor. Some of the men rose to tip their hats to her, or murmured, "Good day, Mrs. Adams." Esther had made up the fire in the bedroom, but like every other room in the house the place still smelled of damp plaster, and the clammy atmosphere made her body ache, as it had at sea. Through the window she could see a slave-gang, clearing away some of the rubble around the new stone Treasury Building, the closest structure to the Executive Mansion and still half a mile away. They were dressed in rags and barefoot. She couldn't imagine how they could work outside in cold like this. A white overseer sat nearby on a stump, watching them. They worked slowly, though not nearly as slowly as the few white workers hereabouts that Abigail had observed.

Like the slaves on Mount Vernon—Abigail suspected, like slaves anywhere—they had no reason to care if things got done or not.

She was taking off her hat when movement in the mirror caught her eye. Turning, she saw John, a letter in his hand. He held it out to her, and taking it, she put her arm around his waist, pressed herself to him. His face told her what it said, before she read it.

Charley was dead.

The Federal City
Thursday, January 1, 1801

"It is a shocking mix-up," declared Meg Smith, wife of the editor of the new *National Intelligencer,* at Abigail's New Year's Day reception. A rather horse-faced young lady of twenty-two, she, like everyone else, was a newcomer to the Federal City. "Why no one ever thought what would happen if *everyone* who voted for Gentleman A as President would also vote for Gentleman B as Vice President . . . Giving Gentleman B the same number of votes as Gentleman A . . ."

"They were assuming that—er—Mr. B— actually *is* a gentleman," replied Abigail. "And would, as a gentleman, step aside. Though I suppose they all refer to one another as 'Citizen' in good French form and the concept of such a distinction as 'Gentleman' is a dead letter among them."

"You do the authors of the Constitution too much credit, Mrs. Adams," purred Sophie Hallam. "I'm sure they never gave the matter any thought at all. Just as they didn't consider the fact that in other circumstances the man with the *second-highest* number of votes stood a good chance of holding views radically different from those of the man with the *highest* number of votes."

There had been times, John had told her, during the worst of the "Pseudo-War" with France, when he and Tom Jefferson would pass each other on the streets of Philadelphia without speaking.

It comforted Abigail somewhat to reflect that her husband had done better in the election than either of them had thought he would. He'd carried New England, and had garnered a total of sixty-five electoral votes. Only eight votes behind Jefferson's seventy-three.

Equally, only eight votes behind Aaron Burr's seventy-three.

"Well, of course everyone meant for Mr.

Jefferson to be President and Mr. Burr, Vice—"

"Vice" being an apt title for Mr. Burr, reflected Abigail, but she merely agreed, "I think there is no doubt as to who is the greater genius."

Young Mrs. Smith beamed. Though the *Intelligencer* concentrated on news rather than personalities (or invective), she clearly worshipped Jefferson. Sophie Hallam, elegant in silver-gray silk in the new French style, remarked, "Perhaps not everyone. Mr. Burr is a New Yorker, and it was New York that made the difference in the election. He brought it to Mr. Jefferson as his dowry."

Abigail followed Sophie's sardonic gaze across the overcrowded levee-room to Tom Jefferson, surrounded as usual by his supporters—charming, warm, unpowdered, untidily dressed, and radiating a quirky scholarly brilliance. She remembered how diffidently he'd stepped into that family gathering in her uncle Isaac's parlor, and had had all those stiff dark-clothed New England patriots eating out of his hand before the end of the afternoon.

Remembered the many afternoons he'd come to dinner with them, at that preposterous mansion on the outskirts of Paris; the evenings he'd walk with her in the gardens, talking of architecture, flowers, the inherent rights that God had given to Man.

What had gone through his mind, she wondered, when word came in November of Bonaparte's coup that had ended once and for all even the pretense of the Revolution in France? Or because a Corsican tyrant was on the throne now instead of a French dunce, did he still pretend to himself that the Revolution had ended in victory instead of defeat?

All around them men kept crowding into the Mansion, darting up the makeshift wooden stairway in the rain to straighten their coats and refurbish their hair-powder in the oval hall. Fires roared in every fireplace, but the evening was still wickedly cold. Abigail wondered that Sophie, slender as the girl she'd been in Paris, didn't freeze. The new French style seemed to consist of diaphanous silk, no petticoat (and the French Minister's wife was clearly not wearing a corset either!), high-cut in the waist and so shockingly low in the bosom that Abigail was hard-put not to blush for some of the ladies who wore it, although Sophie herself managed to make the disgraceful costume seem elegant.

Of a piece, thought Abigail despairingly, with the libertinism that the Revolution had brought in its bloody wake.

"I hope your husband will offer his support to Mr. Jefferson, when the voting in the House begins in February." Meg Smith was, Abigail knew, a faithful attender of Congressional sessions, sitting in the gallery with the most amazingly motley crowd of society women, free blacks, idlers, and prostitutes to observe the debates and cheer during speeches. Had the weather not been so raw—had her grief for Charley not weighed so heavily on her heart—Abigail might have gone herself: *Who knows?* Sophie had said cheerily a few weeks ago, *We might see another brawl.*

But though once Abigail would have done murder for a chance to attend sessions of Congress, it seemed to her now a hollow victory. *Vanity of vanities, all is vanity. . . .*

The truth was, she suspected she would simply become too angry.

"My husband is a firm believer in the separation of powers," replied Abigail. "He says it is a matter for the legislature now, and that it is not his business."

"One's heart might almost go out to Mr. Hamilton." Meg giggled like a schoolgirl behind her fan. "He has to choose whom he hates least. Whichever way the Federalist votes go, that man will be placed above him. And between Mr. Jefferson and Mr. Burr, I'm not sure that he can choose."

"Mr. Hamilton will lean toward Jefferson." Sophie smiled her slightly malicious smile. "He knows Burr, and Burr knows him, through to his marrow-bones. Hamilton believes he can talk his way around Jefferson, given time."

"Obviously," remarked Louisa, coming up to join the little group. "A man who would believe Citizen Genêt would believe anyone."

The others laughed, but Abigail wasn't so sure. Craning her neck a little, she returned her gaze to Jefferson, wondering if she had ever truly known him. If anyone did. He would almost certainly pardon that pack of foul-minded journalists who'd been jailed for Sedition, not seeing where their lies would lead and perhaps not caring. As a Virginian, and like all Virginians desperately in debt to English tobacco-factors, he might very well repudiate not only the treaty with England but the power of the central government to make any such treaty.

The man is dangerous, she realized. *His followers, more dangerous still.*

A part of her wished with all her heart that she was back in Quincy again, back on the farm that was now the rock on which their lives were founded, with Louisa and little Caro and Susie. Nabby's boys would join them, too, when they were done with school for the summer. Johnny would be home from Europe next year, with his bride—

But a part of her wondered, *Should John step down? Or should he make a stand against what is clearly the beginning of ruin for this country?*

⚜

The voting in the House of Representatives took place on Wednesday, the eleventh of February; Abigail was already packing to leave. After weeks of pounding rains, the sky had cleared. Though the cold remained arctic, the northward roads were drying. Whoever won the House vote, Abigail knew, it would not be John. The thought of staying on in the Federal City—in a hotel? As a guest of one of Martha Washington's grand-daughters?—was more than John, or she, could bear.

If John had ever entertained the thought of not stepping down, of not leaving the country to the mercies of a Jacobin dema-gogue, he never spoke of it. And since John spoke to her of whatever entered his mind, it was safe to believe that it hadn't. At one point he had considered resigning in protest a few days before the inauguration, but Abi-gail had talked him out of it. It would not do, she said, for him to appear a bad loser.

"I *am* a bad loser," he'd replied. "Tom . . . Well, Burr would be worse. Tom may be a Deist, and a Jacobin, but Burr is . . . Burr is nothing."

He'd come down to the great East Room where Abigail was taking down the laundry, which took two days to dry in the clammy cold. *Only politicians could have designed this house,* Abigail reflected, flexing her aching shoulders. It had no service court-yard, nor even a fence around it, and the stables were nearly a mile away. Going back and forth to the Presidential Necessary-House was bad enough. Weeks of rain aside, she wasn't about to hang the Presidential linen out in full view of the likes of James T. Callendar's spiritual brethren.

"Burr is all technique." John's breath puffed white in the silvery window-light. "All slick cleverness. He's the kind of lawyer I used to hate coming up against in court because he's half an actor. He has all the facts but moves them around like chess-pieces, to whatever angle will look best to the jury. Tom, at least, there's a real man inside. A good man. But whether that man's decisions can be trusted . . ."

His breath blew out in a sigh. "Well," he said after a moment, "I've done what I can. And will do what I can." At the far side of the great chamber, Charley's tiny daughter Susie ran giggling among the clothes-ropes, hotly pursued by little Caro Smith. It was a relief, to see how John's eyes brightened at the sight of the girls.

He went on, "At least the Senate approved the treaty with France. Jefferson can't tamper with that, though the Good Lord only knows what other tricks Bonaparte has up his sleeve. And, thank God, they passed my proposal to increase the number of circuit courts, so at least there'll be responsible Federalist judges to interpret whatever laws the Republicans dream up. Including," he added, with the grim ghost of a smile, "John Marshall as Chief Justice, now that Ellsworth has resigned."

"John Marshall?" Abigail stood for a moment, sheet over her arms, startled out of her depression. She remembered how the handsome Virginian had bent his head to listen to John at the New Year's levee—how furiously Tom Jefferson had protested when his enemy (and third cousin) had been named one of the chief negotiators of the French treaty. A slow smile spread over her face. "Well. There's one Mr. Jefferson won't be able to talk his way around."

"Nor," said John, handing her the laundry-basket, "without dismantling the Constitution—the very thing he accused *us* of wanting to do—will he be able to get rid of him."

⚜

Now, as she folded the crisply ironed petticoats into her trunk, Abigail heard hooves on the hard-frozen gravel of the drive. Looking out, she glimpsed her nephew Billy Shaw—Betsey's boy, hired as John's secretary and assistant—limping up the makeshift stair. *So it's done,* she thought, and whispered a prayer, because John was perfectly right about Burr. Was an honest Jacobin more to be desired than a man who'd sell his support to the highest bidder?

Footfalls on the stairs. Billy's halting, John's firmer tread.

Abigail looked up.

"It's a deadlock," said John.

Abigail had been braced for any news but that. "I thought the House vote was supposed to *break* the deadlock." *Honestly, couldn't they even get THAT right?*

"The Federalists still control the House," said John grimly. "The new Congress hasn't been seated yet. This is the *last* session that's voting. And the Federalists who aren't under Hamilton's control trust Burr. Tom has eight states—" He ticked them off on his chubby, chilblained fingers. "Kentucky, Pennsylvania, Tennessee, Georgia, Virginia, New Jersey, New York, and North Carolina. That's one short of a majority. Burr has six, and Vermont and Maryland are both deadlocked. They've cast six ballots already. Nobody's moving."

By eleven o'clock that night, when the Representatives were starting in on their eighteenth or nineteenth ballot, the situation was still the same.

And still the same when Billy Shaw came back in the morning from the all-night session. Men were sending out for food, he said, and for coffee and some for clean linen.

And the vote was still tied. The sky was still clear. The road home still open.

"Fools!" John shoved his breakfast porridge from him, struck the table with the flat of his hand so that all the glasses jumped. "Don't they see what they're doing? Weren't any of them paying *attention* to what happened in France?"

His face suffused with anger, the "ungovernable temper" that all his life his foes had exaggerated, though Abigail had never found it ungovernable at all. One just had to let him shout himself breathless, and later he'd be perfectly sensible.

"It was divisiveness that brought France to ruin, every man pulling his own way! Stabbing one another in the back! Hamilton's still holding on to the votes of the men who support his party. He won't back Burr under any circumstances and he won't back Tom unless Tom will give him assurances of what to expect, which I don't think is an unreasonable request. Just the assurance that he's not an outright advocate of anarchy would do!"

⚜

"They'll all feel very silly," remarked Sophie Hallam, when she came by later in the day with word that on the twenty-first ballot the House was still split, eight to six to two, "with all the flags put up for the inauguration, if they don't know who to inaugurate." She sounded pleased.

⚜

The short winter day was drawing to a close and the last of Abigail's few callers had departed, when Jack Briesler tapped at the upstairs parlor door. "Mr. Jefferson to see you, ma'am."

Jefferson looked as if he had not slept last night. Spots of pink showed high on the Virginian's elegant cheekbones, and on the end of his long nose. In a year or two his faded hair would all be silver. Abigail had sat next to him at dinner just after the New Year, but this was the first time they had seen one another alone since . . .

She tried to calculate, running the years back in her mind.

Since London. They'd gone to the theater together, on a night when John had been obliged at the last minute to meet with the Portuguese Ambassador. They'd walked home through the chilly March mists, talking of fossil bones and Indians and mesmerism and the education of women . . . What one always talked about with Tom.

Everything except what he truly thought on any subject, or the contents of his heart.

That was the evening she'd given him Nabby's sketch of the garden of the Paris house.

You will be welcome in our home, she had said to him that evening, *as often as you care to come, as long as you care to remain, at whatever hour you make your appearance.*

Like so many last times, she had been unaware that it would be the last.

She had not realized how much she had missed her friend.

Tears filled her eyes and she blinked them away. *Weak,* she thought, furiously. *Losing Charley has made me weak—*

"Mrs. Adams." He bowed over the hand

she held out to him. "Is there any service I can offer you, before you take your leave?"

Not urging your journalist friends to call my husband a fat dotard before all the nation? Not lying about him behind his back to the President he served?

Perhaps giving him support he could trust?

Or had these acts been only Tom's view of how politics should be conducted? Part and parcel of his inability to see any inconsistency in hating slavery and giving his daughter twelve families of living human beings as a wedding-present?

For a moment silence hung between them in the shadowy parlor, chilly with the sinking of the fire. Only her own chair remained unsheeted near the hearth.

They had met in a crowded room, she recalled, looking across at the tall man before her. Life and promise glinting like the diamonds on the frame of Martha's French mirror. The War over, the world of sea-voyages and new romances ahead. *Journeys end in lovers meeting. . . .*

Now there was nothing but stillness, and

shadow, and years that could never be recovered.

She sighed, and said, "None that I can think of, sir. We've been living here like a couple of vagabonds, John and I. It only remains to bundle our tooth-brushes up in our spare shirts and be on our way. . . ."

And Jefferson laughed. Slipping easily into the banter of friendship, as if the more recent past had not existed. "Perhaps I could offer you a cow to take along, as you did to France?" He looked around him at the oval parlor. A beautiful room, Abigail thought, with its gold-starred wallpapers, but like everything in the house, too big to be really comfortable. "To tell you the truth, this house has always appalled me," he remarked. "It's a palace—it would swallow Versailles and have room left for the Dalai Lama. My heart bled for you, trying to heat it."

"I always wished," said Abigail quietly, meeting his eye, "that those wretches who called us 'monarchial' could have seen how we actually lived here. With six servants and no way to get wood, in spite of the fact that there were trees whichever way we looked.

Of all the accusations, that was the most unjust."

Another small silence fell. Just for a moment, Jefferson's eyes avoided hers. "On behalf of the men who supported me," he said at last, "I do apologize, for causing you pain. Of which, this year, you have had enough."

It was all he would say, concerning politics, concerning the election, concerning his supporters who were still in jail for trying to whip up hatred against the President. Concerning all the blood spilled in France, all the lies told and trust violated, only to put a dictator on its throne.

Jefferson is a dreamer, thought Abigail. Who had said that to her once? And his dream today was, before she took her leave, to reestablish something of the friendship they had lost. To pretend that all was actually well.

Briesler brought fresh tea, and candles, and another log for the fire. They drank together and Abigail pretended, for the sake of the man she'd once called her friend.

As she listened to his footfalls retreat down the echoing hall, she realized there was little likelihood that she would ever see Thomas Jefferson again.

The Federal City
Friday, February 13, 1801

As dreams went, Abigail reflected—as fairy-tales went—"happily ever after" was not, as Martha Washington had often said, "all it was cracked up to be."

She stood in the long French window of the downstairs entrance-hall, waiting for the carriage in the gray chill of dawn. The furniture was gone. Louisa sat by one of the fire-places cradling a bored and sleepy Susie in her arms.

We fought our war—we won our free-dom . . . Journeys did end in lovers meet-ing.

Only the lover Nabby met turned out to be a good-for-nothing, and the freedom we fought for turned out to be freedom for dirty-minded newspapers to call John names while he battled to keep the country out of a war it couldn't win.

And the prize for all our striving was the privilege of living in a world that we do not understand.

And along the way we lost our daughter's hope and happiness, as surely as we lost poor Charley. As surely as John and I lost our dear friend Jefferson.

Abigail pulled her cloak tighter around her shoulders, watching the black-cloaked, slender figure that had to be Sophie Hallam walking toward her along Pennsylvania Avenue from the Capitol.

"They just finished ballot twenty-three," she reported, as she arrived. "Still nothing. Some of the Federalists talk of asking the President Pro Tempore of the Senate to take over the position of Chief Executive if the deadlock cannot be resolved; or possibly Chief Justice Marshall . . . In which case, Mr. Jefferson says, he will call for another Convention to rewrite the Constitution *again*—presumably more to his liking."

"Which is *precisely* what they did in France," said Abigail bleakly. "Over, and over again. Whenever one faction didn't like what was going on."

"I understand militia is gathering in Virginia."

Abigail shook her head, and for a long while was unable to speak. Unable to frame into words the anger and sickened pain in her heart. At last she said, "It's just that I sat on Penn's Hill and watched the fighting before Boston. And now, after all our struggle, it seems I'm going to see the Republic break into pieces within my lifetime, after seeing it born."

"Mrs. Adams . . ." Sophie's expression of sardonic amusement was gone. "You know Hammy isn't going to let it happen. He wrote the *Federalist Papers,* for Heaven's sake, if for no other reason than his pride won't let him stand by and watch the Constitution *he* championed be swept away, completely aside from the fact that without General Washington to dote on him he has less control now over what the Republicans might come up with on a second try. He'll back down, and give the election to Jefferson."

"So that's what we have come to," asked Abigail bitterly, "in so short a time? To be thankful that one man's vanity truckles to another man's pride?"

"At least as things stand there is little likelihood that anyone is going to come posting up to Quincy to demand Mr. Adams return to public life the way they did to poor General Washington."

Surprised into a cackle of laughter, Abigail responded, "*Poor* my grandmother's lumbago! He delighted in being called back to the colors, when it looked as if we were to go to war with France. Poor *Martha,* to have waited for happiness for sixteen years, only to have it end in two—"

She broke off. Remembering that plump, black-clothed figure in the dilapidated parlor of Mount Vernon. The dreadful silence of slaves waiting for her death to bring them freedom. The footworn track that led from the house to the brick tomb overlooking the river. *Where thy treasure is, there will your heart be also.*

Wondering how many years of happiness were left to her and John, when they returned to the stony acres of their farm.

"Only, she didn't wait for happiness, you know," mused Sophie. "I think she was happy every day, just to be with him."

Abigail thought about that. Balancing those grievous winter evenings by the kitchen fire in Braintree against the sparkle of sunrise on the jeweled sea, that first day she woke up on the *Active* and wasn't seasick. Balancing the terror of waiting for British assault, against the salons of Paris in the last days of the Kings. The amazement of Handel's "Messiah" sung in Westminster

Abbey. Her garden in Auteuil and the wind in her hair, as she and John climbed hand in hand up the short green turf of the English downs . . .

Being John's partner, all these years. As if she'd gone along to some vast war with him to stand at his elbow and load his gun. Even were their work to be swept away tomorrow, the fact that they had done it would remain in God's heart, where all things were eternal.

And perhaps, too, in the minds of both women and men.

"I haven't been happy every day," she told Sophie. "But you know, I wouldn't have traded a single one of them for anything."

With a rattle of harness the carriage came around the corner of the drive, the wagon behind it heavy with furniture, trunks, servants bound for home. The inner door of the huge cold room opened and John came in. "The barometer's holding steady," he reported, as Sophie faded tactfully through the French window and down the wooden stair. "I pray you'll be comfortable—"

"If I made it in safety across the ocean," Abigail assured him, "I'm sure I'll reach

Quincy in one piece, and have the house snug for you on your return."

"My return." John sighed. "God knows what will happen here in the meantime. . . . And Jefferson, of course, is still refusing to tell anyone a thing about his intentions—" He shook his head, like a horse enraged by a horse-fly. "He could be plotting to abolish religion entirely in this country, the way they did in France—he's completely capable of it—or turn the states loose to do as they please, and undo everything the Convention labored to—"

Abigail put her hands on his shoulders: "It will be all right, John," she said, as she had said to Nabby, when her daughter had clung to her in the blackness of storm at sea, their lives in balance between the world they'd known and a future unforeseen. She wasn't entirely sure she believed it, but Martha's words came back to her mind. *We go where our hearts command us, in the faith that it is God who formed our hearts.* Which included Mr. Jefferson, as well as John. Whether Mr. Jefferson believed it or not.

Perhaps all things *did* return at last, to where they were meant to be.

She said again, more firmly, "It will be all right."

As John walked her down the steps to the carriage, Abigail looked from the dreary, bare expanse of stumps and trees back to the house: enormous, unfinished inside, still smelling of newness, like the country itself. Waiting for what would come.

But that was out of her hands now. And out of John's.

"God willing, I shall see you in a month," John said, and kissed her gloved hands, then her mouth. "And God willing, from that point on, *'I'll go no more a-rovin' with you, fair maid.'* "

The carriage started off; Abigail hummed the old song a little, to the creak of the wheels on the icy road.

A-rovin', a-rovin', since rovin's been my ru-i-in,

I'll go no more a-rovin' with you, fair maid. . . .

Looking back, she saw his stumpy black figure, standing on the steps of the great raw half-finished Mansion, in the muddy wilderness that civilization had barely scratched. Her John. A stout balding patriot who had seen everything of one of the most astonishing events of History—and who had seen it at her side. She sighed and settled back, and hoped they'd make Baltimore by nightfall.

MARTHA

☙

Mount Vernon Plantation
Saturday, March 6, 1801

"On the thirty-sixth ballot, Vermont and Maryland switched their support to Mr. Jefferson," Sophie Hallam reported. "Delaware and South Carolina cast blank ballots, withdrawing their votes from Mr. Burr. I understand that rumor is rife that Mr. Jefferson indeed reached an understanding with the Federalists, though he has been protesting to everyone who'll listen that he did nothing of the kind. I assume that his first act upon taking office will be to propose an Amendment to the Constitution making sure such a situation never arises again."

"After all that ink wasted slandering poor

Mr. Adams." Martha sighed, and rang the bell for Christopher, for the third time.

Nelly said, "I'll get it, Grandmama." She collected the empty tea-pot, and rustled away in quest of more hot water. Her foot-falls echoed in the shabby emptiness of the hall.

"After all that ink wasted slandering poor Mr. Adams, and Mr. Jefferson's real foe was there at his elbow the whole time." Sophie dipped a final shard of bread and butter into the dregs of her tea. "A pity, really. Those frightful newspapermen wouldn't have *had* to make up scandals about Mr. Burr's per-sonal life."

"Did you hear the story the Republicans tried to put about," put in Pattie, "about Mr. Adams sending Mr. Pinckney to France with instructions to bring back four beautiful opera-dancers, two apiece, as mistresses for them? When Mr. Adams heard it, he only said, 'I declare, Pinckney's cheated me, for I never got my two!' "

If the absence of her undivided guidance and care had pressed hard on her elder granddaughters, Martha reflected as they all laughed, at least Pattie seemed to have surmounted its effects. While Eliza still wore dramatic mourning for the General, Pattie had returned to ordinary dress, if one could call "ordinary" the high-waisted, narrow-cut gowns that more and more women seemed to be wearing nowadays.

Martha had long ago given up wondering whether she would have been different, had she, Martha, been able to raise all four of her grandchildren instead of the younger two when Jacky died.

Now Eliza declared, "I have heard that rather than endure seeing his foe made President, Mr. Adams sneaked out of the city in the dark before dawn on the day of the inauguration."

"If one is going to catch the public stage from Baltimore to Massachusetts," said Nelly reasonably, returning, "one had better sneak out of the city in the dark before dawn. Did Mr. Jefferson even think to invite Mr. Adams?"

Sophie said, "I understand Mr. Jefferson— whose inaugural address was perfectly inaudible, by the way—is still in residence at Conrad and McMunn's Tavern, taking his meals in the ordinary with the other guests." She leaned to scratch the ears of Nelly's elderly lapdog Puff, who had come around to sit at Nelly's feet again in hopes of a tea-cake. "Since I've never known him to occupy any building without tearing it down and putting it back together again to suit his fancy, I expect there will be changes in that dreadful Mansion."

"Will he live in it?" asked Pattie.

"Oh, he'll live in it," prophesied Nelly wisely. "It's all very well to proclaim one's Republican principles by living in a cottage, but one can't do one's work properly in one's sitting-room. You know how Grandpapa was driven distracted by people coming to see him. Mr. Jefferson shall want offices and some kind of state rooms to receive Ambassadors in. And once he's got those, whatever he'd replace the current Mansion with would have to be almost as large. And we certainly haven't seen him building a humble little dwelling at Monticello, have we? The question is, who will receive for him? Mr. Jefferson's a widower, and I think both of his daughters have too many small children to come here from Albemarle County to look after things. Will it be Mr. Burr's daughter, then, since he, too, has no wife?"

She glanced at Martha, and Eliza added in her booming voice, "Yes, Grandmama, what would be proper? You were, after all, the first Presidentress. You remain the ultimate arbiter of what is proper in a Republic."

Martha couldn't keep from smiling. Mr. Madison and Mr. Jefferson, and Mr. Hamilton, had all labored to bring forth the *principles* of a Republic. But to the best of her knowledge, only she and George had considered what the actual *practices* would be. Rather like playwrights who didn't give a thought to how the scene would be set or performed, as Dolley would have put it, Martha had long suspected that her dinners at Valley Forge had done more to convince the French that they were dealing with civilized reformers rather than wild-eyed King-haters than had any amount of rhetoric.

"Mr. Burr's daughter was married in February, just before the voting in the Senate began," said Sophie. "To a rice-planter, from South Carolina, a very wealthy man. So I expect Mr. Jefferson's hostess will be Dolley Madison, won't it?"

Martha smiled. "It will indeed."

⚜

Dinner was served at three, as always in Mount Vernon in winter and spring. Nelly saw to it at least that the reduced kitchen staff turned out a respectable meal. To Martha's disappointed shock, during their last return-journey from Philadelphia to Mount Vernon in March of 1797—in that crowded carriage with Nelly and Puff and Nelly's parrot, and young George Lafayette and his tutor and Martha couldn't recall who-all else—their faithful and excellent cook had run away, disappearing into Philadelphia's community of free colored without so much as a backward glance at the masters who'd been so good to him the whole of his life. His replacement wasn't nearly as good. Moreover, bills in the kitchen had risen appreciably since he'd taken over, despite all Nelly's watchfulness.

After dinner Sophie departed in her chaise, and the girls all piled into Eliza's husband's extremely elegant open landaulet, with nursemaids and children. It had been a delight, to visit not only with Pattie and Eliza, but to see five-year-old "Toad," as Nelly called Pattie's bouncy daughter Elinor, and three-year-old Columbia and Little Eliza, playing and tumbling on the brown winter lawn under charge of their nursemaids, with Nelly's toddler Parke.

Jacky's granddaughters.

The heiresses of the Custis estate, which Martha had guarded and husbanded all those decades.

When the carriages were out of sight down the drive, she slipped out of the house, and followed the path worn through the grass of the unscythed lawn, past the smokehouse and the washhouse, the coach-house and the stables, down the steep hill beside the vegetable garden, and so to the brick tomb overlooking the river.

It comforted her beyond measure, to know that he was there.

To know that he wasn't going to be off to Philadelphia, or Cambridge, or the heights above New York. To know that he wasn't going to be shot at by the British or hanged for a traitor or exposed to the filthy miasmas that seemed to hang over cities, like angels with burning swords.

He was home.

Mount Vernon was very quiet without him.

With the freeing of his slaves in December, of course, there was almost no work getting done. All George had ever had to do was look at a slave, and they'd hasten to obey. There were more whippings, she thought, and many more threats to sell them to men bound for the richer soils of the western part of the state. Perhaps last summer's abortive uprising was to blame, but the atmosphere felt ugly around Mount Vernon, and dangerous, even with the early release of those who had previously been scheduled for manumission on her death. Resentment was a stink in her house, like some dead thing, rotting under the floor.

When she walked past the stable-yard, past the clerk's house—past the place where she'd met George that January afternoon in '87, when Jemmy Madison had come to talk him into attending the Convention that had blasted all her hopes of peace—she felt the silence and the tension. As she moved about the house in the late afternoons when the light softened and shadows pooled in the corners of the hall, she found herself listening, convinced that the servants were whispering in the gloom. She had not realized how protected she had felt in his presence.

Only out here, on the brick bench beside his tomb, did she feel safe.

Such a silly thought, "safe," she reflected, blinking at the last shimmer of evening that gilded the treetops on the Maryland shore. Even when she'd genuinely feared that those slaves of George's who saw her as the obstacle to their freedom would find a way to poison her, she'd kept returning to the thought that it probably wouldn't be so bad. Then she'd be with George.

And Jacky, and her beautiful Patcy, after all those years.

But mostly what she looked forward to was seeing George again.

She remained where she was, watching the sun go down above the mountains. Remembering all the sweet days of unremarkable peace here, after they'd returned from Philadelphia for that last time in '97. Crowded years, so that George had been hard-pressed to find time to put his land in order, much less sort through his papers on the Revolution and the years of his Presidency.

For a time Lafayette's son had lived with them, and his tutor—both of whom had shown signs of falling in love with Nelly. Also living with them was George's nephew Lawrence Lewis, his sister Betty's boy, handsome in the strong, quiet way that George had been in his prime. Perhaps be-

cause he reminded Nelly of her grandfather—because beneath his air of strength
he also had a touching vulnerability—when
he, too, fell in love with Nelly, she returned
his love.

To further complicate matters, Wash was
back with them, too, having dropped out of
college. Like his father, he'd gotten engaged to a girl of fifteen, though fortunately
nothing came of it. When poor Fanny had finally succumbed to consumption, after less
than two years of marriage to Tobias Lear,
there had been talk of their four children—
Fanny's three by her first husband Augustine, and Lear's first wife Pollie's little Lincoln—joining the household, but Martha
had simply refused. George contributed to
their support in various boarding-schools,
and that had to be enough.

To add to all that, everyone in the country
still wanted to simply come and see him.
While still President, George had overseen
the laying-out of the Federal City on the
other side of the river. There was constant
coming and going of men engaged in building the President's House, and the Capitol,
and laying out those vast avenues, and of
course George could no more resist talking

architecture than a drunkard could turn his face from the bottle. When in 1798 it had appeared that the country would go to war with France, an army was called up, and George became once again its Commander in Chief. He was too old to take the field, but he trusted Hamilton and forced Congress to make him second in command, and had spent a good deal of that year in Philadelphia and in the Headquarters at Cambridge.

Nelly and Lawrence had married on George's sixty-seventh birthday—February 22, 1799—and George wore his old Continental uniform to escort her down the staircase to the wedding in the dining-room.

Good years, Martha reflected, flexing her hands, which lately had shown a distressing tendency to swell so that her wedding-ring cut into her flesh. What there had been of them. Her feet, too, were swollen, and she found that even the short walk down to the tomb brought her breath up short.

She hadn't told Nelly or Wash about this. If they knew, they'd only discourage her from coming, to this one place in the world where she wanted to be.

Nelly came looking for her, when the last of the daylight faded. Martha found she needed the support of her granddaughter's arm, going up the steep path to the house. The whitewashed bulk of it seemed to glimmer in the twilight before them, the ground-floor windows gently glowing. It was still hard to remember that he wouldn't be there when she came inside. She still flinched a little as she passed the shut door of George's study on the first floor.

She had not crossed the threshold of that room, or of their blue-and-white bedroom above it, for fifteen months, since the night George died.

⚜

"I suppose it's something," remarked Nelly after supper, "that the country's passed another election safely—and one with so much ill-feeling and slander." She shook her head as she picked up Martha's candlestick, and her own, from the table in the Little Parlor. "I'm sorry Mr. Jefferson won. He's turned his back on so much of what Grandpapa tried to accomplish. I don't expect any of us will get many invitations to balls in the Federal City."

"With Dolley Madison writing the invitations?" Martha raised her brows. "Don't you think it, dearest."

They passed in silence through the nursery, where Parke's old nursemaid Moll dozed in her chair beside the toddler's bed. At the top of two long flights of stairs, Martha's maid Caroline waited for them outside the door of the little garret bedroom where Martha slept nowadays. Not as good a maid as Oney had been, Martha thought, with the slight surge of resentful anger at the girl's brazen escape their last year in Philadelphia—and George had scarcely lifted a finger to get her back even when she was known to be living, bold as paint, in Newburyport!

But then, thought Martha wearily, as Nelly helped her into her nightgown and brushed her long gray hair, so many of their people had been spoiled, living in Philadelphia where they could associate with the free colored of that city. And it had been while they lived in Philadelphia that George himself had started to speak of slavery itself as being unjust, though how he thought he'd get his acres tilled without it she couldn't imagine.

Another thing that never would have hap-

pened, had he remained where he belonged, at home.

Jemmy Madison had a lot to answer for.

"Yes, I'm glad it all worked out, dear,"
sighed Martha, as Nelly helped her to bed.
"But from everything I hear, the world
sounds like it's growing very strange, and
stranger by the day. Goodness knows what
will become of the country in four years—or,
God forbid, eight—of rule by Mr. Jefferson."

⚜

Sleeping, Martha dreamed of waking on a
warm midsummer morning eighteen months
ago and going to the dressing-table for her
prayer-book, to read by the window's first
glimmer of light. From the bed she heard the
sudden creak of the ropes beneath the mattress as George turned over, and then his
voice, "Patsie?" And in it, a note that was almost fear.

"What is it?" She hurried back to his side,
saw him turn, lay his hand on her pillow as
if seeking her. Then he sat up, and under the
open throat of his nightshirt she saw him
breathing hard, as though he'd been
shocked awake, the way his eyes would

snap open, panting and alert for years after the War, still listening for the British guns.

He caught her hand in his.

"I am—well," he said hesitantly. "I think. But I dreamed . . ." He shook his head, and she could tell, looking into his lined face, that he still saw the images that had burned their way into his sleep.

"It was vivid, as clear as we sit here. We were in the summerhouse, talking—I remember saying to you how happy we are here, and how I look forward now to many more years with you. Then a light came, brilliant, as if the sun had come down to the earth, and through it I saw a figure, beautiful but dim, an angel I thought, standing at your side. It leaned down to whisper in your ear and you turned pale at its words. And then you began to fade away, like a mist dissolving with the coming of day. Then you were gone . . . and I was alone."

His stricken eyes met hers. God knew, Martha thought in her dream—as she had thought that morning in 1799—each had seen people die, friends and family: Patcy, Jacky, Fanny, Pollie. Griefs that wrenched the soul and crippled one's trust in life.

But she saw in his face that the mere concept of living without her was unthinkable to him. His hand clung to hers as if he truly expected that nearly invisible angel shape to enter the bedroom in its numinous cloud of light, to whisper into her ear that he and she would have to part.

Martha laughed, uncertainly but gently, as she would have laughed to soothe a child's nightmare fear. " 'Twas only a dream," she told George. "How many dreams do we dream, that never come to pass? At least I *hope* I shall never find myself back at the ballroom in Williamsburg wearing only my nightgown, as I dreamed I did the other night!"

"And very stylish I'm sure you were." He touched her cheek with his palm. The grief did not leave his eyes. "You know how often the outcome of dreams is contrary to what we dream. I fear that it is I who will be obliged to leave *you.*"

"Well, to be *truly* contrary, sweetheart, it would be that instead of leaving you in a cloud of light, I shall simply stay," Martha pointed out in her most reasonable voice. "A dream is a dream, General. It is absurd to make a piece of work over a phantom."

But it seemed to her now that, without

transition, for one moment she was standing in that same place in the blue-and-white bedroom, looking down at him less than six months later, as the doctors carried away the bleeding-bowls from his bed. The slaves' overseer had bled him at daybreak, that first morning he'd woken with a throat so sore and swollen he could barely breathe or swallow. At nine, when the doctor came, he'd been bled again, and then a third time by another doctor mid-afternoon. In her dream the room stank of blood. Martha didn't think that in real life the bedchamber had ever been without people in it, but in her dream she stood there alone. Looking down at George's still face, wax-pale against the blood-daubed linen of the bed.

Whether it was the dream that woke her, or the noise, or the light, Martha didn't know, but she was abruptly awake in the low-roofed garret room, heart hammering. In the flickering orange reflection that came through the window she could make out the corner of the Franklin stove, the angle of the ceiling, the curved shoulders of the plain wooden chairs.

Orange reflection!?!

Martha scrambled from her bed, flung

herself at the garret window. The roof of the covered walkway lay below her, and beyond that the kitchen, flames licking out of its windows.

Dear God, if the walkway goes it will spread to the house!

Scooping up her wrapper, Martha stumbled into the attic's central hall. Caroline sat up at once in her nest of pallet and blankets on the floor—"What—?"

But Martha was already across the hall, hammering on the door. "Wash? Wash! Caro, wake Mr. Lewis, the kitchen's on fire—"

Caro said, "Lord God!" and was down the attic stairs like a hare. Wash emerged from his room a moment later, hair hanging in his eyes.

"The kitchen's on fire!" Martha panted, and hurried back into her bedroom and to the window, to see the nightgowned shape of their overseer, Mr. Rawlins, and half a dozen other shadows come running from the darkness toward the quarters . . .

And what she could almost, but not quite, swear was that another shape darted out of the kitchen and vanished into the night.

Mr. Rawlins was shouting in a voice like a

bronze gong. Martha could see the slaves forming up a bucket-line from the well behind the washhouse, and downstairs she could hear Puff barking wildly, Parke wailing in terror. Lawrence's valet cried somewhere, "Come on, Mr. Lewis, just another step," as he tried to coax his half-stupefied master down the stairs.

Nelly almost fell through the door, dark braids flying behind her and giving her the look of the schoolgirl she'd once been. "Grandmama, come on. If it spreads—"

"How bad is it?"

Nelly shook her head. She must have just been waked herself, thought Martha, as she let her granddaughter lead her to the stair. Had the fleeing figure been just her imagination? Or would morning reveal there'd been runaways under cover of the confusion, runaways whose parents or brothers or sisters or sweethearts had been freed by the General's will, and forced to leave?

Outside, the stench of the smoke was overpowering, as buckets of water were hurled into the burning kitchen and onto the near end of the walkway's roof. Though the mansion house was painted and cut to look like stone, it was wood: If wind-carried sparks ignited the roof, the blaze would be almost impossible to put out.

Mist hung over the river, blurred the moon. Martha was fighting for air as Nelly led her out onto the piazza and from there down the lawn to the river, where old Moll already stood with Parke, wrapped in a quilt, in her arms, and Puff running worriedly back and forth around her feet like an agitated milkweed.

"It ain't got a good hold yet," predicted the old woman, nodding up at the red glare that now shone behind the mansion house. "That new cook couldn't bank a fire right if the instructions to do so was written on the chimney-breast. That's the second fire we've had in a year."

That was true, Martha reflected. But it was also true that the first kitchen fire, back in June, had almost certainly been the work of arson—and it had been at that point that George's nephew Bushrod, Lawrence, and Wash had met to discuss freeing George's slaves at the end of the year, rather than waiting for her death.

Hours later, Lawrence finished checking the buildings nearest the kitchen and let Martha, Nelly, and Parke go back upstairs. Charlotte, the headwoman of the plantation, very sensibly boiled water in the little hearth of the room where the sewing-women worked, so that Nelly could make tea, which they drank sitting in the Little Parlor. Parke was already making determined little forays to see what was left of the kitchen: "Cookies," she said worriedly, knowing the kitchen was the place they came from.

"Are you all right?" Nelly asked Martha, when she finally was allowed to lead her upstairs again. "Would you like me to stay here with you for a little while?"

"I'll be quite all right, dear, thank you." Martha sat on the edge of the narrow bed, breathless and a little dizzy from the long ascent. "I should imagine Mr. Jefferson's supporters are lighting bonfires in the streets of the Federal City tonight in celebration, so why should we be any different?"

But after Nelly left, Martha sat up in bed for a time, listening to the house grow quiet again around her. The house she had known, as intimately as she had known George, like a beloved body against whom she had slept for all those many years. Instead of her breath returning, it grew more stifled, until she was panting, as if she had run a mile instead of simply walked down the slope of the lawn. She felt a kind of soft, pushing sensation in the left side of her chest, as if someone were pressing a heavy hand around the muscle of her heart. Dizziness grayed the light of the single candle, until she lay back, gasping, against the pillows.

Then the sensations faded as swiftly as they'd come, like taking off a garment. Except for the dizziness, and the sensation of not being quite able to get her breath.

It was the climb, she decided. *The climb up the stairs.*

She leaned up on her elbow long enough to pinch out the candle. Even that small effort dropped her back limp.

When she dreamed again, it was of George sitting in the latticed shade of the summerhouse, waiting for that sweet blazing light to return again, and with it the invisible presence, who would lead her back to him.

Mount Vernon
Wednesday, May 5, 1801

"It hath been a most difficult spring for everyone, I see." Dolley Madison sighed, removing her black kid gloves to accept the tea-cup Martha handed her. "Poor Mr. Madison's father passed away at the end of February, and Mr. Madison was much taken in settling the estate—and with it, that of his brother Francis, who died this October past. Then he himself took sick—and who could blame him, poor lamb?—with a rheumatism so bad even flannels and temperance could not cure it. And all the while poor Mr. Jefferson like a fly in a tar-box, to have him come and 'set up the shop.' Is there aught that I or Jemmy can do, to speed things here or help with the cooking, until the kitchen is restored?"

"It's good of you to ask, dearest, but no. My granddaughters have the matter in hand." Martha smiled. "That's the advantage of an old-fashioned kitchen, you know. If one is cooking over an open hearth, one can do it almost anywhere and get an edible result. I suspect that those English cooks who've become completely accustomed to closed stoves and Rumford Roasters would find themselves at a loss if they suddenly had to go back to pot-chains and Dutch ovens."

She glanced across the Blue Parlor at

Nelly and Dolley's young sister Anna, who had taken it upon themselves to entertain the three Congressmen, a former colonel of the Continental Army and his wife whom Martha barely remembered, and two complete strangers—a married couple from New York City bearing a letter of introduction from Gouverneur Morris—who had turned up at the door of Mount Vernon to "pay their respects" and gape at Washington's house, Washington's tomb, and Washington's widow.

Though Jemmy and Dolley had paid a visit of condolence just after George's death—in the dead of winter—she had herself been in a state of eerie numbness. It was good to see, among the gawking strangers, a friend she wanted to see.

"Mr. Jefferson intends to have a cooking-stove put in, at any rate," said Dolley. "Not to speak of modern water-closets, so that dreadful little privy can be torn down, that stands in full view of Pennsylvania Avenue, for all the world to see. Mr. Madison and I are staying with him, until we can find a house of our own."

"*Are* there houses available?" Martha's own single view of the Federal City had been of marsh and pastureland, carpenters' sheds and heaps of rubble: a world of cattle, birds, and roving swine through which those sixty-foot-wide avenues cut forlorn swathes leading nowhere.

"Indeed. And more being built every day."

"I own I'm astonished. Of course Eliza's husband speculates in land there, but it appears that's quite a different thing from actually *building* houses for people to live in." She tried to keep the tartness out of her voice and didn't succeed: Mr. Thomas Law was a sore spot in the family. The middle-aged Englishman had arrived in the Federal City five years ago—when it really *was* only a few sheds and a brick-pit—with a dark-eyed half-caste son in tow, who was now at Harvard. Rumor credited him with two more, and Martha could not rid herself of the suspicion that he'd proposed to Eliza only because he knew she was the President's granddaughter . . .

And that Eliza had accepted only because Pattie was on the brink of getting married before her.

Dolley went on, "We shall probably take one of the houses in the same row as the State Department, on the Georgetown road, though Mr. Jefferson would have us stay in the Mansion with him through the whole of his term. I think he doth miss the company of his family. He likes to know there is someone in the house with him."

Across the parlor, Mr. Waln of Pennsylvania said impatiently, "Yes, yes, General Washington was a great believer in the principles of liberty. But he can never have countenanced the license that would result, were girls educated as boys are! We have all seen what comes of that, in France."

"He certainly educated the slaves that he released," pointed out Mrs. Colonel Harris self-righteously.

"That's not the same thing at all! He didn't believe in their *general* education . . ."

"I shall ask Mr. Lear, when next I'm in Georgetown," declared Congressman Waln. "He corresponded a good deal with the President, and should know."

"And I shall write to Judge Washington . . ."

"Of course that 'row' is just six little houses standing in the midst of a marsh," added Dolley thoughtfully, calling Martha's worried attention back. "But while I'm under Mr. Jefferson's roof, I shall attempt to convince him that it is not aristocratical to observe diplomatic protocol, which I gather he came to hate in France. I rather think he feels he owes it to the Democratic-Republicans who voted for him, to have it known that seating at his dinners is *pêle-mêle* and without regard to rules of precedence. But he needlessly sets back his own cause by offending those who are used to it."

"It is a great pity," said Martha, "that he never married again."

An indefinable expression flitted across Dolley's blue eyes. "Perhaps he never found a woman of his own station, who could endure to be his wife." For a moment Martha had the impression that Dolley was thinking of someone specific—surely not that artist's wife in Paris she'd heard rumor of from Abigail? "And whoever she might be," Dolley went on briskly, "I think she would have a struggle of it, to supplant Patsy in his heart."

"Of course," agreed Martha, recalling what she had gathered of the older daughter's fierce protectiveness toward her father. "And understandable, of course . . . But it is a pity that Mr. Jefferson hasn't someone to temper his Republican ideals with a little social common sense."

Her eyes met Dolley's, and Dolley smiled, knowing exactly what Martha meant.

"Mr. Madison doesn't understand either, of course," Dolley said softly. "Though I think, neither doth he understand why Mr. Jefferson is so determined to answer his own front door himself in his bedroom-slippers. I have heard Mr. Jefferson speak many times against women trying to influence politics—having seen how the ladies of the French salons could make or disgrace the King's ministers there. But men will build society wherever they are, and be influenced by it for good or ill. And even a Philosopher King surely hath need of a hostess, not only to make calls on the wives of those who shall be useful to his policies, but to make sure that none who come to his door feel slighted."

"Well," agreed Martha, "it *is* the women who actually run things, you know, whether Mr. Jefferson likes it or not."

Dolley chuckled. "Think what influence Citizen Genêt might have wielded, had he brought with him an amiable wife!"

They both laughed at that, and at the first natural break in the conversation on the other side of the parlor, Dolley invited an opinion of Mrs. Harris, to draw the talk into a general group. Watching Dolley charm the Honorable Representatives from New York and Pennsylvania, Martha reflected again that pro-French or pro-English—and she had certainly entertained enough Frenchmen around the ill-lit dining-tables at Valley Forge and the Hudson Heights—or whatever one felt about alliances and treaties and the National Bank, it took more than a man to govern the country.

There almost had to be a woman beside him and only half a pace behind, to make sure things were run smoothly. Whatever Mr. Jefferson liked to think, politics did not exist in a vacuum. They were a part of men's hearts, and as such, they existed side by side with the other things men kept in their hearts, like the desire for friendship and good company in the evening.

She smiled at the thought of her young friend welcoming diplomats in the blaze of candlelight, and presiding over dinners that were more than simply dinners. Invisibly setting the stage upon which the nation's leader would be seen to speak his lines.

Guard my back, George had said to her, long ago in this parlor: through the soft birdsong of the May morning she could almost hear the sob of that January wind around the eaves. And guarding a general's back—and a ruler's—was a hero's task in itself.

Abigail had guarded her John's, admirably.

And Patsy Jefferson having given over the position in favor of a husband and children of her own, Dolley would, Martha thought, do an admirable labor of guarding Mr. Jefferson's. Or rather, the pair of them, Dolley and Mr. Madison working as a team, Dolley socially and Mr. Madison—that crafty little kingmaker—politically.

As she bade Dolley and the other company good-bye after dinner, Martha reflected she would never have believed she'd welcome into her heart the wife of the man who had stolen her peace.

Which only went to show that one never knew what "happily ever after" was going to consist of.

The Honorable Congressman Waln was still squabbling with Colonel Harris and his wife about whether or not George would have advocated education for young ladies—he'd certainly paid for Harriot's—as they were climbing into their own carriages, each of them quoting examples as if every word George had spoken had been holy writ. The Pennsylvania Congressman's insistence that he was going to ask Tobias Lear about it—the former tutor had spent most of the past year sorting through George's correspondence—brought back to Martha the ugly memory of the private letter Jefferson had sent a friend, in which he'd expressed his opinion of George's support of the British constitution, likening him to Samson having his head shorn by the "harlot England." The friend, good Democratic-Republican that he was, had published it, to score a political point. Completely aside from George's hurt feelings—the matter had very nearly come to a duel—the political implications had been horrific.

The recollection of some of the things George had called various Congressmen over the years in letters to her brought home to her what had to be done . . .

And why.

"Lady Washington?"

She looked up, to see Dolley watching her with concern in her lovely blue eyes. Colonel Harris's chaise, and Mr. Thompkins's rented vehicle, stood already a little way off on the potholed circle of the drive—which Lawrence had sworn he'd given orders *weeks* ago to be repaired. Dolley's carriage waited, with young Anna, and the other two ladies, invited to share the ride as far as Georgetown, already inside.

"Is all well with thee, madame?"

Martha made herself smile, though in fact she felt crushed by the fathoms-deep weariness that had come on her first the day after the kitchen fire. "Quite all right, dearest. But I have something for you."

And from her pocket she brought out the small golden mirror. She pressed it into Dolley's gloved hand.

Dolley turned it to the light, openmouthed. " 'Tis beautiful! Art thou sure? What—?"

"I'm sure. And I'll explain another time." She closed her friend's fingers around it again, and patted her hand gently. "I think this needs to be yours now. Keep it safe. It has a . . . a rather interesting tale. Yes, I should like it to belong to you."

She lifted her hand to them, as the carriages jolted and rattled away.

Guard my back.

There was one thing left to do.

She hated to do it, though she had long

known she must. She remembered, as she passed the door of the Little Dining-Room, how much joy she'd always derived from opening the black wooden chest beneath her bed and reading George's letters. Her own as well, for George—who was not sentimental—always returned them to her when she arrived in winter quarters, or when he got back from Philadelphia to Mount Vernon again. The letters made a sort of diary, a recollection of cares that had seemed colossal at the time, like Harriot completely ruining that straw-yellow muslin dress trying to catch the stable cat, or George's grim despair at trying to extract ammunition from Congress when Congress kept telling him to stop drawing away from the British and attack them.

He'd trusted her, with everything that had been in his heart.

He trusted her still.

And she'd be with George soon, she reminded herself, pausing halfway up the first flight of stairs to catch her breath. Very soon, she thought.

Then she'd be able to talk to him about all that had happened, and to remember it all, good and bad, in its true context.

And nobody else would be able to go prying through their words to one another: what they had thought, what they had feared, how they had loved.

But I can't let myself read even a word of them now, she told herself, as she reached her attic room at last. *If I do I'll be drawn back into that world—of Cambridge, of Valley Forge, of Philadelphia—and Nelly or someone will stop me.*

So she lit a fire in the Franklin stove and gently fed the letters into it, unopened, one by one. Kissing each good-bye and then releasing the past to ashes and smoke: his occasional despair and the anger she'd sometimes felt at him, forty years of love and misunderstandings. The secrets of his heart that he knew she would keep.

The burning took longer than she'd thought. The heat seared the backs of her fingers painfully as she fed and poked, fed and poked, breaking up the fragments until all were consumed: as Prospero had said of his phantoms, *leaving not a wrack behind.*

The stuff that dreams were made of.

When it was done, and the floor around the stove and her chair littered with the faded ribbons in which she'd had the packets tied, she was so tired that she couldn't even rise to walk to the bed.

She bowed her head and wept silently, the furnace-blaze of burning paper slowly fading in the stuffy room. Wept because what she'd done was, like all events in time—Patcy's death or the hesitant smile in George's eyes when first he'd walked into Mrs. Chamberlayne's parlor to meet her—irrevocable.

When she at last raised her head, she saw that there was still daylight in the garret bedroom. Going to the window, she saw the evening's golden brightness beyond the shadow of the house.

Time enough to go down and sit a little with George, before night came on.

The Federal City
Wednesday, May 5, 1801

"*Is* it really the women who actually run things?" Anna, quiet for much of the drive back to the city, turned to Dolley as Mrs. Harris and Mrs. Thompkins waved farewell from the windows of their husbands' carriages and those vehicles pulled away. Both of those ladies had clearly subscribed to their husbands' view—and that of Congressmen Platt and Waln—that men made politics and the womenfolk merely made them comfortable when they got home from more important work.

"Of course it is." Dolley smiled. "Look at Montpelier. Jemmy's father owned the land, and made all the decisions about how much wheat to plant and how much tobacco, and should they buy another mule, but thou knows 'twas Mother Madison who'd say to him in their bedroom at night, 'You've got to do something about getting the kitchen rebuilt,' or, ' 'Tis time to buy new cloth for the slaves' winter things.' And for all Jemmy wrote to the newspapers and to everyone he knew about Mr. Jefferson being elected, nothing would have happened had not Jemmy made sure he knew every one of those Congressmen whilst we lived in Philadelphia. Had *we* not had them to our house there, and later up to Montpelier, to discuss things informally instead of listening to each other's speeches in Congress.

"Mr. Jefferson would rather it were not so, naturally," Dolley went on, shaking her head in kindly affection at the thought of their friend. "Meg Smith told me yesterday that Mr. Jefferson did away with the levees and at-homes Mrs. Adams used to hold. And all the ladies of good society in the city called upon him in a body one morning last week, to force him back into the custom. He, however, went downstairs to them in his riding-clothes, and expressed astonishment at the coincidence of them all calling together like that, at once—and then went right round the room and charmed each one of them individually."

Anna laughed. "He was lucky to get out of the room alive!"

"Mr. Jefferson is an idealist. He would have things be as he likes to think they are, kept separate and pure, like the principles of Liberty or honor, like politics and law, untouched by the realities of the world."

Like his love for his daughter and his love—if love it be—for his Sally?

Like two separate fossil bones, stored in different drawers in different rooms.

Dolley sighed. "But the world is real, Anna. And speeches in Congress tell only half the story, and that not the most important half. Nowadays no man of intelligence believes

Congressional speech in any case. 'Tis what is said in private that counts."

The two carriages behind them turned off down the tree-shaded streets of Georgetown. The gold light of sunset illuminated the woods around them, but already the evening chill gathered under the trees, the peculiarly damp, miasmal cold that seemed to seep out of the ground in this place. Abigail Adams, Sophie had written her, had lived last winter in an agony of rheumatism. And even after only a few days in these marshy lowlands, Dolley was wondering what the effect would be on poor Jemmy.

And indeed, she thought, on Payne. In Philadelphia's muggy summers and damp winters, her son had shown her own tendency to colds and chest complaints. In the mountains at Montpelier he'd been as healthy as a pony. Moreover, she'd already ascertained that there was no such thing as a decent school in the Federal City, and it was getting more and more difficult to get the boy to pay the slightest attention to his tutor. Try as she would not to become one of those fondly doting mamas she had always gently mocked, the thought of losing him filled her with such dread.

She would have to ask some of the older inhabitants of the vicinity—not that there *were* many "old inhabitants" in the city itself!—what they intended for the education of *their* sons.

The trees broke to the left of the road, and Dolley contemplated in passing the six red-brick buildings that stood isolated among them. Like nearly every building within the boundaries of the Federal City, they were surrounded by piles of building debris and a latticework of water-filled wagon-ruts that reflected the limpid gold of the evening sky. The State Department had shut up shop hours ago, its six clerks slogging their way back along the muck of Pennsylvania Avenue to the cluster of boardinghouses, taverns, and small shops that huddled behind the unfinished Capitol, over three miles away.

The house next to the State Department, Dolley knew, would be hers. The headquarters from which she would begin setting up the network of calling and being called upon—the country distances would be a challenge in winter—that cemented the foundations of political support.

She took from her reticule the gold hand-mirror Martha had given her and turned it over in her gloved fingers, admiring the flash of the jewels on the frame—not real, surely?—and the ivory miniature of the sweet-faced lady with old-fashioned ostrich-plumes in her hair. *A tale,* Martha had said. And, *Keep it safe . . .* Which she'd do without being asked, for her dear friend's sake.

In the distance Dolley saw the white-washed walls of the President's House.

"A State prisoner," Martha had called herself, and had dreaded the Federal City that she had herself never seen.

Abigail, Sophie had written to her, had hated the place—Understandably, reflected Dolley, with a pang of pity in her heart for that indomitable Yankee lady who had come to this place only to learn of the death of her younger son.

Yet seeing the white walls, she felt her heart lift, the way it did when she dreamed of flying.

A new city and a new world. A city like none other that the world had known—though she could imagine Mrs. Adams's horrified expression as she agreed with that statement. A city of tulip trees and wild roses, of streams rank with wild grapevines, of open countryside free of the stinking miasmas of Philadelphia's alleys. A city unbuilt, with all the promise of things still within the realm of dreams.

A new city for the new world of Washington's hopes and Jefferson's visions, Mr. Adams's stubborn courage and her own Jemmy's wisdom.

More than Philadelphia, more than the sleepy beauty of Montpelier, Dolley understood that in coming to this place, she had finally come home.

❦ **1814** ❦

❦

Washington City
Wednesday, August 24, 1814
4:30 P.M.

The white sandstone walls of the President's House disappeared behind the trees, and Dolley heard in her mind the whisper of Aaron Burr's beautiful voice: *Has it ever occurred to you that Sophie Hallam might be a British spy?*

Hast thou quarreled? Dolley had asked Burr at once, and immediately felt herself blush for the suggestion that Sophie might be his mistress—which of course Dolley was virtually certain Sophie was, that summer of 1803. Her certainty was confirmed when Burr had grinned, like a wicked older brother to whom Dolley could say anything.

"We have not," he retorted. "Because a

man shares a woman's bed doesn't mean he *has* to be blind to all besides her beauty. And no lovers' spat would excuse a man for inventing such a rumor about a woman. I merely wondered, that's all. She'd make a fine spy."

☙

Stifling in the closed carriage as she fled the capital, one arm draped over the jolting stacks of boxes and bundled papers that threatened to avalanche over her every time the wheels struck another rut, Dolley could see her old friend's face as clearly as if the conversation had occurred yesterday instead of eleven years ago.

☙

"Why should a woman return to this country, whose current government ruined her family, caused the deaths of her father and brother, and drove her and her mother out as camp-followers of the retreating army?" Burr's eyes, brilliant as a poet's, narrowed as if he were reading a court document; he had looked past Dolley and through the oval drawing-room's long windows to the half-built boundary-wall and the inevitable fair of hawkers and hucksters, cockfights and dog-fights, in the grounds behind the President's Mansion that accompanied the Fourth of July celebrations.

The Fourth of July was always boisterous in the Federal City, which was then only be-ginning to be called after its founder. That year—1803—was quadruply ebullient: Pres-ident Jefferson had announced, just that morning, that France had sold the United States all its territory of Louisiana.

There would be no fighting over the West, no threat of Spain once again closing the Mississippi to trade. As a Quaker, Dolley's soul had been deeply satisfied: Fourteen million dollars was less costly than any war she'd ever heard of, and every land-speculator in the country was in ecstasies. Jefferson had held a mammoth levee at the Executive Mansion at noon, and private cel-ebrations were being planned all over the city. Burr had come to the levee alone, and had exchanged no more than a dozen words with Sophie, but turning her head Dolley could pick out her friend Sophie Hal-lam, in very stylish second mourning, deep in conversation with Hannah Gallatin, the wife of the Secretary of the Treasury.

"More curiously," Burr went on, following her gaze, "*how* would she return? Mrs. Hallam's needlework is unexcelled, naturally—" He lifted his punch-cup in salute to Dolley's gown of yolk-yellow silk and silver spider-gauze that had been Sophie's creation. "Yet a woman needs money for materials, to set up as a mantua-maker, much less to purchase a house in Philadelphia—which she did—and another here, which she also did, in excellent parts of both towns. And no one I've ever spoken to has heard of a merchant or banker in England by the name of Hallam. A woman can trade on the capital which, God help them, God gives to women—but it generally leaves its mark, on a woman's soul and on her body also. And I haven't seen it."

Her cheeks hot with anger for Sophie, Dolley drew Burr a little further into the relative privacy of the window—the oval drawing-room which the Adamses had used as an entrance-hall was as full as it could hold—and whispered, "I trust thou wilt understand that should I hear a single word of this ever again from any other source, dear as I hold thee, my friend, our friendship will be at an end."

"I do understand, Mrs. Madison," replied

Burr, inclining his head. "And you will not. I've spoken of this to you alone, solely because of all the women in this city, only you and Jefferson's daughters know the lady well."

Above him, flanked by the rather faded green curtains that Jefferson had purchased for the oval salon, Washington's portrait had gazed into space, as if fiercely disapproving still of Burr after all those years. In addition to the usual Congressmen, speculators, and place-servers, the crowd in the oval drawing-room was enlivened by a number of delegates from Western Indian tribes, in full glory of feathers and paint, and representatives from the piratical Barbary States in a gaudy glory of turbans and pearls.

"However," Burr went on quietly, "those ladies seem to have taken their broods back to Virginia for the foreseeable future. Indeed, it isn't my business to speak of what I cannot prove and only suspect—fond as I am and continue to be of the lady! But as Vice President of this country, I suppose it is my duty to at least let the *wife* of the Secretary of State know that the thought has crossed my mind that there may be an agent of Britain in our midst."

His words returned to Dolley now. Through a haze of dust she watched American militiamen staggering along the dirt road beside the carriage, or straggling in the distance among the trees. Joe kept the horses as close to a gallop as was possible in the ruts of Pennsylvania Avenue: Clinging with one hand to the strap, the other arm fending off boxes, Dolley felt as if her bones would be broken even if they didn't manage to overturn the vehicle.

Through the windows she could see soldiers as well as civilians driving wagons full of supplies. Others rode horses or mules still in the harness of some abandoned dray or limber. There were others, Dolley saw with sudden anger—rough men both black and white in laborers' clothes—driving carts or pushing barrows full of silk dresses, of silver services hastily bundled up in sheets or shawls, even small pieces of expensive furniture or elaborate, imported screens.

Sophie had been right. Such men had probably been just waiting for her carriage to leave the Mansion, to begin looting what she could not save.

Would Sophie wait there, too, for the British troops to come?

Burr may have been a schemer—and later, a traitor—but he had a keen judgment of humankind.

And under ordinary circumstances it wouldn't have mattered what Sophie was in the habit of telling the British Minister. All ministers had informants, who picked up bits of news. It was part of a minister's job. Dolley acknowledged that Sophie—known to be a friend to both Jefferson and Abigail Adams, whose first successes had been due to her friendship with Martha Washington—would be a logical choice for such work.

But these were not ordinary circumstances.

Her mind circled back to Jemmy, sixty-three years old, riding the Bladensburg battlefield in range of the British guns.

I should not have left.

The carriage jolted, veered around a group of stumbling men, without knapsacks or rifles, whose dust-smeared militia uniforms bore the marks of powder but not of blood.

If Jemmy is taken . . .

He won't be, she told herself grimly. *He will have had the sense to flee, when his Army dissolved about him.*

But Jemmy, in masterminding Jefferson's election, had read hundreds of scoffing broadsides that mocked Jefferson's "cowardice" in fleeing Richmond ahead of Benedict Arnold's forces; in getting out of Monticello minutes before Tarleton's dragoons emerged from the woods. The jeers had followed Jefferson for twenty years, never mentioning the fact that Tarleton would almost certainly have hanged the author of the Declaration of Independence, had he caught him.

Would the recollection of the mockery keep Jemmy on the field a few fatal minutes beyond his own last chance to flee?

Please, God, no, Dolley whispered. *Dearest God, hold him safe in Thy hands.*

Horsemen clattered up beside the carriage, the blue of the leader's militia jacket barely visible through the dust. Joe reined in and Dolley put down the window, her hands trembling so badly they could barely work the catches. One of the men she recognized as John Graham, who had been a clerk with the State Department when Jemmy had taken it over—he was Chief there now.

"Where is he?" She thrust open the door,

staggering as she stepped down into the road.

"We don't know, ma'am. But General Winder was defeated. The whole Army's in flight—"

He'll go to the Mansion and be captured. I knew I should not have left.

"Hast heard anything?" Her voice cracked. "Mr. Graham, take me back to the Mansion. I shan't leave him—"

"Mrs. Madison, your being taken will serve him no good—"

"It will if he be taken as well!" She almost screamed the words at him, the whole weight of the day suddenly falling on her, like a dam giving way all at once before the pressure of a flood. Her whole body shook. "I will not leave him! Take the things on to Georgetown, but let me go back!"

"There is no going back," said Graham.

Sukey scrambled from the carriage-box and took her other arm, said with surprising gentleness, "Ma'am, he's right. You can't—"

Like the rolling boom of thunder, an explosion cut across her words. All of them swung around, looking toward the south. Black smoke rolled toward the storm-blackening sky. Even at this distance, Dolley could see in it flickers of flame.

"It's the Navy Yard," said Graham. "Secretary Jones ordered its destruction, to keep our powder and ships out of the hands of the British."

Dolley stood for a long moment, watching the smoke and the flame, as another explosion echoed across those flat green marshes, the scattered buildings and cut-down stumps that made up the Republic's capital. Refugees jostled around them, poured like a dirty river along the road to Georgetown.

More quietly, Graham repeated, "Ma'am, there is no going back."

Dolley let herself be coaxed back into the carriage. Joe whipped up the horses; they clattered on their way.

⚜

Sophie Hallam was still at the Executive Mansion when James Madison stumbled up the front steps. French John, with Pol in her cage and a bottle of the Madisons' best champagne in either coat-pocket, had departed shortly after four, and immediately thereafter looters had broken in, helping themselves to whatever Dolley had left. Sophie had simply retreated to the yellow parlor and seated herself by the window with a pistol and a bottle of champagne—after all, these men and women had presumably paid the taxes that purchased the silver candlesticks and bottles of port and cognac.

She was still there, and the last of the shouting was just dying down in the hall, when she heard Paul Jennings gasp, "Mr. Madison, sir!"

Stepping quickly through the parlor door she saw the little white-haired gentleman stagger, then sink onto one of the hall benches as if he'd been shot. The men with him crowded around, supporting him and jabbering, Sophie thought, like so many frightened monkeys. She crossed unhurriedly to the dining-room, poured a glass of champagne, and brought it back out.

"Drink this, sir."

The thin white fingers could barely keep a grip around the stem, but he glanced up and met her eyes and there was nothing weak or beaten in his sharp glance. "Mrs. Hallam." He shook the others off him—the senior Charles Carroll, whose son had so recently hustled Dolley out of the Mansion, and one of his generals—and stood to bow.

"Mrs. Madison left safely about half an hour ago," reported Sophie calmly—she had always liked Mr. Madison. "And as you see—" She gestured at the shadowy front hall, strewn with Dolley's dresses and shawls, with broken china and sweetly reeking puddles of spilled wine, "—the looters were a bare ten minutes behind."

"I hope you managed to secure something worthwhile for yourself, ma'am?"

"Only memories."

"Ah." Madison sank back onto the bench, closed his eyes. "A woman of discernment." His black clothing was gray with dust, his white hair and dead-white exhausted face, blackened with powder-smoke.

"Dolley, on the other hand, carried off all the Cabinet papers, a small clock, General Washington's portrait, and the drawing-room curtains, so as you see, she exhibited more discernment than I. Will you lie down, sir?"

"Lie down?" exploded old Mr. Carroll. "Dammit, woman, the British are on our heels—!"

"I see no sign of them on the Avenue," Sophie retorted coolly. "And I believe Mr. Madison would be the better for twenty minutes' rest."

"The lady is right, sir," affirmed Mr. Barker, kneeling to hold the wineglass again to Madison's lips. "I think those louts about cleared out the cellar, sir, but I'll have a look round for cognac if thou'rt mindful for it."

Madison shook his head. "I see things have much changed since the days of the Revolution," he murmured. "I would not have believed the difference between a militia force and regulars, had I not seen it today."

"I think it's the British who have changed, sir," replied Sophie. "Since last Americans fought them, they have sharpened their steel against Napoleon. And the generation that has grown up here since that time has done nothing but call one another names."

"They'll rally," said the General bracingly. "Of course they'll rally. And men will come into the city to defend it—"

Madison lifted his fingers, shook his head without opening his eyes.

After a moment, Sophie said, "Mrs. Madison has gone on to Bellevue with your son, Mr. Carroll."

"Too close," Madison breathed. "The British will pass over this city like breaking surf and follow our troops on into Georgetown. Will you be going out there, too, Sophie?"

"Later, yes."

"I must find General Winder—rally the men. Keep the government together." He drew a deep breath and coughed, flinching with pain. Sophie, who had sat with Abigail Adams through bouts of her rheumatism, knew just how agonizing was that net of fire that seemed to clothe bone and muscle beneath the skin. "Should you see my wife before I do, let her know we'll rendezvous at Salona Plantation. It's ten miles up the river and she should be safe there."

"You should rest," said Sophie again, and the old man waved slightly, brushing the suggestion away.

"Since first the British learned they could not hold us by force," he said, "they've been trying to hold us by other means: all the usual tricks that the strong play on the weak. Debt. Extortion. Isolating us from support elsewhere. Bullying. There always comes a time when the bullied must hold the line and say, *No more.* There is never any going back, but what we strive for now is to choose our own path forward, not the path that is most convenient for the merchants and bankers who surround the English King.

"They could not conquer us before but they can break us apart. Once union is sundered—once the government centered in this city shatters—we can be dealt with piecemeal. Each State will go back to being England's handmaiden, now that France and Spain are broken. Sending our men to die in wars of her choosing; paying money to her rather than investing it in ourselves. Tonight—and in the next few weeks—we will need to hold fast."

He sighed, and sat up. An unlikely-looking kingmaker, thought Sophie, to have maneuvered first Washington and then Jefferson into leading the raw new nation in the direction he believed that it should go.

But he was no Richelieu, she thought. When the enemy turned up again, he had mounted his horse and ridden to the battlefield, something not even Washington had done as President. And had it been necessary, she understood, looking down at him, he would have died under the British guns.

"I hope Dolley understands," he said, and Sophie smiled.

"She spoke of defending this house with Patsy Jefferson's Tunisian saber."

His grin was bright as a boy's. "That's my Dolley."

It was yet daylight when they left the Mansion, the last rays of the sun sickly yellow beneath the blackness of the coming storm. Sophie helped Paul Jennings lock up the doors for what she knew was going to be the last time.

Then the young man set off on foot for the Georgetown ferry, and Sophie went back to her house on Connecticut Avenue, to ready her own gig for a drive.

⚜

Not long after that, the British came.

Sophie could see them easily in the thickening twilight. There were about two hundred of them, an advance guard, sailors, not soldiers, with little black hats and tarry pigtails hanging down on their shoulders. Sophie picked out General Ross at their head on a dappled horse, and beside him Admiral Cockburn in his blue Navy uniform. Dust gritted in Sophie's nose and throat.

Where the Avenue crossed Second Street someone fired a single volley from a house on the corner. Ross's horse staggered and fell under him, blood glistening on its neck. The general hadn't even sprung clear of the saddle before men were breaking down the door of the house. A hundred feet away, Sophie saw dark figures dart from the back of the house and vanish into the dusk. An officer came out the front door and called, "Nobody here, sir. And no guns."

Sophie heard Cockburn snarl, "By God, they'll pay for this!" and over his voice Ross's, angry but calm. "Burn the house, Mr. Starrett. Was anyone hurt? Get them back to the ambulance wagons . . . ."

Someone brought him up a fresh horse.

That was the sum total of the capital's defense.

The men set up a rough camp on an empty field east of the Capitol Building. From the trees that surrounded the nearby Carroll Hotel, Sophie watched the detachment led by Ross ascend Capitol Hill, the flares of their torches dripping fragments of tar that burned in the dirt behind them as the Devil's hoofprints were said to burn. She heard the crack of rifles, the shattering of

window-glass. Moments later, scarlet re-
flections flitted in the windows of the two
legislative houses and in the open wooden
passageway between. They must have
either brought powder with them, she
thought, or found it there. The sound it
made when it exploded in the connecting
passageway was unmistakable, and as the
flames rippled up, Sophie saw the men
moving about inside, gathering up whatever
they could to feed the blaze.

They moved on by torchlight up Pennsylvania Avenue, walking in double column
without drum-beat or bugle, muffled footsteps a heavy whisper in the dust. Strange
little gusts of wind had begun to stir the
trees, and overhead the tar-black sky was
streaked with heat-lightning. Like the ghost
of her own parents—or of the girl she had
once been—Sophie followed in her dark
gown, as if she'd been assigned the task by
someone else, to fulfill a rite for those who
were dead.

She stood for a long time outside the President's House, watching torchlight play
through the windows as it was first searched,
then ransacked for whatever the looters had
missed. Since that first winter, when she'd

called on Abigail Adams, the place had gone from a dank and gloomy cavern to a very respectable mansion, thanks to Jefferson's delight in remodeling, and to Dolley's exquisite taste.

They might all have saved themselves the trouble.

As her grandparents might have, back in Virginia, had they known.

She had waited a long time, she reflected, to watch this. And yet she felt almost nothing. She heard the breaking glass as the men smashed out the ground-floor windows, and torchlight flowed around the doors as everyone came out again. By that torchlight she saw Ross line up men outside each window, with poles like javelins in their hands. At the end of each pole was a ball about the size of a soup-plate—oiled rags. The British army had a system for everything.

A torch was borne the full circuit of the house, touching each javelin in turn, until the white sandstone walls were ringed with fire. In the silence Sophie was aware of others, half glimpsed in shadow, among the young trees that Mr. Jefferson had had planted to screen the house from the Avenue. Civilians, watching in silence—listening to the shouts of the bands of stragglers from the British camp who were now roving through the darkness, looking for what they might steal.

General Ross spoke his word of command, and a color-sergeant shouted it. In unison the men threw their javelins through the broken windows, like a well-crafted machine. The whole house went up at once, each window around the lower floor glaring like yellow eyes into Hell. Red flickered, then blazed, in those on the second floor.

For a time they stood in silence and watched it burn.

Thinking what? Sophie wondered. *Feeling what?* The sweet brandy of vengeance? Or just a solid craftsmanlike awareness of a job well done?

Had any man of them been born in these colonies? Watched his own family's house go up in flames, knowing there was no other place of refuge to be had in all the land?

She wondered why she felt so little. Flames licked through the windows, danced over the blazing roof. Yet her only experience was a slight sensation of disappointment: like the much-anticipated embrace of a lover who turns out to be only a man like other men.

She tried to recapture the shouts of the patriot militia who'd torched her grandparents' plantation, but the only words she heard were Madison's: *There is never any going back, but what we strive for now is to choose our own path forward.*

And Dolley: *We all need reminders of who we were and where we came from, if our hearts are to survive.*

But survive to go on to where?

And others behind them, like spectres taking shape within the smoke. Plump little Mrs. Washington, hiding her fears for the General and her grandchildren behind chatty efficiency. Mrs. Adams like spring-steel, ready to shed her own blood or anyone else's for John's sake and for her country's. Sally seeming to appear and disappear through the smoke, a spirit outlasting scandal and time.

If I hate those men and what they did, I must hate the women who helped them—let them—be what they were.

Yet she found she did not. Nor did she feel pity for them. Only the comradeship of those who have passed through the same battle, albeit on different parts of the field.

Liberté—Amitié: Liberty and love, that most ancient of conundra. *Did* all things come at last to where they were meant to be?

Sophie had meant to go to General Ross, when the burning was done, as she'd been instructed to do, and let him know where Dolley and her husband were to be found. A fast-moving company could be at Salona Plantation by midnight. She knew Mr. Madison was right: Without a rallying-point, the scattered militia companies, the fragments of the fast-dissolving government, would disperse.

Without a central focus, the individual States would take up their old position of leadership, and each State—squabbling with the others as usual over debts and privileges and shipping rights as they had all throughout the Revolution and for four years beyond—could be dealt with piecemeal far more easily than the Congress of the whole.

But when the officers barked out orders to form up columns, Sophie turned away.

Fairfax County, Virginia
Thursday, August 25, 1814
1:00 A.M.

From the upper windows of a house called Rokeby, Dolley watched Washington City burn.

Though it lay some ten miles off, she could see the red reflection against the underside of roiling clouds of smoke. The trees around the house tossed and fretted as the winds strengthened. The sky smelled of storm, and of smoke.

Dolley felt very, very tired.

Jemmy at least was safe. Or at least he had been safe four hours ago, when he and his little band of friends had caught up with her carriage on the river road. The team's pace had slowed to a crawl, the way blocked by carts, carriages, wheelbarrows, and dead-tired trudging militia, mostly invisible in the suffocating darkness. Like themselves, everyone in Georgetown had realized that the British would sweep through the city.

Somewhere ahead of them was a family with a wailing baby. Its cries wrenched Dolley's heart. Was there no one there to comfort it? Then Sukey had called down from the box, "Riders comin' behind us, ma'am!" and the next instant, it seemed, lantern-light flashed in the window of the carriage and old Mr. Carroll's voice called out, "Mrs. Madison?"

And a moment later, Jemmy's, unmistakable, "Dolley?"

The drivers behind them cursed as Joe reined the team over. Men and women jostled past with barrows and bundles, sparing barely a glance as the tall buxom black-haired woman nearly fell out of the carriage into the arms of the dust-covered little man.

For a time Dolley knew nothing and cared less, only the grip of Jemmy's arms around her and the taste of his mouth on hers. *Dear God, he's alive! Dear, dear God, Thou has spared him. . . .*

"Move along there!" groused someone behind them whose wagon couldn't pass on the narrow road. "We ain't got all night here!" and another voice added, "Kiss 'er in the carriage, pilgrim!"

"Shut up, Matt, let 'em kiss!" retorted a woman's voice. "Catch me kissin' you, if you was lost."

"I can't stay." Jemmy's hands gripped her

shoulders as he spoke, as if convincing himself against all odds that they were together,
both alive, both unhurt. "We've heard the
men are regrouping in Fairfax County—perhaps at Wren's Tavern, or near there. They
say that's where Monroe has gone."

"Where shall we meet, then?" asked Dolley.

"Salona. If I don't reach there tonight, or
can't reach there, meet me tomorrow night
at Wiley's Tavern near Little Falls. I should at
least know by then what is being done, by
way of counterattack."

"All right." He looked ready to drop, but
there was no time for more, and Dolley only
drew him to her again in fierce embrace,
whispered, "God go with thee."

"And thee." He cupped her face in his
hands, kissed her again, hard. "We'll come
through this, Doll. And come through victo-
rious."

It was only after he'd ridden away, that
Carroll mentioned that Sophie Hallam had
been present when Salona had been decided upon as their meeting-place.

Rokeby House lay about a mile from Salona, and from it Dolley hoped to be able to
watch the road. The house was crammed

already with other refugees, mostly people she'd met at receptions and parties over fourteen years in Washington City. Her very young hostess, Mrs. Love, offered her her own bedroom for the night, and would have found floor-space for herself in one of the already innlike guest-rooms had not Dolley forbidden her to even think of such a thing.

Mrs. Love—Tilly, a connection of Jemmy's by marriage *(wasn't everyone in Virginia?)* who'd been a child in the schoolroom when Dolley first came to the Federal City—slept now on the bedroom day-bed she'd had made up, her pet gray cat in her arms like a doll. Her blond braids hung out from under the makeshift tent of mosquito-netting in the glow of the single candle. The big house had fallen silent an hour ago, save for the restless rushing of the trees outside, like the sound of the sea in the darkness. Even the noises of fugitives on the river road had ceased.

The smell of rain and lightning rode like a seraph on the night.

And what now?

Even with her spyglass, Dolley couldn't see much more of the fires than the red flash of flames, but it seemed to her that they were confined to several wide-separated localities. At least, she thought, no matter how hard the wind blew, flames from one house wouldn't automatically ignite a whole neighborhood, as they would in Philadelphia. She had to smile a little at that, thinking of how everyone but herself had moaned and wailed about Washington City's endless distances and scattered houses. If they wished to torch the city, the British would have to do it house by house.

Her own house, she knew, was one of those in flames. She saw the dining-room again in her mind, all dressed in its white and silver as it had been on those evenings when Jefferson had sent her a hasty note begging her to come and preside at his dinner, as there would be other ladies present.

Even for a philosopher who considered etiquette a worthless nuisance, there were limits.

The thought brought others. She turned to her reticule in quest of her snuffbox, and recalled again she'd left it in the desk-drawer, and with it the Queen's golden mirror. *So it was destined to vanish after all,* she thought, and felt the stab of grief for what could not be retrieved. For some moments it was as if she'd lost Martha again, and all those vanished days, those years of joy and trial, with her.

Burned to ashes, as Sophie's early years had been burned, leaving only stony irony and revenge.

Weeping, strangely enough, made her feel better. *Maybe I just hunger for snuff.* After a few minutes she raised the spyglass again, turned it toward the road. Though the night was pitch-black, she'd been aware that more than refugees prowled the darkness. Twice, since the flow of fugitives had slacked, she'd seen torchlight, and forms moving among the trees. American stragglers or British, she didn't know.

Waiting to ambush Jemmy, as he rode to Salona, thinking to join her?

But when she thought of Sophie, and of the roving bands of British soldiers, she pushed her doubts aside and breathed a prayer for the safety of her friend. It was said that British stragglers had stripped the countryside between their landing-point at Benedict and the city itself. The half-dozen men and boys in the house, including her host, were grouped in the downstairs hall, but in the event of a determined incursion by the enemy their collection of dueling-pistols and hunting-arms could only serve to trigger deadly violence.

Sooner than that, she thought, as torches and lanterns began to gather again on the road beyond the trees, *I will give myself up.* The thought turned her sick with dread.

Even flight out the back door and into the surrounding woods might not serve to save her hosts or their dwelling. And in the woods would be looters, and runaway slaves.

She strained her eyes at the glass, to penetrate the wild darkness. On the road she could only guess at a confusion of movement, but it seemed to her there was a large force there. The roaring of the trees carried away any sound. For interminable minutes Dolley watched, heart pounding, before the flickering spots of fire retreated back into the darkness, in the direction from which they'd come.

A single speck of flame detached itself from the woods. Bobbed through the wind-whirled blackness toward the house.

Dolley took a deep breath, and went downstairs.

Joe the coachman was just opening the

front door when Dolley reached the hall. So-phie Hallam stood on the threshold with a lantern in her hand. "Who was that?" Dolley asked, breathless, and Sophie replied with a shrug, "Merely some gentlemen who'd missed their way. I sent them back toward Georgetown." Sophie's eyes met Dolley's for a silent moment, tired and bitterly sad. Then Dolley stepped forward and took her in her arms.

"That was good of thee," she said softly, and led her to the stairs.

"Are you all right?" whispered Sophie, as they entered the silent bedroom above.

Dolley nodded. "I've seen Jemmy." Hesi-tantly, she added, "Hast thou been to Sa-lona?" and Sophie raised a brow, as if she knew exactly what was in Dolley's mind. Through the open window spits of rain had begun to fall. The wild air outside was sud-denly thick with the breath of the storm.

"I have—alone—and Mr. Madison is not there yet, though I suspect he's safe. The men have marched thirteen miles in the heat from Bladensburg today, *and* fought a bat-tle," she added. There was anger in her voice for the frustrated weariness of the British soldiers—Dolley knew instinctively whom she meant by *the men*—faced once again with the conquest of cities in a hostile countryside far too big to subdue.

They were, when all was said, back exactly where they had been in 1776. And they knew it.

"Now the rain's begun, even the stragglers will turn back." Sophie gazed into the night. Flames flickered through the trees.

"Did they burn the house?"

"Of course. And the Capitol. And more tomorrow, I think."

Dolley closed her eyes, too tired even to think. Remembering Martha, faithfully journeying to all those winter camps. The British had held the cities and the ragged colonial Army had all they could do to keep them bottled up there, in a grueling eight-year stalemate that only France had broken, for reasons of France's own. Remembering Mr. Adams's after-dinner stories of Abigail, trying to keep house and household together in the face of British raids and what the War had done to the country—

We were young then, and the country was young.

"Must we do it all again?" She wasn't even

aware she'd spoken her thought aloud, until Sophie replied, "Would you not want to?"

In her mind, Dolley saw the red coats of Banastre Tarleton's dragoons, like splashed blood against the brown Virginia woods, on their way to sack Monticello. Saw the children and the families that had been left behind when Abigail, or Martha—or she herself—had made the choice to follow a man, and give to their offspring only what was left over, of their hearts, their energy, their too-finite time.

"I am not sure that I could," she answered at last. "I don't mean the fighting. *Ye shall hear of wars, and rumors of war: these things shall come to pass.* But what it costs, to forge a new world. For it doth take the life of a man, and more of his life than he hath in him to give: constant labor and for the most part unthanked. We have both seen this. And if we go with him—whether to wash his shirt and load his rifle, or to preside over a thousand ill-matched dinners, or only to make sure that he hath a safe place at night to lay his head—do we not betray our children, by giving to the new world what should rightly have been theirs?"

"Are you thinking of Eliza Custis and her

sisters?" asked Sophie quietly. "Or poor Charley Adams—and even poorer Nabby and Johnny?"

Or the slave-born boy everybody at Monticello except Patsy called President Tom, and his brothers and sister?

Or—and Dolley flinched from the thought—Payne Todd, Virginia planter's son, currently living a life of extremely expensive dissipation in Ghent?

Far-off thunder boomed. Rain whirled in at the window, pounding hard now, and the two women struggled to close the casement against it. The candle flame on its table leaned drunkenly, then straightened; water poured down the panes as if from a bucket.

"It seems now that it all hath been for nothing," Dolley murmured. "The country we have tried to build with our dear friends hath all but torn itself to pieces, not only with lies but with different truths. The Revolution in France that split us apart hath ended in Napoleon, and now he, too, is gone down in defeat. A King sits on France's throne and the English Army is once again on our shores. After all we have given, we stand where we stood before, having robbed our children to no purpose."

"Had I faith in God," replied Sophie, folding her arms, "I would remark that nothing in this world lies outside His purpose. As I don't, I will only point out that they—those children—*are* the new world. And bear in themselves all the treasure, good and bad, of the old. Payne would be Payne, however he was raised. His sins might take a different form, but he would still sin them, and bring down your heart in sorrow to the grave—if you let him. Abigail's brother was a drunkard, in spite of loving, intelligent parents who *didn't* deposit him with relatives and go running off to play politics in France. I don't think there was a thing she could have done to save either him or Charley, or Nabby and Nabby's children. Maybe there never is."

"No," Dolley whispered tiredly. "No, thou art right. It needs no revolution for sons and daughters both to make foolish choices that lead them to unhappiness. We only think there *should have been* something that we could have done."

"But you'll never get Abigail to admit it," said Sophie briskly. "Do you think we could open the window again a little? The rain seems to be slacking and it's like an oven in here."

Only a trace of the stench of smoke remained in the green sweet magic that filled the room with the opening of the window again. The magic of a summer night in Virginia. Dolley leaned her forehead against the wet window-jamb, breathing in the scent of it, and with it the childhood she'd shared with Sophie in Hanover County, while Jemmy was off studying law and reading Tom Paine and going to Princeton and falling in love with that dreadful Fulton girl who broke his heart, all unbeknownst to her.

The past and the dreams she'd felt, an hour ago, to have been lost with a Queen's mirror in a burning Mansion, suffused the air around her with their living presence, as close as the patter of rain on the trees.

"They may have taken the city," said Dolley, looking out through the blackness where lightning still flickered, but where now no trace of flame could be seen. "Yet Mr. Madison will rally the militia, and the tide will turn. We will drive them out as we did before. And make our new world, in their despite."

A half-smile touched the corner of Sophie's mouth, just before the guttering candle puffed itself out in a whisper of smoke. "Do you know," she replied softly, "I think we will."

EPILOGUE

⌖

McKeowin's Hotel, Washington City
Thursday, December 7, 1815

As she moved through the crowd in the candle-lit ballroom of the largest hotel in Washington City—far larger than either the Tayloe town house that had been their original temporary quarters or the dwelling near the State Department they now occupied—Dolley found herself remembering Martha again. Thinking of Abigail Adams as well: her predecessors in this exacting and curious task of creating the unspoken background against which the President of the United States was perceived to stand.

Even Jefferson, who'd claimed the background of "State" didn't exist, had taken great pains to establish the reverse and paint himself as Common Man Extraordinaire. His only failure in that stage-management had been Sally, still with him at Monticello despite the horrific scandal that James Callendar had trumpeted in the newspapers during Jefferson's second year in office.

To be President was to do more than to simply hold an office. Like it or not, it was about more than simple "presiding." Jemmy had understood from the first that in times of trouble, the President was and must be the man around whom other men would rally, as they had rallied—a little to his surprise, Dolley thought—around him.

She was sorry Jefferson had not come tonight. He had emerged from the quiet of Monticello to greet tonight's guest of honor at Lynchburg, recognizing in him, perhaps, his heir. Jack Eppes was here, somewhere in this mob, and she must, Dolley thought, extend a special welcome to him for poor Maria's sake. After Maria's death, Jefferson's younger son-in-law had wed a very youthful heiress named Miss Jones—and according to Sukey, had taken Sally Hemings's niece Betsie as his mistress. But as this was something that she, Dolley, wasn't supposed to know, she would greet him like a good Virginian: In addition to being an old friend, he was one of Jemmy's supporters in Congress.

Part of the Presidentress's job was not to have opinions, anyway.

No wonder poor Abigail had always had trouble with the position.

As she struggled to move through the crowd—it seemed as if everyone in Washington had jammed themselves into the hotel's ballroom, and more arriving all the time—she spared a smile for that redoubtable old lady, safely ensconced, Sophie had informed her, with her dearest John in Quincy. Abigail did not write Sophie as often now as she had done before Nabby's death from cancer of the breast, but her last letter had mentioned that her John and their old friend Jefferson had resumed their friendship at last.

Despite the raw cold outside, the ballroom was suffocatingly hot. Pomade, candle wax, and wool coats competed with the cloying of women's perfumes. Wax dripped from the glittering chandeliers. Silk gowns made splashes of color in the thick amber light, among the dark clothing of the men. From inside, it was difficult to believe that beyond the dark windows stretched empty acres of frozen marshes and cow-pastures that were still the leading characteristics of Washington City.

For some time after the British left, during those days when even old friends were refusing Dolley's dinner invitations, Congress had debated where to move the capital. Somewhere beyond the mountains, certainly. But, if the British took New Orleans, that would scarcely be safer.

Dolley smiled, as she looked around the overcrowded chamber, and beyond the black windows, to the answering sparkle of candle-lit windows in the dark distances.

It was astonishing, how swiftly that had changed.

Out of the babel of talk all around her, three words kept bobbing to the surface.

"New Orleans."

And, "Jackson."

"Not a Federalist in the room." Sophie Hallam appeared at her elbow, sliding serpentlike from a wall of bodies Dolley could not have breached with a battering-ram. "Nor anyone who has ever been one. Just ask them."

Dolley laughed, and shook her head. "Dost remember that horrid woman at Wiley's Tavern, when we went there to meet Jemmy before coming back to town?"

Sophie set her fists to her hips and mimicked: "Miz Madison! If that's you, get out! Your husband has got mine out fighting, and damn you, you shan't stay in my house!"

"She had the right, alas," sighed Dolley. "And I cannot fault her for speaking her heart. Compared to what those wretched newspapers said later, she was quite refined."

"Mama!" Payne worked his way in from the hall, trailed by Jack Eppes. Blond hair a little tousled, eyes as bright and blue as Dolley's own, and sparkling with pleasure. "What a triumph! You know the downstairs is packed tight as a cheese-hoop, and every one of them singing your praises and Papa's, at least as much as they are the General's."

" 'Tis kind in thee to say so, dearest." She beamed at him and pressed her hand to his cheek, glad to have her son home again. He'd been vague about how he'd gotten along with the younger Mr. Adams—Abigail's Johnny—during the negotiations for the peace treaty in Ghent, but the reports sent by the other delegate, Dolley's fellow Hanover County émigré Henry Clay, hadn't been encouraging. Once the peace had been signed, the younger Mr. Adams had returned to St. Petersburg where he was the Minister. Instead of coming back with Henry Clay, Payne had gone on to Paris.

He'd been home only a few weeks now, but the bills were already starting to come in.

Still, Dolley reflected, her handsome son had acquired a whole new polish in Paris, from the tips of his patent-leather pumps to his shining golden curls. Surely that was something.

"Truly, Mama, it's your triumph tonight." Payne kissed Dolley's hand. "Yours and Papa's." Dolley wondered for an instant if Payne even recalled his first Papa, the Papa who had adored him. . . .

He didn't seem to. He went on blithely, "But Papa just disappears in a crowd, while you stand out as a beacon for everyone I've talked to: *such* a gown! Your work, ma'am?" he asked Sophie. "Mama, Jack says there's to be a gathering of some of the choicer spirits down at Ogle's tonight—just for a little jollification, you know—" He leaned close to her, sliding effortlessly into the real reason for seeking her out, "—and with one thing and another I haven't a sou to call my own. Would Papa mind very much if I stopped by the house on our way there, and fished a little in his desk-drawer? I shouldn't need but twenty dollars or so."

His breath smelled of port and champagne. Dolley guessed that of the fifty dollars' housekeeping money in Jemmy's desk, not a dollar would be left if she said yes, but it wasn't the time or the place for an argument. She said, "*Only* twenty—*and* I shall count it—"

"Mama—" He gave her his angel smile. "I'm a reformed character now! Besides, we need to celebrate! How often have we the nation's savior to entertain?"

As she watched his tall height, his broad shoulders in their beautifully cut Parisian coat weave through the crowd toward the ballroom door, Dolley tried to hope that her son hadn't already helped himself to the contents of the drawer *before* coming here to ask.

She knew there was gambling going on already in the parlors downstairs. There would almost certainly be tables of whist, vingt-et-un, and faro at Mr. Ogle's.

It was something, she hoped, that Payne would outgrow.

But she'd hoped that before she'd sent him off to the Netherlands to learn a diplomat's trade. She'd hoped, indeed, that he could have stepped in as Jemmy's secretary, as Johnny Adams had been the former President's. Dearly as she loved her boy, Dolley was honest enough to admit that only a wittol would appoint Payne as secretary to anything.

It was simply not his skill.

"I trust, at least, there'll be no more talk of moving the capital?" Sophie's voice broke into Dolley's thoughts, and thankfully, Dolley turned her mind from the ongoing, hurtful puzzle of what Payne's skills *were.*

"No, and I cannot say how thankful I am for it. I've a mind to go over to Mr. Clay and General Jackson and kiss the pair of them." She smiled in the direction of the two tall Westerners, whose heads could be seen above the crowd at the far end of the room. Clay, born only a few miles from her father's farm at Coles Hill, was one of the handsomest men she'd ever seen. His tawny brilliance seemed to blaze across the room like fire. Jackson, beside him, had that shining quality as well: cadaverously thin, maniacally intense, gesturing furiously to Clay as he spoke in his hoarse booming voice.

The victor at New Orleans. The man who'd driven the British into the sea.

The one people meant now, when they said "the General."

"They have already begun to rebuild the President's Mansion. Jemmy hath said that he's instructed the commissioners, that the house shalt be rebuilt exactly as it formerly was."

"For 'the General' to come in and put his feet on the table?" Sophie followed Dolley's glance, her gray gaze steely. "And for 'Miz Rachel'—" She imitated Jackson's harsh drawl, "—to serve up hush-puppies and burgoo to the representatives of Europe's Kings? He'll be President, you know." She glanced down at Dolley. "Oh, we'll probably have one last hurrah of gentility in Mr. Monroe, but can you really see a colorless cold fish like Johnny Adams being able to defeat the Victor of New Orleans?"

"General Jackson doth seem to be a force of nature," agreed Dolley.

Sophie sniffed. "The boiled-down quintessence of the worst of the Revolutionary patriots mixed with the worst of the French radicals. No wonder Jefferson came down from his mountain to greet him the other day. You managed to miss him when he was in Congress—Jackson, I mean—not that he was in town long before he resigned and went home in high dudgeon. Jackson and his over-mountain men will run the last of good manners out of the government like a house-fire."

Dolley thought about what she said, as Eliza Custis Law—who had the distinction a few years ago of being the first woman in Washington City to be divorced—came surging out of the crowd to regale Sophie with the tale of her own sufferings and heroism last August.

It was true, as Payne had said, that Jemmy tended to disappear in crowds. Had Dolley not known where to look—in the corner by the chimney—she wouldn't have been able to find her husband at all. As it was, it was only because he was with tall Jim Monroe that he was even visible. What kind of Presidentress would the aloof and sickly Elizabeth Monroe make? An epileptic who hesitated to go out into company at all? Sophie said she'd seen a miniature of young Mr. Adams's wife Catherine—beautiful and accomplished, by all accounts. . . .

"Excuse me, ma'am." A soft voice spoke at her elbow, with the gentle accent of Virginia. "Are you familiar with this establishment? Could you tell me if there's so much as a square foot where I might retire and rest, just for a minute—"

"Of course!" Dolley sized up the woman beside her instantly as one of the throngs who'd come pouring into the town to see the General and his family: a planter's wife from the western counties of Virginia, to judge by the old-fashioned cut of her gown. Her own age, and getting stout, but still very pretty: dark hair framing a soft rectangular face, kindly dark eyes with an echo in them of hardships that had left her weary. "A sort of little parlor lieth just off the stair-landing, that they always set aside for ladies here— at least I hope they've remembered to do so tonight! My experience is that whenever one hath a headache, or had someone step on one's flounce, that's the occasion when one's hosts have decided to put the retiring-room in the broom-closet or a corner of the scullery. . . ."

"At least in a public hotel one isn't going to find the broom-closet's been turned into a dormitory for the guests' servants—"

Dolley laughed, remembering the crowds of overnight guests at Montpelier for Francis's funeral, or at Monticello when Maria wed Jack Eppes.

"To be honest," her new protégée went on, "if I could return to our lodging I would—I'm not much use at parties. And traveling, I'm always afraid our son will wake alone in a strange place—he's only six—"

"What's his name?" asked Dolley, liking the lilt of joyful pride in this woman's voice when she spoke of her child.

"Andrew. For his father." And at the sound of General Jackson's voice from the other side of the room, her eyes softened and changed, and Dolley realized who this had to be.

"Thou'rt not Mrs. Jackson?" she exclaimed.

The woman hesitated, genuinely unwilling to put herself forward, then said, "Yes, I am. I'm sorry—"

Dolley held out her hand impulsively. "And

I'm Mrs. Madison. *Drat* these public assemblies where they haven't a proper receiving-line. I have so wanted to meet thee." She recalled someone—Sophie?—telling her there had been some scandal attached to Rachel Jackson's name—bigamy? But her impression was that the woman had been more sinned against than sinning. In any case General Jackson had already fought a number of duels whose ostensible cause was his wife's reputation.

And this soft-voiced Virginia lady was a far cry indeed from the pipe-smoking frontierswoman she'd been led to expect, although of course it was perfectly possible that Mrs. Jackson did smoke a pipe in the privacy of her own front porch. She herself would certainly have killed for a pinch of snuff at the moment.

"Rot!" She heard Jackson's strange, hoarse voice slash out over the general din. "That's the business of the States, not the Congress. There's no reason on earth why a State shouldn't have the sovereign right to—"

Dolley's eyes met Mrs. Jackson's. The two women wheeled as one toward the far end of the room, where the red-haired General seemed to be working himself up to the point of physical assault on Congressman Webster beside the punch-bowl. Rachel Jackson headed straight for her husband with the air of one who has matter-of-factly defused a thousand such arguments.

Before Dolley could reach the scene, her sister Anna had appeared as if by magic at Webster's elbow; Dolley could almost hear her asking breathlessly, as Dolley had taught her, for some information about farming—specific to Webster's own New England acres. Jackson turned aside at the touch of his wife's hand on his sleeve.

Beside her, Dolley heard Eliza Custis Law's booming voice declare, "*Horribly common—*"

"Yet men will follow him," murmured Sophie, reappearing at Dolley's other side. "I take it the lady in blue is Mrs. Jackson?" Watching the pair of them together, Dolley was startled and touched at the transformation of the General's cold blue eyes, as he looked down into the face of his wife. "I have this for you," she added, taking something from her reticule. Dolley saw that it was her old tortoiseshell snuffbox, the one she'd left in the desk-drawer at the Mansion before her flight.

When Dolley looked at her in astonishment, Sophie went on, "I found it only this afternoon, in a pawnshop in Alexandria, when I went to fit Mrs. Harrison for that red dress she's wearing that makes her look like an animate petunia."

"A looter must have got to the parlor desk," said Dolley wonderingly, "before the Mansion was burned. I wonder if they took the Queen's mirror as well? It was in the same drawer—"

"And is obviously worth twenty times as much," Sophie reminded her. "I believe we can safely assume that in time, the mirror, too, will return to the light. So it might do to alert Mrs. Jackson to be on the lookout for it, when she returns to Washington as Presidentress herself." She glanced sidelong at Dolley, then back at Jackson, and sniffed. "God help you—us—all."

Dolley turned the snuffbox over in her gloved fingers, her own gaze following Sophie's across to the General and his Rachel.

"Yes," she said slowly. "Yes, I believe God will help us all. In spite of ourselves. Jemmy hath always said that the point of the Con-

stitution—the point of all that we have sacrificed ourselves for—is that no matter *who*
is captain, the ship is able to move forward.
And it is the ship, and her cargo, that is important."

She looked back, smiling, into her friend's
eyes. "They shall play their part, as we have
played ours: thou and I both, Sophie. I
trust," she added quietly, "that thou wilt remain to see it?"

"To tell the truth," drawled Sophie, "I came
here tonight intending to tell you that I was
returning to England. Since my business
here seems to be at an end." She didn't say
what business, and Dolley didn't ask.

"But do you know," she went on, looking
about her at the candle-lit room, the illuminated city in the darkness beyond, "I just
might find another business, and stay."

Dolley couldn't resist the urge to say,
"Possibly even dressmaking?" and caught a
sidelong glance of startled enlightenment,
before Sophie's features softened into a
smile.

"Maybe even that," Sophie agreed.

"Gentlemen, I regard it as the duty of the
government to improve the lives and affairs
of its citizens," Henry Clay was saying in

that gorgeous voice, and Jackson's head swiveled in his direction like an artillery-piece sighting.

"It is *nothing* of the kind, sir!"

He surged in Clay's direction. As she, Sophie, and Rachel moved to head off again the volcanic violence that always seemed to bubble beneath the surface of politics, Dolley wondered if anything ever really changed.

Watching the dance of politics and civility, of what is said and what is shown, it seemed to her almost as if the War that she remembered so clearly were in another lifetime, a hundred years ago and not thirty-five. As if the storm of ink and invective had not almost torn the new Republic apart, had not severed friends, had not brought men within a step of tearing up the Constitution and throwing away everything for which they had risked their lives and those of their families. The great patriots had all gone home. Mr. Adams to his Abigail, Jefferson to his Patsy—and his Sally, in their ambiguous private world. General Washington and Martha to their "happily ever after" at last.

And in another fifty years, thought Dolley, *we shall all of us be gone, too.*

But the ship would sail on.

Carrying Payne, she thought with mingled foreboding and love.

Carrying General Jackson and his Rachel, young Johnny Adams and his gently bred bride, the Custis girls and Jefferson's children and grandchildren both white and black, forward into a world she could not even imagine.

New quarrels, new issues, new leaders; new answers to the same questions of Federal and State, taxes and debts, principle and compromise, liberty and love.

She laid her hand on Mr. Clay's arm just as Rachel caught her husband's sleeve once more, unobtrusively, each woman turning the man aside from a quarrel that could transform a celebration into a brawl. By the time Jemmy and Jim Monroe sprang into action from their chimney-corner to head off the fracas they hadn't even seen coming, Dolley had deftly passed Clay along to Nelly Lewis; she heard Rachel making some innocuous query of her husband about the lineage of a horse, and almost laughed.

Jemmy slipped an arm around Dolley's waist.

"I knew I might count on you," he whispered. Then, more loudly, he added, "Gentlemen, a toast." He raised his cup, looked to the General to propose it.

Jackson's glance touched Rachel's, and she nodded shyly. He raised his cup to Dolley, and said, "I shall leave that to the Presidentress."

Dolley caught the smile in those chilly pale eyes, saw how close he, too, kept one arm around Rachel, as if guarding her from harm. Not a complete barbarian, after all.

She raised her glass, and said, "To the world to come."

POSTSCRIPTUM

Rachel Jackson never inhabited the White House. She died in 1828, just after her husband was elected seventh President of the United States.

Abigail Adams died in 1818, at the age of seventy-four. Both the house in which she raised her children in Quincy, Massachusetts, and the one she shared with John after their return from Europe—Stonyfield (later Peacefield) Farm—still stand. The roses and lilac she brought back from England to plant in the garden still grow there.

Her niece Louisa never married, remaining Abigail's companion until the old lady's death. Louisa herself died in 1857, at the age of eighty-four.

Johnny—John Quincy Adams—was elected sixth U.S. President in a four-way split that threw the hotly contested election of 1824 into the House of Representatives. He was the first second-generation President. He was also the only U.S. President to serve in the House of Representatives after his Presidential term, which he did with great distinction, for the rest of his life, literally, dying there after a stroke in 1848.

John Adams lived til 1826, dying at the age of ninety on the Fourth of July, the fiftieth anniversary of the signing of the Declaration of Independence. A few hours earlier that same day, Thomas Jefferson, aged eighty-three, died at Monticello, almost bankrupt and living under the knowledge that his treasured mountaintop haven would have to be sold to pay his debts.

With Jefferson's death, Patsy Jefferson Randolph fled her husband and lived with her daughter Ellen in Boston until Randolph was on his deathbed, in 1828. Monticello was sold after Randolph's death, but can— like Mount Vernon and Peacefield Farm, and Montpelier (in the process of restoration as this book is being written)—be visited today.

Martha's beloved granddaughter Nelly went on to a life of depression and loss, seeing seven of her eight children die before her, and her ailing husband fritter away most of her share of the Custis fortune. She died in 1852, at the age of seventy-three. Wash Custis came into his share of the Custis estate and with it built the house now known as Arlington. His one surviving child by his marriage to Mary Fitzhugh—also named Mary—married the Confederate general Robert E. Lee, and they made their home at Arlington until after the Civil War, when the estate was confiscated for back taxes and turned into a national cemetery. Many Washington family mementos—including a lock of George's hair, and Martha's Sunday-best blue-and-white china—can be seen at Arlington today.

Payne Todd went on to a career of gambling debts and dissipations that impoverished James Madison and exhausted Dolley; in the end Dolley's friends convinced her to tie up her money in a trust so that Payne couldn't get his hands on it. To the end of her life, her son was trying to get from her what money he could, including trying to force her to sign a will giving him the small share she had intended to pass along to her beloved sisters Anna and Lucy, who cared for her in her final days.

Dolley lived til 1849 as the most popular

hostess in Washington, to which she returned after Jemmy's death. She was a regular guest of all five Presidents between Monroe and Polk, and the heartbeat of Washington society, though by that time she was living on the cheerfully offered charity of her many friends. Dolley Todd Madison was given what amounted to a state funeral when she died.

Payne Todd died in poverty and obscurity only three years later, at the age of sixty-one.

James Madison lived to the age of eighty-five, dying at Montpelier a few days before the Fourth of July, 1836.

He was the last surviving signer of the Declaration of Independence.

Aaron Burr outlived him by ten weeks.

SALLY HEMINGS

In the course of putting this book together, I realized that no matter how I told the story of Thomas Jefferson and Sally Hemings, I was going to offend and anger someone.

And yet, in a book about the first First Ladies, to omit the issue would leave a gaping and obvious hole.

I have done the best I can, to re-create one possible version of a relationship whose actual nature is—in the words of Fawn Brodie's romanticized biography—simply "nonrecoverable."

Were Thomas Jefferson to be asked on Judgment Day whether he loved Sally Hemings, my personal opinion is that he would reply defensively that he loved all his slaves: which is not the same thing as saying that he thought they were of the same species as himself. Jefferson is the most elusive (some historians would say, "two-faced") of the Founding Fathers, saying one thing and doing another so frequently that it is almost impossible to pin down what he actually thought or felt.

The Civil War, the polemical arguments for and against abolition of slavery, the bitterness of Reconstruction and the long disgrace of race relations which followed it have so altered modern perceptions of black and white that any re-creation of even a simple relationship would be difficult to achieve, and the relationship between Jefferson and Hemings was, I believe, far from simple.

One of the most striking features I have come across in my own studies of slave accounts of slavery has been the enormous degree to which the conditions of any individual slave's life depended upon the individual slave-owner. Situations of what appear to be warm affection existed side by side with truly subhuman cruelty and jaw-dropping callousness. It all depended on who and where you were, each slave-owning household a microclimate from which, for a slave, there was no possibility of legal redress.

I have made the arbitrary decision, based on the good opinion of Jefferson held by his friends (and in the few recorded instances, by his slaves also—though the ones who didn't like him probably wouldn't have felt able to say so), that he wasn't the kind of man who would force or coerce sex with an unwilling fifteen-year-old girl.

I have also made the arbitrary decision that there was more to the relationship than a bargain for sexual favors in exchange for protection, privilege, and freedom for Sally's children.

Jefferson kept Sally as his concubine despite the scandal in 1802 (their youngest two children were born in 1805 and 1808), and after he took Sally as his concubine in 1788, there is not even speculation that he was involved with any other woman, white or black. Their older surviving sons, Tom and Beverly, simply vanish from the Monticello records; according to their son Madison Hemings in an interview in March of 1873, their daughter Harriet (the second daughter of that name, born in 1801) "married a white man in good standing in Washington City." Madison and Eston, presumably because their features were too African to allow them to "pass," were freed in Jefferson's will.

I have chosen to follow Fawn Brodie (and James Callendar) in portraying Young Tom as alive and present at Monticello at least up to 1800, rather than simply accepting Madison Hemings's assertion that his eldest brother "died soon after" birth. Either way, Young Tom was probably gone from Monticello before Madison Hemings was born.

It must be remembered that Jefferson—and Sally—both grew up in a society in which it was acceptable (among men, anyway) and fairly commonplace—though by no means universal—for men to have mistresses, and for Southern slaveholders to have sexual relations with the women they legally owned. I think it should also be borne in mind that Sally had known Jefferson literally all her life, and that the Hemings family formed a sort of sub-caste at Monticello, somewhere between ordinary slaves and the sort of shadow-families that in French Louisiana would have been free and informally acknowledged.

One can only speculate as to why Jefferson did not free Sally in his will. Patsy Randolph—who left her husband shortly after

Jefferson's death in 1826—freed her, and took great care to solemnly assure her sons that Sally Hemings's children had been fathered by Jefferson's nephew Peter Carr. Sally went to live with her sons Madison and Eston in a house near Monticello, until her death in 1835.

Whether Sally knew anything about Gabriel Prosser's attempted revolt or not—or what she would have chosen to do if she *had* known—I have not the slightest idea.

All writers of fiction about historical personages have to make choices about how to portray events and relationships for which there is little or no evidence. I have done my best to be true to the known facts, about Jefferson and Sally and about the world in which they lived. To those who feel I should have told the story otherwise—and to those who have been offended by my choices—I apologize.

I have used the word "concubine" in its original literal meaning, that of a servant or slave-woman who sleeps with the master on a regular or semiregular basis.

CAST OF CHARACTERS

Real life is not tidy, and the story of any couple is the story of their families as well (and in the eighteenth and early nineteenth centuries, this included servants). I have dates for some; for others I do not. For others I have found several different birth and death dates, with as much as ten years' variation for the same person. Fictional characters are marked with an asterisk*. Though many characters overlap from section to section, I have listed them by the section in which they primarily occur; and by the name under which they are primarily known in the book. A woman's maiden name and alternate married names are in parentheses, alternate first names (either nicknames or real names for those dozen or so women all named Martha) are in brackets.

MARTHA

Anna Maria (Dandridge) Bassett 1739–1777—Favorite sister of Martha, married Burwell Bassett in 1757. Mother of Fanny Bassett Washington Lear, one of Martha's many surrogate daughters.

Fanny (Bassett) Washington (Lear) 1767–1796—Martha's favorite niece, successively married to George's nephew (and secretary) Augustine Washington, then at his death to George's secretary Tobias Lear.

Aaron Burr 1756–1836—The dark star of the Founding Fathers; briefly Washington's aide-de-camp, then Colonel in the Continental Army, Senator from New York, Thomas Jefferson's Vice President (and so far the only United States Vice President to serve while under indictment for murder), and would-be Emperor of Mexico.

Eleanor (Calvert) Custis (Stuart) 1758–1811— Jacky's wife and mother of Martha's four grandchildren. After Jacky's death she married Dr. David Stuart of Alexandria, and had numerous (twelve in some accounts, sixteen in others) children by him.

Daniel Parke Custis 1710–1757—First husband of Martha Washington and father of her four children.

Jacky Custis 1754–1781—[John Parke Custis] Only child of Martha and Daniel Custis to survive to adulthood, father (by Eleanor Calvert) of Martha's four grandchildren.

Patcy Custis 1756–1773—[Martha Parke Custis] Only daughter of Martha and Daniel Custis to survive childhood; suffered from seizures, and died of one at age seventeen.

Eliza (Custis) Law 1776–1832—Oldest daughter of Jacky and Eleanor Custis. Married Thomas Law in 1796.

Pattie (Custis) Peter b. 1777—[Martha Parke Custis] Second daughter of Jacky and Eleanor Custis. Married Thomas Peter in 1795.

Nelly (Custis) Lewis 1779–1852—[Eleanor Parke Custis] Third daughter of Jacky and Eleanor Custis. Semiadopted by Martha and George at Jacky's death. Married George's nephew Lawrence Lewis in 1799.

Wash Custis 1781–1857—[George Washington Parke Custis] Only son of Jacky and Eleanor Custis. Semiadopted by Martha and George at Jacky's death. Married Mary Ann Fitzhugh; their daughter, Mary, married Robert E. Lee. (Thus most of the Washington family mementos ended up at Arlington.) Three of their sons were also generals in the Confederate Army.

Nan Dandridge—Daughter of Martha Dandridge Washington's father, John Dandridge, by one of his slaves. She was employed in the Washington household at Mount Vernon and in 1780 gave birth to a child, William, by Jacky Custis.

"Citizen" Édouard Genêt 1763–1834—First minister sent by Revolutionary France to the U.S., he attempted to meddle in U.S. policy, commissioned American privateers to prey on British shipping, and tried to field, from the U.S., expeditions against France's enemies. When, at Washington's request, he was recalled, he defected to the U.S., married the daughter of the Governor of New York, and lived happily ever after.

Alexander Hamilton 1757–1804—[Hammy, Alec] Washington's Secretary of the Treasury and much-loved surrogate son. Known for his financial brilliance, military and political ambition, wide-ranging amours, and verbal viciousness about his political opponents, a trait which eventually got him shot.

Uncle Hercules—The Washington family cook, trusted and much-favored slave who took the opportunity of being in the North to escape to freedom, waiting to do so until the Washingtons were on their way back to Mount Vernon for the final time in 1796.

Ona Judge b. 1778(?)—[Oney] Martha's beloved and trusted slave maidservant who escaped in Philadelphia to freedom in the North, to Martha's speechless indignation.

Thomas Law—Married Eliza Custis in 1796. Was about twenty years older than she, an English India merchant who had at least three illegitimate sons by Indian women, one of whom he brought with him and sent to Harvard. He and Eliza were divorced in 1810.

Tobias Lear 1762(?)–1816—George's secretary and tutor to the Custis children. A New Hampshire man and Harvard graduate, he was introduced to Washington at the end of the Revolution. After the death of his first wife Pollie, he married Martha's favorite niece Fanny (Bassett); upon Fanny's death, he married another of Martha's nieces, Fanny Henley. After Washington's death, he organized the Presidential papers (and, it was rumored, selectively destroyed some that reflected badly on a quarrel between Washington and Thomas Jefferson): Jefferson appointed him First Consul to Saint-Domingue, and then Consul General to the Barbary States (where he made a great deal of money in bribes). Returning to the United States at the outbreak of the War of 1812, Lear, who suffered from headaches and depression, shot himself in 1816.

Pollie Lear 1770–1793—Tobias Lear's childhood sweetheart from New Hampshire. After their marriage she acted as Martha's secretary. She was one of the first casualties of the yellow fever epidemic in Philadelphia in the summer of 1793.

General Charles Lee 1731–1782— Continental general and soldier of fortune, he was one of Washington's rivals for the position of Commander in Chief.

Lawrence Lewis—Son of George's sister Betty; married Nelly Custis in 1799. A hypochondriac who later in life became dependent upon opiates.

James Monroe 1758–1831—Virginia planter, officer in the Continental Army, U.S. Senator, Governor of Virginia, fifth President of the United States. Was the third U.S. President to die on the Fourth of July.

Thomas Peter—Married Pattie Custis in 1795. Their house in Georgetown still stands.

Dr. David Stuart—Second husband of Jacky Custis's widow Eleanor; father, by her, of many, many children.

George Washington 1732–1799—Virginia planter, Commander in Chief of the Continental Army during the Revolution, and first President of the United States.

Martha (Dandridge) (Custis) Washington 1731–1802—[Patsie] First First Lady. Formerly married to Daniel Custis.

George Augustine Washington 1763–1793—[Augustine] Son of George's brother Charles, George's secretary and overseer of Mount Vernon, first husband of Martha's niece Fanny. Died of tuberculosis.

George Steptoe Washington 1771–1809— [Steptoe] Son of George's brother Sam, of Harewood Plantation. Married Lucy Payne, sister of Dolley Madison.

Harriot Washington b. 1777—Steptoe's younger sister. At their father's death, she was taken to live at Mount Vernon for a time, while her brothers were placed in boarding-school.

ABIGAIL
Abigail (Smith) Adams 1744–1818— Second First Lady, and mother of the sixth President of the U.S. Middle daughter of the minister of Weymouth, Massachusetts.

John Adams 1735–1826—Lawyer, member of the Continental Congress, Minister to

France, and first U.S. Minister to England, second President of the United States.

Nabby (Adams) Smith 1765–1813— [Abigail] Daughter of John and Abigail Adams, married Colonel William Smith in England in 1786.

John Quincy Adams 1767–1848— [Johnny, Hercules] Oldest son of John and Abigail Adams, U.S. Minister to Berlin, helped negotiate the Treaty of Ghent (which ended the War of 1812), sixth President of the United States, afterwards Representative from Massachusetts, and lawyer who defended the mutinous slaves of the slave-ship *Amistad*. In 1848 he suffered a stroke on the floor of the House of Representatives, and died in the Speaker's Chamber shortly thereafter.

Charley Adams 1770–1800—Second son of John and Abigail Adams. He married the sister of his sister Nabby's husband; died of acute alcoholism at the age of thirty.

Thomas Adams 1772–1832—Third son of John and Abigail Adams.

Jack Briesler—[John] Adams family servant. Married Abigail's faithful maid, Esther Field.

Granny Susie (Susanna Boylston Adams) Hall 1709–1797—Married John Hall after the death of John Adams's father in 1761. Lived long enough to see her son elected President; died about a month after his inauguration. Abigail described her as the mainstay of the entire family.

Peter Adams—John's brother and next-door neighbor in Braintree. A third brother, Elihu, joined the Continental militia at the siege of Boston and died in camp.

Samuel Adams 1722–1803—John's second cousin (both were great-grandsons of Joseph Adams of Braintree, Mass.); master propagandist, radical revolutionary, signer of the Declaration of Independence, and eventually, first Lieutenant-Governor and then Governor of Massachusetts.

*Michael Boyne**—Sam Adams's law clerk, Irish, anti-Federalist, and courted Abigail's niece Louisa Smith.

Mary (Smith) Cranch 1741–1811—Older sister of Abigail Adams.

Esther Field—Abigail's faithful maid. Became pregnant by Jack Briesler while in England, married him there, but bore and lost the baby on the voyage home. Briesler and Esther remained in the Adams family's service throughout their lives.

Elbridge Gerry 1744–1814—John's erratic and independent fellow delegate to the Continental Congress, a signer of the Declaration of Independence and a lifelong supporter of John Adams. It was the Republican redistricting of Massachusetts, while Gerry was Governor, in 1812, to rearrange the state so as to have more Republican senators, that gave rise to the term "gerrymandering."

John Hancock 1737–1793—Merchant, tea smuggler, patriot, first signer of the Declaration of Independence, president of the first Continental Congress, and later Governor of Massachusetts.

Jamey Prince—Free colored servant of the Adamses.

Betsey (Smith) Shaw (Peabody) 1750–1815—Younger sister of Abigail Adams. Her parson first husband ran a school in Haverhill, where the younger two Adams boys (Charley and Tommy) were boarded for the four years Abigail was with John in France and England.

Colonel William Smith 1755–1816—John's secretary in the American Ministry in London, married John's daughter Nabby in 1786.

Sarah Smith 1769–1828—Colonel Smith's younger sister, who married Charley Adams in 1794.

William Smith 1746–1787—Abigail's good-for-nothing younger brother.

Louisa Smith 1773–1857—Daughter of Abigail's brother William, taken into the Adams household when John and Abigail returned from England, shortly after brother William's death. She remained unmarried, as Abigail's companion, until Abigail's death in 1818.

SALLY
Aunt Martha Carr 1746–1811—Thomas Jefferson's youngest sister, who married his best friend Dabney Carr in 1765. Carr died in 1773 leaving Martha with six

children under the age of ten. Jefferson gave them all a home at Monticello, where Aunt Carr remained.

Peter Carr 1770(?)–1815—One of Aunt Carr's children, raised at Monticello. Much later in life, Patsy Jefferson claimed that Peter Carr was the father of Sally Hemings's children, a claim disproved by DNA tests in 1998. He *was,* apparently, the father of a son by Sally's sister Critta.

Sam Carr 1766(?)–1855(?)—Another of Aunt Carr's sons, raised at Monticello.

Aunt Elizabeth Eppes—Younger half-sister of Jefferson's wife Martha (Patty). She assumed care of Jefferson's daughters Maria (Polly) and Lucie Elizabeth on the death of Patty Jefferson.

Jack (John Wayles) Eppes 1773–1823— Son of Aunt Eppes and Maria Jefferson's childhood sweetheart and eventual husband; lived for a time with the Jefferson household and acted as Jefferson's secretary. U.S. Representative for Virginia, U.S. Senator. After Maria's death in 1804, Jack married Martha Jones; he also kept as a concubine Sally Hemings's niece

Betsie Hemings, who is buried beside him at Millbrook in Virginia. Martha Jones Eppes reportedly asked to be buried someplace else, and was.

Betty Hemings d. 1807—Mother of Sally Hemings by John Wayles, the father of Jefferson's wife. Prior to becoming John Wayles's concubine, she had three children by a fellow slave—Martin, Bett, and Mary (Mary was the mother of Jack Eppes's concubine Betsie Hemings). She had six children by John Wayles: Robert, Jimmy, Peter (Pip), Critta, Sally, and Thenia. Later, at Monticello, she had a son (John) by one of the white carpenters there, and a daughter (Lucy) by a fellow slave. All the slaves manumitted by Thomas Jefferson were either Betty's children or her grandchildren.

Sally Hemings 1773–1836—Daughter of Betty Hemings by John Wayles, the father of Jefferson's wife; nursemaid to Jefferson's daughter Maria (Polly) on her journey to join her father in France; maid to both the Jefferson daughters and later the servant in charge of Jefferson's private quarters; Thomas Jefferson's concubine for forty-two years and the mother of eight of his children including his only surviving sons. One of her grandsons fought as a Union soldier in the Civil War and died in the Confederate prison at Andersonville.

Jimmy Hemings 1765(?)–1801—Son of Betty Hemings by John Wayles, taken to France with Jefferson in 1784 to be trained as a cook, returned with him to Virginia and was given his freedom, later traveled in Europe but died "tragically" (Jefferson's word)—possibly from the effects of alcoholism, in 1801.

Peter Hemings—[Pip] Son of Betty Hemings by John Wayles, trained by Jimmy as his replacement as Monticello cook.

Critta Hemings—Daughter of Betty Hemings by John Wayles; housemaid at Monticello and mother of a son (Jamey) by Jefferson's nephew Peter Carr.

Young Tom Hemings 1789–(?)—[Little Tom] Oldest son of Thomas Jefferson and Sally Hemings.

Beverly Hemings 1798–(?)—Second son of Thomas Jefferson and Sally Hemings.

Reported to have gone to Washington, D.C., and "passed" for white.

Thomas Jefferson 1743–1826—Virginia planter, philosopher, architect, gardener, author (in committee with John Adams and Benjamin Franklin) of the Declaration of Independence, Minister to France, Secretary of State to George Washington, Vice President, and later third President of the United States.

Martha (Wayles) (Skelton) Jefferson 1748–1783—[Miss Patty] Formerly married (for twenty-two months) to Jefferson's friend Bathurst Skelton, by whom she had a son, John, who died at age four. Jefferson loved her desperately and promised her on her deathbed that he would never marry again.

Patsy (Jefferson) Randolph 1772–1836—[Martha] Oldest daughter of Thomas Jefferson, and his lifelong companion. Married Thomas Randolph, Jr., by whom she had twelve children, and left him shortly after Jefferson's death. Her youngest son was the first Secretary of War of the Confederate States of America.

Maria (Jefferson) Eppes 1778–1804—[Mary, Polly] Youngest surviving daughter of Thomas Jefferson. Married Jack Eppes by whom she had three children, died two months after the birth of the third.

Lamentation Hawkin*—Free black carter from Charlottesville; one of Sally's admirers.

Lacey*—Patsy Jefferson Randolph's maid.

Adrien Petit—Thomas Jefferson's French valet. Originally employed by John Adams, he went to work for Jefferson when Adams went to England. He remained in France at the beginning of the French Revolution, but rejoined Jefferson at Monticello in 1791. I have been unable to ascertain whether the Monticello overseer from 1794 to 1797, Hugh Petit, was any relation.

Thomas Mann Randolph, Jr. 1768–1828—Virginia planter, U.S. Representative of Virginia, twice elected Governor of Virginia despite severe depression and intermittent mental instability. Son of Jefferson's old friend Thomas Mann Randolph, Sr., with whom Jefferson grew up. Randolph junior was Patsy Jefferson's childhood friend, reencountered her in Paris in 1788, and married her in 1790, three months after her return to Virginia. He spent much of his life in debt. Even after he and Patsy were reconciled and he returned to Monticello to live, he had separate quarters from hers.

Anne Carey Randolph b. 1791—[Annie] First child of Patsy and Tom Randolph.

Thomas Jefferson Randolph b. 1793—[Jeff] Second child of Patsy and Tom Randolph. In 1795, when their father had a breakdown, Jeff and Annie were taken to Monticello to live for almost two years.

Ellen Wayles Randolph b. 1796—Second daughter of that name born to Patsy and Tom Randolph; the first, born in 1794, died in infancy.

Cornelia Jefferson Randolph b. 1799— Fourth child (third surviving) of Patsy and Tom Randolph.

DOLLEY
Lizzie (Collins) Lee b. 1768(?)—Dolley's best friend from the Quaker Meeting in Philadelphia; like Dolley, ejected from the Meeting for marrying out of her faith (to

Congressman Richard Lee of Virginia).
Remained Dolley's best friend for life.

Andrew Jackson 1767–1845—First
Congressman and later Senator from
Tennessee, Judge of the Tennessee
Supreme Court, and General of the United
States forces defending New Orleans
against an invading British force in January
of 1815. Seventh President of the United
States.

Rachel Jackson 1767–1828—Daughter of
Virginia planter and politician John
Donelson; later married to Lewis Robards
(who seems to have been something of a
nutcase), who initiated—but did not
complete—divorce proceedings in 1790.
Rachel married Andrew Jackson in 1791,
in Spanish territory, under the impression
that she was a free woman, which turned
out not to be the case until 1793. Jackson
and Rachel remarried in 1794—as soon as
they legally could—and Jackson
subsequently shot several people in duels
for calling Rachel an adultress. This
became a major target for mudslinging in
the Presidential elections of 1824 and
1828.

Paul Jennings b. 1799—James Madison's slave valet and writer of the first "behind-the-scenes" account of White House life. When in desperate financial straits in later life, Dolley sold Paul to Daniel Webster for a ridiculously low sum so that Paul would have the opportunity to easily work his way out of slavery.

Dolley (Payne) (Todd) Madison 1768–1849—Third *and* fourth First Lady of the United States, she acted as Thomas Jefferson's hostess through much of his administration (except for one season when Patsy Jefferson Randolph was able to come to Washington). Formerly married to Philadelphia lawyer John Todd, Jr., by whom she had two sons, Payne and Willie.

James Madison, Jr. 1751–1836—[Jemmy] Virginia planter, father of the U.S. Constitution, U.S. Representative of Virginia, Secretary of State for Thomas Jefferson, fourth President of the United States.

Old Colonel Madison 1723–1801—[James Madison, Sr.] Virginia planter, father of President James Madison.

Mother Madison 1731–1829—[Nelly (Conway) Madison] President James Madison's mother. She and the "Old Colonel" shared the house at Montpelier Plantation with James and Dolley.

John Payne 1740–1792—Dolley Madison's father, formerly a small planter in Virginia, then a starch-maker in Philadelphia.

Molly (Coles) Payne 1745–1807—[Mary] Dolley Madison's mother, a devout Quaker.

Anna (Payne) Cutts 1780–1832—Dolley's favorite sister and lifelong companion. Her granddaughter Adele married Stephen Douglas.

Lucy (Payne) (Washington) Todd 1778–1846—Dolley's younger sister, who married George Washington's nephew (George) Steptoe Washington in 1793. After Steptoe's death in 1809, she married Judge Thomas Todd.

"French John" (Jean-Pierre) Sioussat— Steward at the White House during Madison's administration. Formerly steward to British Minister Anthony Merry;

had studied for the priesthood, then been a sailor for a time.

Jamie Smith—James Madison's free colored valet.

*Sophie (Sparling) Hallam** b. 1765—Childhood friend of Dolley's, daughter of a Virginia doctor and granddaughter of a Virginia planter, both Loyalists. During the final year of the Revolution she worked as a nurse, then fled with her mother to England and, later, France. Returned to Philadelphia, then to the newly built Federal City, as a dressmaker.

Sukey—Dolley's enslaved maidservant.

John Todd, Jr. 1765–1793—Philadelphia lawyer and Quaker, first husband of Dolley Madison.

Payne Todd 1792–1852—Dolley Madison's aptly named oldest son by John Todd: handsome, charming, much beloved, an alcoholic and a gambler.

Willie Todd 1793—Dolley Madison's second child by John Todd, born during the yellow fever epidemic and died within a few weeks, on the same day as her husband.

James Todd—John Todd's brother, who seems to have tried to push Dolley out of some or all of her inheritance from her husband and father-in-law. He eventually embezzled three thousand dollars from a Philadelphia bank and ran off to Georgia, never to be heard from again.

BIBLIOGRAPHY

It is of course impossible to list all the books (to say nothing of Internet sites) that went into the making of *Patriot Hearts* over the two-plus years of research, writing, rewriting, and editing. As a historian, one constantly picks up bits and pieces of information about how people lived—cooking, laundry, dances, what one did and didn't do in company—and this information, some of it acquired decades ago, is virtually impossible to trace down. Similarly, a good deal of research is non-written: visits to Monticello and Mount Vernon and Williamsburg to see how far it actually is from the house to the river, the marvelous re-creations of slave quarters and kitchens, the invaluable expertise of docents and re-enactors to whom the eighteenth century is as real as the twenty-first (and makes a good deal more sense). (My special thanks to Jefferson's law teacher George Wythe, and to Williamsburg magnate Robert Carter, for taking the time to chat with me in the Apollo Room of the Raleigh Tavern in Williamsburg one afternoon.)

This is a partial list of the books I found most useful in the writing of *Patriot Hearts.* I've arranged them by lady, but there was, of course, considerable overlap. Any or all of these titles can probably be acquired over the Internet.

MARTHA
Bryan, Helen. *Martha Washington, First Lady of Liberty.* New York: John Wiley & Sons, 2002.

Clinton, Catherine. *The Plantation Mistress: Woman's World in the Old South.* New York: Pantheon, 1982.

Kitman, Marvin. *George Washington's Expense Account.* New York: Grove Press, 1970.

Lewis, Nelly Custis and Patricia Brady Schmit (ed.). *Nelly Custis Lewis's*

Housekeeping Book. Historic New Orleans Collection, 1982.

George Washington's Mount Vernon, Official Guidebook. New York: Mount Vernon Ladies' Association.

Schwarz, Philip (ed.). *Slavery at the Home of George Washington.* New York: Mt. Vernon Ladies' Association, 2001.

Thane, Elswyth. *Washington's Lady.* Philadelphia, PA: Curtis, 1954.

Wiencek, Henry. *An Imperfect God: George Washington, His Slaves, and the Creation of America.* New York: Farrar, Straus and Giroux, 2003.

ABIGAIL
Adams, Abigail, and Charles Francis Adams (ed.). *The Letters of Mrs. Adams, Wife of John Adams.* Wilkins, Carter & Co., 1848.

Adams, John and Abigail, and Frank Shuffleton (ed.). *The Letters of John and Abigail Adams.* New York: Penguin Classics, 2004.

Cappon, Lester (ed.). *The Adams-Jefferson*

Letters. University of North Carolina Press, 1959.

Forbes, Esther. *Paul Revere and the World He Lived In.* New York: Houghton Mifflin, 1942.

Levin, Phyllis. *Abigail Adams, A Biography.* New York: Thomas Dunne, 2001.

McCullough, David. *John Adams.* New York: Simon & Schuster, 2001.

Nagel, Paul. *The Adams Women.* Cambridge, MA: Harvard University Press, 1987.

Withey, Lynne. *Dearest Friend: A Life of Abigail Adams.* New York: Simon & Schuster, 1981.

SALLY
Bernier, Olivier. *Pleasure and Privilege.* New York: Doubleday, 1981.

Brodie, Fawn. *Thomas Jefferson, An Intimate Biography.* New York: Norton, 1974.

Burstein, Andrew. *Jefferson's Secrets.* New York: Basic Books, 2005.

Crawford, Alan. *Unwise Passions.* New York: Simon & Schuster, 2000.

Erickson, Carolly. *To the Scaffold: The Life of Marie Antoinette.* New York: Robson Books, 1992.

Hall, Gordon. *Mr. Jefferson's Ladies.* Boston: Beacon Press, 1966.

Jefferson, Thomas, and Edwin Morris Betts (ed.). *Thomas Jefferson's Farm Book.* Thomas Jefferson Memorial Foundation, 1999.

Jefferson, Thomas, and Edwin Morris Betts (ed.). *Thomas Jefferson's Garden Book.* Thomas Jefferson Memorial Foundation, 1999.

Kierner, Cynthia. *Scandal at Bizarre: Rumor and Reputation in Jefferson's America.* New York: Palgrave MacMillan, 2004.

Kimball, Marie. *Jefferson, the Scene of Europe, 1784–1789.* New York: Coward, McCann, 1950.

Mercier, Louis Sebastien, and Jean-Claud Bonnet (ed.). *Tableau de Paris.* Mercure de France, 1994.

Poisson, Michel. *Paris, Buildings and Monuments.* New York: Harry Abrams, 1999.

Randall, Willard. *Thomas Jefferson, A Life.* New York: Henry Holt, 1993.

Robiquet, Jean. *Daily Life in the French Revolution.* New York: MacMillan, 1965.

Shackelford, George. *Thomas Jefferson's Travels in Europe 1784–1789.* Johns Hopkins University Press, 1995.

Stein, Susan. *The Worlds of Thomas Jefferson at Monticello.* New York: Harry Abrams, 1993.

DOLLEY
Allgor, Catherine. *Parlor Politics.* University of Virginia, 2000.

Côté, Richard. *Strength and Honor: The Life of Dolley Madison.* Mt. Pleasant, SC: Corinthian Books, 2005.

Ketcham, Ralph. *James Madison: A Biography.* University Press of Virginia, 1990.

Madison, Dolley, and David Mattern and Holly Shulman (eds.). *Selected Letters of*

Dolley Payne Madison. University of Virginia Press, 2003.

Pitch, Anthony. *The Burning of Washington.* Naval Institute Press, 1998.

Smith, Margaret Bayard, and Gaillard Hunt (ed.). *The First Forty Years of Washington Society.* New York: Frederick Ungar, 1906.

ALSO:
Bernier, Olivier. *The World in 1800.* New York: John Wiley & Sons, 2000.

Boatner, Mark. *Encyclopedia of the American Revolution.* Mechanicsburg, PA: Stackpole Books, 1966.

Garvan, Beatrice. *Federal Philadelphia.* Philadelphia Museum of Art and University of Pennsylvania Press, 1987.

Roberts, Cokie. *Founding Mothers.* New York: William Morrow, 2004.

Seale, William. *The President's House.* White House Historical Association, 1986.

Unger, Harlow. *The French War Against America.* New York: John Wiley & Sons, 2005.

Much tiny detail about the eighteenth century I gleaned from the various volumes of Muzzleloader Magazine's *The Book of Buckskinning,* edited by William Schurlock.

ABOUT THE AUTHOR

BARBARA HAMBLY is the author of *The Emancipator's Wife,* a finalist for the Michael Shaara Award for Excellence in Civil War Fiction. She is also the author of *Fever Season,* a *New York Times* Notable Book of the Year, and seven acclaimed historical novels.

Patriot Hearts: A novel of the Founding
Mothers